Items should be returned on or before the last date shown below. Items not already requested by other borrowers may be renewed in person, in writing or by telephone. To renew, please quote the number on the barcode label. To renew online a PIN is required. This can be requested at your local library.
Renew online @ **www.dublincitypubliclibraries.ie**
Fines charged for overdue items will include postage incurred in recovery. Damage to or loss of items will be charged to the borrower.

*runul*

**Leabharlanna Poiblí Chathair Bhaile Átha Cliath**
**Dublin City Public Libraries**

| Date Due | Date Due | Date Due |
|---|---|---|
|  | 06 IAN 2020 |  |

D1513556

# Lucian Dan Teodorovici

# MATEI BRUNUL

Translated from the Romanian by Alistair Ian Blyth

**DALKEY ARCHIVE PRESS**

Originally published in Romanian by Editura Polirom as *Matei Brunul* in 2011.

Copyright © 2011 by Lucian Dan Teodorovici
Translation copyright © 2018 by Alistair Ian Blyth
First Dalkey Archive edition, 2018.

Library of Congress Cataloging-in-Publication Data
Names: Teodorovici, Lucian Dan, 1975- author. | Blyth, Alistair Ian, translator.
Title: Matei Brunul : a novel / Lucian Dan Teodorovici ; translated by Alistair Ian Blyth.
Other titles: Matei Brunul. English
Description: First Dalkey Archive edition. | Victoria, TX : Dalkey Archive Press, 2017.
Identifiers: LCCN 2017036707 | ISBN 9781943150236 (pbk. : acid-free paper)
Classification: LCC PC840.43.E58 M3813 2017 | DDC 859/.335--dc23
LC record available at https://lccn.loc.gov/2017036707

INSTITUTUL
CULTURAL
R O M Â N

Partially funded by the Translation Publication Support Program of the Romanian Cultural Institute.

www.dalkeyarchive.com
Victoria, TX / McLean, IL / Dublin

Dalkey Archive Press publications are, in part, made possible through the support of the University of Houston-Victoria and its programs in creative writing, publishing, and translation.

Printed on permanent/durable acid-free paper

# Preface

So many excellent novels have been written about life under communism in Soviet Russia and the countries of Eastern Europe that it difficult for any writer today to find an original way to depict the oppressiveness, inhumanity, and institutionalized injustice of those regimes before they began to collapse in 1989. But Lucian Dan Teodorovici has succeeded in *Matei Brunul*. The title is the name of the book's hero, though that term seems inappropriate to a man so meek and mild in nature. At the age of twenty-two, he rashly returns from Italy, where he lived during the Second World War, to his native Romania, only to fall under the suspicion of the State for no reason he can understand or repudiate. In consequence he suffers long periods of brutal imprisonment and forced labor, ultimately so traumatic that he loses his memory. Rehabilitated with a job at the local puppet theater, he carries a wooden doll around with him as a surrogate companion, but is too innocent to perceive the motives of the human beings he interacts with, especially the Party official who is his minder. Bruno is a kind of Holy Fool, with whom the reader cannot help sympathizing, while at the same time deploring his naivety. The novel is therefore both exquisitely comic and movingly tragic by turns, while its shifting perspectives in time and narrative point of view keep the reader constantly involved in the story. It is a remarkable achievement by a writer who was born in 1975 and had no personal experience of the era he describes, bearing comparison with classics of the genre such as Milan Kundera's *The Joke*. Such books are salutary reminders to English-speaking readers of how lucky we are never to have lived in a totalitarian state.

David Lodge

# Chapter 1

THE BUILDINGS LOOKED dazzling from up there on the Trancu Bridge. By the new housing blocks, even the stale mid-March snow showed seamless and white, concealing the mud, the roads, the back alleys. The snow concealed a city whose structures were, in that district at least, very different from the gray building in which for months, for almost a year, he had regathered memories; only on his release had he discovered, to his amazement, what it looked like from the outside. On seeing the exterior of the building, Brunul had been left stupefied, and from his right hand Vasilache had dangled inert for a long space of time.

Now, hanging below the arch of the bridge, Vasilache gave a twitch.

It was the same now as it had been then: riveted by the landscape, his mind elsewhere, without gathering any word, any thought. And then the hand on his shoulder. He turned around; below, over the edge of the bridge, Vasilache began to move erratically, jerking upward a few inches, then farther, perhaps a foot or more. The policeman leaned over the balustrade, looked at the trembling marionette, then at Brunul:

"I asked you what you were doing here."

He knew that he had to answer him. Not the cold, but fear now made him tremble. He knew that he had to say something, lest his protracted silence annoy the other man. But right then his thoughts, all of them, refused to coalesce into words.

He turned back to the balustrade and, by way of explanation, pointed at Vasilache. Silence. The policeman looked over the side of the bridge, and then at Brunul. Who, after a few awkward moments, opened his mouth. Finally. But he opened it to say something that he ought not to have said.

"I came out for a walk."

"A walk," snorted the policeman. "Are you mad or . . . For a walk with a doll!"

"It's Sunday," Brunul straightaway added, as if that explained everything.

He took Vasilache out every Sunday: that is what he meant to say. They didn't bother other people, the people on the street, who thought him crazy; he had grown accustomed to that. Paradise might not be perfect, but if you knew how to conduct yourself there, you didn't come up against very many difficulties. He had learned to pay no attention to the people who sniggered, who laughed, or even to the children who sometimes swore at him, who even threw things at him. But it was harder when it came to the police.

A few months ago, two policemen had even stopped him in front of the State Puppet Theater, where he had been showing Vasilache to the children coming out after a performance. Sunday was his day off, but the actors had performances to give. At the time, he had still been fearful of venturing into town; on his day off he came to the front of the theater, which was in the yard of the Catholic church, and waited for the children to emerge after the performance. He would show them Vasilache. In the end, one after the other the children began to sneer at him because his marionette didn't move or talk like the other puppets, in other words, the ones onstage, which they had just seen, and so Brunul gave up that custom of his. But at the time, that Sunday, he had not yet started feeling offended and unwanted; he had not yet taken to weeping in his one-room apartment, pouring out his bitterness to Vasilache, who, silent and expressionless, listened to him on the bed, propped against a pillow. At the time Brunul had still hoped to win over the children. When the first signs of their dissatisfaction became apparent, when they began to comment that a real doll could move by itself, without anybody holding its legs and moving them, he had not known what to say to them; he had frozen in that stooped posture of his, holding Vasilache slightly raised, with the marionette's legs dangling in mid-air, clasping its waist in his right hand, and looking fixedly at the astonished, perhaps even disappointed, faces of the three or four children and their parents. When one of the children had clutched at his mother's hand, asking to leave, because that puppet did not know how to talk, did not know how to move its hands, did not know how to move its legs, because it was just a lump of wood, Brunul had panicked and begun to speak, abruptly, supplying his lips with thoughts that seemed to come out of nowhere, as if he were reciting them, thoughts without life, without intonation, highly unsuited to a conversation with children. Thoughts about the soul of marionettes. He had somehow spoken those words as an excuse, as an explanation. Or else he had spoken them merely because he felt the need to say something, to fill the void engendered by the marionette's lack of articulated movement.

"Every marionette has a soul." Thus began his speech, there in front of the State Puppet Theater. "But you have to know how to discover it. It is to be found, perhaps the same as in humans, on the inside. But without doubt there will be some who wish to give it a different name, and so we shall call it a center of gravity. The marionette's every movement relies on a center of gravity. If it is manipulated in the right way, if the puppeteer knows his marionette, if he can feel it to the point where he identifies with it, the other parts of the body, which are nothing but levers, pivots, will move in the direction he wishes. The force of gravity does its duty. In man, the soul is an unknown quantity. The soul of the marionette is easy to find, however. It is precisely that center of gravity. And he dictates the movement, the action; in effect he dictates its life. The life of the marionette resides in the puppeteer's hands. You will never be able to manipulate the puppet, never be able to make it live the way you would wish, unless you learn how to control its soul in the profoundest possible way, regardless of where that soul might reside. The soul or the center of gravity . . ."

He then stopped, not because he had espied the two policemen walking over to him, nor because those highly affected, artificial words had finally struck even him as inappropriate to such an audience; he stopped quite simply because he did not know how to continue. An abrupt silence. And it was only then that the men in uniform had come up to him. One of the policemen, who seemed to be the other's superior, took Vasilache in his hand, examined the doll for a short moment, handed it to the other policemen, and demanded Brunul's identity papers. He didn't have them on him. He told them that he worked at the State Puppet Theater as an attendant. "As an attendant of what?" "Of puppets." They didn't believe him, or perhaps they could not comprehend what kind of a job that might be. "So you're not an actor?" said the policeman who seemed to be the superior, with a frown. "Are you engaged in black-market activity here? Taking the children's money for a performance held off the official premises?"

Despite the fact that that very day the theater's puppeteer had signed not only a sworn statement but also a petition vouching that Brunul did not give performances for his own personal financial gain; despite the fact that no less than the director of the theater himself had invited the policemen into his office, providing them with the recipe for the rum coffee he had just served (two cups of russet liqueur to three of coffee, into which were then to be stirred no more than four spoons of sugar) and explaining Brunul's entire situation to them, for half an hour or even longer; despite all this, in the end matters had only been partly resolved. Which is to say, the policemen had been persuaded only to confiscate Vasilache until the situation could be clarified. Clarification arrived two days later. Brunul, who had not left the house since losing his doll, was summoned to sign some forms that he was not given an opportunity to read, after which the marionette was handed back to him without further comment. Indeed, without further warnings. But even though matters had been resolved, without further consequences, the occurrence had frightened Brunul at the time. And the memory of it frightened him even now, as he stood on the bridge in front of the fat, stumpy, red-faced policeman, who was still waiting for an answer.

"Your identity papers for inspection," repeated the man, and the curt, scornful smile that accompanied his growled words didn't dispel his frown. "How about that, you're out for a walk with your doll," he snorted. "Like it's a dog or something . . ."

Brunul looked along the bridge and then behind him. None but the two of them were there. The two of them and Vasilache. He began to wind the strings onto the paddle, and when the marionette's head appeared from below the balustrade, he clutched it to his breast, a protective gesture dictated not by mind but by instinct. As inappropriately as he had once spoken in front of the children, he now began to intone, in the same expressionless voice, as if reciting, with his head bowed, looking at Vasilache, rather than the policeman:

"Every marionette has a soul. You need only know how to reveal it. Perhaps the same as in humans, it resides within. But of course some people—"

"I said I wanted to see your papers," interrupted the man in uniform, raising his voice. "Or how about I beat that soul of yours out of you?" he added, brandishing his fist.

Brunul raised a placatory right hand. With his other hand he clutched Vasilache even more tightly to his chest.

"All I want is that you don't get annoyed."

He took a deep breath, looked along the bridge, and his legs then did what his mind had been whispering he should do from the outset—it was his one coherent idea, which had drowned

out any other whisper in his mind ever since the policeman
stepped up behind him. His legs wrenched him away from that
fear, a fear that made him tremble more than he had trembled
on that cold day thitherto. Clutching Vasilache to his breast, he
let his legs carry him away, fleeing across the little bridge, down
the still frozen street that ran along the Bahlui River, down the
paths between the housing blocks . . . He ran blindly, without
looking back, at intervals clutching his flapping raincoat to his
chest. And only after he began to feel his throat, the pain in
his throat, did he slow his gallop, close his mouth, and inhale
deeply through his nostrils.

He looked behind him only after he ducked into the
entrance of a housing block. The policeman was nowhere in
sight. Perhaps he had not even given chase. Or perhaps in his
gallop he had outdistanced him, leaving far behind that fat
policeman whose sole intention must have been to confiscate
Vasilache.

He looked at the marionette he was clutching to his chest.
He brushed the hoarfrost from the clumps of tow sewn into the
crown of its head. He smiled. And then he opened his mouth
and took a deep breath.

The afternoon was already turning to evening, and still he had
to wait. He knew that Eliza would not leave work any earlier,
but he disliked the thought of waiting at home in the meantime.
What could he have done at home? Vasilache knew about the
incident with the policeman, he too had witnessed the whole
thing, he had even to a large extent been responsible for it, and
so Brunul could not fill the time telling him about it. At home
he would have spent two hours waiting in that room with a
bed, a table, two chairs, and a wardrobe, perhaps he would have
fallen asleep, as so often happened to him, while straining to
salvage some shred of memory, setting off on its trail, fruitlessly,
as ever, before finally being overwhelmed by newer, charmless,

completely pointless memories. He would have fallen asleep, perhaps. And he would have missed his meeting with her.

He began to walk around Union Square, which was almost deserted at that hour, trying to alleviate the numbness of his feet, which his galoshes could not fully shield from the frost. First, he traced the concrete pattern on the ground, upon which the snow had left only faint traces. After about an hour, during which he stopped at intervals, as if trying to hasten the time, he put the bag with Vasilache on the ground and stepped inside the perimeter of the now snow-covered patch of grass at the back of the Square.

He crossed the rectangle of snow, carefully counting his steps, and headed toward the brick-red building at the other end. Having reached it, he turned around and looked. There were seventy-four footprints in the otherwise undisturbed snow. It had taken him exactly seventy-four paces to traverse the small park. And now he would have to take not one step more or less on his way back.

Halfway back across, as he gauged it by sight, he had already taken forty steps. He looked behind him in amazement. Had he trodden on a footprint from the first crossing? He continued, more carefully. He planted his right foot slightly ahead of the footprint in front of him, then his left foot, taking a somewhat longer stride. Only slightly longer. Imperceptible to anybody else, but clear to him. Slightly longer, long enough to enable him to cover the remaining half with only thirty-four steps. He neared the pavement. He still had another ten steps to take. He counted the footprints from the first crossing. Something was wrong. He had room for another five steps. Maybe six. He had gone wrong somewhere. A few moments later, he gave up. He trod six times on the unbeaten snow, without taking account of the gaps. Seventy-six steps.

In the end, it wasn't important, thought Brunul. It wasn't the number of paces that mattered. Anyway, on the third crossing, he wouldn't be able to use the previous footprints as a guide. Seventy-four, the first time; seventy, the second time. In total . . . In the end it wasn't important, he told himself once again. The point of it was the path, not the footprints. How many times did you need to cross the snow to make a beaten path, a smooth, even a glassy path? He set out for the third time, following the trail of footprints, without counting. He concentrated on the snow, on the raised, fluffy parts between the footprints.

By the fourth crossing, there were no more fluffy remnants, only a tamped trail. Over the next hour, he crossed back and forth another fourteen times. Eighteen crossings in all. Eighteen. He looked up. The path didn't look much better than it had on the fourth crossing. Too much untidy snow.

How many crossings would it take to produce a beaten path through the snow, a smooth, even a glassy path? More than twenty crossings. Certainly more than twenty. He set off down his path again, slightly annoyed. He would not know the exact number of crossings. In the end, it wasn't important, he said to himself through gritted teeth.

Perhaps another hour, perhaps longer. That was how long it took before, weary, frozen, he nodded his head, more or less satisfied, looking at his path. It was sufficiently beaten. Perhaps not yet smooth. Certainly not glassy. But it was a path made by him and him alone. One you could walk down. One that even Vasilache, with his little wooden feet, could tread without sinking up to his waist in snow. Without soaking his trousers up to the waist.

He took Vasilache out of the bag, which he had left on the pavement before his first crossing of the park. Around the back of his neck he hung the paddle to which the strings were attached, he grasped the right leg with his right hand, the left leg with his left hand, he bent over and began to move the marionette along the path. One step, two, three . . .

Vasilache advanced with difficulty; the way seemed much longer. At about the halfway point, Brunul almost gave up. He stood up straight, pressed his hand to the small of his back, where it was as if a sliver of ice had lodged between his vertebrae, he gritted his teeth, bent down, and continued. A little farther along the path he helped Vasilache to make a huge leap through the air, but then, ashamed, he returned to the take-off point of the unnatural leap and, chastened, resumed his Lilliputian progress along the path, sighing at intervals.

In order to reach the other end of the park it took Vasilache two hundred and ninety-four steps. At the other end, after straightening his back with further sighs, Brunul lifted Vasilache level with his eyes, examined him closely, and smiled, satisfied at the fact that only the wooden feet were wet. He went back down the path across the park, this time treading lightly.

On the other side, he picked the bag up off the ground and stuffed Vasilache inside. Only now did he look at the wristwatch comrade Bojin had given him almost a year before. His eyes bulged and he hurried off to the right, trying, in the semi-darkness that had already settled over Union Square, to pick out one of the shadows in front of the door to the Victoria Hotel.

They met once every two weeks, on Sundays, the Sundays when she was on duty at work. That was because he had never ventured to visit her at home, nor had she given him to understand that he might do so. He only ever waited for her after she finished work, although he knew where she lived. He always walked her from her place of work to the building where she lived. They seldom met on weekdays. Her schedule was quite irregular, but Brunul would have been able to memorize it had she asked him to. Even if they saw each other only at intervals, he sometimes imagined, lately in particular, that she was his closest friend, since neither the actors at the State Puppet Theater, nor the woman who painted the marionettes, nor the seamstress, nor the electrician who also assembled the stage sets, nor the theater manager, with whom in any event he had spoken no more than twice, could be called friends, although he liked all of them, and he was sure that he could have spent hours, even days, in their company and not have grown bored. But he never met with any of them outside an official setting. Besides Eliza, perhaps comrade Bojin was his friend too. He could hardly view him otherwise, given how much he had helped him over the last year and a half. But even he, the only man who ever entered his one-room apartment, once every few days, sometimes once every few weeks, always bringing a bottle of wine, which they drank together, even comrade Bojin crossed his threshold with an official sort of motive—Brunul sensed it without ever being told overtly. In a way he couldn't fully understand, he sensed that they were working visits. Not for him, obviously, but for comrade Bojin.

The woman clasped his arm lightly, and Brunul responded by gently lifting her hand to his chest. And then, almost without letting any further moments elapse, he told her, impatiently:

"You know, today I ran away from a policeman."

She stopped in her tracks, her wide eyes fastened on his; she pulled her arm from under his.

"It wasn't anything serious," he reassured her. "He just asked to see my papers."

"Didn't you have them on you?"

"Yes, I did. But he would have taken Vasilache away from me."

"Why would he have taken him away from you?"

"I was trying to . . ."

He smiled, lowered his eyes, shrugged. The expression of alarm had not faded from the woman's face, but she nodded, took his arm once more, shivered, which caused her to cling to him more tightly, and rested her head on his shoulder. She started walking once more, gently pulling Brunul after her.

"How did it happen?"

"I ran away," he said with another shrug. "If it happened to me again, I'd still run away. It's better like that. I can run very fast," he said in a tone not lacking a glimmer of pride. "He was fat. He couldn't keep up with me."

"Did you start to show him your papers?"

Brunul shook his head.

They continued on their way, and by the time they reached Yellow Gulley, he had told her the whole story. She listened in silence. Until they reached the bottom of the Gulley she asked no more questions, she didn't interrupt him with so much as a sound. But at the bottom she stopped, for the third time. She stopped when she thought he had finished his story, she raised her hand to her mouth, as if thinking of something, and then she frowned.

"Listen," she said, lowering her hand. "You want so much to learn how to work this marionette. I've never understood: how is it that nobody from the theater has taught you? Why don't you ask them, instead of standing on bridges and struggling to untangle the strings and . . . and having to run away from policemen?"

"Because the people from the theater don't know how. They have hand puppets. They don't work with marionettes."

"How can they not know? I mean, what kind of puppet theater is that? I think it's you who doesn't know how to ask. Or whom to ask," Eliza added, and the right corner of her lips twitched upward, a sign of affection, but as she again pressed her cheek to his arm, it might equally have meant that she did not wish to talk any further about it, at least not there, at the bottom of Yellow Gulley, with them standing stock-still and exposed to the cold.

He frowned, ran his fingers through his hair. He wouldn't have been able to gainsay her. Nor was he able to come up with any explanation, although not because he did not want to find one. In May, when comrade Bojin brought him to the State Puppet Theater to get him a job, he had thought it strange that the puppets on the posters pasted in the large yard of the Catholic church, which was also home to the theater, didn't look like Vasilache in the slightest; they had no strings, no paddle. They too were living puppets, it was true, and later he had seen how they moved, he had even imagined that he might master those movements, and quite easily too. But even so, the puppets were different. Vasilache couldn't be worn on the hand, Vasilache didn't have arms stuffed with tow, arms stuffed with straw, Vasilache had wooden arms, which flexed at the elbows, like a man's, Vasilache wasn't moved about by means of rods, Vasilache had legs on which he could walk, Vasilache had strings, Vasilache was different. And Vasilache was his. He had been told so: Vasilache had been his since his previous life, the long period of more than twenty years, which he could no longer discover among his memories. And if he were his, then certainly he had once been alive, the same as he himself had once been alive, in a different way than now, living a different life than he did now. And only his memories, or rather the lack thereof, prevented him from being with the living Vasilache once more, the Vasilache from the previous life: such was the conclusion he had reached by himself.

But he now knew as little about Vasilache's previous life as he did about the two cursed decades of his own previous life. To be precise, he knew next to nothing. He had been provided with an explanation as to the difference between his own puppet and others: his was a marionette, so he had been told, and the word "marionette" sounded very familiar to him; the others were hand puppets. Later, perhaps on a Sunday the same as this one, after Brunul had made an attempt to perform to the children coming out of the theater, one of the young puppeteers had taken him aside, he had suggested they take a walk together around the church, and he had told him about himself. He told him about how he had come to work there eight years previously, in the autumn of fifty-two; about his first show, in which the puppet he played had been a Russian tsar, a beastly character, evil to his very stuffing, as the puppeteer quipped; about what it meant to love your puppet, even when it was as bad as that tsar, and to possess it to the very depths of its existence, to possess it from the pit in which the puppeteer crouches, to possess it in such a way as to make it appear full of life and feelings and thereby convey life and feelings to the children. Brunul had listened without a word; he was happy merely that one of the actors was paying him the attention he had craved from the very first. He had listened to him in fascination, without asking questions, without being surprised that the man had taken him on a walk around the church merely to talk about himself and his passion for puppets. But when they reached the opposite side of the church, from where the entrance to the theater was no longer visible, the young man lowered his voice, telling Brunul that his Vasilache wasn't the real Vasilache, because the real Vasilache was a Romanian fairground puppet, whereas Brunul's marionette, with its white clothes and big nose, with its black domino and tall, pointy hat, didn't resemble Vasilache in the slightest. Although what he had heard upset him, angered him even, it was only then that Brunul divined that the actor's purpose had not been to tell him his life's story. His purpose had been to convey a message that none other should hear. And anger had given way to curiosity. He had asked the young man whether he knew anything about his past, the past he was unable to discover among his own memories. And the puppeteer had dolefully shaken his head, telling him that he did not know, that he had no way of knowing. Other than the fact that Vasilache couldn't be called Vasilache, the puppeteer did know one more thing: Brunul could not really be a storeroom keeper, or puppet attendant, as he himself put it. For, such a job did not exist, or rather it existed, but not there, at the State Puppet Theater, where each actor looked after his own puppets. The job, said the puppeteer, had come into existence with the arrival of Brunul. Thitherto it had never existed; it had been created specially for him. Storeroom keeper? Puppet attendant? Why would the puppets need tending, when there was a painter who brought their colors back to life, when there was a seamstress who darned and patched their clothes when need be?

Brunul had been saddened for the second time; he had even been angered, again for the second time. But after that conversation, abruptly broken off when they arrived in front of the church once more and met another three puppeteers, he had begun to ask himself certain questions. The most important of those questions was the first: Why could Vasilache not be Vasilache? What life had his Vasilache previously led if his past couldn't be told openly and for all to hear, but only whispered behind the Catholic church?

As time passed, he tried to discover more. But he received no further answers. When he asked the puppeteers, they shrugged. Not even the young puppeteer who had talked to him behind the church wished to add anything more, he even seemed to regret what he had already said. By way of an answer Brunul received a stern frown one evening. He was talking with comrade Bojin and they had already drunk half a bottle of wine. As they drank the wine to the last drop Brunul repeatedly found himself forced to refuse to reveal where "that information," as comrade Bojin put it, had come from. He didn't understand why exactly he had to maintain his reserve with the man who, once every few days, sometimes once every few weeks, visited him carrying a bottle of wine tucked under his arm, but from the hushed, secretive voice of the puppeteer who had told him all those things about him and about Vasilache, he understood that such matters were not to be spoken of with just anybody. Not even with comrade Bojin, or perhaps, and this was merely a whisper in his mind, which arose after his interlocutor had reacted with a frown, perhaps with comrade Bojin least of all. And so, after striving to persuade comrade Bojin that these were things he himself had been wondering about, since his job seemed so strange to him, given there were other members of the staff to look after the puppets, and since Vasilache's name also seemed so strange, given that he had found a stuffed Vasilache among the theater's puppets (this was a lie he invented on the spot, even rejoicing in it having come to him as an explanation), Brunul abandoned any further search for answers. But since it would have been difficult for him to part with a name to which he had already grown accustomed, he let Vasilache go on being Vasilache.

Time passed, and in the months that followed the need to discover why Vasilache was so different from other puppets faded, and in its place came the obsession with discovering the movements best suited to his marionette, and the obsession with not being late for his meetings with Eliza. Merely by her question, Eliza had now stirred an eddy of recent memories in his mind, along with doubts he had for a time striven to consign to the past.

They came to a stop in front of the apartment block where she lived, in the place where, over the last few months, Brunul had always bidden her farewell, sometimes ceremoniously, sometimes with a mere wave of the hand, before walking, for another half an hour, to his own one-room apartment. The same as on the other Sundays that winter, he now checked the bag in which he kept Vasilache, as if worried he might have lost him on the way, he tugged at the ends of his scarf, he clasped the flaps of his raincoat shut, not finding any other more natural gestures of parting.

This time, however, although as usual she drew herself slightly away, Eliza didn't release his arm. For a few seconds she gazed at him intently, perhaps in slight amusement, and then said:

"Usually I don't invite you up."

"Never," nodded Brunul, without a shadow of reproach or eagerness.

"But today you were chased by a policeman."

"I was," he confirmed, and his cheeks flushed, as if they understood more quickly than his mind that an invitation was about to follow.

"And I think that after such a hard day, you wouldn't refuse if I invited you up for a cup of tea," Eliza concluded.

Brunul made no reply. But without being prompted by any thought, his lips opened and closed a few times, like a fish's. Only after a few seconds did he give a slight, fearful nod of the head. But by the time his head made that faint inclination, the door was already open, his feet were already in motion, stepping over the metal threshold embedded in the cement floor of the entrance hall, and he had already lifted his right hand toward his chest and was lightly gripping the woman's arm.

# Chapter 2

THE INTERROGATOR WAS around forty-five years old and had a face whose gentleness he was apparently making efforts to disguise by scowling repeatedly, but without managing to keep it up throughout the interrogation. He knew his entire personal background. There was no point in contradicting him even where the minor details seemed incorrect.

He had tried. No, his father was not a traitor, he loved his country—but here a fresh scowl from the other man cut him short. No, he did not want to lead him astray, he yet again felt obliged to explain, it was true that his father had never joined the Party, but in his youth he had been a communist sympathizer, which is why he sent him, his son, back home to Romania. "Yes, true," he said, allowing the interrogator's counterargument, "in forty-five democracy hadn't yet been fully established in Romania, but the Petru Groza government had been in power for a few months; the signs were good."

Such exchanges did him no favors, however. Whenever he tried not to contradict him, but merely to fill out a detail, to make it clearer, the interrogator, sitting behind his desk of unvarnished planks (the only item of furniture in the room apart from two chairs and a lamp), muttered to himself, glanced through the dossier in front of him, and then steered the discussion back to what interested him.

"But even so, you left in thirty-seven. Didn't you like Romania anymore?"

"My mother was Italian."

"That's not what I asked you."

"Even if I hadn't liked it, would that have been a problem? In Romania, at the time, there wasn't . . . At the time, there wasn't the democracy there is now."

"That's not what I asked you."

"I was barely sixteen years old. I didn't want to leave. I didn't want to leave at all. Up until then I had only ever lived in this country. All my friends were here. It was my father who made the decision."

"Didn't your father like Romania anymore?"

"My mother's family insisted on it. He went to take over the running of their business."

"But according to the declaration he gave in 1945 . . ."

At this point the stifling quick-fire exchange came to a stop. The interrogator paused, but only for a few moments. He needed to look through the file. And then he recommenced, in the same harsh voice.

"But according to a declaration he gave in 1945, he left the country because he wanted you to go to university over there."

"No, actually he didn't give a declaration, it was a letter, which he was asked to write by Mr. . . ."

His lips stopped moving; the sentence floundered. It was definitely not a good idea to steer the conversation in that direction. Although the interrogator surely must know about it already, thought Bruno. It was better to let him ask the questions; it was better not to broach matters that were of no interest. The man sitting opposite him confirmed his fears. The interrogator knew very well what Bruno was talking about.

"That's not what I asked you. We've got all the time in the world to talk about that declaration, or rather that letter to Lucreţiu Pătrăşcanu."[1] Here he smiled, or perhaps it was a faint grin. "Don't you worry: we'll talk about everything." The half-grin became a full grin, a forced grin, although the gentle face

---

[1]    Lucreţiu Pătrăşcanu (1900–1954), Communist intellectual and politician, arrested during a purge in 1948, and finally executed after a show trial. — *Translator's note.*

was not at all suited to the menacing expression the interrogator was striving with all his might to compose. "We'll talk. But right now we're on the subject of patriotism: yours and your father's. And so let me say it again: he declared that that was why he left, because he wanted you to go to university over there. Is it true?"

"I don't know."

"How can you not know?"

"I was sixteen. My father wanted me to become a lawyer, but I didn't yet know what exactly it was I wanted to do. And so I don't know. But I don't think he was thinking about my going to university at the time."

"But even so, that's what he wrote."

A sigh on Bruno's part, a moment of capitulation, and then a gleam in his eye: an explanation.

"I think that . . . I told you: he was a communist sympathizer. But he had to take over his in-laws' businesses. I think he mustn't have wanted to talk about his businesses, perhaps . . . Perhaps he was embarrassed."

"So you're telling me he lied."

Once again, Bruno had let slip something he ought not to have said. Nevertheless, he tried to regain his composure. The man behind the desk certainly knew about his father's businesses. But even so, it wasn't good; it wasn't at all good that he himself had brought up such details. Despite the interrogator's forced glower, despite the kindness that he could almost read behind his grimaces—all right, perhaps not kindness; despite the willingness to understand that lay hidden behind the scowls, subsequent to the scornful curling of his lip and the threatening insinuations in his voice; despite the willingness, there was something that made Bruno say things that would have better been left unsaid.

"No. I mean: I don't know. I don't know what he said back then. Nor do I know why he had to declare anything about his leaving Romania."

"That's not what I asked you."

"I know, but . . . All these questions . . . Try to understand: my father died last year. Even if I wanted to find out what his intentions were, I wouldn't be able to now."

"Aha," grunted the interrogator, with a nod of the head.

He then paused once more, biting his lower lip, shaking his head in dissatisfaction. Nor did Bruno say anything more. It would have been hard for him to find something to say.

"He's dead, and so the slate's wiped clean, that's what you think. If he's dead, he's taken the past to the grave with him, that's what you think," the man muttered to himself after a time.

And then, all of a sudden, scowling, changing the subject, shifting the focus of the discussion a few years ahead and taking Bruno by surprise:

"Tell me what you know about—" here, he looked down at the file and read out the foreign name syllable by syllable "—Heinrich von Kleist."

Bruno had been brought there early that morning and left alone for a few hours. Had they gotten hold of his manuscript? Had they read it already, in just those few hours? It was the only explanation. As far as he could remember, it was only in his manuscript that he mentioned Kleist and his brief but so important essay *Über das Marionettentheater*; he referred to him the same as he referred to so many other playwrights and theorists, the same as he referred to some of the world's oldest texts, to the *Ramayana*, for example. For a marionettist it was impossible not to mention him. Would he be asked about the *Ramayana* too?

"I wrote something about Kleist," admitted Bruno Matei, staring at the floor.

"Really? You wrote something?"

"Yes."

"Where? In a newspaper? In some almanac?"

"In my manuscript."

"What kind of manuscript?"

"An . . . an essay. Or a kind of course. Something personal."
He emphasized the final word.

"A course . . ." The interrogator raised his hand to his chin,
pensively. "A course isn't something personal, Mr. Matei Bruno,
a course is taught at school, at university." He suddenly stood
up and walked around the desk. He sat down on the edge of the
desk, in front of Bruno. "A course is taught at school!" he said,
slowly, stressing each word, and leaned threateningly close to
Bruno's face. "Which school did you want to teach it at?"

Bruno gave a shrug; the interrogator gave an angry grimace.
The interrogator then snorted and began to pace up and down
that dark, almost empty room deep within the Ministry of the
Interior. He did not stop pacing after he commenced his tirade:
he walked round and round the chair on which Bruno Matei
was sitting. From time to time he placed his hand on the back
of the chair, and then he would walk from wall to wall, forcing
the young man to twist and turn in his chair to show he was
paying attention to what he said.

And during the tirade, Bruno gradually felt his breathing
quicken; he felt his eyes tire and bulge as they sought a point
on which to rest. Not because only now did his fear find its
justification in the words of the man walking up and down
past him, not because only now did the threat of which he had
become aware a few months ago fulfill itself in the gestures
of the man with whom he was pent in a dark, dirty, sparsely
furnished room. Rather it was because only now, during the
man's speech, did he sense how alone he was, not only in that
building, where he had found himself for the last few hours,
but in the whole of that country, which, in Italy, he had always
regarded as his own. He had never felt so foreign. In a strange
way, he was foreign even to the language he was hearing in that
cold, dark room, with its reek of damp wood, although it was

his native tongue, the language in which he had continued to think throughout his time in Italy. He was completely foreign and therefore completely and utterly defenseless.

"I know," began the interrogator, but then corrected himself, emphasising the pronoun, "we know that you were invited here, to the country that nurtured you to the age of sixteen, because you could lend a helping hand in the creation of an institution that Romania needed in the country's new era. We know that you came back to Romania, at the expense of the Romanian state," he said with renewed emphasis, "in the capacity of so-called expert at the Puppet and Marionette Theater. That was in 1945. We know that you had a task that you were able to complete, and so nobody thought of checking up on you before now. We know that recently you were thanked for the task you had completed and you were sent to find another job, like any other honest citizen. What we didn't know—" here he raised his voice, stressing the "didn't." "—is that you were intending to recruit a band of fascists and bandits here in Romania, to work with them against the state and to the detriment of the nation that raised you. To be more precise, we didn't know, but we found out." Here, the man made a long pause, sat down on the edge of the desk once more and looked fixedly into Bruno Matei's eyes. "I'd like you to explain it to me: instead of minding your own business, what the hell made you strike at your own nation, the nation that raised you? You come over here, a shitty expert from Italy, and you tell me, who have worked all my life for this country, that you're cleverer than me? You come over here and write your shitty course, a load of nonsense in which you shove some German's reactionary ideas down my throat, the ideas of that Kleist of yours, and you say you're going to teach them to students? What students, you animal? You expect me to believe that the wretched fascists you recruited came to see you so that they could play with puppets? The same men whose hands once held pistols and rifles? Go on, tell me, you bastard, is that what you expect me to believe?"

Bruno made no answer. But by the time the man in front of him had finished what he had to say, all the empathy of which he had up until then believed him capable, the whole of that atmosphere engendered by the face that had seemed to harbor gentleness beneath its glower, the whole of that air, almost breathable up until a few moments ago, rushed into Bruno Matei's lungs, as he heaved a deep sigh at the end of the interrogator's speech, and then it choked off all further sighs, almost suffocating him.

He made no answer. He merely shook his head, mechanically, from left to right. One of his hands rose, as if wishing to speak in his stead, but a few moments later it fell back down, in a gesture of renunciation. His shoulders sagged, his body slumped, his neck drooped, relinquishing his head to the pull of gravity, and his chin came to a rest on his sternum.

Nor did the interrogator say anything more. His eyebrows rose slightly, and his scowl gave way to sincere amazement. His eyes remained fixed on the young man's head. His amazement having turned to curiosity, the interrogator got up from the desk, hoisting himself with the help of his hands, and stooped to look at Bruno's face.

Aged just twenty-two, with his as yet fresh acting diploma in his pocket, unconcerned about a war which, since he wasn't officially Italian, he didn't have to fight alongside the Italians, and, given he didn't live in Romania, not having any reason to return and fight it alongside the Romanians, Bruno stubbornly insisted on viewing his life as he saw fit, ignoring the wishes of his family, who, without his knowing it, had in the end dealt with the formalities that had spared him being called up and sent to the front. In the view of the Romanian authorities, which had nonetheless taken an interest in his fate, the young Bruno was incapable of fighting on any front whatsoever, because he suffered from an infirmity of the back, solemnly known as Marie-Strümpell disease, which caused him dreadful pain in the shoulders, arms, and legs, and which, according to his grief-stricken family, would, due to stiffening of the shoulders and joints, turn him into a human *burattino* within a few years.

Despite this disease, confirmed by Italian physicians in various documents sent to Bucharest, the same physicians who recommended he stay in the house for long periods, taking only brief walks, Bruno did not give up the passion he had discovered in Italy. Nor did he relent even when confronted with his imploring family and yelling father. Quite simply, he couldn't see any kind of future for himself in the central office of Macellerie Pignatelli, an *azienda* established more than half a century previously, thanks to the efforts of his maternal grandfather, Antonio Pignatelli, who had gone on to open a whole chain of butcher's shops that extended far beyond Salerno.

Nor would he end up a human *burattino*, since in his case Marie-Strümpell's disease progressed only on paper, in the documents sent to Bucharest, rather than taking its course there in Italy. And after he found out about those documents, which the family, with the assistance of some doctor friends, had sent without his knowledge, the whole story seemed almost comical to Bruno. To an extent he even regarded it as a token of fate, since from *burattino* to *marionetta* was but one short step, one he had already taken.

In fact, it had not necessarily been fate that drove his family to opt for such a disease, but rather the choice that Bruno himself had made not long before. With his wonted stubbornness and aided by a trust fund from his rich grandparents, he had enrolled at the Silvio D'Amico Accademia Nazionale d'Arte Drammatica rather than studying law, as his father would have preferred. Acting was not at all in keeping with a management position at the central office of Macellerie Pignatelli in Salerno, but in the end, even his unyielding father, George Matei, or Giorgio Matei, as he started signing his name in 1937, had been forced to yield, consoling himself with the thought that his son would later regain the wits mislaid during his belated adolescence. Ultimately, an acting diploma wouldn't be such an impediment to an office job, particularly given that the office would be part of the company run by the father himself.

But mere acting did not completely satisfy Bruno, although he had started out with the enthusiastic notion that such a life would, in the not-too-distant future, bring him closer to the actors he had idolized in childhood and adolescence, the likes of Warner Baxter, Wallace Beery, and Clark Gable. During his three years of studies, which had been more mechanical and less passionate than he had anticipated, studies he had completed with dwindling enthusiasm, he discovered puppets. He had fallen in love with a marionettist. The affair had ended quickly, but it left him with an enduring love for the stringed creatures that the young woman had brought into his life. After he left the Silvio D'Amico Academy, he went south, not to Salerno, where his family were waiting for him, but much farther, all the way to Sicily, where he had another family, with whom he had corresponded during his last year at acting school. They had accepted him as one of their own: a family of eccentric puppeteers, but famous and well loved withal, a family who, in the homeland of the *Opera dei pupi*, with its oversized paladins, were trying to preserve the tradition of the *teatro delle marionette* with smaller, older puppets that had come into being in the ancient Orient and been carried along the routes taken by wars all the way to the Roman Empire, which passed them down to the whole of medieval Europe and Italy in particular.

In a plain letter, without going into detail, he informed his parents of this new passion, which had led him to bypass Salerno on his way to Sicily. This was during the period when it was becoming apparent that Romanian citizen Bruno Matei was being sought for enlistment in the Romanian Army. One evening, on the terrace of the Pignatelli family villa in Salerno, after they had drunk a few glasses of wine and smoked a few cigars, a doctor friend described to Bruno's father George Matei, also known as Giorgio Matei, a number of possible diseases that would guarantee Bruno's exemption from conscription. More amused than determined, Bruno's father had picked Marie-Strümpell's disease, his attention drawn to the word *burattino*, whose stiff, jerky movement the physician had compared with the effects of the condition. George Matei had only just received his son's letter, and so the doctor's words suggested to him the idea of an ironic punishment for Bruno. It was the least he could do, since his son's stubbornness left him no other alternative. After a few more glasses of wine, Marie Strümpell was declared the winning disease.

However, the portent glimpsed even by Bruno in the symptoms of that disease, a gift from his family, did not come to pass in his life after he became an apprentice. True, his apprenticeship was quite brief, but long enough for him to acquire the art of manipulating a marionette and to become highly learned in the history of that theatrical genre, or at least so it seemed to him. He became learned at least in that part of history to which the family of puppeteers ascribed the most importance and which he managed to absorb in the time he spent with them: the history of the Orient, where all the world's puppets originated. He had been obliged to read and listen to Italian translations of countless Indian, Egyptian, Chinese, and Persian stories, more often than not handwritten on loose leaves of paper, although he had not found this remotely as arduous as his studies at the Academy, since he had never lacked a passion for stories. And within those ancient, mythical worlds, reborn thanks to his patient, methodical teachers, he began to breathe life into his marionettes, string by string, step by step, movement by movement. Although satisfactory, his progress alongside the puppeteers on the way to consummate animation of his puppets and an applied knowledge of more recent history encountered an obstacle a little over half a year later, at the beginning of forty-three. Based on what he had learned during his study of the art of Antiquity, no sooner had he begun to understand the traditional Italian marionette play, which traced its origins to the *Commedia dell'Arte*, than the family of puppeteers came into conflict with the authorities, which were not at all amused at certain performances that made not very subtle reference to *Sua Eccellenza il Duce*, and they found themselves forced to flee north. Bruno was not part of their escape plan, and fortunately for him, nor had he been part of the incriminating performances, given that he was not yet skilled enough for such a test. Nevertheless, to reward his assiduous apprentice, the head of the family of puppeteers had, before their unavoidable separation, given Bruno Matei a document that could substitute for a diploma, a document that did not confer on him the title of master puppeteer, but which attested to the period he had spent alongside masters of their art, albeit eccentric masters now fallen into disgrace.

With his diploma from the Silvio D'Amico Accademia Nazionale d'Arte Drammatica and the document from the head of the old family of puppeteers, the young man returned to Salerno. Not necessarily because he saw a future for himself there, but because even he had begun to sense the hard times everybody else was complaining about, and therefore a reconciliation with his rich family was not to be neglected at such a moment. He brought with him a host of hopes, and so he was not discouraged in the first months when he failed to find work appropriate to his qualifications. But as time passed and the failures mounted, the desk waiting for him in the central office of Macellerie Pignatelli became a clearer and clearer threat.

The moment which, not even he himself knew why— perhaps because the document attesting that he had formerly been the apprentice of puppeteers now in disgrace acquired a different value, or perhaps because he had adopted the broader hopes of those around him—he regarded as a turning point in his life, namely the rebellion within the Great Fascist Council, was of no great help to him. The broader history, no matter how exhilarating, did not always have an effect on the narrower history of the individual, thought Bruno at the time, in disappointment. Moreover, he had not been able to foresee that the *Opera Nazionale Dopolavoro*, already considerably weakened by the war, would, after the overthrow of Mussolini, give up the ghost altogether, and the arts, including that with which Bruno was in love, no longer seemed to be of interest to anybody. In the months that followed, his attempts to find employment held not even the shadow of a chance. Other than looking for a job, Bruno had nothing to do but abandon himself to his reading. He read more and more books, more and more widely, constantly striving, this time all by himself, to perfect his knowledge of the marionette artistry he had begun to learn alongside the puppeteers from Sicily.

But although they don't always have an effect, there are still moments in which the broader history can intervene decisively in the narrower history of the individual. This is what Bruno thought when his own history changed dramatically. For the small empire the Pignatelli family had founded on pork and beef, and which had existed for more than half a century, the autumn that followed brought problems such as they had never faced before. When the company's central offices were reduced to rubble in September 1943 during fighting between the Germans occupying the city and the American Fifth Army, the Pignatelli family took refuge in Rome, where they rented a house using money they had set aside for just such dark days as they were now experiencing, and they boarded up and left behind their butcher's shops in the south of the country.

For George Matei, his native land once more became a solution, although to tell the truth it had never been absent from his mind. But his attempts to persuade his wife to abandon

her family and return to his native Romania failed, despite his
insistence. In Romania they now had only a very few friends,
a handful of very distant relatives, and not even a home to call
their own. Why should he go back? For whom? Furthermore,
as his parents-in-law said, the Americans would soon enter
Romania, the same as they had Italy, wiping the German army
from the face of the earth.

After August 23, 1944, reading news about Romania in
the liberated press in Rome, George Matei discovered that his
friend Lucrețiu Pătrășcanu was now a Secretary of State. They
had studied law together at Bucharest University and although
George Matei had not joined the Communist Party, thanks to
his friendship with Pătrășcanu he had come to know and agree
with some communist principles. In the two years before he left
the country he even attended a few meetings, of which he still
had good memories, since his friend, the former communist
undesirable, newly returned from Moscow, had maintained his
enthusiasm, and it rubbed off on the apolitical George Matei,
whom Lucrețiu Pătrășcanu roped into his future plans. The
plans came to nothing, however, since in the end George Matei
had been drawn more strongly to the directorship of a chain
of Italian butcher's shops. But thanks to those conversations
and those plans, the hopes of the George Matei of 1944, the
businessman without a business, responsible for a family made
up of a wife, parents-in-law, and a son who had never done
a day's work in his life, took on a new outline, albeit a faint
one, which in the first instance concerned only his son and his
dreams of being a puppeteer.

Through intermediaries, he managed to contact his
erstwhile university friend. Not quite straightaway, but after a
good few months, by which time Lucrețiu Pătrășcanu was no
longer Secretary of State, but Minister of Justice in the new
Petru Groza government, which had come to power in March
1945. Finally, George Matei received a friendly letter—even an

enthusiastic letter, as he saw it—from the Romanian minister, providing a telephone number, which Lucreţiu invited him to call, mentioning the days and hours when he could generally answer. At the beginning of May 1945, a few days after he too took to the streets, alongside countless citizens of Rome, tossing his hat in the air and celebrating the end of the war, even if there was little else to celebrate in Italy, George Matei telephoned Lucreţiu Pătrăşcanu in Bucharest. After they congratulated each other on the end of the war, after they briefly reminisced about the times they had spent together, after George, out of politeness more than anything else, asked a few questions about Lucreţiu's work as a minister, and after Lucreţiu answered the questions, also out of politeness, the topic of Bruno Matei at last entered the conversation: according to his father, it was the young man's wish to return to his native land. The situation had become too complicated for the head of the family to take into account any eventual opposition on his son's part.

Inquiring as to the young man's aptitudes and education, and then expressing his slight disappointment that under the circumstances it was hard to believe that he would be able to find a job for him in the ministry, Lucreţiu Pătrăşcanu nonetheless assured his old friend from Italy that he would think of something. Here the conversation came to an end, since other business, which was of national importance, demanded the attention of Romania's Minister of Justice.

Near the end of the year, as well as near the end of the money left over from the Pignatelli family business, George Matei had still received no news from the old friend, who had in the meantime become a minister. It was not until mid-November that an envelope arrived from Romania, but without any official markings. He opened it, not suspecting who the sender might be. First of all he glanced at the signature at the end of the letter: the simple signature of an erstwhile classmate and friend. That signature was appended to a text urging him to send his son to Bucharest, where Lucrețiu would find him a position as an adviser at the Țăndărică Puppet and Marionette Theater. In fact, as the minister took pains to emphasize in the letter, it was not he who had found the job, but rather his wife, Elena, who was a set designer at the theater and who, during one of her few free evenings, on hearing the story of her husband's old friend, had clicked her fingers, astonished at the coincidence, since the newly established theater was in great need of a man knowledgeable about marionettes. The only thing the minister asked of George was to send his son the marionette expert to Bucharest as quickly as possible. Nonetheless, in the final paragraph, he made the following request: that besides his university diplomas Bruno Matei should also bring an explanatory letter from his father, since although his departure from Romania eight years previously was not a serious matter, it still might give rise to certain questions. He promised him that such a letter would not have any repercussions, but would merely be kept on file, once he, Minister Lucrețiu Pătrășcanu, had vouched with his own signature that its contents were in accordance with the truth.

A week later, Bruno Matei alighted on the frozen platform of Bucharest's Northern Station, lugging a voluminous suitcase, in which he had also stowed a Pulcinella marionette, which he had bought after parting with his Sicilian family, during the time when he was striving to achieve mastery of Italian marionette artistry by himself. He had not objected to the plan, far from it; he had accepted with a joy surpassed only by his amazement that it had come from his father. For the first time in Bruno's life, his father had taken account of his wishes and, as if this were not an event in itself, he had also found him a job. A job suited to his dreams, which, at the time, had been all but obscured amid a host of disappointments.

On his way to the apartment that had been allocated to him, on which he was to pay rent once he received his wages, he pressed his cheek to the window of the car that had been waiting for him in front of the station, and his enthusiasm melted into a kind of amazement, perhaps even sadness, since he was now rediscovering places that his distant memory of childhood had painted completely differently, in shades less gloomy than those he was now given to see, in the aftermath of a war that had buried colors beneath dust and rubble, seemingly lowering the sky and making it grayer than he remembered.

But not only Bucharest had fallen victim to disaster.

In the days, weeks, and months that followed, he did not meet his father's friend, the minister. He was never to meet him. Not that he particularly wished to: his work at the Puppet and Marionette Theater occupied his time and was enough for him. On the day when he entered the building of the new theater for the first time, he handed his father's letter to the minister's wife, Elena Pătrășcanu, a voluble woman of thirty, a woman perhaps a little too affected, a little too self-confident, and, in a way not exactly pleasant, a little too overbearing toward other people, although to Bruno such details did not matter greatly, especially given that from the outset the woman showed him an odd sort of gratitude, as if he had done the theater a favor by coming to work there as a marionette expert. As if it were not she who had been instrumental in finding a position for a twenty-two-year-old man who had done nothing in his life except dream.

The work then opened up to him. The work he had long been waiting for, the work he had somehow feared, but from which he did not flinch in the months that followed, months that elapsed without very many changes, but with plenty of satisfactions for him personally and for the troupe of marionettists of which he felt himself part, months that became a year, and then two years . . .

Rather than exhausting itself, his enthusiasm only increased with the passage of time. Perhaps also because at the beginning of forty-seven a satisfaction he had thitherto never imagined was added to his work at the theater, work that was in itself rewarding, since although he was an adviser, he studied alongside his colleagues, created with them, shared their excitement at every success of the marionette section: at the request of a colleague, he agreed to give private lessons to that colleague's nephew, who, although an acting student, was drawn to marionettes, under the obvious influence of his uncle. Bruno accepted the challenge, not only from a nostalgia awakened by that young man's destiny, so similar to his own, but also from pride that he, the apprentice of Italian puppeteers just four years previously, had at last officially achieved the status of instructor, teacher, master. Toward the end of forty-seven, the private lessons began to occupy more and more of his time, since meanwhile his pupils, his apprentices, had increased to four, and with them had increased the self-respect of the fledgling master of marionettes.

Forty-eight brought radical changes to Bruno's life. But not political changes: he had learned to pass over them in silence and experienced only the vaguest curiosity, enough only to make him buy a Bucharest newspaper perhaps once every two weeks, sometimes more often. In the last two years or so he had noticed that the political articles had begun to sprawl, taking up more and more column inches, but he read them last, after scanning the cultural listings, rejoicing at even the most fleeting reference to the Țăndărică Theater.

The first change in his personal circumstances occurred in late spring: a tragic change. His father died in Salerno, having returned there in 1946 in an attempt to revive the Macellerie Pignatelli. A heart attack, without any prior warning signs. Bruno's situation was only made the worse when the Romanian authorities refused him permission to return to Italy for his father's funeral. They gave him no official reason, and the only explanation he received came from a scowling functionary, who told him that in any event he would miss the funeral, since no train would be able to take him to southern Italy so quickly.

Bruno knew this already, but he was duty bound to spend at least a few days with his mother and grandparents, who he couldn't help but imagine must be devastated by the event. And so he was forced to reply by telegram, having to choose his words carefully, since another functionary, this time from the post office, rejected his first missive, declaring that Bruno's explanation about his being unable to leave the country was unnecessary, all the more so given that it laid the blame on the Romanian authorities.

The second change came before Christmas 1948. It ought not to have been unexpected. Various events during the year now coming to a close, events that Bruno had tried to pass over, immersing himself in his work and thereby allaying his own disquiet, which was part of the general disquiet, ought to have prepared him for it: the sacking of Lucreţiu Pătrăşcanu's government in February, and then the arrest of Elena Pătrăşcanu, whose surname could not but provoke a reaction on the part of her theater colleagues, and to whose name Bruno in particular could hardly have remained indifferent. But even so, he took the second of these blows as if it had come from nowhere. In December, in an office that was not Elena Pătrăşcanu's and in which not she but somebody else was waiting for him, he was thanked for his contribution to the development of the arts section of the Ţăndărică Theater, after which that same somebody informed him, without any attempt to soften the blow, without any glimmer of a guilty conscience, without even adopting a different tone of voice, that his assistance was no longer required. The man in front of him didn't hold any managerial position; he wasn't even an employee. He was merely a man whose visits to the theater, not for performances, but for random discussions with various employees, had begun that summer; a man who merely had to utter, albeit in an incantatory fashion, the name of the institution to which he belonged: the Ministry of the Interior, in order to be given his own office in the Țăndărică Theater building. The man had used his office there as a base where he was able to turn his random discussions into longer talks, far from the eyes and ears of the others, talks of which the theater employees made no mention on emerging from that room. Those who had not yet entered the office nudged each other and exchanged whispers, sometimes jocularly, whispers that lent the room in question a name: the confessional, since all those who emerged from it looked like they had been relieved of a burden they had been carrying on their shoulders, otherwise it was inexplicable that their shoulders should become so light, so disburdened that they instantly rose, sometimes even moving up and down repeatedly if you asked the visitors to that office what they had talked about within.

Although Bruno Matei had entered the office thinking that it was his turn to engage in one of the discussions, when, in clipped sentences, the man communicated to him something else entirely, he was not taken aback; he asked no questions; he didn't react in any way. He spoke no word. He merely nodded his head, almost in approval, or perhaps he merely wished to convey that he understood all that had to be understood, and then he turned on his heel and went out.

He gathered his things together, silently, neither expecting nor desiring further confirmation of his dismissal. With two bags full of materials he had purchased over the course of time and with the white-clad marionette that had been tucked under his arm when he arrived from Italy, he went to his apartment near the Simu Museum, a building that resembled the Hephaesteion at the foot of the Acropolis. He had visited the museum as a child and it had provided him with a landmark from the very first day of his return to Romania, a unique, distinct landmark that enabled him not to mix up the streets of Bucharest, where, in the beginning, he was liable to get lost whenever he turned a corner.

He spent the holidays there, leaving the apartment only to buy a loaf of bread or a liter of milk. Prior to this self-imposed solitude, Bruno had nonetheless bought all the newspapers he found on the street stalls. For it was only then, in the winter of 1948–49, that he began to understand that the broader history always wielded an overwhelming power over the narrower, personal history, even if often it was too late by the time you realized it. And in those days, the broader history was written between the lines of the newsprint.

After the New Year, Bruno stopped reading the newspapers. Instead he began to write. He wrote not for the broader history, since a table with a few sheets of paper spread on it, in a nondescript apartment in Bucharest, was not sufficient for that, but perhaps for his own narrower, personal history. Or perhaps just for his own narrow present, crammed into the space of that rented apartment, from whose window could be seen a wide, gray street and the tops of a few columns of a museum that resembled the Hephaesteion at the foot of the Acropolis.

He began to write about a passion for which he had renounced a career in an office in Salerno, for which he had renounced Italy, and for which, lo and behold, he had renounced even his parents. A history of marionettes, as he himself had discovered them, a history which, as he wrote it, came more and more to resemble a long essay, perhaps even a course on marionettes, although he held out no genuine hope that his own personal experience, which he was now putting down on paper, would ever be passed on to any students.

The audience Bruno Matei addressed was from a different history, an audience prepared to listen to him, to understand him, even to ask him questions. And he sought answers to those potential questions, he provided the answers firstly in his mind, and then turned them into considered sentences, aimed directly at that receptive audience, which he couldn't see anywhere around him, when he looked out of the window at the passersby, for example, but which, in those icy days, he greatly needed. In that imagined audience he sometimes saw his students, who were four real reference points, but whom he had given up teaching at the beginning of forty-eight, after his father's death. He craved that audience, but he knew it would be hard for him to find it ever again.

Then came that morning in March 1949. Scarcely had he awoken, after sitting up late at his writing table. He was somewhat satisfied, but at the same time saddened that his ideas had almost run out. In the pages on the table he could already see his manuscript in its final, tangible form. He counted the last of the money he had been keeping in reserve. He gloomily ascertained that he barely had enough to pay the next month's rent. At one point he stood up, perhaps slightly surprised, but more bothered by the repeated knocking on the front door.

An ordinary morning in March 1949. At the door, two men in uniform invited him to accompany them, that he might make a statement. Bruno didn't ask what kind of statement. He didn't even change his clothes, there was no need; he had fallen asleep in his outdoor clothes, which he had put on the previous afternoon when he had gone out to buy milk and bread. He didn't get changed, but merely asked for a moment so that he could put his boots on, because otherwise the puddles on the street, as he told the men in uniform, even essaying a smile, otherwise that wretched slush on the street would not spare his feet, shod in house slippers as they were.

# Chapter 3

IT WAS AFTER half past eight when Brunul, frozen, entered his one-room apartment. When he turned on the light, from the hall he saw comrade Bojin seated on the bed, holding the customary bottle of wine. Comrade Bojin's frown abruptly reminded Brunul of the note he had been handed at the entrance to the theater, the same as every other time previously, a note which informed him that today, Sunday, he would have to be home by eight at the latest. There was no question but that comrade Bojin was usually late, sometimes half an hour or even a whole hour late. However, it wasn't because of comrade Bojin's wonted lateness that Brunul had failed to arrive home on time, but rather because of the unexpected event of that evening: Eliza's invitation for him to come up for a cup of tea, which had so unsettled him that for the first time ever he had forgotten all about comrade Bojin.

"What time do you call this?" he asked, without getting up. "It's me who's got to wait for you now, is it? Didn't you get the note or what?"

He mumbled, "Yes, I did," and was about to tell him that he had walked Eliza home, but stopped short, embarrassed, knowing that the story would have had to continue, that the explanation would have perhaps also touched on details that he felt belonged to him and him alone, at least then, that evening. How could he have told him that after he had drunk the hot tea, after Eliza had looked steadily into his eyes and said that he was a good man, she had moved close to him, placed her hands on his burning cheeks and kissed him? First she kissed him above the eyebrows, in a place that still felt colder than the rest of his forehead, but cold in a pleasant, slightly burning way, a sensation that even now still preserved the shape of her lips. Then, lowering her right hand, Eliza bent her head and kissed him on the cheek, curtailing his momentary embarrassment, but not his excitement, with a smile such as Brunul had perhaps never seen before, a smile that made up for the many evenings, including the chilly ones, when he had waited for her to finish work, when he had walked her to the entrance of her building, before returning, as lonely as ever, to his own one-room apartment. He wouldn't have been able to tell comrade Bojin any of these things now, although on other occasions he had told him about his meetings with Eliza without reserve of any kind, and even with pleasure. And so instead of continuing, after his initial mumbled answer, Brunul merely shrugged, by way of apology. He then silently took off his raincoat, hung it on the hook, and beneath it placed the bag containing Vasilache.

Only after they had emptied the first two glasses did the tension subside, giving way to the friendliness that had sprung up between them in the last year and a half. The change in atmosphere was due to comrade Bojin, who, after chiding him for a good few minutes, and after securing a firm promise on Brunul's part that such an incident would not be repeated, gave a resigned, placating wave of his hand and said:

"I've got something for you. That's why it was important that we see each other now. But you had other business," he said, repeating the reproach for the last time. "Never mind. We'll pass over that. I had a hard time getting hold of this present, it's important to you, and so I'll forget about the rest."

He put his hand in his chest pocket, pulled out an old, greenish piece of paper, no larger than a lottery ticket, and handed it to Brunul, who first looked at the drawings: on the right, a group of three men and three women, each holding an open newspaper and reading with obvious interest. Above the drawing was a hammer-and-sickle emblem, framed by sheaves of wheat and R.P.R. in large letters. To the left was a drawing of a building site below various captions. After studying these drawings, which meant nothing to him, Brunul began to read from top to bottom: "Series D – LEI 20 LEI – twenty – toward The House of the Spark." Curious as to why his friend had given him this piece of paper, Brunul lifted his eyes questioningly. Comrade Bojin told him to read what was written in the bottom right-hand corner, and only now did Brunul feel a surge of excitement: there in the corner were printed the words "Deposited by," followed by a name in pencil. It was his name, the same name as appeared on his identity card.

"It was nine years ago," said comrade Bojin. "A national subscription was held to raise funds for the House of the Spark in Bucharest. A beautiful building. Maybe you'll see it one day. And you gave some money toward it. Twenty lei. No small sum. You were generous, in other words. A man of labor, first class," he said, with a smile.

"So, I went back to Bucharest, I didn't come here to Jassy . . ."

Excitement gripped his vocal cords; he was barely able to articulate the whispered words. Comrade Bojin's eyes bulged. He hesitated for a few seconds, apparently surprised. He then shook his head and recomposed his self-assured mien.

"Wait a minute . . . Didn't I say it was a national subscription? You could have subscribed anywhere. I've already told you that. When you returned from Italy, you came here to Jassy, after your parents died in a bombing raid. I don't know why you came here. I really don't know. But I found this in the archives. And even then, only by chance. I told a friend about you and when I said your name, he said: 'I know that name, comrade, I saw it on a national subscription ticket for the House of the Spark from 1950.' Here in Jassy. Not in Bucharest."

It had been clear from the very first that comrade Bojin had not taken at all kindly to Brunul's deduction. If Brunul had been more attentive, he would have wondered when he heard

his friend rattling off the story about the national subscription as
if he had learned it by rote. But a whole host of other questions
were now gnawing away at Brunul.

"Is that my signature?"

"It's yours."

"How did people pay over the money?"

"At their place of work."

"So, I was working?"

"You were employed, yes. What, still harping on about that?
Is it possible for anybody to be out of work in this country?"

"Where did I work?"

"How am I supposed to know? Can't you see it doesn't say
anything on the ticket?"

Brunul's eyes narrowed and he looked aside, dissatisfied.

"Would you look at him! What's your problem? I thought
I would make you happy, showing you something from your
past, whereas you . . ."

"It doesn't tell me anything," said Brunul shaking his head.
"It doesn't say where I worked. It doesn't even tell me what town
I was living in."

"You were living here, for God's sake."

"I don't know what use it is to me."

"Do you really not get it? It shows that back then, before
everything, you were upstanding, you contributed to society
and wanted what was best for it. How can it not be any use
to you? It clearly shows that at least your intentions were
good, that you wanted to help the people, the country. What
happened after that, I don't know. But in the end, it's intentions
that count the most."

"Hmm, yes," agreed Brunul.

"'Hmm, yes,' he says! A little more enthusiasm, man! Be
happy you've found something out about yourself."

"I'm happy."

The ticket lay on the table, between the two glasses, which
comrade Bojin now refilled with wine. They clinked glasses.

"You'd think you were a child," said Bojin, after smacking his lips. "I go out of my way to give you a present, and you have to pick faults. You're not satisfied. What is it you want? In time, slowly but surely, you'll receive other pieces of information, you'll find out more . . . But why don't you tell me what you did today?" he asked, suddenly changing the subject.

"A policeman chased me," answered Brunul, absently.

"What?"

Eyes bulging, comrade Bojin put his glass back down on the table, although he had been about to raise it to his lips. Brunul shrugged, without looking at him.

"What's wrong with you? Are you completely out of your mind? Here I was praising you for being such an upstanding citizen, and you come out with this. Phooey," he exclaimed, rolling his eyes. "What the hell did you do?"

"Nothing. Nothing really. I was on a bridge, with Vasilache."

Comrade Bojin struck the table with the palms of his hands and stood up, in annoyance. He walked over to the wall, leaned on it with both hands, his back turned to Brunul. He then turned to his host and, wagging his raised finger chidingly, he began:

"I've told you before: don't take that stupid doll with you when you go out, because people will say you're insane. That stupid doctor should've taken that doll away from you!" he muttered to himself. And then to Brunul: "And what did you do? Did he take you to the police station? Am I going to have to run around after you again?"

"When have you ever run around for me?" asked Brunul in surprise, lifting his eyes to look at comrade Bojin.

"Don't give me that nonsense. Tell me what happened."

"You mean it was you who talked to the police the last time, so that they would give Vasilache back to me?"

Comrade Bojin sat back down, raising both hands and shaking his palms in Brunul's direction, seeking thereby to calm himself more than to temper the other man. Brunul for his part, sitting motionless, suddenly felt a surge of gratitude toward his friend. He had not previously made the connection, but now he wondered how something so obvious could have escaped him. From the very beginning, from the first meeting with comrade Bojin, at a time when he didn't even dare look at him, let alone speak to him, his friend had told him he had been assigned "by the Party" to look after him, to provide him with whatever he needed, to help him whenever he needed. Everything had lived up to that promise. The one-room apartment where they now sat was thanks to comrade Bojin, with whom he had crossed the threshold for the first time. Comrade Bojin had given him the key, keeping one for himself, in case Brunul ever lost his. It had been comrade Bojin who had taken him to the yard of the State Puppet Theater. Comrade Bojin had asked the director to give Brunul a job. How could he have not realized that it had also been comrade Bojin who had intervened to release Vasilache when Brunul first got into trouble with the police?

"Tell me what happened," comrade Bojin said, his voice now mild.

"There's nothing much to tell. I ran away."

Comrade Bojin's eyes bulged once more; he raised his hand to his brow and then slumped forward, so that his elbow leaned on the table, propping up his head.

"Man . . ."

"No, wait, don't worry! He was fat and couldn't catch me," Brunul reassured him, with a hint of pride in his voice.

"Ah, so you got away. He didn't take your papers . . ."

"No."

"And he didn't catch you? You got away from him?"

"I hid in the entrance to a building until I was sure he was gone. And then I left. Nothing happened. There's no reason for you to worry."

Comrade Bojin breathed a sigh of relief, nodded, and reached for his glass of wine.

"Haven't you got anything better to do? Isn't there anybody you can spend your time with in a normal way, like normal people? Get rid of that damned doll! Stop carrying it around with you!"

His arched eyebrows relaxed, and with his right hand he made a gesture as if to banish unpleasant thoughts. His eyes narrowed in curiosity, accompanied by the shadow of a smile, and his tone became friendly once more.

"On the subject of dolls . . . What's new at that theater of yours?"

"*Sînziana and Pepelea.*"

"Seen it."

"They're going to put on *The Emperor's Rabbits*, they're working on it, but I don't know when it will be ready."

"Rehearsals?"

"Yes. Almost every morning."

"In the morning?" said Bojin with a frown. "I'm at work in the morning."

"There's also a rehearsal on Sunday. The performances aren't until the afternoon."

"Are there animals too? What I mean is dolls, but animal dolls."

"It's mainly historical. But there are animals too. That's why it's called *The Emperor's Rabbits*."

"Historical . . . That's good," said comrade Bojin, with a nod of the head, abruptly becoming grave and even clearing his throat. "History is good. Generally speaking, you can learn things from history. But the best history is the history that's being made today. Look at the Soviet interplanetary rocket. Isn't that history?"

Brunul made to look as if he agreed, but without really knowing what it was all about.

"Phooey," exclaimed comrade Bojin, rolling his eyes. "You see? I keep telling you: read up on it. It's for your own sake I'm doing this. I keep bringing you the newspapers, man, but you should buy them for yourself too. A newspaper costs just twenty bani, hardly anything. How can you expect to be able to read again, like me, if you don't work at it? And if you read, you learn things. Is it insignificant to know that an interplanetary rocket built by the Soviets is flying above our heads? It's the first artificial planet, man, and it's orbiting the sun. All the newspapers wrote about it at the beginning of the year, but you don't read, you sit around playing with your doll; what do you care about history? And this is real history!" comrade Bojin said, wagging his raised finger at him again. "And that's why history is good when it's combined with art. Because art is good if it's done intelligently. What, isn't building a rocket still art?"

He nodded his head in dissatisfaction, but if Brunul had been more attentive, he would have discovered in his friend's dissatisfaction something just as artificial as the claims to there being a planet on the part of the Soviet rocket orbiting the sun. But comrade Bojin gave him no time to make such an observation, he rose to his feet, ready to leave, and without any connection to what he had just been saying, he asked:

"On Sunday?"

"Pardon?" said Brunul, looking up at him.

"That rehearsal with the rabbits: is it on Sunday?"

"Sunday is over already," said Brunul with a smile.

But the smile was not directed at comrade Bojin. To tell the truth, he had not been paying much attention to the conversation for a while, ever since comrade Bojin had asked him whether he had anybody else he could spend his time with. The smile he now let slip arose from his memory of the hours he had spent with Eliza. That Sunday, despite the fear he had experienced when running away from the policeman, had ended better than any other Sunday he could remember.

Now that the bottle of wine on the table had been emptied, comrade Bojin's Sunday visit came to an end, which, this time, could not have pleased Brunul more. The reason for this was that even as he was walking home, he had pictured the evening he was about to spend, with an impatience that made him quicken his steps: an evening in bed, with the light out, with Vasilache beside him, with thoughts that would fill the hours before sleep, since this time he was convinced that not minutes but hours would pass before he fell asleep.

"Stop taking that doll with you everywhere you go," said comrade Bojin, standing next to the front door, before he put his hat on. "You don't solve things like that by running away, man. You were lucky today, but you might not be the next time."

Brunul assented.

After closing the door behind comrade Bojin, he took Vasilache out of the bag and straightened the marionette's hat. He went to the bed and sat down. He held Vasilache's head in his hands and gazed at it for a long moment. He pulled down Vasilache's black mask and for a few seconds pressed his lips to the varnished wood of the marionette's head. He then lowered his right hand and tilting his head slightly he kissed Vasilache next to his carved wooden ear, beneath the curls that tumbled over his face.

He was still smiling as he carefully laid the marionette next to his pillow. He went to change into his pajamas, turned out the light and, having climbed into bed, lay with his back to Vasilache. That evening he wouldn't tell even his wooden friend anything about Eliza, although Vasilache would have liked to find out what had happened in the woman's apartment, since Brunul had not taken him out of the bag even for one second.

Giving way to puddles and mud the snow was thinning day by day, dissolved by a wave of warmth nonetheless feeble for late March. Besides his usual tasks at work, Brunul occupied his week with the national subscription ticket. He wasn't particularly enthusiastic about it; there was no date on the ticket, and in fact it provided almost no information at all about him. Of course, after his initial disappointment had passed, when he woke up and found it on the table, between the two empty glasses, he remembered what comrade Bojin had said and for a few moments he was carried away by a wave of warmth that filled his body from head to feet. It was good to know that in his past, about which he knew so little, he had been the same person, he had loved his country as much as he loved it now, he had seen with the same eyes the paradise that was being built all around and in his own small way he had contributed to the building effort. Perhaps he had contributed more than that? If just one ticket had been found, that didn't mean that there had not been others. But that happiness, which deserved to be experienced to the full, was not enough for him. And so, after a short while, instead of helping him, the ticket began to prompt further, niggling, torturous questions, because he realized how far he still was from any answer. He didn't calm down until evening, when he decided to content himself with the sole item of information provided by the greenish piece of paper: his signature beneath the sum of twenty lei toward the construction of the House of the Spark.

Therefore he would not have sought other details, for the simple reason that he himself could see how pointless such a search would have been. But he did have a reason to keep his mind occupied, and the ticket was a good pretext. Otherwise his mind, sometimes impelled by an excitement that culminated in a feeling of suffocation, would have led his steps to the Victoria Hotel, Eliza's workplace. He would have found her there, yes, and he would not have done anything out of the ordinary, since sometimes, seldom, it was true, he sought her out during the week, not just on the Sundays when she was on duty; he had sought her out on days that had seemed too long and too uneventful to him, and his going there always seemed to be a pleasure for her. But now Brunul felt something different. Although he would have liked to, although his mind, impelled by impatience, would have directed his steps to Union Square, whenever he was about to let himself be led there, a strong emotion, which instantly transformed his heartbeats from the ticking of a clock to the flutter of a dove's wings, told his mind to calm itself, to let itself be carried away by other preoccupations, to wait for the usual evening, Sunday evening, when the emotion would be just as overwhelming, perhaps even more so, but at least it would not be self-induced. For, it was as if the Sunday evenings, even if they did come once every two weeks, when Eliza was on duty at work, had always been dedicated to her, they were obligatory, they could not be avoided, not even now, when his desire to hide himself somewhere, in a place where she would never be able to find him, was just as strong as his desire to see her again, to have her kiss him again. On the forehead. On the cheek. Even on the lips.

When he asked them, not one of his colleagues could tell him anything about the national subscription ticket. Not even the actors. In the end, it was not at all surprising; most of them were young, most had not been of working age in 1950, when, as comrade Bojin had told him, the ticket had been issued and Brunul had signed it, with the same name as that inscribed in his identity card.

On Friday afternoon, however, as he was getting ready to lock up the puppet storeroom and go home, the cleaning woman, whom he had not gotten around to asking, came up to him and said:

"I hear you're interested in a subscription ticket. Can I have a look at it?"

Brunul took the ticket out of his trouser pocket and showed it to her.

"Hmm, yes," said the woman, chewing her lips. "Just as I thought. Me and my husband subscribed. Twenty lei each. We were working at the cloth factory at the time, if you know it. I was a cleaning woman there too. He still works there. He's a foreman. I got transferred here two years ago, because I was ill, in April of fifty-seven: the work would be easier here, or so I thought, at first. But you know what? It's not at all easier," said the woman, waving her hand in disgust. "But no matter," she added, "because I'll be able to retire in another three years, and if it hasn't killed me by now, it won't kill me by then."

"What about the ticket?" asked Brunul.

"Ah, yes. The management summoned us one day and said there was a voluntary subscription. Voluntary it may have been, but it still meant you had to cough up. We didn't have any choice, and so we paid. It wasn't up to us. Me and my husband, that is. It wasn't any big deal; we were hardly going to starve, because twenty lei isn't very much money. But anyway, I wanted to tell you, since I heard you were asking. They told us about the House of the Spark, but I've never set foot in Bucharest in my life, and so what use is it to me? Maybe the country is nicer with it there. I've seen it in photographs. But they could have told us: comrades, if you want to make the country nicer, contribute twenty lei. And I would have paid, really I would. But as it was, the management summoned us and said: sign here. We signed and they deducted the money from our wages. But I'm not sorry. I just wanted to tell you, because I heard you were asking."

Brunul's brow wrinkled. He thanked the woman and went outside into the large yard of the Catholic church. He looked at the greenish piece of paper and then angrily crumpled it up and tossed it onto a heap of frozen snow, which had survived the warm spell of the last few days. Not even his initial joy now remained.

He walked a few dozen paces and then turned back. He

searched for the ticket, he picked it out of the dirty snow, he wiped it and smoothed it against his knee, and then he put it back in his pocket. It had not brought him any advantage, not the slightest advantage. It had brought him nothing but further disappointment, at the end of a week in which he had consoled himself with at least the thought that he had found out what kind of man he had been nine years previously. But even so, it was a present from comrade Bojin, and on remembering that fact, a few moments before, he had felt guilty enough to turn back. In the end, even though it was of no use to him, nor could it do him any harm.

At the end of the rehearsals for *The Emperor's Rabbits*, which he had watched from backstage next to Brunul the following Sunday, comrade Bojin was not at all temperate in his applause. Quite the contrary. In that moment, had Brunul asked him what he thought of the performance he had just seen, comrade Bojin would have told him the truth, for reasons he himself would have been hard put to explain.

The fact of the matter was that comrade Bojin never lied. The principle behind it was no great matter, but such as it was, it had served him well in life. And in recent years, it had helped him enormously, so much so that he applied the principle in every situation, including conversations with his wife.

Quite simply, he had begun to believe that in addition to the lie, there was not a single truth, but two broad truths. One truth was the truth in his mind, which most of the time was better off staying there. And the other truth, which had become increasingly important in his life, was the openly expressed, official truth. There was no hypocrisy behind it: for comrade Bojin, the official truth held exactly the same importance as the unofficial truth in his own mind. He believed with equal firmness in both truths, and he was not at all bothered that most of the time the one was at odds with the other, so long as the one was openly expressed, while the other was tucked away in a corner of his mind, kept under close guard by the experience that he had gained over a lifetime now approaching forty-six years.

In time, the consistency of the two types of truth had come to seem completely normal to him, governing his every move, so much so that after a given point even the concept of the lie had been completely erased in his mind, without it further troubling his conscience in any way. Who needed lies, when the simple truth, or rather the simple truths, solved absolutely everything and could extricate comrade Bojin from any difficult situation whatsoever? Or rather, who needed lies, when the truths shielded comrade Bojin against any difficult situation?

When, a week previously, for example, he had told Brunul that history was good, just as good as art, comrade Bojin had, in good faith, applied his second type of truth. The words had flowed from his mouth easily, smoothly, evenly, without encountering the slightest obstacle. That was because he had not doubted what he was saying for an instant.

According to the truth in his mind, however, comrade Bojin found art unutterably boring. But that thought could not be voiced. It was a good thought, a healthy thought, no question of that; it was a true truth, but only as long as it stayed in its own place. It would have been utterly stupid to let others hear that thought, particularly when art meant, for example, a theater performance he had seen years ago, in which two arrogant kulaks had been put in their place by a heroic Party member. Or, to give another example, when art meant paintings of Comrade Joseph Vissarionovich Stalin, at the opening of a section or gallery, or whatever it was called, of the new museum in town, which he had been obliged to attend. Experience prevented comrade Bojin from making such stupid mistakes. As was only natural, in such situations his words had been guided by the other type of truth. On every such occasion his words had been lofty, full of praise for the things he saw;

his words had been superabundant, since true words cannot be hesitant, their natural flow cannot be staunched.

When it came to history, the truth in comrade Bojin's mind was equally simple: he hated it. This wasn't a recent thing; he had hated it ever since he was at school, when he had been forced to memorize dates and names that would never be of any use to him in his life. As for the new history, which up until a few years ago he had been taught even at work, at the compulsory courses where they read *The Spark* newspaper and discussed the articles, there was no doubt about what type of truth impelled him to applaud at the end of each lesson and then passionately discuss with his classmates the political doctrine to be drawn therefrom.

That morning, nothing obliged comrade Bojin to activate the second of the truths in which he believed. But even so, he was backstage at the State Puppet Theater, watching a puppet show, with a pleasure that only someone familiar with comrade Bojin's philosophy of life would have found strange. A show in which art combined with history. A show titled *The Emperor's Rabbits*.

The truth, of whatever type it might have been, was that comrade Bojin had seen such a show a few weeks previously. Or rather he had seen the rehearsal to a show. He had come to inform Brunul about something. At the theater they were rehearsing for a show called *Sînziana and Pepelea*. Comrade Bojin had not paid any attention to it at first, but gradually he neglected his discussion with Brunul, the very reason for his coming to the theater, and he had been carried away by what was happening onstage. Not by the story. Such nonsense for children could hardly have captured his attention. Rather he had been distracted from his discussion with Brunul because of the actresses, who, giving voice to the characters, seemed to be indulging themselves, puckering their lips, lisping and talking in a childish, affected way, which had annoyed comrade

Bojin at first, and had then seemed strange to him, and finally irresistibly attractive. His eyes had bulged and after a while he gestured for Brunul to stop talking. For twenty minutes he had not taken his eyes off the actresses; he had had ears only for the sounds coming from their mouths. He had then left, without resuming the discussion, merely making sure that Brunul had understood what he had come to tell him. Since then, he had been looking for an excuse to return to the theater. But he was constantly busy with his work. His meeting with Brunul that Sunday had been the first since the rehearsal.

That morning in late March 1959, immediately after the rehearsal for *The Emperor's Rabbits*, if Brunul had asked him what he thought of it, comrade Bojin would not have been able to say anything. But because of an emotion he was not yet fully able to explain, he would have allowed a third type of truth to coalesce into words, a truth that he had not discovered thitherto. In fact, precisely because he had never before had to deal with such a truth, comrade Bojin would not have been able to staunch it. This was because it was a truth that had accumulated neither in his mind nor in his words. It was a truth that had bunched up in his ribcage and made him believe, at least at the time, that he was in love. Not with the puppet theater or the show in itself. But with the voices and the bodies of the women moving behind the screen. With all of them at once and with each of them singly.

But because he had never seen his friend pay such attention to the puppets, even imagining that he hated them, given his attitude toward Vasilache, Brunul did not ask him any question, fearing that an answer, any answer, might curtail the wonderful moment he too was experiencing, thanks to the unexpected reaction of the man who had come to the theater with him.

Once outside in the open air, comrade Bojin managed to turn his thoughts elsewhere and to banish from his ribcage that strange new type of truth, which, since he was unable to control it, he found dangerous, perhaps the most dangerous thing that had happened to him in the last few years. By the time he parted from Brunul, no more than a hundred meters from the theater, he had fully regained control of the only types of truth he knew in life, and he swore never to cross the threshold of the State Puppet Theater again. Unless, of course, he was required to do so because of his work.

# Chapter 4

ON MARCH 17, 1950, in the tribunal at no. 3 Strada Negru Vodă in Bucharest, the trial of five bandits was held behind closed doors. The bandits were headed by Bruno Matei, a young Romanian who had returned from Italy for hostile purposes, the result of the fascist education that the investigative organs had proven beyond any shadow of a doubt.

The charges were no longer any surprise to Bruno. He had been made familiar with them from the very first day of his interrogation, held within the Ministry of the Interior. The interrogator with the gentle face, or rather gentle as it had seemed to him at first, had brought the charges to his knowledge one by one. Charges more numerous and terrifying even than those with which he was to be confronted during the trial, for in the meantime, after more than a year in Military Prison No. 1 on Strada Uranus, Arsenal Hill, most of the initial accusations had been dropped. Or at least they ought to have been dropped, since Bruno's innocent and often completely naïve answers had managed to infuriate the interrogators, who concluded, sometimes aloud, in front of him, that the young man from Italy didn't have a clue about the acts they were trying to convince him of having committed.

Before the trial, Bruno had nonetheless agreed to the charge of a plot against the state. He had acted alongside his four former students, of whom two, Mihai Rotaru and Octavian Padina, had been proven to be members of the Brotherhoods of the Cross. With regard to them at least, nobody would ever have believed that in just a few meetings over the course of six months they had turned from bandits into puppetry enthusiasts. After the interrogation period, not even Bruno himself believed it anymore or wanted to believe it. And because he no longer believed it or wanted to believe it, at one point he had signed a declaration, which had been dictated to him word for word, from which it emerged that the organization he had created in his rented apartment aimed, if not to overthrow the regime, then at least to undermine it, by spreading counterrevolutionary ideas via manifestos and other reactionary writings and materials.

It was a small compromise, so it had seemed to him, in comparison with the other declarations that had been placed in front of him over the course of time, ready-made statements that included many unfamiliar names, as well as names he recognized from his years in the theater, such as Lena Constante, Harry Brauner, and Elena Pătrășcanu. Not even after being beaten and threatened had he been able to sign such statements, above all else because during the interrogations he had not known what to say. A number of times he would have been prepared to invent things, just to be left alone, just to be taken back to his cell. But even inventions had to have some real starting point, which Bruno was unable to find in his memories since returning to Romania. The second reason for his not signing the statements was his continued gratitude to Elena Pătrășcanu and, although he had never met him, to her husband. He realized that anything to which he might have put his signature would have added to the charges brought against his benefactors, who he suspected were still being held under arrest. And so, his own innocence aside, he took care to avoid making any reference to the Pătrășcanu family, no matter how innocuous.

The morning after the first interrogation, as he was being taken by Jeep to another center, as the man from the Ministry of the Interior informed him, Bruno tried to shift his thoughts from what was to follow and instead concentrate on the journey.

He had imagined he would be taken to one of the prisons near Bucharest, perhaps Văcăreşti, perhaps Jilava, perhaps even Tîrgşor, names that he had heard other prisoners whisper in the last few months and which, probably because of the tone with which those places were pronounced, terrified him. But when in front of the new Municipal Theater the Jeep turned onto the Izvor Bridge, passed the magnificent building that housed the State Archives on the other side of the Dîmboviţa, and then climbed Arsenal Hill, Bruno gave a sigh of relief. He knew they must be heading to the Army barracks: this must be the "center" that had terrified him so much, and the fact that it lay within Bucharest, in an area quite familiar to him, made him feel somewhat safer. Nothing bad could happen here, so he thought or at least so he sensed; nothing traumatic, nothing terrifying.

In the first few days, the feeling of safety that had welled up in him on the way to the redbrick prison was not dispelled even by his cellmate, a man of thirty-four from Tîrgovişte, a former Iron Guard member, as he was later to discover, who, as soon as the cell door opened, went to stand with his face to the wall, turning his back to Bruno and the warder, not daring to look at them. Only after the warder left did the man turn around, with fear still in his eyes, begging Bruno before all else to tell him what prison he was in. In the hours that followed the man recounted how he had been blindfolded, bundled into a car, and brought there—he had suspected from the start that it was a prison in Bucharest, firstly because the journey had not been very long, secondly because he could hear the hum of the city, and lastly because a few days previously, when they had taken him into the yard for half an hour's exercise, although he wasn't allowed to speak or look up from the ground, he had glimpsed from beneath his eyelashes the steeples of a church.

Over the week that followed Bruno got used to obeying the instructions he had received at the very beginning: during the day he was to sit on a stool or stand facing the spyhole, so that he would be visible if the warder looked inside. At the end of that week, a different warder than the one who had brought him there took him from that cell, which, such as it was, had begun to lend him a feeling of safety, precisely because, apart from the spyhole, mealtimes, and the two visits a day, morning and evening, when he and his cellmate were taken to the toilet wearing blinkers, nothing bothered him. Bruno began to believe that he would stay there in that cell for perhaps a few weeks, perhaps a few months in the worst case, after which somebody, one of the guards or even the interrogator from the Ministry of the Interior building, would enter, call out his name, inform him that the investigation had reached a conclusion and his innocence had been proven, whereupon they would release him. Perhaps even offering an apology.

Although it was only just past lunchtime, on the eighth day of his confinement, because he could tell from the warder's eyes that that day was not to bring the release he dreamed of, Bruno presumed that he was going to be taken to the toilet, all the more so given that the warder made him put on the all-too-familiar glasses with matte black lenses. He was taken out of the cell alone, which for a few instants made him think yet again that he was about to be released. But after walking down various corridors, they entered a room where, after his blinkers were removed, he found himself face to face with a man in uniform, whom the warder saluted with the utmost deference before going out again.

After perhaps two hours, which, however, seemed endless, Bruno Matei was taken back to his cell, trembling, with his tearful eyes still bulging, with his feeling of safety shattered into tiny pieces, with suffocating despair bunched in his throat. The bones of his back and chest felt like the branches of a tree tossed in a storm almost to the breaking point. The interview with the second interrogator in his life had come to an end after just a few minutes, after Bruno's first few denials. The man had punched him to the floor with heavy fists and then proceeded to kick him in a fury, with hatred. He had kicked him all the harder whenever Bruno had been unable to supress a moan, a groan, a yell. And when he began to weep, when the pain was transformed into imploration, the interrogator turned him face upward and kneeling on his ribcage asked him, almost casually, almost humanely, whether he now felt the need to confess his crimes. At the same time, he assured him that even if he did not confess now, he would do so the next day, or the day after, or the day after that, before the end of time or before the end of his life, the life of Bruno Matei the bandit, who thought he could mock an entire people and the democratic regime that had liberated the country from villains like him.

In the evenings that followed, each time he was brought back to his cell from the interrogation room, he prayed to God. The God in whom he had taken no interest since childhood, when, in the house of his grandparents, who had raised him till he started secondary school, his nanny, an old maid from the village, had often made him kneel beside her in fervent prayer: woman and child would whisper together as they begged for succor against Baba Samca and her army of ghosts, who, in the fearful mind of Bruno's nanny, were to blame whenever young people died in the village, coming down from attics or from the forest when the moon was full. For Bruno at the time, God was faceless, secondary to Baba Samca, and it was only his terror of her red eyes, which moved like two lanterns swaying in the wind, and her long, thin hair, which reached to the ground, that made him mutter in unison those prayers to the only being capable of banishing the danger, even if He was invisible and featureless.

Baba Samca, whom his grandparents drove away in the end, along with the nanny, when the child's terrors could no longer be held in check by the old maid, had now appeared in a different guise, there in the Uranus Penitentiary, for he had also learned from his nanny that that creature more dire than the devil himself had the power to change her appearance at will. Even if Bruno had in his mind long since consigned the monster to the realm of silly legend, the harsh walls of the cell now brought her back to life. Perhaps she no longer had red eyes like glowing lanterns; perhaps she no longer had disheveled hair that reached to the ground. But she made her presence felt with a terror as great as that of childhood, and her menacing breath seeped from behind the heavy cell door, enveloping Bruno, poisoning him.

And now that Baba Samca had come back to life, he once more felt the need to speak to that unknown being capable of driving out evil spirits. His communication with that being was mainly in his mind, as he lay in bed, his lips barely moving. In precisely worded prayers, Bruno implored God for the interrogator to ask him questions to which he would be able to give an answer. He prayed for the interrogator to question him about his father and about his leaving Romania—he would even admit that his father had not been a patriot. He prayed to be asked about his mother, although there was not much he could say about her, or to be asked about his maternal grandparents. He was willing to admit that they had been capitalist exploiters, and would even have gone so far as to tell the interrogator about how in Salerno his grandparents had advised his father to give the German soldiers, the Nazis, little gifts: packets of beef, pork, and other Macellerie Pignatelli products on sale in southern Italy. If it had come to that, he would have admitted that he himself, after his return to Romania, had never, not even once, bought a copy of *The Spark* newspaper prior to the day when he was sacked from his job at the Țăndărică Theater. He would not have hesitated even to lie about himself, albeit only a little, to lie, for example, about having wept when King Michael abdicated more than a year previously, although in reality the event had not made much of an impression on him: he was completely uninterested in politics and he didn't know enough about the king to have genuinely suffered on his account. He could have lied, and he was certain that he could have made such a lie convincing, about having been a National Peasant Party or Liberal Party sympathizer before he went to Italy, although at the time he had been only a child.

He might have said such things. But the interrogator, always the same man, day after day, week after week, impervious to any attempt at changing his questions on the part of the God to Whom Bruno prayed, stubbornly insisted on trying to discover from him something completely different. He wanted to know how exactly Bruno Matei might have helped Lucrețiu Pătrășcanu flee the country. He wanted to know what connections existed between the Pătrășcanu family and the Iron Guard group Bruno had convened in his apartment. He wanted Bruno to tell him how much money his bourgeois traitor of a father had paid the former minister in order to find his son the spy employment in Romania. All the questions were connected either to Pătrășcanu or to Iron Guard students Mihai Rotaru and Octavian Padina, who had already identified Bruno Matei as the head of their organization. Or else the interrogator's questions combined both of these *idées fixes*. And the young marionettist quite simply did not know what to answer. He had never heard of Lucrețiu Pătrășcanu's intention to leave the country, or of any intention to do so on the part of Pătrășcanu's wife, even if she had been his colleague. He had never asked his students about their political past, for the simple reason that it never entered his head that they might have been Iron Guard members. He had never even imagined that his father might have paid the former minister to find him a job at the Țăndărică Theater in Romania. Not one of the interrogator's questions found any answer in his mind, even less so an answer that he might have put into words.

One day, more than two months later, his cellmate was brought back from interrogation and sat down on his stool facing the spyhole. He began to sob, muttering about his brother and, after a good few minutes, giving Bruno to understand that he had broken down and signed a declaration. One in which the brother, whose name was barely intelligible through the sobs, became the chief of an Iron Guard group, whereas in reality he had never had anything to do with them. The cellmate sobbed long into the night. But for Bruno it was the next day that was to be decisive. The next morning, to be precise, when the warder took the man from Tîrgovişte out of the cell and a few moments later shoved a new prisoner inside. Before closing the door, the warder winked at Bruno, grinned, and said:

"See? Those who confess their sins get out of trouble. Doesn't it say in that fucking Iron Guard Bible of yours that the truth will set you free?"

That day, Bruno withdrew into himself; he exchanged not one word with his new cellmate. Late at night, lying in bed with his hands in view and facing the cell door, as he usually slept, this time without being able to fall asleep, he felt different. Full of energy and long-forgotten hopes. The next day, during the interrogation, the little lies he might have told, but had not had the opportunity to tell, were to turn into big lies, which provided unequivocal answers to the interrogator's questions. In the end, as Bruno assured himself that night, his students themselves had admitted they were Iron Guard members, and what was more, they themselves had declared that he, their teacher, had formed the group to fight against the regime. Therefore what further harm could he have done them? If the lie offered up as truth would set him free, then the price was extremely small.

Bruno spent the following weeks with that thought in mind, transforming it into veritable theatrical performances, which he pictured, embellishing them, creating various scenes. For, strangely, whenever he was taken out of the cell, it was not to the interrogator's room. At first, wearing the black glasses, driven by the thought that obsessed him, Bruno instinctively changed direction after the usual number of paces, turning to the right, down the corridor that led to the interrogation room. But when the warder swore and hit him with his truncheon, he straightaway turned around, in the direction of the toilet.

Another five weeks, during which his cellmate was twice replaced, elapsed before he was at last brought to the room where the interrogator was waiting for him. And there, before the man in front of him had time to raise his fists against him once more, Bruno confessed. He confessed briefly, without being asked any question, without even waiting for the interrogator to open his mouth. Yes, he had known from the start that his two students were legionaries. Yes, he had suspected that Octavian, who had been the first to come to him for private lessons, and afterwards his friend Mihai, wanted to use the group in order to spread hostile, counterrevolutionary ideas. Even in his presence, the two had sometimes talked about the Captain's ideas, trying to win him and his other two students over to their side. And yes, he too, Bruno Matei, was to a certain extent guilty, as he had not opposed those ideas, but rather, from a desire to hold on to his students, he had allowed them to think that he would be willing to support their line. This would explain the declarations made by the two legionaries, according to which he himself was the head of the entire organization, and which had come to his knowledge via his own interrogator. This conclusion was also perhaps justified by the fact that, as he was older and more experienced, he had encouraged them, saying things that were otherwise innocuous, but which, as he had to admit, might also be interpreted differently. So, he was guilty, he acknowledged his guilt, he begged forgiveness for that guilt. He had unwittingly fostered the idea that there was an organization, but he could also say in his defense that, after the death of his father, under the pretext that he was in mourning, he himself had put a stop to the group's activity, he had ended the so-called private lessons, precisely because he had grown alarmed at the direction in which things were going.

The next morning, after yet another sleepless night, this time due to an impatience he could barely suppress, Bruno stood trembling in front of the door until it opened and the warder stepped into the cell. He let the warder put the blinkers on him without asking any questions, even though his first cellmate, the one from Tîrgoviște, had been removed from the cell without being blindfolded. And not even when he heard the door to the latrine did he lose hope, thinking that perhaps this was standard procedure, that perhaps he would have to sign various documents, that perhaps the formalities of his release would last half a day, or all day, and so it was preferable that he should relieve himself beforehand.

When he heard the bolt of the cell door he realized that things were taking a different course than they had in the case of his erstwhile cellmate. But during the days that followed he didn't lose hope completely, especially since nobody came to fetch him to the interrogation room. After a few weeks, he even managed to convince himself that the investigation was proceeding with difficulty in his case, probably because they had to gather more evidence, and a mere declaration was not enough. At first, he had been worried on account of this presumed evidence gathering, inasmuch as it was possible that the investigators might get wind of some falsehood. But he quickly remembered that his two former students had also confessed the same thing, at least that was what he had been told, and this quelled his anxiety, allowing him to cling to a hope.

This hope, albeit one that grew increasingly slender, gave him strength throughout the summer of 1949 and for the whole of the autumn that followed. Each day elapsed in exactly the same way. Reveille was at five o'clock in the morning. Seated on the stool or standing up, facing the peephole. Then the door would open and he and his cellmate would turn to face the wall. They would stand with their backs to the warder. They would be taken to the toilet. They would be brought back from the toilet. Face the peephole. The door. Face the wall. The first ration of food: a piece of bread and boiled beetroot juice. Hours spent sitting on the stool or standing up, facing the peephole. And finally the door would open once more. Face the wall. The second ration of food: cabbage juice, which he had not been able to stomach during the first days, since the rancid stench had made him ill, but he had grown used to it in time. A few bits of pearl barley floated in the so-called soup. Then more hours spent sitting on the stool or standing up, facing the peephole. Again the door. Again face the wall. The third ration of food. The same cabbage juice. From time to time, instead of pearl barley, a few peas. Face the peephole. The door. Face the wall. The toilet. Bedtime at ten o'clock. Facing the door, hands in view, on top of the blanket. From time to time, the door would open for some other reason. Once a week, sometimes more seldom, they would be taken outside for half an hour, into the fenced enclosure. Otherwise, over the course of the summer and the autumn, the door opened only when a cellmate was taken away permanently and another took his place. Days that elapsed in the same way, over the weeks, over the months. But during all this time there was not one day in which he did not think that eventually, sometime soon, perhaps when he was least expecting it, the door would open for some other reason. For some completely different reason.

When the frost came, which would have been enough in itself, for seldom were there moments when the two men stopped shivering, when the stools on which they sat stopped clattering on the floor in time to their shivering, it put an end to Bruno's rash thoughts once and for all. It was not only the torture of the cold, not only the long moments in the cell when he blew warm, warmish, almost cold breath into his palms, onto his shoulders, sometimes onto his toes, pulling his feet up to his mouth, that exhausted his hopes.

Sometime in early December, the warder roused him from his bed at one o'clock in the morning. And Bruno's first nocturnal interrogation, although it did not conclude with a beating or any physical pain—an interrogation whose sole purpose was to introduce his new interrogator: a tall, broad-backed man of around forty, whose eyebrows joined together above his nose—his first nocturnal interrogation put an end not only to his dreams and his expectations, but also his naivety, which, in various ways, had succored him up until then. He discovered from the new interrogator, whose speech was a mixture of grammatical errors, obscenities, and menacing chortles, that the declaration he had made in spring was good, useful, even interesting, but not nearly enough. That declaration was a start, he told him, but it was a start that must continue with "textbook" confessions, and in those confessions he, the interrogator, who was ultimately a kind of priest, was expecting to hear the lost sheep of the flock, as he put it, "bleating about Pătrășcanu," to hear him "bleating about the group of fucking legionaries" that he, the sheep, and he alone, had trained. And having said that, the new interrogator chortled, he told him that he could go back to living in clover the same as he had for the last few months, but that he should be prepared, because that night was "only the beginning," and there would be others to come, and then others still, until he had yanked the very last word from his mouth, as he wasn't so stupid as to waste his nights like that without getting anything to show for it.

And the promised nights were not long in arriving. In addition to the grammatical errors and the obscenities, those nights brought with them different kinds of torture, which made Bruno look back on the other interrogations almost with nostalgia. The previous beatings and kickings, as he was to learn in the winter of forty-nine and fifty, had not been nearly as painful as these new tortures.

Baba Samca had altered her appearance yet again and in this new guise she commenced a new, more ingenious, more agonizing phase of Bruno's torture.

During the first series of the promised nights, they beat the soles of his shod feet with a crowbar. And when the crowbar ceased to thrash his heels and toes, when he imagined that it was over and managed to staunch his tears, Bruno was lifted to his feet and made to run from one wall of the room to the other. Twenty times. Thirty times. Forty times. And as he ran the torture proved to be crueler even than the blows from the crowbar. Afterwards, once he was taken back to his cell and laid on the bed, the frost continued the work begun by the interrogator, transmitting the pain from his feet to his throat, and thence all over his body, a pain that was like a snake coiling around his organs, biting them, rending them, crushing his liver into his lungs, his lungs into his heart, his heart into his spleen, until Bruno felt that all his innards had coalesced into one, huge organ, burning inside him, suffocating him.

But the interrogator was still not satisfied. The night between the first and the second of January Bruno spent in the torture chamber, suspended by his arms from a kind of coat hook, positioned very high up the wall. Hands bound, feet dangling above the floor. In the first few moments, after the interrogator left the room, Bruno had had the strength to picture how his tormenter had spent his New Year's Eve, clinking a glass with the family, then going into the larder, taking a cured ham from a hook, abruptly coming to a halt, thrilling to the pleasure of the idea that had just struck him, returning to the dining room and telling the rest of the family how he intended to punish those bandits thenceforth, by suspending them from a hook like ham shanks, being congratulated, perhaps even receiving a warm kiss from his wife, clinking another glass, then another, then another, and finally going to bed contented. The first few moments had been bearable. So much so that Bruno had been able to conjure up this theatrical performance in his mind, with the interrogator's house as the stage set. But after half an hour, perhaps even less, his desperate attempts to touch the floor with his feet began to strain the bones in his arms, and the snake that on other nights had rent his vitals moved to his shoulders, entered his brain through his neck and nestled there, devouring not his body, but his brain, shooting venomous darts into his eyes, shoulders, and nape, maddening him, consuming him. And when at last the interrogator unbound him, summoning two warders to haul the almost unconscious Bruno back to his cell, all his thoughts, terrified by the snake that had made its nest inside his cranium, huddled up in a recess of his mind, a single nook, a single all-encompassing thought, which cried out to him that he should confess to anything, to absolutely anything, only to escape.

And perhaps that thought, which the snake had pursued through the recesses of his mind on so many other nights, would in the end have placed the final confession in his mouth, would have given voice to the connections between his Iron Guard organization and the Pătrășcanu family, had not his former interrogator, rather than the brute, inexplicably appeared in his cell at the beginning of February. This time, Bruno looked on him as an old friend. And when he asked him to bring his declaration up to date; to confess to having had Iron Guard sympathies even from his early youth, later augmented by the fascist sympathies he had become contaminated with in Italy; also to admit to the fact that he was the originator and head of the counterrevolutionary group, as not only the two legionaries adamantly claimed, but also in the meantime his other two former students, Bruno nodded his head, confirming that this was the truth, the whole truth, and nothing but the shameful truth. And he whispered that he regretted it. With all his soul he regretted his errors. Then he asked the interrogator to dictate his new declaration, for his mind was weary, his memory was weary. He would write what was dictated to him. He would write it and sign it without hesitation.

On the morning of March 17, 1950, when he was taken from his cell in the Uranus Penitentiary and led to the van that would transport him to court, Bruno Matei was no longer able to feel any sense of relief. He had left his naivety behind in the interrogation room, clinging to the crowbar that had crushed the soles of his feet, hanging from the hook that had elongated his arms. And so, on the way to the court, his mind no longer conjured up any theatrical performance. In his mind there was no longer any room for a stage set. There was no room even for so much as a crumb of curiosity about a future which, at the most, held in store nothing but a change of cell.

The trial did not last long. The verdict seemed already to have been decided for each of the five accused. Even before they entered the courtroom of the people's tribunal, the prosecutor told them to expect heavy sentences. And the lawyer appointed to them confirmed it with a kind of impotent smile, with a slight nod of the head. That same short, puny lawyer, who cannot have been more than twenty-five years old and who seemed more afraid even than the accused, told them in an imploring half-whisper that it would be well that they spoke only if asked a question, in other words after the clerk read out their statements on file and the presiding judge asked whether they still maintained their declarations, at which point it would be very well if each of them answered "in the affirmative," because otherwise things might turn nasty.

And so, bereft of all hope, Bruno's main preoccupation was now looking, as much as he was able, at the faces of his former students, who stood beside him in the dock, and trying to divine the extent to which each had admitted to his share of guilt. But whenever Bruno furtively glanced at them, the four young men turned or bowed their heads lest their eyes meet his. As if they were ashamed. Their former puppetry teacher felt the same shame, although his was tempered by the other men's faces, since to Bruno it quickly became clear that his interrogators had not lied to him, that each of his former students had capitulated, the same as he himself had; each of them had cast the blame on the others, and all of them, very likely, had cast the blame on him. As he began to realize this, Bruno felt strangely closer to them, he felt a greater understanding for what had happened, and somehow he felt more tranquil in the face of what was to come.

Without any emotion he then listened to the prosecutor's long summing up. The prosecutor was a man of thirty-five, perhaps older. Bruno was more attentive to his forked, somehow repulsive beard than he was to his words. Nevertheless, he did register the prosecutor's fury, peppered with the same labels to which he had become accustomed during interrogation: "bandits," "enemies of the people," "criminals." The other thing he registered, since he discovered it only now, was that he had come to the notice of the "organs" in the first half of 1948, his cursed year, and the initial reason for this had not been the group of students that had gathered around him, as the interrogators had given him to understand, but rather his "dubious association over the course of three years, starting in 1945, with a former minister and his family, deviationists who betrayed the interests of the Party and the working class." In that instant, his feeling of guilt returned, and he realized that even after he gave up the private lessons, the investigation had led the secret police to the four young men now standing next to him in the dock. But fate was more to blame for that, Bruno reassured himself, a dark, insane fate, to which both he and his former disciples had fallen victim.

After the prosecutor finished reading the indictment and the clerk started reading the statements, Bruno's attention increased, since the statements of the other four men in the dock concerned him directly. And at the end of the statements, interrupted only when the accused each answered the presiding judge's question, each acknowledging his statement and his signature on the page, Bruno looked at his former disciples with satisfaction. He could now hear and acknowledge his own statement without concern, since he had not been deceived as to the guilt he had read on their faces from the very beginning.

When the lawyer's turn came, Bruno experienced a different kind of curiosity. He was in a way impatient to hear what the small, frightened young man would say; the lawyer didn't even dare look up at the presiding judge. His curiosity quickly turned to disappointment, however. He wasn't disappointed at the defense, since he had expected nothing better and had never even imagined that he would be assigned a lawyer who might challenge any of the accusations. Rather, he was disappointed at the brevity of the speech, which was no more than a few sentences. The lawyer acknowledged that before the people's tribunal stood five class enemies, five revisionists, five bandits who had intended to do great harm to the Romanian people, but he asked for "a certain amount of clemency, if possible," given that four of them at least had been too young to know very well what they were doing during the period of their counterrevolutionary activities. And that was all. Not a single word more, nothing to demonstrate that in the most hidden recess of his heart there might still exist a speck of courage.

Only when the sentence was read out was Bruno finally overwhelmed. He had felt nothing when the two former students who had had no proven links to the Iron Guard were sentenced to three years' imprisonment for "the offense of machinating against the social order"; seeing their faces in that moment, he realized that they themselves had been expecting worse. Nor did he feel anything when he learned that he and the other two students had been convicted of not an "offence" but a "crime," in accordance with article 209 of the Penal Code, which obviously entailed heavier sentences. He felt nothing, perhaps because he was prepared for it, even when he heard that Octavian Padina had been sentenced to eight years of harsh imprisonment. And because the punishment was the same, he would have felt nothing when Mihai Rotaru was sentenced, had his former student not let out a howl and shouted at the judges that his statement had been coerced, that nothing in it was true, that all of them were dogs, that they would have made such statements too, longer ones even, if they had been tortured for more than a year as he had been. And when the young man tore open his prison fatigues, baring his chest, and shouted: "I weighed eighty kilos when they arrested me, now I weigh fifty and you can see my every rib!" the lips of his former teacher began to tremble, he clenched his eyes shut, as if trying to protect himself from that sight, and his shoulders hunched forward, as if trying to free themselves of the burden that once more weighed down on them.

Bruno learned his own sentence only after the warders had dragged Mihai Rotaru out of the courtroom. The same charge as that leveled against his legionairy former students. But aggravating circumstances meant that he had to prepare himself for ten years of hard labor.

# Chapter 5

HE WAS NOW sorry that he had not been able to take Vasilache to the Maxim Gorki Cinema too. Because Eliza asked him to, he had agreed to leave Vasilache at home; he had even become accustomed to doing so. Vasilache was dear to her as well, but they also needed time to themselves. Their friendship had turned into something else, so she told him, without expatiating, and when two people felt that their friendship had turned into something else, it was well, at least every now and then, that they should make time for just themselves, time that made no distinction between working Sundays and weekdays, time that was theirs alone and in which the two of them existed independently of the calendar and even past, present, or future.

And so he had grown used to going out without Vasilache. In a way, he had even grown to like coming home and finding him in bed, resting on the pillow; he had grown to like telling him about events at which he had not been present. But that evening, as he walked Eliza to her apartment, from time to time murmuring a vague answer to what she said, but otherwise unable to articulate any thought that might express the enchantment he shared with the woman at his side, Brunul regretted not having brought Vasilache. Since he was now unable to find words to describe what he had seen, to convey Eliza's enthusiasm, he knew that he would not find words to describe it to his wooden friend.

It was difficult for him to talk to Eliza. Even if in the last two weeks or more their meetings had become not only more frequent but also completely different, with kisses on the cheek, caresses, and embraces taking the place of timid and respectful touches, every step closer to him she took, every change, brought with it a whole different set of emotions for Brunul. And feelings. Emotions and feelings different from anything he had felt thitherto, different from anything he could ever remember having felt. The friend into whose eyes he had gazed for so many months was gradually turning into a woman at whom only seldom did he now dare to look, from beneath lowered eyelashes, a woman whose words made his cheeks flush, regardless of whether they were outside on some chilly evening or inside, in her warm apartment, a woman in whose company his words failed, sometimes catching in his throat, sometimes barely escaping through half-closed lips.

And the invitation to the cinema had turned out the same way, eliciting not many words, just an acceptance. She then asked him whether he had seen many other films. Yes, when he was a child, or rather during his second childhood, after he arrived in Bucharest. He had seen many films; he remembered it now, although he hadn't thought about it before. He had even been fascinated with the cinema; it had been a means of protecting himself against his mother's oppressive, niggling silences and his father's harshness. He remembered that well. He remembered well the happiness he used to feel when he went to the cinema, most of the time alone, but on rare occasions with one or another friend willing to waste time with him rather than playing in the park with the other children, who pretended to be Germans and Romanians in the Great War, shooting each other with wooden pistols, taking each other prisoner, killing each other. Merrily killing each other. He remembered that too. What he did not remember were the plots of those films. Amazingly, however, that evening, prompted by Eliza's question, he now remembered well the names and the faces of the actors on the big screen; they seemed very familiar, so much so that they must have remained with him even through his nebulous period: Wallace Beery, Emil Jannings, Katharine Hepburn, Clark Gable, Warner Baxter, Norma Shearer, Bette Davis—these had been his favorite actors, he didn't even know when, each of those names seemed to tell him something, they were there, inside him, they spoke to him, but without his being able to hear what they had to say. Names, but not stories. Only vaguely: a story from a Romanian cartoon, in which Haplea (Greediguts), carrying a knotted kerchief on the end of a stick, walks to Hăpleşti (Greediville), and then, after a lapse of a few years, the same character's son and daughter: Hăplişor and Hăplina. Nothing palpable, but even so, it was the only film about which he could remember more than just the faces. In fact, there were no real faces to remember, they were just cartoons, and maybe that was why a few snatches of the story still clung to his memory.

But he didn't mention any of those names to Eliza. He merely answered that he had seen films, but he couldn't remember anything more than that, and that he would like to see a film with her, yes, of course he would, yes. And then, the newspaper: Eliza reading in an official-sounding voice, mimicking solemnity, inviting him to choose.

"At the Maxim Gorki, opposite where I work, *My Dear Man* is showing. At the Ilie Pintilie, *Wrong Paths*. That must be good. To judge by the title, it's a film about revolution. *The Girl with the Guitar* at the Pushkin also sounds good. What do you say? Or what about this: at the Youth Cinema, *In Moscow We Became Friends* is showing. I've never been to the Ion Creangă Cinema: *Deadly Game* is on there, if you like, we can go and see it now . . ."

He listened, looking at her from beneath lowered eyelashes; he shrugged, smiled.

"Oh, look at this, *My Dear Man* stars Alexei Batalov. You must know Alexei Batalov; he was in *The Cranes Are Flying*."

Brunul didn't know him.

"How silly of me. Of course you don't know him, the film came out just two years ago . . . A pity it's not on at any cinema now; it's really wonderful. But we can still see Batalov in *My Dear Man*, what do you say?"

A shrug, a smile, a lowering of the head—he had nothing to say beyond those gestures.

"You'll like it."

But now, after they left the Maxim Gorki Cinema, it was not a lack of words, not his bashfulness in front of Eliza that prevented him from speaking. Rather it was because too many words were whirling in his mind, and too many thoughts behind those words. He would have wished to give voice to that myriad of words and to join them with Eliza's excited words, but they remained lodged somewhere, perhaps in his chest, perhaps higher up, in his throat, where it was as if the images from the film had formed a lump of sensations that barely allowed him to breathe.

How was he to tell Vasilache about the feelings created by the images? about how powerfully Dr. Vladimir Ustinenko had spoken of heroism when fighting on the front line? about how modestly he had turned down a job at a city hospital, because of his love of the common man, asking instead to be transferred to a village in the middle of nowhere? How could he have expressed what he felt when, rather than moving to the town with Varvara, the woman he had loved since his youth, the doctor sacrificed his love, separating from her rather than make any compromise? How could he have described the tears that filled his eyes as he watched the terrible scene where Ustinenko saves the life of the still smitten Varvara, but then treats her with a coldness that emanated painfully from the big screen? A coldness perhaps unjust, but understandable, since the doctor had no way of knowing the truth, he had no way of knowing that all the while the woman had remained faithful to him and him alone.

Brunul felt that none of this could in fact be described. Of course, with a certain amount of effort, it could be put into words. But none of it could really be described, in such a way as to rekindle the feelings he experienced while watching it, to make them as vivid and as strong. It was the same as with the puppet theater. A while ago, just after he got a job there, he had tried to describe to comrade Bojin a performance that his new colleagues were trying to revive, one that had not been staged for a long time and which they had been rehearsing for a number of weeks. It had been the first performance, or rather rehearsal, he attended. *Nikita the Brave Russian.* But Brunul had bored his friend, even if he had stood up and begun to move around, mimicking now the Emperor of the Seas, now the boyar Ignatius, even making his voice shrill when he tried to talk like the Fairy of the Seas or Marfa the serving woman, making his voice deep when he acted out the part of Nikita. "You've gone off your nut again," concluded comrade Bojin. Such things could not be described; they had to be seen.

After parting with Eliza, lying in his bed, with his back to Vasilache, on the stage set of his mind he allowed his thoughts to put himself in the place of actor Alexei Batalov: Brunul fighting in the war in Dr. Ustinenko's place, performing surgery in Dr. Ustinenko's place, sacrificing himself in Dr. Ustinenko's place. After more than an hour of sleeplessness, after long adventures, after all the sufferings arising from his love for Varvara, who on his mental stage set wore the face of Eliza, a single thought then kept him awake for the rest of the night: What if, during the hidden years that refused to yield any memories, he himself had been a surgeon? Perhaps not so good a surgeon as Dr. Ustinenko. Soviet medicine was far ahead of Romanian medicine: "We have so many things to learn from them," as Eliza herself had told him outside the cinema, resting her cheek on his shoulder. But what if he, Brunul, had been a good surgeon? What if he had saved lives?

These thoughts brought a smile to his face, a broad smile. For the first time in his life, the darkness, the void of the past, which up until then he had always experienced as an illness, gave him pleasure, protected as he was by such thoughts. Precisely because he knew nothing about the time before his illness, he could have been anything; he could have been anyone. Even a "man among men," as Eliza had called Dr. Ustinenko after they left the cinema.

But those good thoughts, the thoughts with which he strove to fill the void, soon proved to be feeble, ineffectual, uncertain. They were swallowed up by darkness, this time a different kind of darkness, the darkness of a prison cell. And the broad smile froze on his face, his lips contracted in alarm, an alarm that he had long been trying to fend off, but which, now that his relationship with Eliza had turned into something else, he could no longer avoid. Dr. Ustinenko would never have been sent to prison, and certainly not for any political reason. And even if he had, due to some error, of which ultimately he himself was perhaps not completely guilty, Dr. Ustinenko would never have lied about his past to Varvara for months on end, for almost a whole year, he would never have tried to hide it from her, he would have openly and frankly admitted it to her, with that gentle but at the same time unflinching gaze of his, and he would have surrendered himself to her judgment.

What was even more certain was that Dr. Ustinenko would have made an open and frank admission as soon as he felt the joy that his relationship with Varvara had turned into something else.

After sipping the customary and, as always, pleasant cup of tea that Eliza gave him, Brunul asked her to bring him up to date about Manolis Glezos. He had never done so up to now; it had always been Eliza who, when their stories about what they had done that day petered out and the silence of evening became too enervating, opened the newspaper and read to him about the progress of the Greek revolutionary's trial. They would both declare their disgust at the villainy of the Asfalia political police, at the villainy of the prosecutors and the entire Greek judicial system, which was capable of behaving in such a bandit-like manner. Such villainy outraged not only those close to the patriot who, eighteen years previously, had torn down the flag of fascism that flew from the Acropolis and fought for the independence and freedom of his country, but also the whole world, which with baited breath read the press reports on the sittings of the Athens military tribunal.

That evening, however, it was not curiosity that prompted Brunul to bring up Manolis Glezos.

Fear is like a spider, it sits hidden in a corner on the ceiling, in a shadow, behind a small web, which you don't notice, and then, one night, when its legs have grown long enough, when its body has hardened, it comes out from behind its web, it stalks across the ceiling, it descends the wall, and there, right next to you, it reveals itself in all its hideousness. It is even worse when it's not an ordinary spider, but a spider that cannot be squashed, that cannot swiftly and with a single, revolted swipe be transformed into nothing but an unpleasant memory, a vague trace on the wall, a spider that descends and above you weaves a huge web that holds you prisoner night after night, without your being able to break it, without your being able to sleep, because you are constantly aware that it's there, that you are there, at the mercy of that loathsome arachnid.

Such a spider, such a fear had not allowed Brunul to sleep for the last few nights.

Why had he not told Eliza from the very beginning, almost a year ago, about what he remembered of his adult past since his accident? On the one hand, he blamed himself, but on the other hand, he knew that Eliza had been merely a kind stranger at the time, like so many other kind strangers. And for all strangers, no matter how kind, his story was short and clear: he had been discharged from hospital with that illness, the result of an accident, a very rare illness that manifested itself as a complete loss of memory. There wasn't even any reason why he should tell anybody more than that. His very illness spared him further details. Where had he worked before? What was the accident that now held his past captive? Had he had a family? Had he had friends? Had he lived in Jassy or somewhere else? No, those were things that could not be told; Brunul himself had no answer to such questions. But he did have a few answers to other questions, answers that he had construed throughout his time with comrade Bojin and in which the truth that could be told was interwoven with the truth that had better be left unsaid. Was it necessary that anybody else from the theater, apart from the director, should know that the accident had happened in a prison? No. And therefore the truth could remain between the few people who needed to know it. Was it necessary that he should explain who had helped him resume his life after he left hospital? Yes. And here the truth became simple, it could be told, because this was the change that the Party had brought about in people's lives during the last decade, the Party didn't allow anybody to perish, the Party stepped in and gave you the chance of a future. For any stranger, no matter how kind, such explanations were sufficient, so comrade Bojin had told him firmly and on numerous occasions. And to Brunul too such explanations had seemed sufficient at the time.

But now, in the last few days, Eliza had ceased to be merely a kind stranger. True, she had ceased to be a kind stranger a long time ago. All the countless Sundays he had waited for her in front of the Victoria Hotel had changed that little by little, but after the explanations imparted in the beginning, their friendship had not required further details. Now that the friendship had become something else, however, even if it did not demand anything of Brunul through Eliza's voice, it demanded it of him through a new voice, the one that had entered his mind thanks to the moving example provided by Dr. Ustinenko; it demanded that he unburden himself of a truth that previously had not proven necessary.

The dramatic circumstances in which Manolis Glezos found himself at that very moment might somehow ease the path for Brunul to unburden himself. Or at least they might help him to bring up a subject which otherwise would not have arisen. How could he have made such a confession out of the blue, after a sip of tea, after an embrace, after one of Eliza's smiles?

There was no news from Athens. The military tribunal had not yet reconvened. The paper provided only the familiar story of that infamous trial, starting with the night of August 16–17 the previous year, when, in the house of his sister Vasilikia Dolianitis and her husband, Glezos was supposed to have met with Koliannis, the so-called "representative of the Communist Party espionage apparatus." A patriot like Glezos and a communist like Koliannis could not have had anything to do with espionage, but in wild, savage Greece such miserable lies were possible. The evidence, provided in a written statement signed by Vasilikia Dolianitis and her husband, had certainly been extorted by the Asfalia, using their own methods. The ultimate goal was more than obvious: the harsh punishment of the hero who opposed the villainous Greek government, thwarting them in their dirty affairs, and perhaps even the ultimate punishment: a death sentence.

But there was news from outside Greece: demonstrations held by the working class in the Soviet Union, in Hungary, in Czechoslovakia, and even in Denmark and Italy; letters of protest from Jassy, signed by factory workers, university teachers, and representatives of the local Red Cross. Through his huge strength and the example he set, Manolis Glezos had mobilized positive energies everywhere, and behind the hopes of the protestors could be sensed clenched fists, gritted teeth, and tensed muscles, out of justified hatred toward the villainy that forced its way into a world in which the desire for progress had taken concrete shape in those countries that were deciding their own destinies, and among the ranks of those peoples who had thrown off humiliation, tyranny, and exploitation, choosing by their own will the straight path to follow. Above all else, those peoples had a voice, a resounding voice, gathering the separate voices of all their members into a cry that struck terror into the world's remaining tyrants. And that voice could no longer be ignored. The destiny of Manolis Glezos could not be cut short; he could not perish behind bars, because in the end that voice would make itself heard even there, in the courtroom of the villainous military tribunal in Athens.

"What if they still put him in prison?" asked Brunul after Eliza finished reading.

"He has been in prison before; he will survive. But it won't come to that," said Eliza confidently, "they can't go on pretending to be deaf indefinitely."

A new fear suddenly came to augment the fear with which Brunul had entered Eliza's apartment. The subject to which he had been clinging seemed to be slipping away from him. All of a sudden he no longer had any arguments whereby to compare his own prison past with the arrest and possible condemnation of the Greek patriot, although he had been certain that his conversation with the woman who had become so dear to him would, proceeding from the word "prison," which linked him to Glezos, move in the direction he had prepared for it. But one problem that had not struck him until a moment ago was that the word in question was, alas, the only possible connection between himself and the Greek patriot.

"Not everybody who ends up in prison is guilty," Brunul nonetheless ventured, blurting out the words, fearful lest Eliza say something that might place a further impediment in the way of the confession he had prepared.

"What's that you say? Of course Manolis isn't guilty," said Eliza, somewhat amazed.

After a few moments in which Brunul lowered his gaze, defeated, not finding anything else to bolster his courage, Eliza's palm caressed his cheek and restored in him a vague hope, as he waited for words on her part that might make his own words come more easily. And come they did, as if spoken by kind fate.

"What's with you?" asked Eliza, "What's bothering you so? We've talked about Manolis lots of times before, I've read to you from the newspapers before . . . Did something happen this evening?"

"No, not this evening."

And then, with a sigh and not looking at Eliza for an instant, he began to tell her what comrade Bojin had asked him not to tell any stranger, no matter how kind. He began to tell Eliza about how less than two years ago he had woken up in a hospital. Not knowing where he was, not knowing how he had gotten there, not knowing even who he was at first. Up to this point, he provided nothing new; they had of course spoken about his memory loss before. But now he was going further than that; now he would not pass over the subject superficially. And so he told her about Dr. Petrovici, who had tried to restore his memories, his past. He then told her about that piece of paper from his past, which, when he left the hospital, the same doctor had given him and whose words, after he had gotten used to reading once more, he had recited so many times that he came to know them by heart. "Every marionette has a soul. You need only know how to reveal it . . ." He had learned the words as a mnemonic exercise, as an exercise in speaking, although they meant very little to him, even if the doctor had assured him they were his own words, that he himself had set them down on paper. At the time he wouldn't even have known what a marionette was if Dr. Petrovici had not given him Vasilache when he left the hospital. Of course, Vasilache didn't have a name at the time; he was to discover it only later, in his conversations with comrade Bojin, but he had been overjoyed, since the doll came from a past of which he had no memory whatsoever.

As he continued his story and neared the moment of which he was so afraid, Brunul kept expecting Eliza to interrupt him, that her words might at least give him another chance. He didn't know what that chance might look like, but he sensed he had great need of it.

But the chance did not come. Taking a deep breath, Brunul therefore moved on to comrade Bojin, the Party representative and, apart from the doctor, who had visited him a few times, the only person who had helped him after he left the hospital; he had mentioned him to Eliza a few times before, but without telling her about where they had first met. And when there was nothing left to say apart from that part of the story that terrified him, the part where the hitherto faceless comrade Bojin would have to take tangible shape and enter a prison cell, Brunul's prison cell, he lifted his gaze, convinced that Dr. Ustinenko too would have lifted his gaze at such a moment, convinced that Manolis Glezos too would have lifted his gaze, and he haltingly said what had to be said. He had been in prison. The accident had taken place in prison. After he left hospital, he had gone back to prison, for almost a year. He didn't know why exactly, but . . . In that moment his boldness, although it did not abandon him completely, could no longer prevent his eyes filling with tears. He didn't know why exactly, but he had learned from comrade Bojin that it had been for political reasons.

Shame welled up from the depths of his soul, rushed up through his chest, burst forth, rising like a balloon up to the lightshade, where it exploded and then pattered down like a red powder, settling on the table, the armchair, the bed, the carpet, the cup that Eliza had suddenly dropped, the tea stain spreading over the pattern on the carpet, her legs, her arms, her face, her lips, her bulging eyes, her chestnut hair; it then settled on his chest, seeped through his clothes, into his skin, pervading the depths whence it had sprung.

For the last few days, the actors from the State Puppet Theater had been assigned to lend a helping hand to the culture brigades at two industrial units; some had been sent to the Ilie Pintilie Romanian Railways Workshops, others to the Carpet Factory. The workers at those factories required a performance to mark May Day, and a professional one at that, and so the assistance the actors from the theater provided to the amateurs from the factory culture brigades was priceless.

Nobody now stepped outside for a cigarette in the yard of the Catholic church. The only ones who remained during working hours to exchange banter or commonplaces when they met on the corridors of the theater were the woman who painted the puppets, the seamstress, and the electrician.

Since the actors' departure, Brunul had been spending hour after hour shut up in his storeroom. He had no reason to go backstage now that there were no rehearsals, now that the atmosphere was so unlike that of an ordinary day. There was no question but that the people left behind in the theater were, in a way, those closest to him. Or rather, it was with them that he worked most often, with them that he talked most often, although ever since he came to work there he could hardly say that he had talked at any great length with them. He minded his own business, learned, and, most often, acquiesced. And when it came to acquiescence, it was to those three that he acquiesced most often. He was the one who went to the painter to inform her that the eye of a lioness puppet in his storeroom had smudged or faded, that the lips of a princess puppet required a touch of red, that the cheeks of a servant puppet had cracked and that the skin needed repairing. It was he who informed the seamstress that a puppet had lost a chest button, that the sleeve or even hand of another had come unstitched. Normally, he would not have had much to do with the electrician, but since the latter was also in charge of the stage scenery, and since Brunul looked after not only the puppets, but also the settings in which they moved, he was constantly around him, was even his right-hand man, and always assisted him when he assembled the sets.

But even so, for the last few days, Brunul had preferred not to come face to face with any of them. He preferred to shut himself up in the theater storeroom and for an hour or two he would spend his time reading and rereading the ledger of puppets' names, which listed all the mute faces of which he was in charge, supplying the characteristics of each separate puppet: how it should be handled, its stage voice, its different costumes, and so on. After reading the ledger in the storeroom of puppets frozen in their fusty world, and once he was sure that the others had gone about their own business elsewhere in the theater and were not interested in what he was doing, Brunul would begin to speak, in a whisper naturally, since he had no reason to raise his voice and be heard outside the storeroom. And most often his whispers referred to the events that had taken place recently in his life.

He didn't tell the puppets what he felt; he didn't even tell them about the events themselves. But when he was sure that nobody was listening, that nobody could hear him outside the storeroom, he placed his hand inside a puppet that had brown tufts sewn into its scalp and whose large eyes he thought resembled Eliza's. He had dared to make a tiny scratch above the puppet's lips, on the right side of its face, nothing noticeable, nothing that the painter would have to repair with a single dab of the brush, a tiny scratch on the painted skin, which resembled the mole above Eliza's lips. He would place this puppet on his right hand, and then he would insert his left hand through the none too clean skirts of another puppet, with glossy black hair, whose masculine features he thought resembled his own. His whispers would then pass to their lips, to the lips of Eliza on his right hand, and to the lips of Brunul on his left hand.

In those days in the run up to May Day, a moving story would begin to unfold between the two figures embodied on each hand, a story in which the brown-haired puppet would more often than not take a defensive stance: helped by the index finger and thumb within it, the puppet would join its hands imploringly or else raise them in fright; sometimes the thumb would rest above the puppet's heart, while the finger touched its face, signaling shame and repentance. The words no longer even mattered; they came in barely a whisper, words of forgiveness, of hope. All the while, the puppet on Brunul's right hand employed Brunul's fingers to signal fright: the forefinger and thumb rose to its cheeks, but without touching them, freezing in mid air as the shrill voice rang out: "I can't understand why you hid all that from me, I can't understand why you lied to me." And then the forefinger would come to a rest on the chestnut hair, stroking it, stroking the bowed head, thereby showing that the puppet was lost in thought, overwhelmed by feelings it was unable to express, showing that the puppet was thinking about all the things it had heard.

Sometimes Brunul would stop there. He would stop, since no matter how much he would have wished not to know what happened next, his mind extracted it from the very near past, from just a few days before, from the evening when he had confessed to Eliza the truth about himself; his mind presented him with it before the puppets could recreate it for him. He would stop and his two hands would slowly fall, make their exit, almost with sadness, leaving his field of vision, as Brunul fixed his gaze for a few moments, sometimes for a few long moments, on the storeroom window. He gazed in no particular direction, but at the end of his gaze was Eliza's apartment at the bottom of Yellow Gully, out by the railway station. In such moments the puppets dangled lifelessly, an extension of Brunul's lifeless arms, which were separate from his body, his hips, his legs, although they ought to have been enacting the culminating moment. Only then, as if after a necessary dramatic pause, when the man's eyes suddenly tore themselves away from Eliza's apartment, from the window, and returned to the puppets once more, only then did they regain their quivering movement, only then did they rise and, straining to recapture the mood, sometimes repeating the dialogue, with the puppet on the right hand declaring, as if it had not already said the words: "I can't understand why you hid all that from me, I can't understand why you lied to me," and the puppet on the left hand answering: "I was afraid," only then did the hands timidly, slowly move toward each other, as if the distance between them were miles and miles, and when they came close enough, the puppet with the chestnut hair, helped by the forefinger, stroked the black hair and, unexpectedly, surprising even Brunul himself, flung itself into an embrace. A long, trembling embrace. And when the embrace finally ended, something extraordinary happened, always the same thing, on each of the days that had elapsed since the actors from the State Puppet Theater had left to assist their amateur counterparts at the Carpet Factory and Romanian Railways Workshops, on each of the days when the puppet painter, the seamstress, and the electrician met in passing on the corridor as they opened or closed a door, exchanging banter or commonplaces as they went about their tasks.

After the trembling embrace, the puppets drew back from each other, perhaps two centimeters, perhaps three. They moved slightly away from each other and stood face to face, supported by two hands frozen in expectation, they looked at each other for a few moments, as if seeing each other for the first time, and then the brown-haired puppet quickly closed the gap between them once more. And her lips met the other puppet's, in a long-awaited kiss, which offered more than mere forgiveness, which traveled up through Brunul's hands, up through his shoulders, up through his throat to his cheeks, causing them to throb, suffusing them with a burning heat such as he had never before felt.

On the day when the actors returned to the building in the yard of the Catholic church, their voices and their laughter blotting out the emptiness of the days that had gone before, Brunul didn't take the black-haired and the chestnut-haired puppets down from their shelves. As never before, he even forgot about the storeroom for a few hours and with great pleasure he joined the actors, albeit mostly as a listener, when they talked about the May Day performances. His only regret was that he didn't have a close friend among his colleagues whom he could have told about how he had spent the first day of the month, his day off. He would have had a lot to tell. He had told Vasilache about it the evening before. But somehow he felt that it was not enough, and he felt this now for the first time. Vasilache was not enough for him. Vasilache didn't know how to react. Even the puppets in his storeroom had begun to react, but Vasilache remained completely impassive, so it had seemed to Brunul the night before, with Vasilache resting next to his pillow, as if there were nothing in the story Brunul was trying to tell that could move him, absolutely nothing.

As for the other puppets, only now, that day, did he realize that no matter how involved they might have been, no matter how obediently they had allowed his hands to move them, they would not have been able to reproduce the events of May Day with the same enchantment. For, the kiss of forgiveness on the evening of his confession had been transformed, on the day off he spent with Eliza, into more kisses, many more kisses. The something else that their relationship had become, to use Eliza's phrase, now became clear to Brunul; he now understood it in all its importance. And the two puppets on his two hands could not have encompassed that importance. What he was experiencing was more than a performance that he might create, perhaps more even than a performance that the professional actors of the State Puppet Theater themselves could have created.

Listening to their stories, enjoying the actors' jokes, laughing along with them, Brunul at the same time felt a certain degree of sadness. And he thought he too needed a friend, on that day at least. A friend in the flesh and blood. And even if he was not very sure that comrade Bojin was that friend, even if he was not sure that he could have told comrade Bojin everything or that he would have understood everything, Brunul was slightly disappointed when, at the end of the working day, he asked at the entrance whether he had been left a note, a note to announce a meeting with comrade Bojin, and the man at the door merely gave him a bored shrug.

# Chapter 6

PORTHOS, AS SOMEBODY had nicknamed him, rather appropriately given the man's broad shoulders and the chatter he spouted when unchecked, was annoying to many of them primarily because of his constant hunger. In the end, they were all hungry, but they complained about it less. And it was not only his complaining that irked the others so much, but also his eternal harping on his sporting past, regardless of the topic under discussion. When he started talking about the kinds of food he used to eat, the diet that had built up his muscles, as he liked to boast, sometimes trying to convince them that beneath his skin, which now sagged in places, having been aged by all the prisons through which he had passed, could still be found the same muscles that had helped him and his team win fifth place in the 1936 Berlin Olympics; when he started describing to them the recipes of said food, then nobody wanted to listen.

Nobody, that is, apart from Bruno Matei. In the large dormitory into which were crammed two brigades, in other words eighty men, Bruno Matei's blanket was next to Porthos's. Sometimes, despite the ban on talking and even despite his exhaustion, he would listen to Porthos whispering, until he fell into that brief sleep from which he would soon be woken, before first light, by the wretched bugle. He would listen and sometimes he too would talk. It was in Porthos's endless stories about his sport that Bruno found a channel for communication, because it all came down to passion. Bruno's part of the conversation was about passion and came from passion, his passion for marionettes, although it was hard for him to get a word in edgewise amid the other man's extraordinary tales.

They talked the most when there was no guard near enough to hear them: when they were being marched to Taşaul or when they were hacking away at the glossy black vertical bank of the lake with their pickaxes, hollowing out little by little, blow by blow, deep vertical channels, in which they also took shelter when the rains were too heavy to allow work to continue.

Every day, Bruno discovered a world in which he had once lived, in childhood, in early adulthood, but which had been wholly unknown to him. To him, sport had meant tennis, which his father sometimes played with friends, it had perhaps also meant soccer, which he had heard of, but had no interest in, knowing only that it involved two teams of eleven men kicking a ball around. Until he met Porthos he had not heard of handball, "Grossfeld Handball," as his new friend emphasised, "which is completely different to Hallen Handball or Česká Házená," as if Bruno might have had the faintest idea about those different versions of the game so dear to Porthos. After he completed his sentence, eleven-a-side handball played on a large, soccer-sized pitch would provide Porthos with a future, even if his age no longer allowed him to play. But his experience would definitely be useful in one way or another, three years from then, as much as remained of the sentence he began to serve in forty-eight, after an attempt to cross the border into Hungary.

To Bruno Matei, the names his friend kept repeating in his stories had become not only familiar but had acquired faces and even heroic stature, not so much because they had won fifth place in Berlin—not exactly an honorable result, given that only six teams had been competing and the only team the Romanians had managed to beat was the U.S.A., with a score of 10-3, to which Porthos himself had not made any decisive contribution, unfortunately, since he had been very little in play—as much as because of the mere fact that they had set foot in that vast,

120,000-seat stadium, the *Olympiastadion*, which Hitler had had built for the greater glory of Germany.

Bruno, on the other hand, when he was able to get a word in edgewise, was unable to evoke such grandeur. By way of compensation, he began to construct a mythical world, of which he himself had not been part, but which he knew, at least from the books and stories he had stored up in his memory, a world enriched over the course of time and particularly during the period he spent with the family of Sicilian puppeteers; it was a world he knew as well as Porthos knew his, from his own memories. In the place of Halmen, Fesci, Kasemiresch, and Orendi, the sportsman's teammates, alongside whom he had paraded in the *Olympiastadion*, Bruno Matei evoked names from fairy tales, from literature, from the history of oriental puppet theater, such as Vatapi and Ilvala, the two demon brothers who, in the legend of Prince Rama, deceived their guests, luring them into a fatal trap.

The first time he told him this story, during a storm at the beginning of autumn, in the shelter and semi-darkness of a hollow in the sheer lake bank they were excavating, Bruno found pleasure in becoming an actor once more, for a few minutes, recreating the dialogues he had once learned, reciting them boldly, hoping that his voice would be drowned out by the rumbling thunder outside. Vatapi, who had the gift, granted by the gods on high or by the demons of the forest, of always being able to come back to life, no matter how many pieces his body had been chopped into, wore Bruno's face that afternoon, he wore his tattered clothes, he laid down his pickax and began to move his hands frighteningly, showing his demonic visage, attempting to terrify Porthos. After which Ilvala took his turn wearing the faded old fatigues and, barely able to move in that narrow space excavated from the earth, began to seek victims left and right. When he found one, he all of a sudden adopted a gentle, honeyed voice, inviting him to enter his "humble abode" and partake of "food consecrated to the spirits of the ancestors." When finally a sage, a brahman of ancient India, accepted the invitation, Ilvala led him to his "humble abode," taking tiny, barely perceptible steps through the mud in which their feet sank, and served him a very tasty meal, but cooked from pieces of the cursed Vatapi, who, once in the hapless sage's belly, brought to bear his magical powers. Having re-embodied himself, Vatapi burst out of the sage's organs, through his skin, tearing apart his body. The blood-red Vatapi now reappeared in his original form. Here, the narrow space prevented Bruno from making the gestures that that performance for an audience of one required. But nor was there any need, since Bruno's gestures, facial expressions, and words, emphasized where they needed emphasizing, were sufficient to allow the other man to understand the wider meanings behind the story, meanings appropriate to the situation that not only they but also the entire country, outside the penal colony, had been experiencing for the last few years. Sometimes, on other days at Taşaul, on other nights in the dormitory, his friend asked him to repeat the story, albeit without acting it out as he had the first time. Those were the few moments when Porthos reined in his memories of glory and even forgot his hunger, contenting himself to listen in silence.

Both Porthos's nostalgic tales and Bruno's mythical tales were rare, however. They depended on those moments when it was possible for prisoners to exchange words. Sometimes, a story would begin one day and might not end until the day after next. Apart from that, during the day, during working hours, the guards demanded silence, barking the order; and at night, in the dormitory, the anguish of the other prisoners, more often than not manifesting itself as fits of nerves, cut short the whispers.

The only dialogue allowed there in the Peninsula penal colony was group dialogue and it took place in the morning, on the long journey to the labor site, and again in the evening, on the way back to the huts. But it was a dialogue that gave nobody pleasure, apart from the guards. It began with the forward brigade of forty-five men singing in chorus. The jaunty, almost soldierly, heroic song they sang was intended to break the silence of the march, but was in fact a song of atonement:

> We wash away the black stain
> Of our heinous past crimes,
> Digging the canal we regain
> The promise of future times.

After the forward brigade set the tone, another brigade had to synchronize with them, under the watchful eyes of the guards, which hinted at dangers none wished to bring down on himself, continuing the song as follows:

> Tomorrow a free man you'll see,
> On one goal our minds are set,
> Worthy of the Republic we'll be,
> And we'll break our quota yet.

Finally, the song was taken up by another forty or fifty voices, who made another promise, not to wash away their sins, but to provide something of benefit to the whole nation:

> And soon the glad news will go out,
> All along the water's streams,
> And to the homeland we'll shout,
> We've built the canal of our dreams.

A sung dialogue, which sometimes ended in the commotion of the guards' yells and curses, and which in the morning was repeated over and over until the prisoners reached the work sites

and in the evening until they reached the barbed-wire fences
that surrounded the barracks.

At the end of June, when Bruno Matei arrived in the Peninsula colony, the huts were far from finished. The few H-shaped
buildings, made of planks and rush panels and roofed with
tarred cardboard, were crammed with prisoners, and so the first
duty of the newly constituted brigade of which he was part was
to build a shelter for themselves. He had been lucky from the
very start: during the days in which they had been busy building
the hut, there were never more than two or three clouds in the
sky, not one of them a raincloud, and so the nights he had spent
in the open air, sleeping on rushes spread on the ground, had
not been too torturous.

All that labor in the open air, after more than a year spent
in a cell, was also a kind of luck, or at least so thought Bruno.
Even when he had left the courtroom, accompanied by the little
lawyer, who was rubbing his hands almost joyfully, boasting that
only thanks to his speech had he obtained so short a sentence
for them all, since the crime, as he had shouted to Bruno
before they shoved him into the van, the crime demanded a far
greater punishment; even when he had left the courtroom at
no. 3 Negru Vodă Strada, he had been able to think of nothing
except the place where he was to do hard labor, and his biggest
fear was that he would be taken to a mine, to a hole deep in
the mountains, and that there his bones would remain forever.
The months of waiting, first in the cell in the Uranus district,
where they tossed him once more after the trial, and then in
Jilava Prison, where in vain had he asked prisoners in a similar
situation about his possible final destination, had been torturous
in a different way. He had been almost happy on the day when
a bus took him to the south of the country, to the Canal, which
was not completely unfamiliar to him, since in the meantime,
in communication with other men under arrest, which was

difficult but nonetheless possible, he had found out about the numerous prisons and labor camps that had been set up around the country. The Canal was not a mine—this simple thought kept coming back to him, strengthening him throughout the journey. The years of his sentence would pass there differently than in a mine; they would be shortened by labor.

He viewed those first sunny days in the penal colony, days alternating with mild nights, as a sign that confirmed his hopes. A kind of God, whom he had never needed in Italy, whom he had discovered only for a short time in his cell, but whom he had pushed away once he saw that He did not listen to his prayers, once more began to find His way into his thoughts and, little by little, even into his heart.

It was also in those first few days that his friendship with Porthos began. Porthos had not yet gained his nickname at the time. It wasn't that Bruno had been drawn to the other man's stories about Grossfeld Handball, but rather it was out of necessity that they had both ended up sharing the same rush mat for a number of nights. Afterward, when the shelter was almost ready, they had managed to place their beds next to each other. That had been Bruno's second piece of luck: not that they had beds next to each other in the hut, but that their brigade had received beds at all. But they did not become conscious of this piece of luck until November, when the onset of the cold winter winds and rains began to torture the other prisoners, who still slept on the bare ground, sheltered only by a roof and thin walls, in huts that still had no windowpanes. True, nor did their hut have windowpanes, even though it had long since been built, and the wind whistled through it, but the blankets they had been given in the summer took the edge off the cold: you could wrap yourself up in them like a cocoon, after which it was as if the wind whistled only outside.

He did not become close to anybody apart from Porthos. He would have liked to be close to the others, but on one of the first labor expeditions—not to Taşaul, where they were to be taken a month later, but to the embankment of the railway line under construction—while he was pushing a wheelbarrow, he had tried to strike up a conversation with a frail young man, himself struggling with a wheelbarrow laden with earth, pushing it along a runway sixty or seventy meters in length. Through gritted teeth, barely able to talk as he pushed the wheelbarrow and not even glancing at Brunul, the young man said: "Don't talk to me. I'm a student; I came here from Piteşti." At the time, Brunul didn't know what to make of those words spoken under strain; Piteşti didn't mean anything to him, and so the young man's slightly threatening tone amazed rather than frightened him. He then asked the young man why he was so impolite. His answer, coming after he stopped pushing the wheelbarrow and rested, leaning his hands on the load of earth, made Brunul become more wary of the other prisoners, made him fear some of them to the same extent that he feared the guards, sometimes even to a greater extent.

"Don't you know anything?" asked the young man. "You're lucky. But for your own good, avoid speaking to me. Avoid speaking to any student in our brigades, because anything you say will reach other ears, of that you can be sure. And if you don't know what's going on, then it's better you never find out."

But he found out not long thereafter. Firstly from Porthos, who also pointed out to him the brigades in question: numbers thirteen and fourteen. He then heard other whispers. The brigades were largely made up of students brought from Piteşti Penitentiary, where, so the whispers went, they had stood out for their re-educational zeal, for the torture they had endured and which, as part of a pyramidal system, they had in their turn inflicted on others, on their fellow prisoners. In the penal colony, their brigades occupied barracks that were clearly set apart from the others and surrounded by barbed wire. Later, what he heard about what the fearful prisoners had come to call "the thirteen-fourteen," as if it were a single whole, began to be borne out by deeds. In the winter of fifty, fifty-one, there were prisoners who, for a time, for a few days, sometimes for a few weeks, vanished inside the perimeter occupied by the student brigades. And when they returned, having been tortured, beaten to a pulp, the other prisoners avoided them, even if they felt pity for them. In the others' whispers, "the thirteen-fourteen" gradually became a bogeyman more terrible than the guards, and the name of the brigade's head, Bogdănescu, himself a prisoner, but more zealous even than the colony commandant, came to be uttered with a hatred that equaled the horror. He was responsible for re-education, not only that of the students in the brigades of which he had taken control, many of whom had already undergone self-denunciation and re-education, but also that of all the prisoners in the Peninsula colony, in all seventy H-blocks, which, little by little, had ceased to provide shelter of any kind, or at least not any shelter from the mistrust that had taken over each hut.

And then there was the accordion. The first night he heard it coming from the barracks of "the thirteen-fourteen," Bruno rejoiced, the same as all the others in the shelter rejoiced, even if they were unable to sleep for the noise, and even if another exhausting day of toil awaited them. But those merry, sometimes devilish, tunes were a miracle, nothing less, and in various corners of Bruno's hut could be heard men crooning along to the strains of those songs, remembering the words from back home, from a not very distant past.

The accordion played night after night. But later the rumors made the prisoners cover their ears and hate the merry strains that broke the silence of the hut. For, on the third or fourth night, the real purpose of the music came to be known by all. The accordionist didn't expect anybody to sing along with him; he didn't play so that the prisoners in the other huts might join in the merriment. He was the accompaniment in fact.

An accompaniment whose sole purpose was to drown out the groans of the men beaten by Bogdănescu and his henchmen, the screams of the men undergoing the re-education that a student from Pitești, himself a member of "the thirteen-fourteen," had wished that Bruno might never discover.

Over the spring of fifty-one, not only Bruno Matei, but even his garrulous friend Porthos learned to hold their tongues. Even between themselves, without it weakening their friendship, their silences grew longer; there were moments when, even though no guard was nearby, they communicated only by looks and gestures.

Sometimes, but seldom, they also communicated by smiles, such as one March morning, on the plateau at Tașaul, when a cat and a bird made the men from almost half a brigade forget for a few moments where they were, why they were there, and where they would be returning at the end of their day of toil. A mangy cat, which by some miracle had turned up in that field far from any village, had started whimpering at a sparrow sitting diffidently in the branches of a shrub that had not yet been uprooted. The cat had then engaged in the most comical antics, rolling around in the dust, creeping through the undergrowth, arousing the men's amusement when, suddenly, it stopped whimpering and started clattering its jaws, croaking like a bird, in a last desperate attempt to attract the attention of the sparrow up in the branches. At no point did it try to climb the shrub; it probably realized that the sparrow would take flight before it could reach it. And so it contented itself with an almost languorous attempt to woo the bird, and throughout the scene the men in the brigade, including Bruno and Porthos, merely went through the motions of swinging their picks at the ground, for the benefit of the guards standing quite a way off; they moved like mechanical toys, without their picks making a sound, furtively watching the cat and the bird all the while. But the approach of a guard put an end to the scene, smiles turned to frowns of concentration, and the picks once more struck the ground. The sparrow took flight, and the cat darted after it, vanishing over the plain, heading for a horizon at which no man had any reason to look.

For Bruno, friendship with Porthos, the sky, the stories, the little hiding places excavated from the bank at Tașaul, the swarm of men, the endless plain, the summer verdure, the autumn rains, the gleam of the snow, the smell of spring, a cat and a bird, all these made the other things bearable, the things that did not allow him for one moment to forget that he was still a bandit, a class enemy. The other things: the exhausting labor; the four cubic meters of earth a day, loaded into a wheelbarrow, lugged down narrow paths, unloaded; the frozen earth in winter; the miry earth in autumn and spring; the hunger that commenced after a breakfast of something resembling coffee, a crust of bread, and a tiny piece of marmalade, and which continued after a lunch of soup that was nothing but brackish water in which floated dried leaves and rancid pickled cabbage plonked from a ladle into a mess tin, but which was impossible to eat, especially after he once saw little boiled snakes slither from the ladle; the hunger that did not vanish even at night, after the supper of peas or beans, one spoonful per man; the curses that erupted out of the blue; the winter frost, given that windowpanes had not been fitted in the huts until the beginning of February, when a stove had also been cobbled together at the narrow end of the twenty-meter-long shelter; the accordion from "the thirteen-fourteen" huts, which howled in the place of the prisoners . . . But even so, for Bruno, the first nine or ten months he spent in the Peninsula colony, which many prisoners called Black Vale, after the nearby village, had been different enough from the more numerous months spent in the cell in Uranus (a period whose daytime and, above all, nocturnal interrogations still caused him nightmares) for him to take silent contentment in the fact that he had been able to survive and that the greatest dangers had passed.

His silent contentment, which quelled any other natural urges, was shaken for the first time in early April 1951. One evening, after the column headed back from a day's labor; after they had sung in unison for the umpteenth time: "And to the homeland we'll shout, / We've built the canal of our dreams"; after they had entered the gate, passed the administrative building, the barracks of the soldiers who guarded them; after they had arrived in the open space in the middle of the huts, where they usually stood for roll call or for the colony commandant to address them, the brigade was made to halt and the head of the brigade, having spoken with the guards, ordered them all to spit on the traitor bound to a post. The traitor's face was bruised; clotted blood could be seen through his tattered clothes. His legs were shackled to the post with heavy chains. He had tried to escape, so said the head of the brigade. And then, one by one, the prisoners in the brigade spat at him. Some closed their eyes as they did so, some tried to miss the target, some quite simply spat on him. Bruno spat the way his childhood nurse used to do when warding off the evil eye: when they walked through the village on a holiday and he was wearing his navy blue suit with the light blue necktie, if somebody complimented him, she would pucker her lips, pretending to spit three times. Bruno now spat not to ward off the evil eye, but to drive away the evil that had engulfed the poor man bound to the post, to drive away Baba Samca and her ghosts, which, for the first time since he had arrived at the colony, he not only suspected, but could sense: they had been let loose after having been concealed by the accordion for many months. The next day, at work, the whispers went from mouth to mouth, rounding out the story of the man put up against the pole of infamy. He was a prisoner from the area who had gained a certain amount of trust on the part of the colony administration and had sometimes been sent into town to buy various materials. Nobody knew how he had gained such a liberty, but he had enjoyed it for quite some time. On one of his trips, he had forgotten to come back, however. They had caught him and brought him back. And after the guards had finished with him, he fell into the hands of the re-educators. And he had ended up being spat on by all the others, thereby paying for his betrayal.

But the payment was costlier than any had believed, costlier than Bruno could ever have imagined. The next evening, the man, seemingly weaker, seemingly more bruised, was back in the same place. But the ritual spitting, resumed at the order of the heads of all the brigades, no longer affected the man bound to the post. He didn't flinch; he didn't even look at the men spitting at him. He remained motionless, barely breathing, showing only vague signs of life, as if nothing could harm him anymore.

And on the third day after the erection of the pole to punish the traitor, Bruno Matei became convinced that Baba Samca and her ghosts had indeed found their way from Uranus to the Peninsula penal colony, ensconcing themselves there, taking a different guise, claiming dominion over the place, furiously demolishing the mental structure he had built in which to store his years of hard labor, years he had thought he would be able to survive by clinging to the little details.

On the morning of the third day of the public punishment, the traitor no longer lay next to the pole of infamy, but next to the barbed-wire fence, face upward, a bullet having put an end to his torment. They told the prisoners that he had tried to escape, thereby compounding his treachery, and that the bullet had been merely the final punishment for his abjection. Bruno might have believed this explanation, he might have clung to it in the final hope that the ghosts of which he was so afraid had not found their way there, if the legs of the corpse had not still been shackled with the same heavy chains. No matter how desperate, no matter what strength he might have found, nobody would have tried to escape over that murderous fence with his feet shackled in heavy chains. The chains would not have allowed him even to stagger for a few steps.

Then a few days of calm. Calm during labor, calm in the evening on their return, calm during the night. A calm in which Bruno divined nothing good, however. They knew now that he was there; the forces he hoped had been left behind, enclosed within the walls at Uranus forever, had not dispersed except perhaps only to regroup. In the surrounding calm, Bruno sought signs of the evil he now expected not to lurk nearby, but to swoop down on him.

Without confounding Bruno's expectations, Baba Samca and her ghosts took their time, however. It was not until a month later that they swooped down on his shelter. But first they came for Porthos, on the evening of the first day when their brigade returned, exhausted, from the new sector to which they had been assigned, breaking rocks and loading them into railroad trucks. The guards took him just as they were getting ready for bed. And the bed beside Bruno's was left empty.

During the day, among the rocks, without any hollows in the bank in which to hide, without any green plains, without any cats hunting birds, with the trucks creaking along the railroad tracks under the weight of the broken rocks, Bruno missed Porthos less. And sometimes his mind allowed him to believe that Porthos had been transferred to another brigade, that perhaps he was back at Taşaul, digging clay. But at night, because the accordion had again begun to play, Bruno thought he could hear, behind the villainously merry strains, the groans of the man who had until lately lain at his side.

Days, nights, a week, a fortnight. And then, at last, when he returned from labor one evening, he found Porthos in the hut, just when a third possibility had arisen in Bruno's mind: that his friend had left the colony, that he had been transferred to some other penitentiary. That evening he found him there. His back turned toward him, enclosed in a silence contrary to his nature, in a muteness that Bruno was unable to pierce.

When, the next day, at the railroad trucks, Porthos asked a guard to move him to a position farther away from the rock his friend was breaking, Bruno was gripped by a desperation such as he had not felt in the penal colony thitherto, a desperation that overflowed with questions. The other man's muteness was directed not at the others, but only at Bruno. The last two weeks had brought not only an unpleasant change in the site where they were forced to labor, but also an unpleasant, inexplicable change in Bruno's friend.

At noon, he managed to approach the erstwhile sportsman. He had time to whisper his amazement. Why didn't he want to speak to him? Was he guilty of anything in his friend's eyes? He had time to press him. And before a guard arrived to demand silence, he had time to receive an answer, an unwhispered reproach that Porthos was unable to supress:

"Why the hell did you have to tell me all that rubbish about those two devils? Why couldn't you keep it to yourself?"

At first, Bruno didn't understand the meaning of the reproach. It wasn't until after the short break at noon, when he resumed hacking at the boulder with his pick, on the opposite side to Porthos, that his mind made the connection. He recalled that all those who came back from the hut with the accordion were shunned by their former comrades, viewed with suspicion, enveloped in silence. The music of "the thirteen-fourteen"—he had heard about it, but he had not for one moment wished to believe that it would be the same with his friend—drowned out not only the groans, but also the confessions. The music drowned out a complicated re-education, whose starting point was named, simply, "unmasking."

There, in "the thirteen-fourteen," Bruno realized, the unmasked demons Ilvala and Vatapi, moving from his story to the tormented story of Porthos, had met Baba Samca and her ghosts, to the accompaniment of merry tunes from the accordion. No matter how powerful the creatures brought back to life by the story of Prince Rama, it was a battle they could not have won there, inside the barbed-wire fences, in a corner of Romania where not even the bravest brahman would ever have ventured.

# Chapter 7

As he stepped outside the theater, Brunul was almost blinded by the dazzle of the Catholic church, upon which every ray of late-May sunlight seemed to be focused. After taking just a few steps, he felt the need to take off his beige raincoat, which he had worn the whole autumn, the whole winter, the whole spring, and remained in just his pullover.

Outside the churchyard, he saw comrade Bojin leaning against a telegraph pole, puffing on a cigarette. In front of him stood the theater manager. Brunul's friend seemed somehow diffident, detached, and was saying something to the manager, who nodded in agreement. Hesitating for a moment, since neither man had noticed him yet, Brunul walked over to them. He knew very well that he alone was the connection between the two, and his curiosity made him hasten his steps. Comrade Bojin smiled when he finally saw him, not more than ten paces away. He winked and gave a short wave. The manager turned around too. No smile appeared on his face, however. Quite the contrary: he gave him a frowning, cold, bothered, embarrassed look. Or maybe it only seemed that way to Brunul.

The manager shook comrade Bojin's hand and then walked away without another word before Brunul could reach them.

"What's happened?"

And comrade Bojin dropped his cigarette, carefully crushing it under the heel of his boot.

"Let's go. We'll have a little talk. I'm supposed to be at work, so I'll take you to a café," he said with a laugh, looking up at Brunul. A somewhat unpleasant laugh.

He put his arm around Brunul's shoulders, as was natural between friends, guiding him down the broad street, making small talk. Or rather, not quite small talk, since to comrade Bojin it was probably very important that he had bought himself a Record television set, paying twelve monthly instalments to the O.C.L. shop on Strada Republicii Boulevard. It was obvious from the pride with which he said it, as if to impress Brunul. But Brunul knew about television only vaguely, from conversations he had overheard at work, he was unable to imagine what that miracle of Soviet technology might look like, and so he felt no need to reply to comrade Bojin. He remained just as silent when his companion changed the subject, telling him about another marvel, this time one he had only read about: the radiophone invented by an engineer from Moscow, he couldn't remember his name, but obviously it was somebody important. An apparatus weighing half a kilo, but as big as a packet of cigarettes, and here comrade Bojin paused to take his packet of cigarettes out of his pocket and waved it in Brunul's face, an apparatus like you wouldn't believe: no wires, portable in other words, but even so, you could connect with any other telephone using it, you could talk on it as you walked down the street. Bojin's tone ought to have impressed Brunul, if not the achievement in itself, but his mind was still on the theater manager, on the fact that he had left before Brunul reached them, without even saying hello.

They entered the café on the corner of the street. Comrade Bojin went to stand in the line, while Brunul sat down at one of the tables. He returned five minutes later, during which interval Brunul had sat staring at the Pobeda wristwatch his friend had once given him, counting almost every second that elapsed.

"We're good boys," he said, placing two small plates of cake and two bottles of soda on the table. "We don't drink during office hours!"

And again that laugh, as clipped and as unpleasant as the other one, from when Bojin made his invitation. On hearing it

Brunul lost any appetite for the cake. He merely lifted the bottle of soda to his mouth. His tongue felt dry against the inside of his cheeks. He took a sip and put the bottle back down.

"What's happened?" he asked once more, seeking to assuage his alarm.

Bojin frowned.

"What's up with you? Nothing's happened. What could happen? We just wanted to talk about this and that."

With his spoon he scooped up almost half his piece of cake and started munching it, without looking at Brunul. He was still frowning; the cake did nothing to change his mood. He swallowed the mouthful and quickly put the spoon back down on the table, making a clattering noise.

"You know what?" he said, with a scowl. "It's all your fault, with that doll of yours. You have to take it with you everywhere, show it to everybody. What, are you mad? You've got a bit of a problem up here," he said, tapping his temple with his forefinger. "Yes, but it's something else. You're not completely mad. I know you, after all. But what do you need that doll for?"

"Are you going to tell me what's happened?" asked Brunul for the third time.

His friend shrugged, and then shook his head. He was trying to remain calm, to hide his annoyance.

"Nothing much has happened," he said, lowering his voice and cocking his head slightly to one side. "Nothing much has happened," he said again, this time with a kind of bitterness, waving his hand. Then he looked at Brunul once more, he frowned, took a deep breath, and his tone of voice returned to normal. "But let me ask you this: what kind of job is this? Aren't you sick of it by now? A storeroom keeper for puppets . . . Who in this country needs storeroom keepers at puppet theaters? I've told you what's happening over there, in the Soviet Union. The people are building something, a great country, a future. Something. Television, radiophones, who knows what else, stuff we've never even dreamed of. They're

sending rockets into the cosmos. That's what building something means. Not that we're sitting around doing nothing in
this country. Look around you. What's going on here is no mean
feat, is it? Here a building site, there a building site. The city
is getting newer and more modern with each passing day. Everywhere roads and all kinds of buildings popping up, see for
yourself . . ."

Caught up in the torrent of his own words, comrade Bojin
pointed through the large window, over which hung no curtain
of any kind. Only a few seconds later did Brunul glimpse
what he was pointing at: the only building visible through the
window, albeit almost concealed by the trees, was the theater,
half a century old, whose only new feature was that it had been
renamed the Vasile Alecsandri two or three years ago. Bojin
lowered his hand with a grimace and then turned back to
Brunul, raising his voice slightly:

"And what have you been doing all this time? What have
you been doing, man? Looking after puppets! Who ever heard
of such a job?"

The short moment in which, had his mood allowed, Brunul
might have been amused by the incongruousness between what
his friend had said and what he had been pointing at, was now
of no use to him. The other man's words caused his shoulders to
sag even lower and his reply almost died on his lips.

"You brought me there."

It was a kind of apology, although thitherto he had never
felt the need for one; it had never even crossed his mind that he
might have cause to apologize for his job.

"Not because I wanted to," muttered comrade Bojin. "I had
to; it was demanded of me. But it was only for a start, just so
that you could adapt to the world. You wipe a puppet, you
blow the dust off another, or whatever the hell it is you do in
there. For a while it was all right for you to do that. But maybe
people have decided that in the end you yourself might want

to become more useful to society. That you might want to do something else. That you might take inspiration from what people of labor are doing. People who genuinely labor, rather than dusting puppets that nobody is interested in. You know what people like you are called? Leeches. How does that term suit you? Leeches! Don't you want to become important to the nation?"

Comrade Bojin didn't at all like the words he was saying. Yes, if he hadn't come to know Brunul so well, it would have been easy to tell him all those things, even to say a lot more than that. Ultimately, it was part of his job. And the second type of truth in which he believed allowed him sometimes to be harsh, much, much harsher even. When appropriate. But he had grown close to the man sitting on the other side of the table. In a way. He had grown close to him perhaps because, in other situations, he wasn't assigned to talk to various people over a glass of wine, over a few glasses of wine. He had grown close to him perhaps because other people weren't as childish as the man now sitting opposite him, who, despite being thirty-eight years old, was like a babe barely out of swaddling clothes, who could remember nothing of its life in its mother's womb or before that. Comrade Bojin wasn't satisfied with this comparison, which had just come to his mind, first of all because to compare the mother's womb with a prison was going a bit too far, and secondly because he had once used it in a discussion with his wife, Torița, a discussion that had grown more and more heated and strayed from the subject, since his wife, fastening on the comparison, had started to fantasize, asking him whether the soul existed before birth, and such questions, which unfortunately came to his wife quite often, sometimes even in public, irritated him. They came from her peasant upbringing, in a house full of icons, an upbringing he had tried to rid her of, without any prospect of success, however. It had irritated him. Comrade Bojin had intended only to tell her about how he viewed Brunul, even though he rarely talked to her about his work, but that evening he had also been a little drunk, and Brunul's lack of any memory had struck him exactly like that: like a baby that remembered nothing of what had happened in its mother's womb or even before it got there. To be more exact, he had felt sorry for him. But he didn't want to tell his wife that he felt sorry for him. Especially since it wasn't the first time he had had such feelings toward Brunul. He had felt a kind of pity from the very beginning, during those discussions in the prison cell where he had met him, after the accident, since the prisoner's reactions to the truths of the second type that he had told him, enthusiastic reactions, which sometimes conveyed a huge happiness, had made him wonder after a while whether it would not be better to tone down his stories. Then, after Brunul's release from prison, that kind of pity had gradually transformed into real pity, an increasingly large pity. Sometimes he even imagined, but only in the moments when he was content to listen to his thoughts in complete silence, thoughts capable of interweaving the first type of truth in which he believed; sometimes comrade Bojin imagined that were God to emerge from the phantasmagorias of the priests, were He to decide really to exist, then comrade Bojin would have a lot to gain not only in his war against people in general, but also even in the smaller war with his superiors, a war on the subject of poor Brunul, with his debilitated brain. That was what comrade Bojin imagined from time to time, when he felt sorry for Brunul. And that May afternoon, at a table in a café, he experienced one of his moments of pity, all the more so given that he was not entirely in agreement with all the orders he had received regarding Brunul, which caused him puzzlement at the very least, although after asking repeatedly, he had finally received some vague explanations that he had been obliged to accept. First of all, they had allowed him to keep the puppet, and then they hadn't wanted to allow it. In the end, they had relented, since Brunul had grown too attached to that lump of wood, and what was more, in a way that was innocent and innocuous. Then, he had received the order to get him a job at the State Puppet Theater, but now, also at the order of his superiors, he found himself obliged to take away from him all the things to which he had become accustomed, to tear him away from it all and send him off in a completely different direction. Even if he had been given explanations, to him none of it added up. But it added up somewhere in the higher echelons. Not in the higher echelons of a God created by the phantasmagorias of the priests, but at the level from which those orders came down to him. Orders which, however, he would never have disobeyed, not for anything in the world, no matter how much pity he might have felt.

Brunul did not at all like the words he heard. But he didn't blame his friend for them in any way; he completely understood him. In any event, he didn't even have to be told, he himself wished more than anything else to become important to the nation in general and to the Party in particular, and also to the man on the other side of the table, so much so that it now filled his eyes with tears. The fact that he had been released from prison after the Party had already shown him, through comrade Bojin, so much understanding and offer him so much support often made him dream that the moment would come when he would be able to pay back so much trust. He was ashamed of his past, and the goodness that surrounded him only increased his shame. Why had he been put in that cursed prison? His memory was of no help to him. He had tried to find out. First of all from Dr. Petrovici, to whom he was so grateful. And then from the prison guards, who had refused to talk to him, however. "You must have done something," was all he had gotten from comrade Bojin from the very first day he entered his cell. Nothing more. Nobody had ever provided him with anything more than that. It was not until much later, during one of the first evenings he spent in his one-room apartment, after he had drunk a whole bottle of wine with his friend, that Bojin had told him he had been a political prisoner, from what he had been able to discover. And the news had devastated Brunul. Then and there, and during the days that followed, with all his soul he hated the past he was unable to remember. He would take the shame of it with him to the grave, that he knew, and sometimes he was even afraid his memory would come back to him, he desperately wished to discover that his error had been minor, to discover that other than that he had behaved like a good Romanian, like a good Communist, even, that he had achieved things of which he could be proud. But apart from recently with the subscription ticket, which, unfortunately, had provided him with only a few days in which to feel proud, nothing else helped.

"Well, there it is. Any minute now you'll start wailing like Dona Siminică," Brunul heard comrade Bojin say.

Dona Siminică was a folk musician, about whom Brunul knew nothing except that whenever comrade Bojin reproached him for some weakness, he would always say the same thing: that he wailed like Dona Siminică. Brunul had once asked him and found out that it was a singer who keened in such a sorrowful way that you would think he had no reason to live. But Brunul had never heard him sing.

He raised his hand to his face; his cheeks were wet. He wiped his eyes and then his cheeks with the back of his hand.

"Are you a man or what? What are you crying for? There are other things you can do; don't worry. You just have to want to. Look, I happen to know . . ."

Comrade Bojin paused, smacked his lips in dissatisfaction. He raised his hand to his brow, then ran it through his hair, wiping the beads of sweat from the bald patch that had appeared a few years ago and which had been spreading lately, relentlessly engulfing his hair strand by strand.

"Come on, that's enough. Stop crying. Calm down; you

don't want to throw a fit again. That's enough. Eat your cake, drink your soda . . . And then we'll talk man to man."

Brunul raised his eyes, mechanically picked up his spoon, scooped a piece of cake and swallowed it, along with the lump in his throat.

"So this is what I was saying," resumed comrade Bojin, having taken a deep breath, which helped him regain his composure. "I've found out that they need people to build an esplanade along the bank of the Bahlui. Just think: you'll be building something that will last. You'll be laying stone, pouring cement. Thousands, hundreds of thousands of people will pass over that stone, over that cement, from now to all eternity. And if you like, you'll contribute to it. People will walk along the promenade, they'll take delight in how it looks, they'll talk about the people who built it that way. And you'll be one of the people who made that future possible . . . Well, what do you say?"

"What about the theater program?" asked Brunul, almost in a whisper, and Bojin rolled his eyes.

"You just can't get it into your head. What theater program? Forget it. Do you want me to tell you all over again? What are you doing here? You look after puppets. But there you'll be looking after our future, everybody's future. I'm talking about another job, man. One in which you'll be doing something good, something important . . ."

Again the lump in his throat. He tried to swallow it along with another mouthful of cake. But his tongue, his cheeks, the roof of his mouth rejected the cake, just as the thoughts in his brain rejected his friend's words. A mouthful of soda, a refreshing mouthful of soda. He emptied the bottle. And then a refreshing thought. The thought of sacrifice. Regardless of his own wishes, things had to be done. His own good was not above the common good. The puppets were not above mankind. Sacrifice, the example of Manolis Glezos, the face of Dr. Ustinenko, the man who had become dear to him, the man for whom duty to his fellow man overrode his own desires. Brunul wasn't being asked to give up anything very important; he wasn't being asked to give up Eliza, for example. Comrade Bojin had not even asked him to give up Vasilache, but merely a job, one which, if he thought about it, really wasn't all that important.

Finally he nodded his head, repeatedly, up and down, up and down, and his lips no longer held back the words comrade Bojin had been waiting for. Without smiling, without smacking his lips in satisfaction, even without one of his usual grimaces, which betrayed his mood one way or the other, comrade Bojin stretched out his hand and laid it on top of Brunul's.

The first change: departure from his grandparents' village, so that he could go to school in Bucharest, where his parents lived. The large house, with the huge salon, where, always in semi-darkness, an unused piano stood, inscribed with large, gilt letters: Thék Endre—Budapest. His silent mother, who had never learned Romanian, not even as much as would have allowed her to talk to her son. Italian lessons. Not even with the help of the lessons had he been able to pierce her silence. He couldn't remember his mother's face, and for that he bore her no ill feeling. For that she was to blame, a shadow in that large, cold house, a shadow whom only his father and the servant gave a name: Clara. But it was not her name. He was to discover his mother's real name only later, when he saw it written on his birth certificate. His mother's real name was Chiara. Clara in Romanian; Chiara in Italian. A shadow whose face he could no longer picture, no matter how hard he tried.

His father only came home late in the evening. George. He could see his face before his eyes even now, a harsh face, one that never smiled. In a voice just as harsh he would demand that he study. As far as his father was concerned, his future was decided. He was to become a lawyer. Would he become a lawyer? His father's confidence led him to believe so, but his thoughts later, in early adolescence, thoughts he could clearly remember, caused him to doubt it. At the time he was preparing for the confrontation, the big confrontation. One decisive day he would tell him that he did not want to become a lawyer, that he could not accept it. It was not the profession for him. What profession, then? That was the problem. For that reason the confrontation was late in coming; he had not yet thought of another profession. But it would not be the legal profession. Had the confrontation ever come? A vague memory, an image that blurred into whiteness, into the nebulosity of his twentieth year, told him that a quarrel, a scandal, a confrontation had nonetheless taken place. Nothing more. If it had taken place, the subsequent darkness obscured its traces. If it had taken place, he no longer knew how his father had reacted.

The first change. The first immense sadness. At school. The village of his childhood, left behind among his memories. The first days, saying hello to all the people who passed on the street, but receiving no answer. The first weeks, the first months. Different people around him, a suffocating Bucharest, passageways and buildings, broad streets, motorcars. The Italian lessons with a sour old woman. Refuge in the books that filled the cases of his parents' house, a second new world, that of fairy tales, parallel to the real world, but in which he loved to hide away. Somewhat later, a third world, one even more fascinating, peopled with a different type of character, embodied in people like any others, but springing from a beam of light streaming above his head: the cinema. In the early years, all those people, from books, from films, replaced the friends he had been forced to leave behind in the village of his early childhood.

Then a few real friends, who did not cause him to abandon the friends of his solitude, the ones in the pages of books or on the big screen, but who did help him to move and to breathe more naturally, who helped him to forget the change. Secondary school, games, friendships hidden from his parents' eyes. The years passed more easily. The city became more intelligible, closer to him. The beginning of adolescence found him a fully-fledged native of Bucharest, with a life of his own, a different life than the cold life he led in his parents' house.

The second change. First heralded by his grandfather's death. And then, just a few months later, by his grandmother's death. The winter of 1936 to 1937, in the graveyard, after the funeral of the woman who had raised him. Walking down the path, unable to hold back his tears, a question mark: he heard his father, as they all were walking from the grave, say to his mother: "*Le cose hanno preso la piega che volevi. Adesso ce ne possiamo andare. Non c'è più niente che mi trattenga qui.*" At the time he did not understand what it meant; he realized only later, a few months later. The next spring. When his father summoned him for a talk in the living room. Seated on an armchair, holding his knees carefully pressed together, with a gaze that floated somewhere above him, above his father, as if there were nobody there apart from her, as if not even she were there: Clara, Chiara, Mama. And an hour elapsed, at the end of which a small confrontation occurred. Or rather an outburst. A rather cowardly outburst, oscillating between the child he was striving to leave behind and the adult he was striving to become. Shouts of rebellion. Harsh words, the first he had ever dared utter to his father, and then sobs. Sob after sob. The child in him categorically rejected the new change. Italy. He had never been there. His maternal grandparents. Yes, he had met them; he had met them twice in his life, once in childhood, in his grandparents' village, the second time in Bucharest. But even his mother was a shadow. How could people he had known for a total of two weeks mean anything to him?

The beginning of the train journey he remembered. Over the course of that journey something had snapped. Had he confessed to his father in the train how much he hated the way in which he controlled his life? Perhaps. Otherwise he would not now have sensed it had happened. Perhaps he had confessed to him. And then perhaps the train had entered a tunnel or perhaps he alone had entered the tunnel. He now remembered only his immense desperation before he entered the tunnel. He was in the train and there was nothing else he could do. Departure was inevitable. That he remembered. An overwhelming pain. For the second time, he was leaving behind him the life he had managed to create for himself, heading for another life from which he expected nothing good. He could not even speak Italian very well. The sour old woman who had taught him for two years had not inculcated in him any respect for the language. His conversations with his mother-shadow had had no depth and did not demand a good knowledge of Italian. He couldn't even speak Italian very well, and they wanted to cast him into a completely different world, one he hated with all his might, before getting to know it. The tunnel . . .

About the third change he was unable to speak. A hospital. An aged face, seen in a mirror a few days after he had re-awoken to life. And then, after a brief, shocking explanation, he had had to accept an idea: that he was in hospital only temporarily, and that from there he would return to prison. He did not know why; he didn't have the slightest idea. Only the desperation prior to the tunnel. And almost nobody believed him apart from the doctor who tended him. No, about the third change he was unable to speak. Because it came after more than twenty years devoid of memories. And everything around him told him that it could only be the third. In the lost years, in the years that his voided mind was unable to locate, many other changes must have taken place. Otherwise, he could not have arrived there. There was no way he could have arrived there.

The changes in his life could no longer be listed in numerical order. There was no point. When two decades of your life go missing, when you have lost those years without knowing how it happened, why it happened, you can no longer talk about a change. Because everything is something else.

The change of job that comrade Bojin had decided on his behalf provoked in Brunul a terror similar to that he experienced in adolescence in the train taking him to Italy with his parents. But this time, the thought that the change nonetheless had a purpose helped him not to plunge into the tunnel in the days that followed the meeting in the café.

"Just think," comrade Bojin had told him: "You'll be building something that will last." And he was right. Theater was transient, all the more so puppet theater. A day. The premiere. Then weekly, for a few months, maybe a year, maybe five, different shows, for the children's enjoyment. After which the puppets go back to the storeroom, scratched, weary after so many performances. The children grow up; they forget. New scripts, new performances. The labor dies with each show. "Just think: you'll be building something that will last. You'll be laying stone, pouring cement. Thousands, hundreds of thousands of people will walk over that stone, that cement, from now to all eternity." Comrade Bojin was right.

On his last Friday at the State Puppet Theater, at the beginning of June, Brunul was unable to gain much solace from the thoughts that had heartened him lately. They were good thoughts, they were thoughts he needed, but when he went out into the yard of the Catholic church, with Vasilache, whom he had brought with him so that he could bid farewell to the other puppets, so different to him and yet so similar, sitting on a curb, an hour before the end of the show, Brunul had not been able to remember those thoughts. They arose in his mind, rounded out, filled by the days in which he had taken comfort in them, they seemed to be in charge, but when he tried to harness them to drive away his suffocation and his tears, Brunul lost them, as if they had never existed, as if their roundness had popped, like a soap bubble, vanishing in the air without trace.

He looked at Vasilache. He gently moved his wooden arms, without the aid of his strings. He moved the arms toward him, as if in an embrace, and then a sob rose up within his chest, choking him. A sob that was half laughter, half tears. And with the sob came other thoughts. Vasilache was a puppet, a pathetic wooden creature. That was the first thought. Vasilache was insensible; he had never felt anything. That was the second. Vasilache lived only when Brunul made him live. The third. Followed by many others, incapable of joining together to form sentences or ideas. An avalanche.

He stood up as those incoherent thoughts came in an avalanche, he stood up suddenly, and his arms, swinging like pendulums, hurled Vasilache in front of him, his hands released the wooden creature. In the very next instant, Brunul's feet took two, three, four steps, reaching the puppet that lay sprawled on the cement; his right foot rose and violently came down on the puppet's neck. His left foot then did likewise. And then both feet together began a dance on top of the hard body, they began to crush Vasilache's neck, his ugly face, hidden behind its mask, they began to crush the puppet's twig-like arms and legs. The pendulum motion now spread to Brunul's middle, he bent down, his hands grasped Vasilache once more, swung him through the air and hurled him at the State Puppet Theater. And his eyes lingered on the body of the marionette lying at the bottom of the wall for no more than an instant. Brunul's eyes fell on the entrance and his feet were dragged toward it. He did not stop to look at the empty stage, on which the electrician who assembled the sets was tinkering as usual; he did not stop to look at the woman who painted the sets or the seamstress, whom he only just avoided bumping into, thereby sparing the nicely folded pile of cloth she was carrying. Brunul's eyes dragged him behind them all the way to the office of the director of the State

Puppet Theater, and it was also his eyes, perhaps assisted by his arms, perhaps by his feet, perhaps by his torso, that opened the massy wooden door, bursting inside, taking in the whole room at once, and seemingly crashing down on the man behind the desk, whose large, frightened eyes were unable to quell Brunul's glare. Only his words, arising from some place other than the zone in which his thoughts still whirled, only Brunul's yelled words quelled that glare:

"I know why you didn't want to talk to me by the telegraph pole! I know you were ashamed!"

Only after he had released those words did Brunul notice he was trembling, only then did he realize that his brow was soaked with sweat, the same sweat that trickled down his back, plastering his clothes to his skin. Only after he had uttered those words did he feel the avalanche of thoughts settle, as quickly as it had arisen. And feeling all those things, he regained control of the pendulums and at last he was able to lower his eyes, to raise both hands, with their palms facing the director, by now his former director, in a gesture that begged forgiveness or, perhaps, offered it. And then, not waiting for the answer that remained caught in the other man's throat, he said goodbye in a low voice, turned around, and closed the door behind him. Likewise, without looking at the people he passed on his way, but feeling their eyes on him, he bade all the others farewell, in the same low voice. He left the building of the State Puppet Theater, stopping only for a moment to pick up Vasilache from beside the wall, shaking off the dust, winding the strings around the filthy body. And then he headed for the gate of the churchyard.

He leaned against the telegraph pole, took a deep breath. And over the next half an hour, or perhaps more, as he waited for comrade Bojin, he gradually recalled all the thoughts he had constructed over the last few days, he regained his confidence in what was to come. Brunul, or Bruno Matei as he was called in his official papers, was henceforth to be useful to the society that loved him, to the society to which he had long been indebted and which in some unknown way he had once betrayed. In another corner of the city dozens, hundreds, thousands of people awaited him. Millions of people awaited him, most of them not even born yet, but who were to walk on the cement he was going to pour as they strolled along the Bahlui River, without ever knowing that at the beginning of the summer of 1959 a man had made his contribution to their so pleasant outings, thereby requiting his debts, old and new.

Comrade Bojin found him smiling.

"Well, how was your last day?" he asked.

"Fine," said Brunul.

And then they both slowly walked down the cement road built by other unknown men, who had perhaps thereby requited their own debts. And as they walked, comrade Bojin told him once more about the Record-make television set he was buying in twelve monthly instalments from the O.C.L. store on Strada Republicii. And he promised him that one day he would invite him to his house to see the marvel with his own eyes.

# Chapter 8

BECAUSE THE DAYS passed without bringing anything new, leaving only the threat of the accordion to consume his mind, and because his old friend Porthos maintained the same muteness, which made labor at the railroad trucks even more difficult, Bruno ventured to approach another prisoner: a scrawny young man who somehow reminded him of his final memory of one of his students, Mihai Rotaru, who at the end of the trial had yelled his indignation at the presiding judges.

He was from Maramureş and on the first night when they heard the accordion he had been the one who had regaled the other members of his brigade with songs from back home, accompanying the music that came from "the thirteen-fourteen" huts. He was serving a three-year sentence, and as the two of them grew closer, thanks to the fact that they worked next to each other by railroad trucks, he granted the modicum of trust that was so necessary after recent events. Thus Bruno learned that in addition to the young man's appearance, there was another similarity between him and his erstwhile student Mihai Rotaru: he had been a member of the Brotherhood of the Cross, "but only so that I could act the hard man, 'cause all the boys in the village had fallen in with the Iron Guard," as he said, somehow regretful that he had let himself be carried away with the crowd. And as soon as he sensed the Communists were on his trail, he had fled to the mountains, where he had spent two or three months looking for a band of resistance fighters he might join. Not because he was driven by dreams of heroism, but because it would have been the only way he could come by food without dying of fear: while on his own he had suffered terrible hunger, and only in moments of sheer desperation had he dared go down into a village to knock on doors in the middle of the night, begging a crust of bread or a lump of bacon fat. And it had been during one such solitary attempt to assuage his tortured stomach that they had caught him, before he was able to find comrades or lay hands on a gun, although now he said that he had been lucky, because otherwise his sentence would have been far harsher. Probably he wouldn't even have been tried, but rather he would have been "swakin' awa' i' th'erde" by then or lying in some ditch, "scran for the corbies."

That was what Bruno liked about that guy from Maramureş more than anything else: his soft-spoken dialect, the words that were as if from another language, which he always had to ask him to explain. It was as if he were from a marionette performance. His words were like those of a character, or rather they seemed perfect to place in the mouth of such a character. He was somehow unnatural, there among the rocks hacked apart by pickaxes, but that was what made him fresh, attractive. His words, uttered gravely, but which were ultimately so comical, made Bruno forget the menace that stalked him, particularly in the evening, when any footfall outside made his heart start to thud, and he would cower beneath his blanket, closing his eyes and expecting to be hauled outside the hut at any moment.

One afternoon, at work, he plucked up courage. And amid the din of the picks Bruno told his new friend about Ilvala and Vatapi, fearfully awaiting his reaction. The other man's laughter calmed him somewhat. If he saw no hidden meaning in the story of the two demons, if to him it seemed nothing dangerous, perhaps the men from "the thirteen-fourteen" would take it to be a mere legend, and perhaps everything was just a figment of Porthos's frightened imagination. Precisely because he did not want to talk about what had happened there during those two weeks, Porthos conveyed to Bruno a part of the terror he had felt during interrogation. Perhaps the story that he had confessed to the prisoners who had been transformed into re-educators had acquired in his mind meanings far deeper than Bruno himself had intended to convey, and along with those meanings fear too had taken hold. And shame. And regrets. Behind those feelings, in order to confront which Porthos had plunged himself into a self-isolation that Bruno had gradually begun to understand better and better, there was probably nothing else.

And the detached reaction of the guy from Maramureş had provided additional confirmation in that respect. And thus it would have remained if, on the way back to the penal colony, amid the din of the songs, the young man had not approached Bruno and said:

"Do you ken what the trouble be? I've thought about it and here's the thing: if you want to stay safe, don't tell anybody what you told me, about them devilocks, because even the stones here have lugs. If somebody else hears, then he'll think, like I thought, that the devilocks are the communists, who trick you with scran, and then murder you. They'll say you're a counterrevolutionary. And it won't go well with you after that."

The next day he told the guy from Maramureş about Porthos. All the men in the brigade knew that he had fallen into the hands of the re-educators, but nobody knew that during his confession he had let slip about Bruno's story. And after he heard that, Bruno's new friend nodded pensively.

"God preserve you, but maybe it's not as bad as you think. It's just a story, after all. And you told me that your job was with puppets. Aye, that's what they'll say too: that it was a story for your puppets. Tell them nothing except that."

And after a moment's thought, the young man waved his hand, attempted a smile, and concluded:

"Then again, maybe they'll not take you."

With a glimmer of worry on his face, which did not escape Bruno, he then turned his back to him and continued to work in silence.

The hope contained in the words with which he seemed to have been trying to encourage Bruno was not aimed only at him. For, in the days that followed, after they grew close, he recounted not only his previous life, not only about how to tell penny buns and morels from poisonous mushrooms, but also his own prison experiences before arriving there in the penal colony. And one of those stories began amusingly and was worth telling, since for a time, for four weeks, that peasant from the northern corner of the country had been mistaken for a student. "I think they must have seen by my face that I'm a good learner," laughed the young man, after which he confessed that he had had just four years of schooling. Even though he could barely read or write, he had been mistaken for a student of the same name and sent to the prison in Pitești. But the story didn't end there. Nor did it end before Bruno, about whom the guy from Maramureș had discovered too late that he had come to the attention of the men from "the thirteen-fourteen."

The story of the four-week mix-up, before his real identity papers removed him from inside the walls of the prison and sent him to the Peninsula penal colony, quickly became less than amusing, once a character named Eugen Țurcanu made his appearance: "A stark mad prisoner who'd signed a pact with the high-ups that let him do what he liked with the others." The guy from Maramureș had heard that Țurcanu had caught his own brother sleeping with his wife, which had made him even more vicious, quite apart from the cowardice that had made him agree to anything just to get on the good side of the authorities.

The "unmaskings" that Bruno had heard of there in the Peninsula also featured in his new friend's stories, in forms he could never have imagined, so terrifying that he would have wished to hide them away in the darkest corner of his mind, where they might never rear their heads again. The tales told by the guy from Maramureș, with all their strange words, which otherwise would make him smile, quickly turned into images

in Bruno's mind, pictures of the wretches tortured by the re-
educators, who burned their arms and legs with cigarettes until
the flesh fell away, prisoners forced to eat their own feces, grim,
moving pictures in which erstwhile theology students were
"converted," re-baptized by having their heads immersed in the
urine bucket, while others were forced to recite passages from
the Bible commingled with obscenities, in keeping with the
new religion they had to embrace.

The guy from Maramureș had not taken any direct part in
these things, but his four weeks in Pitești had been long enough
for him to come to know them. Despite all the restrictions and
threats, the rumors were transmitted through the prisons along a
wire that nobody could break, a wire alloyed from the prisoners'
fears and harder than any metal. Finding out about all this,
Bruno had never thought of the other chain with which even
there, in the Peninsula, the prisoners had begun to be shackled
together: that of the stories that ought never to have been told.

As soon as he heard his new friend trying to reassure him,
although seemingly trying more to reassure himself, Bruno
realized that he had become a link in that chain. With his own
story, Bruno was already linked to Porthos. With his story, the
guy from Maramureș was linked to Bruno. Elsewhere were
men who joined the links together. And just a few days after
that, Bruno had to confront the two kinds of silence that had
surrounded him: that of Porthos, his old friend, a silence already
guilty, and that of the guy from Maramureș, his new friend, a
silence that cast upon him a future guilt.

That summer day in 1951, Bruno made no protest of any
kind when the guards entered the hut to take him. However,
he did manage to close his eyes to the frightened silence of
Porthos, thereby trying to send him a signal of forgiveness. He
also managed to make the same gesture when faced with the
frightened silence of the guy from Maramureș, this time trying
to convey to him his trust. As he was carried off to the huts
of "the thirteen-fourteen" he was convinced that the chain of

stories, which ultimately had no other purpose than to lend a meaning no matter how small to the evil days, would finally be broken having come to him.

Two nights and the day between them. Two faces. Two separate attempts to persuade him.

The first attempt was almost polite. Under other circumstances maybe he would have laughed when confronted with such an approach. The hulk who was trying to get a confession out of him, based on the one he had gotten from Porthos, didn't remember anything about Bruno's story. So much pointless worry, so many other stories superposed on the first, merely to conceal beneath them the demons from the legend of Prince Rama. And the hulk who feigned politeness didn't remember a thing. Except:

"We've been informed that you instigate people to revolt. That you tell them parables from the Bible about devils that you compare with our guards."

Parables from the Bible. He would have laughed, if he hadn't remembered the other story, which he had to keep hidden no matter what happened, the story told by the boy from Maramureş, in which the men who made the mistake of talking about the Bible had ended up being re-baptized in the shit bucket.

"Look, we're here for your own good. You're on the wrong path, but we know how to put people back on the right path. You can come with us down that path. All you have to do is tell us who else accompanied you down the wrong path, so that we can rehabilitate them, so that we can bring them with us, on the right path. We're not asking you for much. Just some names. We're doing you a favor; you'll be doing them a favor. Together we can cleanse ourselves of our past mistakes; we can start a new life. Don't you want to take the opportunity? Don't you want to give others the opportunity? All of us have to return to a state of guiltlessness, don't you think?"

The second attempt came after Bruno refused to give himself or to give others the opportunity to set off down the right path. The polite hulk withdrew after less than an hour, not before thanking Bruno for taking the time to talk to him. And then the second face. A face almost pleasant at first sight. But a face that lost every last trace of humanity in the moment when the man brutally abolished the hulk's polite words, cursing, punching, kicking. Having wearied, panting, the second re-educator then sat down on a bunk.

"You've got thirty seconds to start talking."

And he started counting. One. Two. Three. Four. Five. Six. Bruno, who was counting ahead, heard the number seven only in his own mind. In the same instant came the crash of a cudgel on his back. Bruno hadn't seen the cudgel lying on the bunk. And then he heard other numbers. Ten, in the moment when the cudgel struck the muscles of his legs. Twelve, when his ribcage cracked beneath the blow. Sixteen, when the cudgel broke his shoulder, lashing his right ear as it did so. Twenty, as his kneecaps sent a hellish pain up into his throat, like the roar of a wounded beast.

Immediately after the intervention of the second face, he remembered Kleist. The Kleist he had forgotten among the pages of his manuscript, left in the hands of his first interrogator. The Kleist he had refused to think of anymore, associating him with the moment of his arrest. As a result of the two very different approaches, however, Heinrich von Kleist once more seeped into his thoughts, Kleist and his *Über das Marionettentheater*, which he had read in Italian translation and for which he had loved him so much in the past. And he remembered what he had read word for word. He had made use of it so many times, in his talks with his students, in his own manuscript. Just as the image in a concave mirror, said Kleist, after moving away into infinity, reappears to us all of a sudden enlarged, so too grace reappears, after knowledge has passed through infinity.

He remembered, for there was no way he could forget, even if he had been forced to do so. And grace, as Kleist said, appears in its purest state in the body that either has no consciousness at all or has infinite consciousness. Which is to say, either in a marionette or in a god. So all that remains for us to do is to eat once more of the Tree of Knowledge in order to regain the condition of primal innocence.

How could Kleist have ever imagined that one and a half centuries later, in order to regain innocence there would no longer be any need of a Tree of Knowledge; there would no longer be any need of a passage through the infinite? In order to regain innocence, men had been found who could reduce everything to thirty seconds. Simple. Easily counted. The infinite was no longer an option; thirty seconds were sufficient. The first twenty were so that the body's pain would subjugate the mind; the next ten so that the mind could relay confessions to the mouth, the only requirement there was in order that innocence might be attained once more.

After two nights and the day separating them spent in "the thirteen-fourteen," if anybody had listened to him and if he had felt the need, Bruno would have had much to tell. About one thing only would he have been unable to say anything. Not for the life of him would he have been able to say whether, even for one second, he had heard the accordion. He would have wagered that not one of the prisoners who had been taken there would have been able to say the same. The music of the accordion could be heard only in the rest of the colony. It was impossible for the man to whom it was played to hear it. Perhaps because his ears were deafened by the screams of the man beating him. Perhaps because his ears were deafened by his own screams.

On the morning when he was sent back to his hut Bruno did not feel any need to say anything, however. And nobody felt the need to ask him to talk. Not because he had become a link in that chain of which no prisoner wished to be part—the

thirty seconds, repeated more than once, had indeed forced him
to confess, but in his confessions he admitted his own guilt,
not others'. He felt no need to talk because the whole colony
was already talking about something else. About somebody
else. The whole colony was talking about the death of Dr.
Simionescu, who was lying curled up next to the barbed wire,
with his dried-out eyes still gazing at the huts, just as a few
months previously the prisoner who had managed to escape
had also lain there. But neither the guards who had shot the
doctor nor the heads of the brigades had dared to name him
traitor.

Ioan Simionescu, who had once been a member of a
government, had not been able to endure the torture to which he
had been subjected in "the thirteen-fourteen." And his desperate
act, his running toward the barbed-wire fence the previous
night, ignoring the guard's furious demands to halt, before he
was mowed down by a bullet, that act of his had been Bruno's
third piece of luck since he reached the Peninsula colony. It was
a blessed piece of luck, since by his sacrifice Dr. Simionescu had
released Bruno from the hands of the re-educators, allowing
him to return to his hut before his confessions could make
another man become a link in the chain.

Sometimes, no matter how hard it might be to believe, and
Bruno understood this the same as all the prisoners in the Peninsula colony had understood it in the period that followed, the
broader history allowed the narrower history to drag it down
roads it would otherwise never have trodden. The death of Dr.
Simionescu, at first just one death among all the other silent
deaths past which the broader history walked without turning
its head to look, cast fear and trepidation over the H-blocks of
the camp. This fear and trepidation would have remained in the
colony if a breach had not existed in the broader history, which
Bruno had thitherto believed to be all-powerful.

Perhaps that dry, scorching wind that the natives of that region called the Kara-yel, or Black Wind, and which had tortured many a prisoner, on days when clouds of stone dust burned their throats, had finally relented and borne away the news of the wretched end that Dr. Simionescu had met; it had borne it over the Bărăgan steppe as far as Bucharest. Perhaps there it had entrusted the news to the Foehn, which bore it farther, crossing the Carpathians, before leaving it in the care of the Auster, which blew it over borders that only the winds can cross without fear of being shot by the guards. Perhaps this conjuration of the winds, or perhaps only men's powerlessness in the battle against whispers, bore the news thousands of miles from Romania, over the English Channel, and thence Radio London broadcast it throughout the world, bringing it back to Bucharest along with various international protests. What is for sure is that from the end of July, the nocturnal strains of the accordion ceased to be heard in the other huts. The narrower history had, at least this once, shown its power over the broader history.

But without knowing the conspiracy of the winds and even before it led to major changes in the students' huts, the prisoners themselves reacted to the death of Dr. Simionescu. They were driven by fear, by the thought that if it could happen to a member of a former government, an important man, not only because of what he had achieved in politics, but also, above all, because of what he had achieved as a physician, then nobody would have the power to protect them, the anonymous, from the onslaught. Among the huts, at the labor sites, the voices of discontent, albeit scattered, took on a new note; one day, an entire brigade refused to go to work: the men knelt down before they went out of the gate, next to the administrative building and the guards' barracks, enduring kicks, punches, and blows from rifle butts until other prisoners, at gunpoint, carried them back to their hut. The men from another brigade went on hunger strike for three days in protest at what was happening to them. But none of these revolts spread.

For Bruno, everything came from somewhere within, not from the example provided by the other rebels. Immediately after the two nights of torture in "the thirteen-fourteen," he rediscovered, perhaps even on the short journey back to his own hut, his center of gravity. He rediscovered it, as if thinking for the first time about the teachings of the family of puppeteers with whom he had once lived, for half a year; as if it were only then that he had remembered the books he had read for pleasure, rather than the obligatory books demanded by the Accademia Nazionale d'Arte Drammatica Silvio D'Amico; as if it were only then that he had hastened toward it, from a void that had swallowed the years of teaching and experience at the Țăndărică Theater, along with friends concealed by a mist that he had never attempted to dissipate. Everything came from within, as if it were a rediscovery.

And with the rediscovery of that center of gravity, thitherto lost among the pains of his body, a smile was more and more frequently to be found on his face, accompanying words that were no longer held back by any fear. His rebellion, lacking sufficient power of example, but possessing the power daily to increase the doses of courage that sprang from his center of gravity, manifested itself through stories, new stories that added to the one about Ilvala and Vatapi, in which this time he deliberately sought their core meaning, in which he hoped to be understood, stories told aloud not only in the presence of other prisoners, whether they were listening or not, but even around the guards, as long as they permitted him to talk. Stories gleaned from the books he had read, stories he had written and then unwillingly left to their fate in the manuscript of the course he had once taught. Stories that pieced together a history of puppets from ancient times, stories that no Hindu *dalang* or Persian *morshed* or storyteller or puppeteer of olden days had ever intended or imagined would have a "counterrevolutionary" future in a labor camp near the Black Sea. In Bruno's meaningful stories characters such as the Egyptian Aragoz or the Indian Vidushaka or the Persian Pahlavan Kachal or even Princess Joruri, born at the ends of the earth, born in faraway Japan, puppets that had for hundreds or thousands of years performed to the delight of the unwashed crowds of the Orient, acquired the features and the speech of the present, they fought the enemies present around them. To these were also added younger figures such as Punch and Judy, Guignol and Lafleur, Hanswurst and Kasperle, Kašpárek and Petruşca, all of whom fought side by side in the battle to which Bruno Matei had summoned them from memories both hazy and clear.

Baba Samca and her ghosts had hidden themselves away, however. Nobody knew why; nobody understood why the accordion had fallen silent. Vague, stray words about inspectors from Bucharest, a consequence of the death of Dr. Simionescu, formed an explanation and gave rise to hope. But for Bruno, who had regained his center of gravity, none of this meant anything. On the contrary, as his stories gathered more and more courage, the lack of any answer on the part of the guards or those who had filled his nights with terror, the men of "the thirteen-fourteen," began to disappoint him more and more with each passing day. His rebellion sought a confrontation. The very fact that he had succeeded in breaking the chain, that he had not become another link reinforcing it, demanded that he did not stop there. After two years of hopes and fears squandered one by one, during which his pain had coalesced into a patience that he had thought infinite, he now needed to strike blows in his own turn, and he needed those blows to be felt. And he began to strike. His stories, sometimes uttered under his breath, beneath hostile gazes, were in his own mind equivalent to the blows he had been struck in his stomach, on his legs, in his face, on his shoulders; they had the power to make up for the humiliations he had endured up until then. But they needed to be felt by others, otherwise they would be nothing but punches thrown at the empty air . . .

It was then that he found Ghatotkacha among the lines he had written at the beginning of 1949 and which he now gathered from his memory. Not that he wished to draw upon Ghatotkacha, with his millennial history, a demigod who, having been brought back to the present and reanimated, reminded Bruno of the accusation that had cast him behind barbed wire: the charge that he had been the leader of an Iron Guard cell. Despite his lack of any interest in politics, Bruno had had time to form an opinion about the Iron Guard. He had never been able to view its members with any understanding. He despised zeal when it was not placed in the service of any artistic or professional idea; he had despised it ever since the time of Mussolini and his sickly, hysterical speeches; he had despised it when he rediscovered it in Romania, among the Iron Guard, who, even after falling into disgrace, still spoke in the name of the ideas with which they tried to fill their own emptiness. If he had ever heard his two disciples speaking in the name of those ideas, rather than out of a passion for marionettes, he would probably have put a stop to those meetings far earlier. It was precisely for that reason that his arrest and the accusation brought against him had been all the more painful and absurd. But that was already the past.

No, Bruno didn't wish to introduce to his vengeful stories the demigod Ghatotkacha. For his story, which had once been simple, was now charged with a powerful, limpid symbol. That symbol was the hero's enchanted shirt, and the possible reference to the green shirts of the Iron Guard that might have quenched the red lava, gave Bruno no pleasure. Nevertheless, he sought the taste of revenge. And that revenge was against the shoddily constructed grounds for his arrest.

One afternoon of dreadful scorching heat, when the stone dust mingled with the sweat that poured off the men's faces and dripped into their mess tins, Ghatotkacha nonetheless emerged from Bruno's lips, at first barely in a whisper, but then in the full force of his story. Ghatotkacha shook off legend and firmly planted himself in the present, rising before one of the guards, who had just hit Bruno in the face, after he had discarded the stinking contents of his mess tin in the dust.

"Are you on hunger strike or what?" yelled the man in uniform, before hitting him. "You fucking bandit!"

Bruno stood up, started to smile, rolling his eyes left and right to look at the others, who did not so much as dare glance up at him.

"Sit down!" shouted the guard.

Bruno raised his arms, like a prophet of old or like a puppeteer behind a screen, stretching before revealing his puppets to the audience.

"Sit down!" yelled the guard once more, looking to the other guards for assistance.

In their kingdom of Sulalaya, the gods were at a loss as to what to do. On Earth, a huge volcano had erupted. Cursed red lava poured over town and village, annihilating thousands and thousands of men.

"Sit down!" screamed the guard a third time, as he saw his two comrades approach.

Mankind's only hope was Ghatotkacha, to whom the gods had once given an enchanted shirt of immortality. That shirt would be their only salvation: if it were cast into the flames that erupted from the huge crater, it would quench the red cataclysm.

"Sit down!" shouted the other guards, who had now arrived.

After long hesitation, Ghatotkacha finally agreed to the sacrifice. And with that sacrifice, hearing the approval of his fellow prisoners who had been members of the Iron Guard, Bruno knew he had at last succeeded in striking a blow. He continued to smile even after the blows of the guards felled him; he smiled as if the blows had not touched him. The confrontation he needed now began at last, even if he had had to resort to a weapon he had never thought would be necessary.

That night he remembered another story, this time from his own childhood. The garden of his paternal grandparents in the country. He and a friend whose name he could not remember. They were playing. The other boy had climbed an old pear tree, which his grandfather had been threatening to chop down for many years, but forgot to do so every autumn. The tree produced a few pears at the beginning of every summer: five, perhaps ten. They were therefore all the more precious to little Bruno. That day, which now came back to him, his friend had climbed the tree, trying to reach its scanty pears. Bruno had tried to dissuade him, nicely at first, but then throwing a potato at him. Although he had never been a good thrower, the potato hit his friend in the eye. The boy had fallen to the ground, crashing through the branches. He had howled in pain; one arm had swollen up and turned purple. In fear, Bruno had run away and hid. That whole afternoon, the whole night, trembling whenever he heard the increasingly worried voices of his grandparents and his father calling to him. In fear, he had spent the whole night behind the woodpile at the back of the shed, finally falling asleep where he sat. Nobody had thought of looking for him there. A tortured, terrifying night.

And he remembered that story there in the penal colony. A different kind of night. A different kind of shed. A tall, narrow wooden chest with no roof, into which up until then two prisoners had been crammed face to face for purposes of re-education. The two barely had room to breathe, let alone bend their knees. But Bruno had been placed inside all by himself; they hadn't found a partner in punishment for him. And so instead of another man they had placed a plank inside the box to narrow the space. Bruno leaned his face against the plank and braced himself against it with his knees, trying to fall asleep standing up. But without success. A terrible night, but which he had endured aided by the thought that confrontation meant blow and counter-blow. A satisfying thought. It was sufficient.

Sufficient until around noon of the following day. It was not his trembling muscles, nor the dryness of his throat, nor his final tears, which had turned into a greasy trickle that glued his eyelids together, but the stabbing spear of the sun, boiling, churning his brain, that caused his desperate screams to erupt. He had the sensation that the scorching sweat from the crown of his head was biting through his skin, into his skull, flooding his mind, blotting out every other thought than that of escape. Like a red lava erupting from a volcano that nobody, not even a hero from the past or present could now staunch. And his screams, his cries, the rattling of his chest gradually began to combine with pleas and with words of repentance.

After the second midnight the door of the wooden cage opened. Bruno fell into the dust and was dragged to the hut. Limp. Incapable of any movement. Barely able to exhale promises through his cracked lips, addressed to those dragging him, but heard only by him. Promises that quelled in him for all eternity any further attempt to revolt.

The time Bruno spent in the wooden cage was sufficient for him to understand that all mankind's stories, regardless of the form in which they were couched, had been conceived in order to meet a need for storytelling in their listeners. It wasn't the stories in themselves that were weapons, but the manner in which they transformed their listeners. But there in the labor camp scorched by the Black Wind, by the village Black Vale, near the sands of the Black Sea, part of the listeners, those in whom that need might have been met, were too exhausted, too dispirited, too pain-wracked, too helpless to be touched by stories. And in the others that need no longer existed. For them, it had been blotted out by the bigger story, the new story that was administered drop by drop, to the point of saturation, in the political slogans.

Bruno's center of gravity, rediscovered after he had escaped from the clutches of "the thirteen-fourteen," did not get lost again, among the pains of his body. From the moment he rediscovered it, he never lost it again, not for an instant. But now his revolt had come to an end, Bruno understood that the trajectory he had been seeking, that the parts of his body might follow it like pendulums, was more rigid than he had imagined. And it was not a trajectory he could control.

# Chapter 9

THEY HAD AT first thought of taking a taxi. Three years ago the Communal Electricity and Transport Department had placed a few motorcars at the disposal of the town's citizens, and the unveiling of the service had been reported with so much pomp in the press that every local wished to take advantage at least once of the wonderful Pobeda and Volga taxis available to them. But in front of the station you could seldom find a taxi, and even then only when a long-distance train was due to arrive. They had waited around twenty minutes before deciding to climb aboard a horse-drawn cab. As soon as he found out where they were going, the cabbie warned that it would cost them extra, since the roads there were bad.

"What do you want to go to Ciric for anyway?" he asked. "It's a building site, as far as I know. They're building some restaurants and all kinds of other stuff out there."

Eliza wanted to see the lake. She wanted to get out of the sweltering city, which had been languishing in a heat wave for the last few weeks. She had brought a blanket for them to sit on. Somewhere away from the building site they would have a picnic of boiled eggs, peppers, and the cheese she prided herself on, which she had been sent by some relatives from a village near Stalin City, a yellow cheese fermented in a sheep's bladder and then wrapped in fir tree bark. They would have fun that radiant day, a kind of holiday, which, said Eliza, they both could do with, especially Brunul, because for the last two weeks, since he had changed job and started working on the new riverside park, he hadn't been himself; it was as if he were submerged in his own weariness and had lost all desire for anything.

In an attempt to get back the Brunul she used to know not long ago, Eliza had jokingly asked him to take Vasilache with him, to show him the lake: "Maybe we can let him go for a swim." But Brunul categorically refused. Lately he had not been interested in Vasilache; he had not even washed his dirty clothes after he had stomped on him in the yard of the Catholic church. Vasilache came from a different time, he belonged to a different time, and so he had now been put away in a cupboard, among Brunul's few clothes. For Brunul, the future was linked with the building site on the Bahlui embankment, with his workmates there, and with Eliza, of course. In other words, with people, not puppets.

The cab came to a stop by the edge of the forest. The cabbie didn't want to go any further, telling them he was afraid of getting bogged down. Not that there was any chance of that: the earth was dry, as it hadn't rained for days, but to Eliza and Brunul it was clear there was no point in their insisting. Eliza paid the cabbie; she had invited Brunul on the outing and she refused to take his money after they climbed out of the cab. They walked along the road that had been built for trucks transporting various building materials. Eliza wanted to see the building site before they did anything else. A few minutes later, the lake appeared in front of them. On the lakeshore there were a number of buildings, some finished, some clad with scaffolding.

They went closer. Eliza asked Brunul to wait for her while she went to talk to the engineer. Brunul sat down next to a tree, with the bag of food on one side of him and the blanket on the other. He watched as fifty meters away Eliza spoke to a laborer, who then hurried away, returning less than a minute later with a man of around fifty, wearing a pair of overalls over his suit. Probably the engineer, thought Brunul, wondering whether Eliza would manage to persuade him to let them visit the building site. Ultimately, they might disturb the men at their work; he and Eliza had come there on an outing, whereas the others had a quota to meet, the same as he himself did on the Bahlui embankment.

A few moments later, Eliza took something out of her handbag. Probably her identity card, thought Brunul. If he were going to let them see the building site, then the engineer would have to know whom he was dealing with. She showed it to the man, who, after glancing at it, nodded. Eliza put it back in her handbag and then turned in Brunul's direction, waving for him to approach.

The site manager greeted Brunul ceremoniously, even raising his hand to his brow in a salute.

"Live long!" he said, then smiled and introduced himself.

Brunul said his name and shook his hand.

"You want to see what we've achieved, from what I gather."

Although he noticed the difference in attitude between this site manager and his own, who was always in a foul mood and almost never wanted to be disturbed, Brunul didn't have much time for amazement since after the introductions were over the engineer offered Eliza his arm and with the same amiability invited the two to visit the site.

"Here we have the main restaurant, with an outdoor dining area," he told them, making a sweeping motion with his arm. "The outdoor area will be large and have a view of the lake. Very elegant. It's patriotic labor and we're in a hurry to finish it before the August 23 anniversary of the Red Army liberation. Most of the holiday complex will be ready by then," the engineer assured them, with the same amiable smile.

"That means less than a month," thought Brunul filled with admiration for the engineer. The buildings were up, true, but the scaffolding, the wheelbarrows full of earth or cement dotted around the place, the two trucks waiting on the road, the workers idling here and there, and the tools scattered on the ground all gave you the impression that it would be at least a year until the job was finished. The engineer assured them that the complex would open within a month, however, and Brunul could not help but give an admiring whistle, as he had sometimes heard comrade Bojin do when he saw a new building, after which he would heave a sigh of satisfaction and come out with something of the following sort: "Look at how the country is being renewed! Before long we won't even recognize it anymore." A similar pleasant amazement now washed over Brunul, causing him to whistle. Both Eliza and the engineer turned to look at him. Eliza's face was expressionless, she merely raised her eyebrows, but the engineer's smile broadened.

"You can hardly believe it, can you?" the man asked. "Just imagine," he added, releasing Eliza's arm and raising his own arms in the air, waving them dramatically as if caressing the panoramic outline of the restaurant building: "Just imagine what it will look like against this fairy-tale backdrop once we've put up the beautiful bas-reliefs. The working class will love it; they'll be coming here not just from our town but from all around. But what am I saying? You don't have to imagine it; you just need to wait patiently for a few more weeks. Come back on August 23 and you won't have to strain your minds imagining it. You'll be able to eat here, relax here, enjoy the natural surroundings . . ."

"And the bas-reliefs," blurted Brunul.

"And the bas-reliefs, yes, of course."

Eliza went over to him and held his arm. The man's enthusiasm didn't seem to have infected her. Quite the contrary.

"Perhaps we should be going," she whispered to Brunul.

But Brunul did not hear her, or at least he acted as if he hadn't heard her. If he had heard her, if he had noticed the expression on her face, he would have had reasons to be amazed. After all, it had been Eliza who had insisted on the outing; she had been the one who wanted to visit the building site. What was more, she had been the one who had wanted Brunul to shake off the dark mood that had been hanging over him for the last few weeks, and that was precisely what was now happening. So, had he observed her sullenness, it would have seemed strange and incomprehensible to him.

Brunul was not paying attention to Eliza, however. He had been won over by the engineer and so he followed him around the building site, becoming more and more excited at each achievement pointed out to him. And as he listened to the site manager's words, his imagination, which the engineer had said would soon not be needed in order to see the place in all its splendor, constructed a corner of paradise, like the one comrade Bojin had once passionately told him about. In Brunul's imagination, the scaffolding vanished, sinking into the walls, the wheelbarrows melted away as if they had never existed, outdoor dining tables sprouted from the earth, along with chairs on which people appeared from nowhere, hosts of people with smiling faces, who had come there after a week of labor to relax in the enchanted surroundings. Along the path there appeared booths selling soft drinks, like a row of toppled dominoes flipped back up by an unseen hand; there would be no fewer than fifteen of these, the engineer promised. The noisy children that Brunul's imagination had placed around the booths were now running back to the café tables holding bottles of soda. The clinking of glasses blended with the burble of lake water. From the restaurant the sound of traditional music filled the bracing air of the Ciric. The sun shone down on the lake, its light flooding the outdoor café, pouring over the delighted faces of the people of labor there to enjoy themselves. Allowing his imagination to construct scenery for the vast stage set of the building site, in keeping with the words of the very friendly works manager, Brunul understood comrade Bojin, without thinking, merely by allowing his soul to take in all the things he saw or imagined around him; only now did he truly feel how important his own work was too, on the dusty Bahlui River embankment, which, however, in a not-too-distant future, would become an esplanade, to which he, Brunul, was to make a small but very real personal contribution.

The building site, even if it was impressive to Brunul, was not, however, very large, and so their visit didn't last much longer than half an hour. At the end, the engineer did not neglect to invite them back after August 23, and Brunul promised to return, seeking Eliza's agreement with a glance. But Eliza's face, whose expressions Brunul by then knew so well, concealed behind a smile a kind of sadness which only now did Brunul notice, at the end of their walk around the building site.

Although surprised, he did not try to elicit an explanation. He was accustomed to her silences, to the way in which she hid within her own thoughts, answering monosyllabically until the end of the discussion, particularly when he tried to find out more about her. Before confessing to her the secret that had been eating away at him, Brunul had been content with that attitude of hers for a while. In a way, it even suited him: Eliza's silences justified his own. And in time, even if he would have liked to understand her better, even if he had disburdened himself of his own mysteries, at least those to do with his memories, he lost the boldness to ask her for explanations. On the other hand, he knew something else, which he had learned in the months they had spent together, namely that Eliza herself did not delay very long in broaching a subject, if it was something genuinely important.

For almost an hour they had not spoken to each other. After they walked around the lake, Eliza had spread the blanket in the woods on the shore opposite the site where the recreation center was under construction. Still silent, lost in thoughts that Brunul did not dare to interrupt. On embroidered cloths she laid out the food they had brought with them: the eggs, sliced peppers, and the round of sheep's cheese wrapped in fir bark, whose not very encouraging odor Brunul had first begun to smell on the other side of the lake, when he picked up the bag as they left the building site. When she placed the cheese on an embroidered cloth, Eliza noticed the expression on Brunul's face and assured him that it was edible; it had grown warm, and the smell was normal, natural. They were the first words she had spoken since they parted with the engineer, her only words, in fact.

The words were followed by a few agitated gestures. Her laying of the blanket, the embroidered cloths, and each item of food taken out of the bag had been accompanied by abrupt gestures, arising from some dissatisfaction on her part, of which Brunul could make no sense.

"The Manolis Glezos trial ended a few days ago," Eliza finally said, and, having seated herself on the blanket, she attempted to regain her calm by taking a deep breath. "I forgot to tell you. They passed sentence on July 23. Five years' imprisonment, followed by four years' hard labor."

After his confession to Eliza, Brunul had to a certain extent, although not even he knew why, lost interest in what was happening to Glezos the revolutionary in Greece. Nor had Eliza dwelt on it. The evenings when she read about the trial to him from the newspaper had dwindled. They had found other ways of spending their time together. But now, all of a sudden, she had brought up the subject, although it was as clear as could be that the moment was not right, that this was not in fact what she wished to tell him, that she was merely trying to hide her mood, which otherwise would have spoiled their picnic.

Although he understood her need to strike up a conversation, Brunul stubbornly refused to relinquish what was eating away at him: he wanted to know what he had done wrong. And so he finally made bold enough to say it.

"What's wrong? Something upset you when I was talking to the engineer and you haven't been yourself ever since."

"What about you? What's been wrong with you these last

two weeks?" she retorted, raising her voice. "There are things that upset me, the same as there are things that upset you. But I never get upset for more than an hour or two, and then I let it go . . ."

Brunul sighed and said no more. This was why he had long since given up questioning her. It always ended up with her chiding him, after which there would be a tense silence. The same as there was a silence now, although this time it seemed much tenser. It was as if Eliza's voice was more determined, more accusing.

After a minute or perhaps longer, Eliza started eating, still not saying anything. Brunul did likewise. After all, that was why they had lugged the bag of food there. Then, since the silence within which Eliza had enclosed herself left him at liberty to listen to the sounds around him, Brunul focused on the limpid, multifarious twittering of the birds, the soft, uniform burbling of the lake water, the intermittent rustling of the leaves in the faint summer breeze. All these things distanced him from the not at all pleasant mood of the moment, carrying him away at a leap beyond the dark, forgotten period of his recent past to the village of his grandparents, on the bank of a river he had not thought about for so long a time. It had been so long that he could no longer remember; perhaps he had never once thought about that river since he woke up in hospital after the accident.

His memory bore him away to that riverbank, to another blanket, or perhaps it was a rug, with a picnic laid out beside it, but in that mental leap back into the past, he could not tell what food his grandmother had brought. There was a meadow behind, where the birds were twittering, the same as now, and there was water in front, also the same as now, although back then it was flowing water. He saw his grandmother, standing in the river with the water up to her knees, stooped over a bench, on which she was washing rugs, carpets, and caparisons for Grandfather's horse. She was holding a thick bar of soap, which caused his mind to make another leap, this time in space, since the time was more or less the same, with the few days separating the two memories dissolving in his mind: he found himself in the yard of his grandparents' house, where in a cauldron were boiling animal remains and various other stuffs, the terms for which he could no longer remember. Once boiled down, they produced a strongly smelling yellowish-red paste, which was left to dry. His grandmother then cut the hardened paste into thick slices, which they used for soap. They even washed their hair with it. He now returned to the riverbank. His grandmother was coming toward him, wearing that apron of hers, wet almost to the waist. She was happy, and in her hands she held a fish. "It's your fish. I caught it for you to play with." The words came to him out of nowhere. Never until now had he remembered his grandmother's voice with such clarity, with such familiarity. That whole afternoon spent by the little pond, the enclosure of pebbles he built for the struggling fish. His boyish laughter. He intended to release the fish, he remembered it very well, he intended to release it before he went home that evening, when his grandmother loaded the rugs and carpets and caparisons into the wheelbarrow. He would have made a breach in the dam of pebbles and the fish would have swum free, back to its parents and siblings, perhaps preserving only a memory of that afternoon spent in a narrow pond, perhaps telling all the other fishes about its adventure and the peril it had faced. But before his grandmother could load the wheelbarrow with the rugs laid out to dry on the rocks, the fish had done something that the child he was at the time could never have imagined: after swimming madly from one end of the little pond to the other, the fish suddenly turned belly up. He had poked it with a stick, then touched it with his hand, but it stubbornly refused to move. It remained floating, belly up, despite the child's implorations and tears. Even after his grandmother tossed it into the river, promising that it would recover there, the fish still remained belly up, floating downstream, completely oblivious to the pleas of the little boy, who followed it, running along the bank for dozens of meters, until his grandmother's shouts brought him to a stop.

That memory had been lost somewhere, behind the mist that blotted out twenty years, and now, on the bank of Lake Ciric, it came back to him, making him smile sadly. Although he himself was unaware of the smile, Eliza saw it and did not allow it to pass unremarked.

"What are you thinking?" Eliza's words forced Brunul's mind to leap back to the present, traversing the mist once more. Having returned, he immediately noticed that Eliza didn't seem so upset or angry as she had been a few moments ago.

"Nothing important," he said, but then, because Eliza insisted, he told her, in a few words, the story of the dead fish from all those years ago. Probably not even its bones remained, but still it clung to the sorely tested memory of a man, as if that had been the whole point of its existence.

"Such things happen," murmured Eliza, sad and pensive once more, as if Brunul's story had contained something solemn and full of wisdom.

She then looked in his eyes, until he felt the need to lower his head.

"I'm not upset with you, you know," she said. "It's just that I don't understand you. I mean I don't understand this happiness of yours, which comes from next to nothing. Do you really like what's happening? In the last two weeks, since you changed your job, it seemed to me that you were sad. And I didn't like to see you like that, but at least you gave me the impression that you understood what was happening to you and refused to accept that everything had to be like that. The same as your fish: it struggled and wanted to escape, didn't it? Like you: two weeks ago, it seemed to me that you were struggling to escape, that you refused to let somebody else decide your life for you."

"The fish died," said Brunul, although he didn't understand what the story about his childhood had to do with anything.

"Never mind the fish. This is about you. I thought you were fighting it somehow. And then you come here, you talk to an engineer about . . . To hell with it all. Him and his achievements. Their achievements. And I look at you and I see you wide-eyed, happy, ready to accept it all, your new workplace, your new job. Don't tell me you didn't think about your own building site while you were visiting this one. You were thinking about yourself. I know you by now. You convinced yourself that everything would be fine, that you could forget about puppets, about the shows you told me about, as if you never cared about anything else except being one of them."

"Is that why you were upset?" asked Brunul, stunned.

"That's why. Not at you . . ."

She waved her hand and lowered her eyes.

"But it was you who wanted us to visit the building site. I don't even know how you managed to persuade the engineer to let us . . ."

"Yes, obviously it was I who wanted to!" agreed Eliza, making a sweeping motion with her arms, and once more Brunul sensed that behind the words there were others, unspoken.

But he did not seek out those unspoken words by asking another question. He tried only to find his own words, to gather them together into an explanation. He realized, however, that he had no explanation, that Eliza was right, but behind the fact that she was right there lay other things, which were hard to put into words. There was the sense of duty he felt toward comrade Bojin, his duty to the Party. Even if the Party had never acquired any concrete shape, he had so many times felt it intervene, in the one-room apartment where he had stayed since before he found his first job, and even before that. He had felt the Party's forgiveness when he was released from prison, where he had been sent for an act he could no longer remember, but which must have been serious, shameful even, given that comrade Bojin told him the reason for his arrest had been political. It wasn't even a matter of duty, but rather the desire for atonement. He had to atone for his sins, no matter what they might have been. He had to atone for them at all costs, if he was to breathe freely, without the burden of guilt, in the new society that had so benevolently provided him with a place. And in order to do so he was prepared to accept anything, he was ready to sacrifice anything, the same as Dr. Ustinenko had sacrificed his love. He was ready to accept any task, as long as he could be rid of that suffocating, excruciating knot of feelings that lodged in his throat night after night, when he relinquished his selfishness and gazed accusingly, and at the same time terrified, into the mist of the twenty years of which he had no memory, but during which, as he had to accept, he had at one point, in one way or another, been unjust toward all those who now showed themselves to be so good.

He could tell Eliza none of these things, however. Not because she wouldn't have understood—she certainly nurtured the same love toward the Party as he did, and she had demonstrated that love to him so many times—but because the thoughts could not be put into words; they were rather feelings, a welter of inexpressible feelings.

But Eliza wasn't waiting for any explanation. She went on talking, as if her initial words had taken a long-standing weight off her soul. Having been released from that weight, she now allowed other complaints to flow more freely, with less hindrance than her previous words had met.

"You told me just now about something from your childhood. There's another thing I don't understand. I've heard you talking about your grandparents before, about the village where you grew up. But even so, the way you behave now, it's as if the illness erased it all not just from your memory but from the face of the earth. That village must be somewhere, mustn't it? Don't you want to go there? Are you content to stay here, without searching for anything from your past?"

"My grandparents are dead. You know that."

"You also told me about your parents. About Bucharest."

"They're dead too."

"You can't be certain."

"Why not? You know very well that comrade Bojin . . ."

Eliza threw up her hands in annoyance. She snorted.

"Comrade Bojin. Of course!"

"He would hardly have lied to me about something like that," said Brunul, not because he really believed for one moment that comrade Bojin might have lied to him, but because he wanted to convince Eliza that it would be impossible for anything of the sort to happen.

"How does this comrade Bojin of yours know that your parents died in Italy in the war, but can't tell you anything about what happened after you came back to Romania?" blurted Eliza, and then shook her head, as if realizing how pointless the question was.

Brunul frowned for a moment, trying to put in order the things comrade Bojin had said. He had quite simply never thought about it. Even after he returned to prison following the accident, he had accepted unquestioningly what the Party's representative said, especially since the last memory he had was of leaving for Italy. Had his parents died in the war? They must have, otherwise they would have come looking for him here in Romania; otherwise they would maybe even have come to visit him in hospital. He had accepted that they were dead. In the pain that had overwhelmed him, rising from his memories that ended at the age of sixteen, he had never asked himself the question that Eliza now put to him so angrily. Even so, how did comrade Bojin know his parents were dead, when he hadn't been able to help him discover anything about his past subsequent to his return to Romania, apart from that subscription ticket? There was no information in the prison archives. He had accepted that. The information had been lost somewhere. Things get lost. It happens. But comrade Bojin had told him on another occasion about a different archive, about other archives, where he worked, the Party archives, presumably. Might there be information about his parents in those archives? Why had it never occurred to him to ask? He promised himself he would do so the next time he met comrade Bojin. The thought of this assuaged the vague disquiet aroused by Eliza's question. He would ask comrade Bojin at their next meeting, and then he would discover the answer.

Eliza stood up. She looked up at the sky. A few clouds had appeared. They weren't at all menacing, but Eliza took the opportunity and pointed at them.

"We'd better be going," she said.

Brunul stood up and helped her to put away the blanket. He had not even tasted the much-lauded cheese. He wasn't sorry, however. He hadn't really fancied it, particularly given the odor it had started to exude when he picked up the bag after they finished their visit to the building site.

"We'll have to walk back into town," added Eliza.

Even so, they still had plenty of time. It was barely noon, but Brunul felt that there was no point in their extending the picnic after the discussion that had arisen between them.

The journey on foot and then by tram took a long while. By the time they reached Eliza's building, the afternoon was almost over, and the clouds that had started to gather in Ciric now blotted out the sky, threatening rain. It had been an awkward journey, with each of them attempting to strike up a conversation that might help them forget the failed outing. Each attempt ended in an abrupt silence, however, the kind of silence that transformed any other sound, no matter what the source, into a blessing.

Eliza embraced him in front of the main entrance, thereby

indicating that Brunul should not accompany her to the door of her apartment. Having released him from her embrace, rather than entering the building, Eliza placed her hand on Brunul's cheek, pensively, obliging him to stand there stiffly, waiting, pointlessly, so it seemed to him, although he could hardly break free as long as she held her eyes fixed on him.

"I want to ask you something," she said finally. "I want to ask you to think about your parents. To think about whether at least one of them might still be alive in Italy. Maybe they died in the war. Who knows? It may be like they told you," she said, and then hesitated for a moment. "But I still want you to ask yourself at least this much: What if the people who told you aren't well informed? Not that they lied to you, but what if they're not well informed? It's no great thing, I'm not asking you very much . . ."

Brunul nodded, not because he really thought that he should ask himself that—he was convinced that comrade Bojin had the answer—but because standing there stiffly, awkwardly in front of Eliza's building, all he wanted was to be alone, to be on his way home, so that he could think in peace about all the puzzling ways in which she, the woman for whom he already nurtured feelings difficult to put into words, had reacted that day.

"And another thing," Eliza went on. "We two have . . ." She searched for the right word. "Between us—how can I put it? A lot of things are happening, aren't they?"

Brunul responded with another nod of the head, which didn't seem to satisfy her completely, but which helped her to continue.

"That's why I would like to ask you to keep what we talked about today between us. I mean, don't tell anybody else, not even a friend. What we talked about is between us . . ."

"Naturally," Brunul quickly assented.

For a few moments, she seemed about to add something else. But instead she grimaced and shook her head. She then pressed her lips to his in a brief kiss. She turned her back, waving goodbye with a limp shake of her hand, and entered the building.

Slowly rousing himself, Brunul set off down the street, still unable to remember all the things Eliza had said to him, but rejoicing, at least temporarily, at having been released from the awkwardness and misunderstandings of the day, the accumulated exhaustion of which he only now began to feel. After a few minutes, the clouds made good on their threat, soaking him to the skin. But he did not quicken his steps. On the contrary, all the way back to his own apartment he rejoiced in the rain, allowing it a free hand.

# Chapter 10

FOR A TIME, history washed its hands of Bruno Matei, who, going through a rebellion whose meaning had been so personal that nobody but himself had understood it, realized he had no control over the trajectory created by his own center of gravity. History washed its hands of him and threw a veil over his face, making him one more anonymous face among others covered with similar veils, without any power to act on his own behalf, a mere mechanical body among hundreds of other bodies, within a machine whose very last cog was controlled by those whom history had provided with the knowledge and above all the necessary power to exert such control.

During the last two years he spent on the Peninsula, there was nowhere Bruno could have gathered memories, or stories, or faces, or friendships. Even friendships by then already old, shaken by the events of the summer of fifty-one, no longer had their original taste, no matter how dusty that taste might have been. The forgiveness Bruno proffered Porthos didn't rekindle the former exuberance of his first friend in prison. The two weeks Porthos spent in the students' huts had quenched his hunger, his appetite to share stories about Grossfeld Handball, and even his memories. Then, one autumn morning, as fate would have it, the former handball player was taken away to another prison, where perhaps he regained his appetite for food, memories, hopes. But whether he did so or not, nobody on the Peninsula found out.

With regard to the boy from Maramureș, Bruno didn't attempt anything much. Even if the accordion was no longer heard from the students' huts, they all knew that the forced confessions continued there in some manner, albeit now among the students themselves. And the fear of that place did not end after the death of Dr. Simionescu and its aftermath. The boy from Maramureş knew it, the same as the others did. And the fear that his closeness to Bruno had brought, after the days the latter spent in the thirteen-fourteen huts, made him forget about his own stories from Piteşti, the stories he had garnered for as long as he was mistaken for a student; they even made him forget his wanderings in the mountains, in search of wild mushrooms. They made him forget, and they made him hold his tongue, especially since the autumn of fifty-one was to bring the end of his three-year sentence. And even if, the same as it had caused him to be mistaken for a student, fate played him another trick, delaying his release for a few months, until the end of winter, not even in this extra time allotted to him did he become close to Bruno.

Bruno didn't seek to become close to anybody else. He was content to lose himself among the others, at the edge of the road where history had abandoned him for a time. He merely counted the days until his own release, crossing them off on the calendar he had made in his own mind, without taking fright at the numbers, even rejoicing in silence when he skipped over a hundred-day stretch: two thousand eight hundred, two thousand seven hundred, two thousand six hundred . . .

Then, when he had already started thinking about the number two thousand, glimpsing it on the horizon with a certain amount of excitement, history once more picked him out of the unknown mass into which it had cast him, thrusting him into the ranks of those it dragged along behind it, according to its own calendar.

That spring morning, on the way to the labor site, bells could be heard tolling over the horizon, from over the hills, not the usual, scattered chimes that came to them only from the direction of Kara-yel, not the chimes that in past summers had made him screw up his eyes, as he walked up on the plateau, peering at a single point, straining to descry the steeple of a church through the shimmering heat. That morning, the distant sound of bells enveloped him, it came from over the horizon, not from a single direction, but as if from everywhere at once. The horizon itself had become rounded, forcing you to wheel around in order to sense the circle traced by that long, cadenced thrum, which came from everywhere at once and seemed to shake even the clouds, causing them to stream downward oppressively, releasing faint shadows tinged by sunlight.

The seven angels had at last decided to blow their trumpets, all at once, as many of the prisoners seemed to think. But not even the angels' trumpets, descending from the belfries of the churches, could stop them in their journey guided by the duty to erase the stain of their past sins, as the guards were at pains to remind them. The prisoners continued their march, to a different music, one that not only they knew very well, but also the air around them, lashed by their vocal cords, the air that filled their lungs only to be released as the same shout as ever, the same song, now intended to drown out the sound of the bells.

But before lunchtime, as they labored, the sound of the unseen steeples turned into a rumor, bringing with it an explanation for the encircling chimes of that morning. From one bowed face to another, from one pair of cracked lips to another, as they raised their pickaxes for yet another blow, giving their ears a momentary chance to hear a different sound, the rumor spread to all the prisoners, one by one, words which seeped through the eardrums, down the throat, and into the muscles of their arms, freezing them, making it impossible for them to raise or lower their pickaxes anymore.

"Stalin is dead!"

Nobody knew whence the rumor had originated or how it had reached the prisoners. But for them, the agitation of the guards, which had preceded the rumor, an agitation aroused by the hasty arrival of a soldier who had come running from the penal colony, was confirmation in itself. And so too was the fact that immediately thereafter the soldiers who had been guarding them ordered them to stop work and then, after consulting with each other out of the prisoners' earshot, decided that they should return to the huts. Nothing like it had ever happened in all the days, months, and years that had gone before.

The guards said nothing to them. They gave no explanation. They merely ordered them into single file and gave the signal to set off. And on the way back they no longer ordered them to sing or felt the need to remind them of their duty and the price they had to pay to the Romanian Republic. The guards were, in those moments, preoccupied with something that was happening far away, but nonetheless very close, in the capitals of the other republics, the Soviet ones, where the great comrade, to whom they had, unawares, hitched their present and future, had left them all on their own, had left them to an uncertainty that had abruptly destroyed any confidence in themselves.

There was a completely different atmosphere in the penal colony. Other labor brigades returned and were left to their own devices among the huts. There was no lining up to form a square, no chief to yell at them. The orderly grayness of up until the day before, the standing stiffly in a line, the military atmosphere, all had dissolved in the space of just a few hours. The prisoners were left to their own devices and nobody knew how to react. They gathered in small groups, from time to time looking fearfully in the direction of the guards, speaking to each other in whispers, gesticulating, which is to say, talking about things they had not discussed for a very long time. Some merely milled around, as if taking exercise, although it was the last thing they needed, having just returned from hard labor. With the force of a bulldozer, the news had destroyed the symmetrical orderliness of the penal colony.

Bruno, who in the last two years had hidden himself in that compulsory symmetry, learning it and wholly depending on it, followed the lead of those who headed for the barbed-wire fence, mechanically stretching his legs, hoping to lose himself amid the crowd of others stretching their legs. He reached the wire, touched a barb, laid his palm over it, wrapped his fingers one by one around the rusty metal, clenched his fist, somehow enjoying the prick of it, trying to feel it with the whole of his body. He needed that pain, not even he knew why. Ever since he arrived in the penal colony, he had viewed the barbed wire as a sign of freedom. The space for the prisoners stopped before the barbed wire, one or two paces before it. He had never been allowed to touch it. The prison wall was not the three- to four-meter-high double barbed-wire fence. It was an invisible wall, but no less tangible for that, a wall built from the guards' yells, from the warning shouts of the soldiers with machine guns perched in the watchtowers. That wall was mobile and went with them to the plateau, where there were no barbed-wire fences. In the years that had elapsed up until the moment when the sentence "Stalin is dead" interrupted all the customs of the penal colony, Bruno had always viewed the barbed-wire fences as the first step beyond. Beyond the wall. And now, amid the dazed confusion, he was able to touch freedom with his own hands: a rusty piece of freedom, with barbs that pierced the skin of his hands, causing him a pain that he desired.

When he heard a soldier shout from the watchtower to the right, Bruno unclenched his fist and withdrew behind the imaginary wall. He did not wait for a second warning. But he smiled as he stepped back. From thousands of miles away, death had allowed him a moment of his own, a moment such as he had never enjoyed in all his time in the penal colony.

After the soldier shouted from the watchtower, the camp

began to seethe; the crowd began to coalesce in an attempt
quickly to rediscover the symmetry demanded. The guards
abruptly awoke from the stupor in which they had been plunged
for the last few minutes, perhaps even the last few hours. Guns
were raised; the soldier's shout was repeated from other mouths,
other throats, turning into screams. Peering over shoulders, over
heads, Bruno also understood the reason why the prisoners,
standing up in the places where they had been squatting,
dispersing from their small groups, were now crowding toward
the exercise yard, with the guards' guns pointing at them. From
the main building, Iosif Lazăr, the camp commandant himself,
accompanied by his adjutants, was striding toward them. He
was a man who only appeared when there was something
important to be said, who merely had to show his face in
order for complete silence to fall, and who was the man most
capable of dispelling the stupor that had descended on them all,
prisoners and guards alike.

Brunul knew him hardly at all. Lost in the crowd of
prisoners, he had not come into contact with the commandant,
who had arrived there as head of the Production Service two
years previously and subsequently been promoted to head of the
penal colony. However, Brunul had heard stories about the head
of the Peninsula and had been able to piece together a picture of
him. Some of those stories told of his brutality, which otherwise
was not apparent in his speeches to the sporadic assemblies of
prisoners he called. It was said that he had mutilated a prisoner
with his own hands, beating him with a rock, smashing his
lips, teeth, cheeks, nose, eyes. The prisoner's skin and bones
had been pulverized beneath the blows, his face transformed
into a hideous, formless red mask. From the wretch's croaks,
the other prisoners had been able to reconstruct the scene: the
guards had held him down, while the commandant calmly,
patiently pounded his face with the rock, the way you would
grind garlic with a pestle and mortar, slowly, firmly, careful not

to leave any chunks. That was the story the other prisoners told about what the commandant had done with the rock. But these were terrors translated into words. The same as other terrors translated into words told of how the commandant had on a number of occasions boasted to the prisoners that he had been a prisoner of war in one of the Germans' harshest camps. To Bruno it was inconceivable: How could you endure hell and then become a supervisor of torments? No, Bruno in fact knew next to nothing about the commandant, and in the last few years he had preferred to hear but not believe the stories, he had preferred to view the commandant as a man who, shut up in his hut for most of the time, didn't have any real idea about what was happening in the camp, as a man to whom, if it came to the limit, you could go and complain, from whom you could seek and receive understanding.

Heading toward the crowd of other prisoners, who were now beginning to form orderly lines, Bruno expected to receive an explanation from the commandant. He even expected more than just an explanation, and this is why he unwittingly hurried his steps and tried to push to the front in order to hear the message about to be communicated to them. Beyond the fences of the penal colony, the death of Stalin must already have had an effect, it must have produced some change, and the hopes that had entered Bruno unawares caused him to see evidence of that change in the gait of the commandant and his adjutants as they approached.

After the man on whom every eye was fixed raised his hand for silence, Bruno heard the eagerly expected words as clearly as all the other prisoners. He heard them and understood them as they were intended to be understood. He also understood that the imaginary walls of the prison, its strongest walls, had not been shaken in the slightest by the news that had traveled from Moscow to that forgotten corner of Romania.

"Bandits!" began Iosif Lazăr and then paused to clear his

throat the better to make himself heard. "Pestilent insects!" he added, with a grin, looking at the faces of the prisoners assembled in front of him. "What did you say to yourselves, eh? What did you say, you pestilent insects? You said: Let's defy the people's regime! Let's defy the will of the people! And did you? Yes, you did! And what became of you, you damned insects? What became of you, eh?" With that he made a sweep of his arms to indicate the barbed-wire fences and the huts. "Do you know why, you insects? Because the people are wakeful, that's why. They're wakeful! But sometimes the people are busy, they have to work, you insects! And what do the people do then? The people send their most illustrious representatives to be wakeful in their stead. That's what the people do! Have you understood what the people do? They send me to keep watch here, because the people are clever! And what is it I keep watch over, you insects? I keep watch to make sure you atone for your sins against the people you betrayed. That's why I keep watch! And to do that, I don't even need the guns you see all around you. I don't need those guns!" here the commandant paused to point at the soldiers and the guards, and then with a scornful twitch of his lips, he turned to the prisoners once more, clenched his fist, and brandished it at them: "I don't need them. All the power of the people is here in this fist. So then, what do you need to fear? The power of the people in this fist of mine, you insects, that's what you need to fear, not guns!"

He waited for a few moments to see how they would react. The abruptly bowed heads did not allow that reaction to be seen, the dry lips did not allow it to be heard. Unclenching his fist and lowering his arm, the commandant continued.

"What did I hear? This is what I heard: that a rumor has been going around. And now what is it that you want? Do you want me to tell you whether it's true or not? That's what you want! As if it would do you any good, you insects. But I couldn't give a shit about what you want. If you didn't know that already, then let me tell you that I couldn't give a shit. The only thing I care about is the will of the people, you insects! And the people have decided that you deserve some mercy for these few days. That's what the people decided. The people have told me that from now on it's forbidden to beat pestilent insects. That's the law of the people! Our people are merciful, that's why they've told me that the guards aren't allowed to hit the pestilent insects. That's what I came to tell you. So be happy about it. Go on, be happy, let me hear you!"

The words were followed by a chorus of murmurs and a few cheers from the guards, rather than the prisoners. The words had come from nowhere, they had in a way confirmed the rumor of that morning, but they were far from what the prisoners had been expecting, from what some of them at least had dared to imagine might come next. And the grin on the commandant's face dissuaded those who were about to lift their hands to clap as demanded.

"You mean to say it doesn't suit you? Too right it shouldn't suit you! You ought to know that through labor you're paying off your debt to the people and through beatings the crimes you committed. But the people are merciful, you insects, and I heed their word. That's why I repeat what the people have spoken: from now on no guard is allowed to beat you! But there's a catch: I'm not a guard. Is that clear, insects? I'm not a guard! And so from now on, in this camp, I'm the only one who'll be doing the beating!"

He raised his fist again, moving it from left to right, to make sure all the prisoners understood the message. His grin spread across his whole face. Without another word, commandant Iosif Lazăr turned his back on the exhausted men, who were dumbfounded by his speech, and went back to his hut, accompanied by his adjutants. The assembly immediately dispersed, with the heads of the brigades shouting as they drove the men back to the huts.

Arriving in his hut, still overwhelmed by the commandant's message, Bruno didn't listen to the whispers of those who, still convinced that Stalin was dead, nurtured renewed hopes, telling each other that the Americans had already crossed the border and would soon arrive. He ignored those who claimed that the Soviet Union had already collapsed, now that the Leader was dead. He no longer allowed his hopes, which had proved so deceptive in the last few years, to lead him to any thought of change. He lay curled up on his bed, trying to forget that day, trying to preserve only the moment when three rusty barbs had pressed against his skin, conveying to him a strange sensation of pain which, for a few moments, had been indistinguishable from the sensation of freedom.

That day did not allow itself to be forgotten. The evening before, after struggling between life and death for more than eighteen hours, Joseph Vissarionovich Stalin had indeed given up the ghost. At midnight on March 6, 1953, history had delivered the news to Bucharest, and then it had traveled onward to hidden corners of the land, where it had not trodden for quite some time, in order to search out Bruno Matei, among many others. It went there to grasp him by the sleeve of his prisoner's uniform and drag him away, although not toward the change he expected, not toward the change created by hopes that had lately always proved deceptive, but ultimately still a change.

The jolting van had left some two hours ago, which meant that they must be halfway there. The three prisoners were alone in the back. One of them, a voice without a face in the darkness, was trying to defuse the tension, telling the other two about the road they could not see, but which he knew well.

"We're crossing the Danube," Bruno heard the voice say. "Listen to the waves."

Then there was silence. All they could hear was the rumble

of the engine.

"It's in my blood. That's why I can hear it. It's the Danube for sure. We're on the good road, past the cliffs. I know this area even with my eyes closed."

"We might as well have our eyes closed," said the prisoner on the bench next to him.

"I know it even in the dark. Oho, how many times I've swum in the Danube here. Shall I tell you about when my boat capsized by Ochiul Dracului? It was pitch black. Nobody would survive there even in daylight. But I survived. Believe me, it's the Danube."

Bruno believed him. There was no reason not to believe it was the Danube, although that didn't help him at all: Couldn't they shoot them by the Danube too?

"Let's see how you swim with a bullet in the back of your neck," said the other prisoner, who from the very start had terrified the other two by telling them what he had heard about the "accidents" that happened during so-called transfers, about how prisoners were taken out of the van and shot in the back of the neck, about how it would subsequently be claimed they had tried to escape.

Although Bruno believed the man from the Danube when he said they were near the river, he couldn't see anything positive in it. Yes, they were obviously on the road to Galați, because how else could they have justified murder? They could hardly have taken them in a completely different direction, shot them, and then said they had been transferring them to Galați. It was obvious they were sticking to the proper route, but that didn't mean they weren't going to kill them.

Listening to the other two, who had even fallen to quarreling about the fate that awaited them, Bruno started thinking about the reasons why he was to be shot. He hadn't done anything. Why then did they want him dead? In the last two years, he had been a model prisoner, both at work and in the hut. He

hadn't even made any other friends, he hadn't complained
about anything, he hadn't annoyed anybody. For two years he
hadn't even received a beating, only a few kicks up the behind,
when he moved too slowly, only a few curses, for various trivial
reasons. He hadn't done anything to make himself conspicuous.
Why then did they want him dead? Why was the transfer just
a pretext?

He had been happy when they told him he was being
transferred and led him to the van. After Stalin's death,
apart from that one day when he had been carried away by
expectation, he had resigned himself. He no longer hoped
for anything. The transfer had come not long afterward, less
than two months afterward, and he had rejoiced. Although he
counted the days until his release, on the Peninsula a frozen
stillness reigned, a dreary eternity, which more often than not
rendered his count pointless. It seemed as if nothing could ever
happen, that nothing could ever change. Sometimes he even
imagined how his count would reach a thousand, and then
five hundred, and then a hundred, he imagined his excitement
when the countdown reached three days, two days, one day,
and how in the final hours nothing would happen, nobody
would summon him to tell him he was free. After that, there
would not be the slightest point in ever keeping count again;
nobody would ever speak to him to inform him of a new release
date. He increasingly came to believe that he would die there,
in the hut, or at work on the plateau, that one day, perhaps after
a year, perhaps after ten years, perhaps after decades, a guard
would nudge his prone body with his foot, realize he was dead,
and order some other prisoners to drag him away through the
dust or the snow. Since he had no family in Romania, since
nobody would come to claim his body, he would be thrown on
one of the stacks of corpses that formed behind the huts from
time to time on the Peninsula. But even to that thought, which
sometimes frightened him, he had begun to resign himself.

Now a new fear arose, one to which he had not had time to resign himself: a bullet in the back of the neck. He tried to calm himself. No, he was too insignificant for something like that. He had been too insignificant, too obscure in the penal colony for that to happen. They had no reason to do it. But did they really need a reason?

The van came to a stop. The argument between the other two prisoners abruptly ended. It was too early for them to have arrived; they all knew it. The door at the back opened and the light blinded them. With the light came a wave of stifling heat, although it was barely the beginning of May. However, it was not the heat that choked Bruno, but the fear.

"Get out and have a piss," said the soldier.

"They'll take us out of the van so we can have a piss," the other prisoner, the one who wasn't from the Danube, had said. He had heard about that kind of thing. "And as we're standing with our backs turned: bang!"

"Get a move on!" shouted the man with the gun.

"We don't need to," groaned the prisoner who wasn't from the Danube.

"If I say you need to, then you need to."

Bruno was the last to jump out of the van, trembling, panting heavily, uncontrollably. He looked at the soldier imploringly.

"What's with that face? Need to take a shit too, while you're at it?"

Bruno shook his head; he was suffocating and couldn't speak.

"By those bushes over there!"

He looked around. The Danube was nowhere to be seen. The local, the prisoner who had swum in Ochiul Dracului at night, who had the river in his blood, as he himself claimed, had been mistaken. Or maybe they had passed the Danube and it was hidden behind the hills. In any event, it didn't matter.

The three of them stood next to each other in a line, glancing at each other, terrified.

"Get on with it!"

"We can't," said the prisoner from the Danube.

"We just don't need to go," said the other prisoner.

"Never mind, I know just the thing to make you go."

The soldier dashed to the cab of the van, leaned inside, and started rummaging for something.

"They're waiting for us to run," said the other prisoner, the one who wasn't from the Danube, in a choked whisper. "It's a trap. Don't move."

All three stood frozen, watching the soldier's legs dangling outside the cab of the van. Watching his rifle. The other soldier's voice then sounded from inside the cab.

"It's not here. It's on the other side. I'll get out and solve the problem."

The other soldier climbed out of the van.

"Don't feel like pissing? Then allow me."

He held up a bottle of water, which the three prisoners noticed only then, and started sloshing the contents. Meanwhile, the first soldier had returned. The soldier with the bottle pulled out the cork.

"Unfasten your flies. On the double!"

They didn't turn around. All three were trembling, but they undid their flies. Bruno could barely hold back his tears. He would have liked to say a prayer, but the words did not come to him, he couldn't find them anywhere. He undid his flies. He heard the soldiers laughing, and he looked up in amazement. The second soldier was pouring water out of the bottle, while the first made a hissing sound.

"Still don't need to go?" said the soldier with the bottle. "Come on, I'm wasting all my water on you, and we've still got a two-hour drive."

Bruno's terror abruptly drained into the ground. The soldier had poured away almost all the water in the bottle. Without turning their backs, Bruno and the other two accompanied the soft gurgle of the water with their own trickling sound in the perfect silence. When the two soldiers burst out laughing once more, it was to a chorus of three restrained chuckles, more a kind of whisper than laughter, an articulation of merriment such as the prisoners had not experienced for a long time. Finally, they heard the first soldier ask them in an almost friendly voice to climb back into the van.

The jolting of the van and the pitch darkness inside were completely different after that. The man from the Danube, whose face Bruno could now see in his mind, told them of his adventures on the river, before he was arrested. The other man, the one who wasn't from the Danube, didn't say anything else about what he had heard, and even tried to crack a few jokes.

Bruno was silent for the remainder of the journey. But from time to time he sensed and pondered that the world was wider and more various than he had been able to imagine in the last few years, and that ultimately his release was something worth waiting for. It was worth holding out for the moment of his release.

# Chapter 11

SELDOM WAS BRUNUL called upon to lend a hand with the labor itself, or rather what seemed to him to be the labor: breaking and lugging rocks, leveling and consolidating the riverbank, pouring concrete. After three weeks in the job, this was his main cause for dissatisfaction. In the beginning, after comrade Bojin brought him there, it had seemed normal that he should be made to paint placards. A young worker, who introduced himself as a member of the Union of Working Class Youth, had explained that it was an important task. In the days that followed Brunul often saw the agitator around the building site: in his overalls pocket he always kept a copy of *The Agitator's Notebook, 1959*, which he would consult, leafing through it to find fresh slogans with which to encourage the men of labor. Once, greeting Brunul with a frown, albeit one that conveyed determination rather than malice, he said that the building site lacked direction when it came to political discipline. Then, confident as to the answer he would receive, he asked Brunul whether he was prepared to assist in solving the problem. Political labor, declaimed the agitator, was more vital to increased productivity than physical labor itself. A slogan, when correctly positioned, above the workers' heads, encouraged them and increased their productivity. The men of labor had to be constantly aware that they were working not for themselves, but for everybody, for the entire community, under the rule and the watchful eye of the Party.

Over the next two weeks, slogans painted by Brunul in large red letters began to dot the building site, along both banks of the Bahlui, between the stone bridge and Trancu Bridge, for a distance of more than a kilometer. He sometimes managed to paint a dozen a day, on pieces of cardboard brought to the site by truck. The young agitator supplied the slogans. Some were overtly political, ranging from "Long live the Romanian Workers Party and the glorious working class!" to the familiar "Workers of the world unite!" Once a sufficient number of political slogans had been painted, the agitator dictated to Brunul specific pieces of advice and exhortations aimed at the working class: "Learn to be thrifty for a life free of worry"; "Discipline at work is the worker's first lesson"; "Improve your qualifications in order to elevate yourself as a man"; and others similar. Brunul realized that the slogans had their importance; people had to be guided by the spirit of communism, as the agitator said. On the other hand, he knew that the slogans painted on those pieces of cardboard were not destined to have a long life; they would not be seen by the people who were to stroll along the new embankment for decades or even centuries to come. No matter how handsomely they were painted, no matter how much care Brunul lavished on each red letter, no matter how much space they occupied on the building site, the placards were doomed to disappear once the workers moved on to another site. Maybe the placards would be taken elsewhere, but even so, in all too short a time, the wind and the rain would erase them and nothing would remain of Brunul's labor, whereas the labor of his fellow workers on the site would be treasured for centuries to come.

Finally, he was rid of the slogans. Before the free Saturday Brunul spent with Eliza at Ciric, the agitator told him that he had painted enough placards and that he had spoken to the engineer to have him transferred to a different job starting Monday. During his two days off, Brunul harbored the hope that at last he would make a visible, lasting contribution. The beginning of the week brought him new reasons for despondency, but he did not let it show. The young agitator had decided that Brunul should continue with the work of maintaining the workers' enthusiasm, but moving beyond slogans. To this end he procured a mobile library, full of copies of *The Spark* and *The Flame* newspapers, as well as books in which the workers might absorb themselves during their lunch breaks, even if only for a few minutes. Brunul was required to push the library cart along both banks of the river, a distance of three kilometers in total. In the time left to him after lunch, he was sometimes called upon to carry a bucket of rubble, to replace broken pickaxes, and generally to assist the qualified workers in constructing the new embankment.

At the end of the week, the agitator did not arrive with any encouraging news for him. Instead, that evening before he left the building site, somebody shouted for him to go to the engineer's hut. Brunul had never seen a smile on the engineer's harsh face. As gloomy as ever, the engineer handed him an envelope, saying:

"A comrade left it for you this morning."

Normally, Brunul would have first thought of comrade Bojin. They had communicated while Brunul was at the State Puppet Theater and it was normal that they should continue to do so at the State Roads and Streets Enterprise. Except that his friend never left him missives in envelopes, and certainly not sealed envelopes. Brunul thanked the engineer, left the hut, and only then did he open it. It was indeed from comrade Bojin, which satisfied Brunul, especially since he had not seen him for the last three weeks and had begun to worry on that account. The content of the note amazed him, however, realizing as it did a possibility that his friend had hinted at but which Brunul had never taken seriously. Comrade Bojin invited him to his house that Sunday, where, according to the note, he would be giving "a small party with friends" to celebrate his birthday. Below, comrade Bojin had written the hour at which Brunul was expected and gave the exact address, seeing fit to add a few words about which tram he should take and the stop at which he should alight.

If he had been asked to describe his house, comrade Bojin would unhesitatingly have resorted to the second kind of truth in which he believed. The first type of truth would have been utterly useless in regard to the history of his house; it would have brought up things that nobody wished to hear and, more to the point, things that comrade Bojin would have been reluctant to recount.

In the period prior to the new social order, the house had belonged to a member of the legislature who had come from Bessarabia with Pantelimon Halippa after the national unification of 1918. Anton Crihan was his name, and the neighbors who had known him spoke of him, mostly in a whisper, as having been a great patriot. The whispers, which he had heard whether he liked it or not in the beginning, since he had been living there for a long time, rather annoyed comrade Bojin, because in his opinion a man who had served the Peasants Party and fled abroad with his tail between his legs in 1948, in fear of the people's justice, could be called anything but a patriot. And besides, activating the first type of truth in which he believed, comrade Bojin sometimes wondered, allowing his thoughts to transmit a slightly mocking smile to his lips, as to what Anton Crihan had ever done for Romania: the unification of those northeastern territories with Romania in 1918, in which the erstwhile owner of the house was supposed to have played a part, had ultimately been all for nought, given that Bessarabia had become a republic of the U.S.S.R. No, comrade Bojin couldn't for the life of him see why some people had uttered the name Anton Crihan with such respect in the years immediately after the establishment of the democratic republic. But ultimately they were just words, and he had forgiven his neighbors for them at the time. After all, not everybody could understand that history was not a matter of opinion, but certainty.

His certainty, on account of which he had to admit, also according to the first type of truth, that he sympathized with

Anton Crihan, was the house in the exclusive Copou district, in which he had been living for more than ten years, since the year after the former member of parliament fled the country, to be precise. It was a magnificent house, which had been allocated to him because it would have been a shame for it to remain empty, a house that was visible from a distance when you walked past Copou Park, along the lane behind the new Church of St. Nicholas, a house with three stories, in which comrade Bojin and his wife resided on the second floor. A single story was more than sufficient, and comrade Bojin was satisfied with the large-windowed rooms, which together were as big as a tennis court, as he liked to say. The ceilings were so high that you needed a stepladder to change a light bulb. He was satisfied with the spacious terrace overlooking the park. He was even satisfied with the narrow room leading off the main bathroom, which he had set aside for his own personal use even before he knew he would use it as an office, since besides his work with people, comrade Bojin also penned various documents.

Because Anton Crihan had gone away and left such a home to the will of the same fate that had ensconced comrade Bojin there without his having to make any financial outlay, the latter sometimes felt sympathy for the former. But naturally his sympathy was unspoken and did not extend to the other things that Anton Crihan had done in his life, things that were, if the truth be told, now just as pointless as the life the former member of parliament was leading far from home in some foreign country or other.

But nonetheless, after so many years, if he had been asked to talk about his house, comrade Bojin would have adopted the second type of truth in which he unflinchingly believed and limited himself to saying that he had bought it with his wife, without mentioning the owner who had abandoned it in times neither very clear nor very certain. The reason for this was that he himself did not know very well at the time how things would turn out when he was allocated the living space, and so he had drawn up a phony purchase contract and had had it officially registered a few years later, once the country's situation had become clear and once the number of friends willing to assist him had multiplied. Now a property owner in the fullest sense of the word, comrade Bojin did not see fit to allow his first type of truth to make even the slightest hint to his second type, the one that issued from his mouth. Sometimes history was better left unsaid, all the more so given that in the meantime, either because they had learned how things now stood with history or because they themselves had, for natural reasons, been caught up in history, even the neighbors ceased to utter the name Anton Crihan.

It was at the second floor of that large house behind the Church of St. Nicholas that Brunul arrived on Sunday evening to celebrate the birthday of his old friend. In paper tied with a red ribbon he had wrapped a Zorki camera, for which he had spent two hours searching the shops the previous evening after he finished work. The present made him happy, and his excitement was all the greater given that he knew his friend's enthusiasm for cameras, whatever their make.

Comrade Bojin's wife opened the front door and introduced herself to him in a manner not unfriendly, but without composing the affable smile required. Torița.

"From Victorița," said comrade Bojin, popping up behind his wife. "Come in! Don't just stand on the doorstep!"

Brunul crossed the threshold and after wishing comrade Bojin a happy birthday in a tremulous voice, he handed him the present. He was delighted at comrade Bojin's smile as he examined the camera.

Comrade Bojin waited while Brunul took his shoes off and then lightly placed his hand on his back.

"Let me show you where I'm having the party."

They went into the next room before Brunul had the chance to get a closer look at the large room he had entered by the front door, since there was no vestibule: a room lined with cases of leather-bound books and at least twice as big as his own apartment. He walked through a wide, sliding door. In the next room there was a large couch on one side and two chairs on the other. The table was laid with food and drink. Two large oval plates of stuffed eggs stood out thanks to the nicely arranged stalks of parsley with which they had been decorated, presumably by Mrs. Torița. Next to the table, on the left, a tall door gave onto the terrace. Also on the left, immediately next to him, Brunul noticed the television set. He realized immediately that this must be the apparatus comrade Bojin had told him about with such delight, describing it in lavish detail. The Record logo beneath the knobs left no doubt. His friend led him through another door, which gave onto a large hall, and then into a room on the left, a little smaller than the previous room but just as tall.

It was the bedroom, but what caught Brunul's eye straight-away were the shelves on the walls, upon which, instead of bibelots, all kinds of electronic objects rested on top of doilies. The shelves stretched along the walls to the left and right, as well as above the head of the bed. With a smile that was almost a smug grin, comrade Bojin pointed to a camera resting on one of the shelves.

"The one I've got already is a Lyubitel, and so I could do with a Zorki," he said, reassuring Brunul, whose eyes had filled with tears of embarrassment.

Comrade Bojin thanked him yet again for the present and then placed the Zorki on the shelf next to the Lyubitel, assuring Brunul that Torița, who had in the meantime vanished down the long hallway, probably into the kitchen, would find a doily for it. He then showed him all the other devices on the shelves. On the first shelf were a number of watches—an entire collection, as comrade Bojin emphasized proudly. Some were pocket watches, Molnia and U.M.F. Ruhla make, others were various makes of wristwatch: Sportivnye, Kama, Iskra,

Pobeda. The Pobeda was like the one comrade Bojin had given
Brunul as a present after he left prison. On another shelf there
was a record player, and on the shelf beneath it was an old
gramophone. Both of them rested on large doilies that hung
over the edge of their shelves. On either side of both the record
player and the gramophone were piles of records; each pile was
of equal thickness, for the sake of symmetry. On another shelf
there were no fewer than three radio sets, of different makes
naturally. As far as Brunul could tell, comrade Bojin was keen
on collecting equipment produced in as many different factories
as possible. This observation finally allayed Brunul's fear that
comrade Bojin might not like his present. One radio set was
inscribed Romanţa, the second was a Strassfurt, and the third,
the most impressive of all, was a Daugava.

"And now let me show you the television set," comrade
Bojin said to his friend, ushering him back to the room where
the table was laid.

But before he could open the door—only now did Brunul
notice his own nervousness in anticipation of this moment—
comrade Bojin was obliged to apologize, thereby prolonging
the wait, when they heard a knock on the front door. Through
the wide, sliding door, Brunul saw a man and a woman enter.
Both were around fifty and seemed to be man and wife.
They embraced comrade Bojin enthusiastically, raucously,
even, and then his wife Toriţa, whom Brunul saw suddenly
appear, although she had not passed through the room where
he now stood waiting. Probably there was another door
connecting the large hallway and the library. Finally, the guests
entered the room where the table was laid and where Brunul
had remained on his feet, since he did not dare to sit down
uninvited.

After making the introductions, comrade Bojin rubbed his
hands in satisfaction, seemingly merrier than Brunul had ever
seen him before.

"Here we all are," he said. "Let's sit down at the table. Make yourselves at home."

Brunul barely had time to wonder at the number of guests. He had expected the word "party" to mean more than five people, including himself. Nonetheless, he seated himself, endeavoring to do so as respectfully as possible.

"No, come over here and sit on the couch," said comrade Bojin. "How will you be able to see the television set otherwise? Never mind them," he laughed, pointing at the couple. "They can watch with their backs turned, because they're sick of television by now. They bought themselves one even before I did," he said, winking at Brunul and giving a laugh that seemed to contain a hint of envy.

"You never stop going on about your Record," murmured the man, and his wife added, directing the remark at Brunul:

"You'd think his was in color, the way he boasts, but don't we see the same thing, no matter what set we're watching it on?" She then turned her gaze to the master of the house.

"Yes, but when I watch mine," comrade Bojin continued, in a teasing voice, "I see something extra: I see that it says Record here, whereas you see that yours says Rubin 102."

He gave a loud chortle and then turned to Brunul.

"Let's turn it on. And then tell me whether what you see isn't more beautiful than the most beautiful puppet theater in the world."

He pressed a button.

After a few minutes' wait, during which Brunul was amazed that apart from a buzzing noise the television set gave no sign that it was working, the sound of violins finally burst forth, after which the screen lit up to reveal an orchestra. Brunul had heard symphonic music on the radio countless times, but the sight of all those people playing violins in synchrony left him agape. He forgot that he was seeing it all on a screen and was carried away by the music, amazed at the manner in which the members of the orchestra were able to create it. Only when he heard comrade Bojin loudly ask for his reaction, for a few words to describe how he felt, did Brunul awake from his dream. He tried to gather his thoughts, regained his wonted awkwardness, and sought the fitting gestures and then words to explain, much to the others' delight, that he could never have imagined such a marvel.

But Brunul addressed his words to the host, realizing that he needed to enhance the present he had given him with feigned enchantment at the apparatus that meant so much to him. It was not the television set in itself that had elicited Brunul's amazement, not the reverie into which he had fallen for a few moments. On the contrary, the measly box, whose screen was so small in comparison with the one he had seen at the cinema, and the blurry outlines disappointed him; he had been expecting much more. A television set could never replace a puppet show. But the music fascinated Brunul, even making him quiver, accompanied as it was by the image of so many people gathered with no other purpose than to weave sounds into harmonies.

And there was something else besides, something far more important, something that could not be articulated, because it plunged Brunul into a mystery whose meanings he sensed, with a sense of suffocation, he could never unravel. Once that image appeared on the screen, a different image entered Brunul's mind, although it was impossible for him to say where it came from. In that image he saw people who he sensed were close to him, but whom he could not name. Some of them were on an orchestra stage, holding violins and playing something that resembled what was on the screen only insofar as their violins, like those of the orchestra, came together in synchrony to produce a harmonious melody with not one note out of place. And alongside them on that imaginary stage that had sprung from nowhere in his mind were other people, who were working puppets that danced on their strings in time to the music. And if such an image were not amazing enough in itself, as if it were not harrowing enough in itself, a glib, faceless voice sounded from a swirling fog, talking to Brunul in Italian, a language that he had not used for so long that it sometimes seemed to him that he had forgotten it. And this is what the voice said: "*Il marionettista è una sorta di musicista: egli domina le corde del pupazzo allo stesso modo in cui il musicista, aiutandosi con l'archetto, domina le corde del violino. In questo modo il marionettista crea una sinfonia, non di suoni ma di movimenti. E la sua sinfonia è addirittura più complessa di quella del musicista, perché ci sono più corde da controllare.*"[2]

During the meal that followed, Brunul strove with all his might to find once more in his mind the images he had glimpsed, the words he had heard for a few moments thanks to the orchestra on the television. The others' merriment, the clinking of glasses, the separate conversations going on simultaneously, to which he was obliged to contribute at least from time to time, prevented him from concentrating on gathering together the shards of words and images to form a whole. Late that evening, when the other two guests, the husband and wife, got up to leave, Brunul sensed that the scene, which for an instant had been so vivid, had been lost once more in the fog whence it had risen.

When Brunul too got up to leave, comrade Bojin, who was by then well and truly sozzled, the drink even having turned the tip of his nose a rather comical red, begged him to stay at least until they finished the last bottle of wine on the table. Brunul accepted. In any event, he had risen only out of politeness; he didn't wish to leave, at least not straightaway. He had some questions, which he would not have been able to ask with the other guests still present.

---

2    The marionettist is a kind of musician: he controls the strings of the puppet the same as the musician, by means of his bow, controls the strings of the violin. In this way the marionnetist creates a symphony, not of sounds, but of movements. And his symphony is more complex even than the musician's, since there are more strings to control.

They went out onto the terrace. Having seen the couple to the door, Mrs. Toriţa had come back and told her husband, in a tone of voice that brooked no objection, that if he wished to carry on drinking then he would have to do so outside. She stressed in particular that she had no intention of cleaning the couch and the carpet if he should suddenly feel sick. She had then set about clearing the table, which in any event did not leave the two men much room for conviviality inside. Brunul realized that he ought to leave, but his questions, stimulated by the wine he had drunk, demanded that he remain at least for another few minutes.

Outside on the terrace, gazing at the rustling shadows of the park, comrade Bojin was not in the mood for talk, however. He took a slug from the bottle and then started whistling softly, before mumbling the words of a song.

> Aş vrea într-o seară să ne întîlnim,
> Dar nu ştiu cînd e mai bine să ieşim:
> Lunea n-are nici un rost,
> Marţi e rău că merge prost,
> Miercuri ştii şi tu că e zi de post.
> (I'd like us to meet one evening, / But I don't know when it would be best to go out: / There's no point on Monday, / Things always go bad on a Tuesday, / You know full well Wednesday's a day of fasting.)

Flies and moths had been drawn to the light bulb on the terrace. Some insects had stuck to the bulb and were sizzling and crackling. Comrade Bojin went over to the light, raised the bottle, clinked the bulb lightly, and continued to sing:

> Joi mi-e imposibil să te întîlnesc,
> Că mănînc c-un unchi pe care-l moştenesc.
> Vineri nu se poate, nu,
> Că postesc şi eu, şi tu.
> Numai sîmbătă putem să ne dăm rendez-vous.

Şi dacă ne-o place, stăm chiar pînă-n zori de zi,
Că duminică putem dormi . . .
(It's impossible for me to meet you on Thursday, / Because
I'm dining with an uncle from whom I stand to inherit. / Friday
is out of the question, / Because we'll be fasting, both you and
I. / Only on Saturday can we make our rendezvous. / And if we
like it, we'll stay up till the break of day, / Because on Sunday
we can sleep in . . .)

He paused to hand the bottle to Brunul, and then changed the
tempo, raising his voice:

Vrei să ne-ntîlnim sîmbătă seară,
Într-o cîrciumioară, la şosea,
Unde cîntă un pian şi-o vioară
Şi-unde nu ne vede nimenea . . .
(You want us to meet on Saturday evening, / In a little tavern
on the chaussée, / Where a piano and a violin play / And where
nobody will see us . . .)

After singing the final strophe, he began to whistle once more,
or at least appeared to do so, since the sound that issued from
his puckered lips was not much different from that of exhaled
breath.

"Who is the song by?" asked Brunul, more as a way of
dampening his host's melancholy upsurge and restoring him to
a mood more appropriate to conversation.

Comrade Bojin froze for an instant, as if suddenly
remembering something which came from that part of his
mind still struggling for breath in the boozy well into which it
had sunk. He raised his finger to his lips.

"Shh!"

After which his mind probably sank to the bottom of the
well once more, bobbing to the surface long enough only to say:

"It's by Jean Moscopol. But he's banned now. The lunatic fled to . . ."

And here he broke off, waving his hands to convey that Jean Moscopol was now far away, in foreign parts.

"I've got an old record by him, from before. But he's banned now." And once again comrade Bojin raised his finger to his lips: "Shh!"

"From before, you say . . ."

There on the terrace, at the end of that evening, for the first time since he had known comrade Bojin, Brunul felt that he was in control of the conversation. It was a feeling that astonished him, but at the same time he knew that he must not let it go to waste; he had to make use of it. And so without further preliminaries, he asked the question to which he was propelled by the avalanche of thoughts released on the day he had spent with Eliza in Ciric.

"How do you know that my parents died in Italy in the war?"

Comrade Bojin froze once more; probably his mind had bobbed up from the depths of the well to gasp for air. The host then wrenched the bottle of wine from Brunul's hand.

"Can you tell me, please?" Brunul insisted, sensing that comrade Bojin had, for the moment, lost the control he otherwise exerted over himself.

"That's what they told me, man!" snapped comrade Bojin.

"Who told you?"

Comrade Bojin's eyebrows lifted. Some unknown person had suddenly burst in on his life story, somebody who seemed to know too much.

"Is there something not to your liking, eh?"

Although he had just taken a long swig from the bottle, comrade Bojin seemed to have recovered from his drunkenness all too suddenly and unexpectedly.

"You've got a home, a job. I've got a job too!" he said, raising his voice. His words carried past Brunul and scattered among the shadows of the park, which seemed to pause for an instant and listen to the conversation of the two men on the terrace. "There are people I've got to answer to. What do you want from me?" comrade Bojin all but yelled, pounding his chest with his hand. "Do you think I like spending my time with you and having to come out with all that stuff? I've got a job to do as well, you know!"

Brunul stood stock-still, leaning with his back against the iron rail that surrounded the terrace, bewildered by comrade Bojin's words and at the same time understanding them very well. Comrade Bojin was now grimacing, his face was contorted, he cut a pitiful figure, his lips were trembling, he was about to burst into tears, the tears of a drunkard, uncontrolled by a mind which, floundering in wine, was unable to haul to the surface the two distinct types of truth that it had long since created for itself.

Right then Mrs. Toriţa appeared in the doorway to the terrace, preceded by her words:

"What are you yelling about like madmen?"

Looking at her husband and seeing his contorted face, her eyes bulged.

"That's enough," she said, with the same determination as when she had sent them both out onto the terrace. Walking over to her husband, she grasped him by the arm. "That's enough. You have to go to bed now."

Brunul hesitated for a moment. Good breeding urged him to apologize and beat a hasty retreat to the front door. But the lump in his throat, which had formed when he stepped outside, caused him to thrust his hand in the back pocket of his trousers. He pulled out the crumpled subscription ticket, which he had almost forgotten about lately. He rushed after comrade Bojin and his wife and planted himself in front of them.

"Is this true?" he blurted, trembling. "Was I here in Jassy in 1950?"

Mrs. Torița cast her husband a reproachful look.

"I told you not to invite him," she muttered.

"They asked me to invite him!" comrade Bojin yelled.

He then snatched the crumpled ticket from Brunul and began tearing it to shreds.

"This is what I think of your ticket! You're killing me! I don't know what you want from me. You're killing me!"

Comrade Bojin's wife sat him down on the couch and then turned to Brunul, who was standing in a daze in the middle of the room.

"Please," she said. "You can talk to my husband about all this when he's in a fit state to do so. But now leave us."

Coming to his senses, Brunul nodded and allowed himself to be ushered to the front door. He apologized in the doorway. By way of an answer, comrade Bojin's wife gave a vague wave of her hand.

He walked down the dark lane. A few minutes later he turned off and crossed the park, heading for the main road, from where he would reach the Foundation and then, passing the building where Eliza lived, the road home. The night, the silence, and the almost complete absence of any other person on the street ought to have calmed his thoughts, given him an opportunity to put them in order. But the things that had happened that day overwhelmed him: the memory that invaded him and which he was certain came from the twenty years erased from his mind, since it was an Italian memory, and comrade Bojin's half and quarter explanations, behind which lurked countless other questions. They made him tremble, although the night was warm. They did not allow Brunul to cling to any meaning, no matter how small, to which he might then join the other meanings for which he had been searching for so long.

# Chapter 12

IN 1953, THERE was only one man you heard talking about the Communists in the past tense and the Peasant Party in the present tense, and if you didn't understand why, you might easily think he was insane. Sometimes you might have felt he was nostalgic, when, after heaving a deep sigh, he started explaining how, years ago, "in the days of the Communists," when he was still a man in his prime, he used to walk the ten kilometers from town to his village. But nowadays, weighed down by sixty years, old man Zacornea, as everybody called him, was content to make the journey by bus. He hadn't given up his job in town, which he seemed to have been doing forever; he was still a guard at the Galați Prison. And in that job could be found the explanation for his strange outlook on history. For old man Zacornea, "the days of the communists" were before the war, when the prisoners he guarded were communist agitators, strikers, and saboteurs. They had even included Gheorghe Apostol, whom old man Zacornea had guarded in person. The guard boasted about Apostol's present position as First Vice-Chairman of the Council of Ministers as if he himself had made some contribution to his political rise, even though Apostol, arrested for communist activities, had only been held at Galați in transit, before being transferred to Doftana. On the other hand, the post-war period was the "time of the Peasant Party" for old man Zacornea. He made no effort to separate prisoners by political category, and for him the political prisoners he guarded were all members of the Peasant Party, even if they had been members of the Liberal Party or even the Iron Guard. Among them Iuliu Maniu and

Ion Mihalache held the foremost place in his memories. Unlike Gheorghe Apostol, he had indeed come to know them well, since they had been imprisoned at Galați for a long time. He could not boast about knowing the two leaders of the National Peasants Party, however, since the times were not appropriate for that, and so he had learned to keep to himself whatever words he might have said about them.

Old man Zacornea had weathered the times, constructing his own history, but only because he had learned to be hard with the "scum" he guarded. As a prison guard, all the more so at Galați, which had become infamous among Romanian prisons, particularly since Captain Nicolae Maromet became governor, it was compulsory to be hard. It was compulsory not to make a single concession to any of the bandits incarcerated there. As a result, for all his years, old man Zacornea knew not to deviate from the governor's hard line. The prison management could cite him as an example of conscientiousness, and they often did so. Nobody was more capable of organizing and disciplining the prison's mass of criminals than that old-timer. Almost without fail, when one of the heads of the prison or even another guard saw Zacornea dealing with a group of prisoners, he could not but notice the harshness and determination with which the old man carried out his duties. The guard flung yells left and right and would not allow the slightest instance of slackness. "You bandit, I'll make mincemeat of you if you step out of line again!" the old man would bellow, and the prisoner in question, who had unwittingly trodden askew, would quickly fall back into line. "You fucking worm! You don't deserve to eat the food of the people if you don't meet your quota! You'll die of hunger, you dishrag, if you keep moving slowly like that!" the guard would roar, and the prisoner who had been trying to straighten his tired back, for example, would immediately bend over and get back to work. Old man Zacornea knew the vilest swearwords. Old man Zacornea flung insults with ease: bandit, dishrag, worm, and others. For the other guards he provided a fund of jibes to hurl at the prisoners: dirtbag, scum, toerag, asshole, louse. Old man Zacornea brandished his fist and, eyes bulging, made threats like no other. Old man Zacornea was a model guard, no doubt about it. For that reason, he was highly appreciated by the management; he was highly appreciated by his fellow guards.

Appreciated by the management and his fellow guards, he was genuinely loved by the prisoners. That was because while the curses, threats, and torrent of swearwords instilled fear as long as there was somebody else around to witness them, as soon as that somebody else went away, the guard's hate-contorted face abruptly relaxed, taking on the features of a genial old man. His eyebrows would lift apologetically, his lips would curve into a smile, and the mouth from which terrible yells had issued but a moment before would now whisper jocular remarks about what had just happened. The terrible fear that had gripped the prisoners would melt away just as suddenly. They would try to restrain their laughter, and here and there a prisoner would remark on the performance in a low voice: "Old man Zacornea, you were in top form today. I liked that bit about 'the food of the people!'" Or: "Old man Zacornea, you really outdid yourself this time: where do you come up with those curses?"

But that wasn't the only reason the prisoners loved him. Those from the Galați area in particular were fond of old man Zacornea because he was the only guard who brought them news from their families. Occasionally, when he got the chance, the old guard smuggled food parcels into jail for prisoners from the local area, which they shared with their less fortunate cellmates from farther-flung regions of the country. The smokers among them were grateful to their guard for the cigarettes he slipped them. To those who fell ill in the prison, which didn't have a physician, old man Zacornea brought sulphamide from the outside. Finally, all the prisoners had reason to be grateful to the old guard because at the very least he constantly provided them with the dose of freedom they craved: he read the newspapers and listened to the radio on their behalf, bringing them the news the next day, which otherwise would have reached them with great difficulty, if at all.

In the first months he spent inside the walls of Galați Prison, months during which, for fear of an accordion whose music might sound from some dark cell, he didn't strike up a friendship even with his cellmates, Bruno Matei grew close to the old guard. This was made easier by a habit for which old man Zacornea was well known to all the prisoners: sometimes, when they were taken outside to work in the vegetable patches or farther away, on the bank of the Danube, to cut rushes, the old man would sit down near the prisoners, in a spot from where he could keep an eye on them all, but far from the other guards, and he would mold faces and even figures from clay. The old man's hobby was viewed with indulgence even by the prison management, since his merits in every other respect were sufficient for them not to deny him this eccentricity, as they regarded it. They were indulgent all the more so given that Zacornea's eccentricity did not detract from his vigilance, with no major incident ever having been reported on his watch. The minor incidents had all been resolved without any bother.

Zacornea's clay figurines, which Bruno could not help but notice, were the subject of their first conversations, which had taken place when other eyes were not looking. One day, while picking tomatoes in the prison vegetable patch, Bruno had asked the guard whether he made the clay figurines for his grandchildren, and although uttered with a certain serenity the old man's answer had seemed to him burdened by other, hidden feelings.

"No, I make them just for myself. To pass the time. Because the Lord Above didn't give me sons or daughters, and so I don't have any grandchildren either."

Then, because the conversation was in danger of petering out, and Bruno did not want it to, above all since it was one of those occasions when prying eyes were not watching, he told the guard about the ceramic figurines of ancient Egypt, which were similar to old man Zacornea's, differing only in their joints and detachable parts. Because he knew about Egypt only from the Bible and didn't often have occasion to talk about that country at the ends of the Earth, the guard let himself be caught up in the conversation, while the tomatoes filled Bruno's basket one by one. Bruno told his story stooped, in a mutter, straightening up only when he had to show with his hands how ancient dolls, whether wooden or earthenware, took on not only shape but life in the rituals of the time. That was the first conversation.

The second conversation came perhaps two weeks later, when old man Zacornea approached Bruno as he was at work in the vegetable garden and, having scratched his head for a few moments, not quite knowing how to begin, asked him whether he could show him how to make one of those moving dolls he had talked about. The thing was, he had filled his house with mute figurines, by way of bibelots, and if his old woman could see that they were good as toys, she might not get annoyed when she was doing the cleaning and toss them in the garbage at the back of the shed. And then, deeming such an explanation insufficient, he laughed, shrugged, and said:

"I make gnomes, to tell the truth. Do you know what gnomes are?"

Bruno thought of the gnomes in fairy stories; no other gnome came to mind.

"My gnomes are made of fired clay, which I then paint. I earn some money from making them," old man Zacornea added, seemingly a little embarrassed. "But the truth is, nowadays, nobody really wants gnomes anymore. Here's what I thought, after talking to you: my old woman doesn't have a pension, because she didn't work in the previous times and she doesn't

now in her old age. And it won't be long before my years are up
and I get sent away to have a rest. A rest will be nice, but I won't
have a very big pension. Like I said, it's not going very well with
the gnomes. Every now and then someone will give me two
bottles of wine for a gnome to put in his cabbage patch to scare
away the rabbits, or maybe someone will put a few pennies in
my pocket for a gnome to put on his porch. But they're few and
far between. You say that I can make moving toys, like they did
in Egypt. And so I thought: if they could do it in ancient days,
why can't I do it now? And if it earns me a little bit on top of
my pension, then so much the better. That's why I decided to
ask you: would you like to teach me?"

Bruno agreed, with a broad smile, and without asking for
anything in return, but merely because he had liked what the
old man had said. Just then another guard appeared and old
man Zacornea underwent an abrupt transformation, yelling
at Bruno like all the devils in hell and threatening him with
a beating. But even so, Bruno had had time to tell old man
Zacornea that for a start, he would like him to find a piece of
young wood, because the most graceful and agile puppets were
not made of clay.

Galaţi Prison, which was in the north of the town, on Strada
Traian, two kilometers from the railway station, was surrounded
by two walls, each almost a meter thick and four meters high.
The outer wall, which ran for more than six hundred meters, was
punctuated, for those on the outside, with light bulbs spaced
fifteen meters apart. On the top of the wall there were search-
lights, pointed at the inside. Between the outer and the almost
identical inner wall ran a river of billowing barbed wire, rising
almost to the top of the two stone walls that encased it. But
Bruno Matei knew nothing of any of this when he arrived in
the prison, nor did he find out during his incarceration there.
What could be seen from the inside of the prison was too little

to enable you to form any overall image of where you were. As Bruno himself concluded during the first few days of his incarceration, without even having been taken out of his cell to work, he might just as well have been back on Arsenal Hill in Bucharest rather than in Galaţi, or on any other hill, or in any other valley, or in any other place in Romania. Perhaps only the Soviet military unit building in the northeast of the prison, where some prisoners were sometimes taken under guard to perform various menial tasks for which the Russians didn't have sufficient personnel, served as a reminder that the enemy was closer there, was more watchful than in the other prisons through which Bruno had passed. If indeed the enemy was the one he thought, the one who, without its recently deceased Leader, maintained, as the way things were going seemed to suggest, its indifference to the rumors among the prisoners that lately gave free rein to fantasies about American soldiers coming to rescue them from the jails.

Even if the location of the prison was unknown to Bruno, in the first few months he quickly became accustomed to the smaller world on the inside. The horseshoe-shaped cellblock had two stories. On each floor, as the newcomer was to discover, there were thirty narrow cells. Rarely were they occupied by a single prisoner; sometimes there were three or even four prisoners to a cell. Bruno was assigned to one of those cells. There were numerous cracks in the concrete, the largest of them extending from the ceiling down the wall. As old man Zacornea was to explain to Bruno a few months later, the cracks were a reminder of the major earthquake of November 1940, thirteen years previously. As Bruno was soon to find out, his suffocating first-floor cell was like an oven, whose minuscule barred window, close to the ceiling, provided him and his three cellmates with all too little air. The sticky heat was even more unbearable at night, because the four men only had two bunks between them, and having to sleep pressed up against a cellmate was more exhausting even than work. During the day, when they weren't taken out to work, they took turns lying sprawled on the two bunks, spreading their arms and legs on the straw mattress, but taking care not to touch the iron bedstead, which the few rays of sunlight that pierced through the barred aperture heated until they were scorching. When the skin of one of the men touched the scorching iron, the accumulated sweat sizzled, causing the others to flinch in expectation of their cellmate's muffled yell. In the torrid summer days, not even the cement floor of the cell held the slightest coolness. Everything around them was scorching, they themselves were scorching, and for Bruno, accustomed to the heat of the Peninsula, where the large open space of the dormitory had allowed the air to circulate, the torture to which his lungs were subjected was almost unbearable.

In such conditions, the constant work schedule was Bruno's salvation, especially during the summer months. Salvation arrived every time a guard opened the metal door, and came to an end in the evening, when return to the oven was inevitable. Unlike on the Peninsula, where labor easily became torment, offering you nothing but the guards' curses and sometimes punches, nothing but the harsh rock dust that always filled the air, here the prisoners were given jobs that varied depending on the agricultural needs of the season. The first few times Bruno was taken out to work it was to hoe the maize. Later, it was to pick tomatoes and peas. Later still, for the barley harvest, Bruno and a host of other prisoners, under armed guard, were taken to a seemingly endless plain. Bruno could sense the walls marked out by the barrels of the guns as clearly as he had on the Peninsula. But the work provided him with a certain satisfaction only on account of its diversity. As he was to discover after his initial joy, the work was not at all easier, and in a way it was more torturous, since agricultural labor forced you to stand bent, to shuffle your feet, to feel the hours weigh down on your back like stone. Whereas the peasant is allowed to free himself of that burden of time at intervals, casting it to the ground and standing straight to stretch his back, for the prisoner forced to become a peasant there in Galați a vertical posture was a privilege granted only to those whose physiological necessities brooked no delay. It was the only solution, to which many resorted, although if the truth be told, the scant water they were given and the heat in which they worked ought not to have placed very much pressure on their bladders.

This was the solution Bruno and Zacornea found, since the requests of the latter, having become a pupil in his old age, resulted in lessons in the construction and manipulation of a puppet that would not languish in the form of a painted gnome, but would be able to move, liberated from the rigidity of its joints. Here in the plain, supervising prisoners that might at any moment become dangerous, given that the specifics of the agricultural labor they were forced to do provided them with a possible weapon, namely the sickle, the guard no longer allowed himself to diminish his vigilance by working on his figurines, and so in the weeks that followed it became his priority to find the time to work on the wooden puppet in accordance with Bruno's instructions.

He worked at home. But the prisoner to whom he had grown close within so short a time, and in whom, listening to the stories he told in that low, determined voice of his, he had gained increasing confidence, told him about the puppet's centers of gravity as if it were something on which he should place greater importance even than the forms of the wood or the final beauty of the figurine. "Beauty doesn't matter," Bruno had told him in one of their discussions, "the marionette becomes beautiful through its movements, and its movements are well sustained only if the centers of gravity are perfectly positioned." Old man Zacornea had difficulty understanding such words, which were like those of the village teacher, whom he sometimes met at the tavern on evenings too fine to spend at home and with whom he took pleasure in conversing, although more often than not it was the teacher who talked, while the old creator of gnomes contented himself merely with listening.

He worked at home on the puppet, limb by limb, and then brought the carved pieces to the penitentiary, waiting nervously for Bruno to give his verdict. There were days when he didn't manage to remain alone with Bruno. Sometimes, after the prisoner weighed up the piece of carved wood, holding it in various positions of equipoise, not even he knew what to say: "Yes," Bruno would observe, "it looks well made, but until we see the whole, until it is plain how one piece combines with another, we can't be sure that it is perfect." And old man Zacornea, in whom the entire operation, the "project" as he had begun to call it in his talks with Bruno, had aroused a passion he could not understand, but which had come to absorb him more than any gnome he had ever made, would become despondent, since it was hard to bring all the pieces of the puppet into the prison to be weighed on Bruno's scales.

The moments in which the talks between them were able to take place arrived mainly in the beds of rushes on the bank of the Danube, where, apart from outings to the vegetable garden or the plain, the prisoners did the bulk of their labor. Because the rushes could be harvested almost all year round, even in winter if required, outings to the riverbank filled all the other days when the generally more pleasant work they did in the vegetable patches and fields was not required. It was there in the rushes that Bruno was most often able to check on the progress of old man Zacornea's puppet, squatting on the ground with his gray trousers around his ankles, mimicking gripes that prevented him from continuing his work. Old man Zacornea would stand next to him, guarding him with a scowling face, listening to all Bruno's indications, memorizing them to the letter, yelling at intervals: "Get a move on, you idler, I can't stand here all day waiting for you to have a shit!" or something similar, and then thanking him in a whisper, winking, and assuring him that he had remembered all his instructions, that he had made a precise mental note of where he had to shave wood off the puppet's arm, forearm, chest, or leg so that it would achieve the desired shape.

Summer was waning by the time the head of old man Zacornea's marionette, with its long, Pinocchio-like nose, was finally ready. It was shown to Bruno, who finally gave his assent for the limbs to be assembled. Bruno promised the guard that the next day, if he could make an excuse to the others, telling them he had a raging bellyache, and if the guard could bring the assembled marionette, joined together at the precise points Bruno had indicated, then he would attach the strings and even give Zacornea his first puppeteering lesson.

For old man Zacornea the prison guard this was the first challenge that genuinely caused him to fear. Up to that point, his fellow guards would have understood him. Even someone from the prison management would have understood him if he had caught him with pieces of wood that could be knocked together into a vaguely human form. They all knew it was his hobby, even if previously he had used only modeling clay, whereas now he had moved on to a different material. But if brought inside the prison, a proper marionette would be a different matter entirely, in the event that he were caught with it. As the poor old guard knew all too well, such a matter could take a course all of its own, including a most undesirable, even terrifying, course. This time, there was no way he could smuggle the puppet in pieces. It would be difficult for him to join them together there in the prison. Not only would he not have the necessary tools, but also he would not be able to find a completely secluded place where he could do the work, which was quite a noisy part of the "project."

The next day, when he walked through the prison gates, old man Zacornea had a long, brown, patchwork scarf wound around his waist, and his heart was jerking like a hen on the chopping block. To those who noticed with amazement, he hastened to explain that he had flints wrapped inside the scarf. He had heard somewhere that flints draw off every illness, completely absorbing it inside them. And when their curiosity was still not assuaged, he gave a silly explanation for that rheumatic backache of his, which had struck at the height of summer, alluding to the exertions he had had to make, despite being long out of practice, when his old lady was filled with an unexpected craving the night before. The treatment with spark stones—the term he used for flints—was the only true thing in the whole story: he had tried them when he suffered rheumatism in the winter, and sometimes they worked. Nevertheless, it was the other things he told them that prompted a flurry of talk. Fortunately, however, such talk, which it was impossible for the old guard to quell, by no means hindered the suggestion he wished to convey. Likewise, his groans were in keeping with his declared infirmity, although some of them were feigned, others less so, being caused by the wooden marionette digging into him underneath the scarf tied with string around his waist.

Having feinted questions he was hard put to answer, old man Zacornea was no longer able to endure the fear that coiled around his heart more tightly than the marionette around his waist, and so, regretting that he would waste another day, or perhaps a number of days, which could otherwise have been set aside for puppeteering lessons, he found an out-of-the-way place within the prison, a hole in the wall where he had previously stashed food parcels he had secretly received from prisoners' relatives. And so in the end it was pointless for Bruno to feign an upset stomach. And his day of labor dragged on more slowly than usual, because without the secret meeting arranged with the guard who had become his friend, only seldom was he able to rid himself of the burden of time, which weighed down on him in the beds of rushes, the same as in the fields and the vegetable patches. What was more, old man Zacornea didn't even come near him that day, since the fear that had accumulated within him since that morning made him avoid any communication whatever with Bruno. It was not until that evening, as they were coming back from the Danube, that the old guard whispered to him that the object was in a safe place inside the prison, but he needed a different time and place in order to carry on with the "project."

The time and place were hard to reconcile to on this occasion. The pointless lapse of days, without his being able to see the puppet he had constructed in his mind, with the exact same painstakingness as old man Zacornea had constructed it for real in a village ten kilometers from Galați, began to torment Bruno worse than the heat in "the oven," as he, like his cellmates, had begun to call the cell into which he was thrust after the hours of labor. And so it was that after more than a week of waiting in vain, he forced himself, as he had grown accustomed to doing all those years, to stifle his hopes this time too, even if his present hopes rested not on his being released in some miraculous way, but on handling a wooden puppet. As Bruno said to himself: he had begun to invest that act of handling with far more than it could possibly mean in reality.

On the night when the cell door opened and the guard uttered his name, he didn't think for one moment about the puppet. Quite the opposite. He got up mechanically and for a few moments he was enveloped by the thought, which arose as if from a nightmare, that Baba Samca and her ghosts had tracked him down there, and in those moments he braced himself for all the bad that he had wished to bury first on Arsenal Hill and then in Black Vale. Recognizing the man who had spoken his name in a harsh voice as Zacornea, his thudding heart grew somewhat calmer. But not even now did the "project" occur to him. Rather, he thought that ultimately, no matter how mild the guard might be, Zacornea would still not be able to shirk his duty. Watching old man Zacornea in silence and not daring to break that silence with a question, particularly since the guard seemed to be wrapped up in other thoughts, Bruno did not feel any surprise until he was thrust inside the washroom. The old guard bolted the door, his face suddenly brightened, and he said:

"You have no idea what I had to go through to get them to put me on night shift again. It's been a year since I last did this shift, as you've seen. They thought I was too old. I didn't complain, because I'm none too keen on sleepless nights. But things have a way of working out . . . I managed to swap shifts with one of the other guards. I'm a bit scared about all this, but at least something will come of it."

Then, he reached inside the scarf around his waist, which only then did Bruno notice was bulging, and from it he pulled the wooden creature on which both had hung their hopes, each in his own way.

But for old man Zacornea what followed was not really a night of initiation into the handling of marionettes. Although he had waited so long for this, the old guard, after watching Bruno demonstrate, like a teacher, the best places to attach the strings to the puppet's body, was content to lean his elbow on the radiator and watch. With a smile barely visible beneath his grizzled, bushy moustache, old man Zacornea was not fearful of the passing minutes, he did not hurry them along, even if from time to time a voice in his mind told him they could be caught at any moment. He drove away such twitching thoughts and freed his mind from the threat that might appear from outside the room. He refused to believe that there was anybody else apart from them in the entire prison right then. Apart from the three of them.

There really were three of them, once the strings were attached, were connected to a living world, and the puppet began to move, taking first one, then two, three, four steps in front of the guard. After bowing ceremoniously before him, like a knight of old in front of a king, he moved back a little way, one, two, three, four steps, and began to limber up. Once he had stretched his muscles and rid his neck of its stiffness, he tapped his foot on the floor and began to dance, taking short steps, long steps. His dance became livelier and livelier, wilder and wilder, more and more caught up in the whirl of music which, no doubt about it, the ears of the puppet could hear just as well as Bruno's. And then, because the magic now filled the peeling washroom, the music also reached the ears of the old guard: his chin began to move in time to the rhythm, to the first violin was added a dulcimer, a trumpet rang out, and the room began to dilate, the dim, grimy light bulb burst, releasing the light it had been holding prisoner, and the light, exhilarated with its freedom, suddenly took on myriad hues, before taking shelter in dozens, hundreds of other bulbs, which engulfed every last trace of darkness.

# Chapter 13

THE "TOWN OF Jassy on the Prut" is supposed to have been mentioned for the first time in a Russian chronicle dating from 1387. There is controversy as to this year, and some say that the first definite historical mention dates from 1408, when Alexander the Good issued a trading permit to some merchants from Lvov, in which a number of towns are listed, including Jassy. Somewhat later, around the year 1476, the Turks burned the city to the ground. This was the first fire to devastate the town, or at least the first to be recorded. The second recorded fire was in 1510, during a Tartar incursion into Moldavia. After pillaging and burning all there was to be pillaged and burned, the Tartars returned in 1513 to destroy what was left of the town. They returned in 1538 to burn down the buildings that had been erected on top of the ruins in the meantime. Perhaps to alleviate their boredom, the Turks and the Tartars seem to have taken turns burning down the town of Jassy. In 1574 it was the turn of the Tartars once more. In 1650, the Cossacks, led by the infamous Bogdan Hmelnitzki, visited Jassy and, inspired by their fellow invaders the Turks and the Tartars, they put the town to the torch, burning down the Princely Court and the Three Hierarchs Cathedral. As if the aforementioned hordes were not enough, in 1686 the Poles joined in, burning down the rebuilt Three Hierarchs Cathedral, the Golia Monastery, and various boyar residences. After that, the invaders either bored or tired of burning the town and so the citizens of Jassy had to set their own fires: in 1725 a major fire destroyed the center of the city, from Main Street to the Princely Court; ten years later, a lesser fire reduced the upper town to ashes; in 1752, the Princely Court and the buildings around it burned down yet again; in 1827, a devastating fire destroyed almost two-thirds of the city; and in 1844, the last fire worthy of historical mention laid waste to the northwest quarter of the city.

It was not only fires that destroyed the buildings of Jassy, however. From time to time, earthquakes also lent assistance. The most significant was the earthquake of May 31, 1739, just four years after the fire that destroyed the upper town, which flattened many buildings and destroyed most of the Golia Monastery. While fires and earthquakes forced people to build their town all over again, plagues, caused by filth and squalor, left buildings intact but placed the very existence of the town in jeopardy. And this more than once.

Arriving in Europe from the vast expanses of Asia in 1347, when black rats disembarked from a ship in the port of Messina, the Black Death reached Jassy only after a large part of its work had been done in the West. This was natural, since the backwardness of Moldavia compared with the West meant that not only fashions but also diseases arrived there only after a long delay. The Black Death reached Jassy in the year 1600, killing countless people and frightening the survivors so badly that in order to rid themselves of the curse they set about building as many churches and monasteries as possible. But even so, toward the end of the century, in 1675, the plague returned to Jassy, unsated, showing that little did it care about either the Orthodox Christian faith or the assiduous building of churches as protection. Since it was unable to rage unopposed in other regions, the plague settled down in Jassy, breaking out from time to time, as was the case in 1717, 1725, 1738, 1795, and even as late as 1829, when the last major epidemic was recorded. Once the plague was left behind, Jassy adapted to the times, finally catching up with the West when, in 1831, it joined the ranks of the European cities ravaged by a new disease: namely, cholera.

The man who narrated these episodes, in a detached sort of way, smiling when he thought a historical event warranted a little humor, sipped from his cup of linden tea. To Brunul's amazement, he recited the dates as if he were reading them from a book. The man was an archivist, a friend of comrade Bojin's, the same friend who, a few months previously, had chanced upon the subscription ticket with Brunul's signature.

"You see," said the archivist, pausing to drink the tea remaining in his cup before he arrived at his conclusion, "this was the Jassy that the Party took over. A city of diseases, squalor, fires, and other disasters . . ."

Brunul could not help but notice, however, that the history of the city that had been presented to him came to an end in the middle of the last century, long before the advent of the savior that was the Party. But he immediately dismissed this thought, firstly because he had no doubt that even if the account skipped a century, the deeper meaning remained the same; he was convinced that the man could tell him about countless subsequent disasters, which would fill the whole period up to the culminating catastrophe of the Second World War. And secondly because he wouldn't even have had the patience to listen to the rest of the city's story, since comrade Bojin had brought him there to find out about his own story.

They sat drinking linden tea in a large room lined with shelves full of files. Neither of the two found anything to say after the archivist concluded his historical survey of the city's disasters. It crossed Brunul's mind that the purpose of the exposition was to persuade him that he was sitting in front of a man perfectly informed; even if a bird collided with the building of the People's Council it would not elude him, and he would duly record it in the archives. But if this was the aim, then it was pointless; Brunul didn't need to be persuaded. Although the incident at the birthday party two weeks previously had raised questions in his mind as to how much truth there was in what comrade

Bojin said, Brunul did not doubt his good intentions for a single moment, and even less so did he doubt the good intentions of the Party, of which his friend was after all a representative. He suspected that he merely wished to protect him. He suspected that he was hiding from him some villainy that he himself had committed before his accident. He had no reason to suspect the archivist. Quite simply, he wished to discover the truth. He was prepared for it. And he had insistently asked comrade Bojin for the truth, especially since Eliza had advised him not to let himself be overcome by doubts, but to ask questions. The questions had commenced the day after the birthday party, when his friend had visited him at home. It was the first time he had arrived unannounced. Comrade Bojin had sat down rather awkwardly and attempted to convince Brunul that the drink had been to blame for everything that had happened the previous evening, that he talked nonsense when he was in his cups, this being the reason why he never, ever drank more than a bottle of wine, but only if he had the luck to be able to share it with somebody else.

This explanation had not been sufficient for Brunul, however. In the days that followed, taking advantage of the fact that comrade Bojin, probably out of a continued feeling of guilt, increased the frequency of his visits, Brunul asked him so many questions that his friend had finally capitulated. This capitulation also included the visit to the archivist, with the promise that Brunul would discover there everything that comrade Bojin and the Party knew about his past.

Now that he was with the archivist, Brunul felt the need for assistance from his friend. After Brunul had sat through the long preliminary talk on the history of the city, the silence in the room grated on his nerves; it filled him with anxiety. He did not dare to break the silence by asking a question, however. Having finished his tea and examining the bottom of his cup as if he found something fascinating there, the archivist finally spoke.

"In 1858, we were nevertheless in step with the rest of the world in one positive respect: gas-lamp street lighting was introduced."

Whereupon he smiled and raised his hands defensively to show that he was joking and did not intend to continue his history of Jassy.

"Well then, comrade, I have been informed about what you wish to find out. And I am of course prepared. I am always prepared."

Now that the discussion had abruptly turned in the direction of what he wished to discover, Brunul felt excitement, but also a certain degree of trepidation. The archivist, who when he had served the tea had come across as jovial, playful even, larding with humor the catastrophes that had befallen the city throughout its history, now adopted an official manner. This did not bode well, thought Brunul. His past must be to blame. He told himself yet again, by way of encouragement, that he was prepared to accept anything; any sin he might have committed in the past would be cleansed in the present and future. But he had to find out, he had to know what he had done wrong, in order to have a starting point, in order to be able to redeem himself in the eyes of the Party, the country, the people. In the eyes of comrade Bojin, even, although he still harbored a slight grudge against him for having concealed the past he was now about to discover.

The archivist opened the file that had been lying on his desk all the while. From it he took a loose leaf; this time, he needed to read from the page what he was going to say. He took a deep breath and drawled:

"Registration form . . ."

He gazed over the top of the sheet of paper at Brunul, who sat frozen, and nodded before continuing.

"Let's see. Name, forename—these you know. 'Born 1921, May 29, in village Buch.'" The archivist looked up at Brunul once more. "That's what it says: 'village Buch.' Village is typewritten on all the registration forms, even if the place is the country's capital, Bucharest. 'Son of George and—'" here the archivist paused, trying to decipher the name. "I can't tell what it is. Is that Chiara?"

"Chiara, yes. We called her Clara."

The archivist raised his finger and waggled it to show he understood.

"Chiara, Clara. That's right. You remember everything up until your departure for Italy . . ."

"Not quite everything," said Brunul with a shrug. "As much as any normal person can remember about his childhood and early youth."

"That's right, as much as any normal person," agreed the archivist. He then turned his gaze to the form once more. "Let's see what comes next. Here's something you didn't know: 'Domiciled in . . .'"

He made a dramatic pause, looking up at Brunul, whose lips were parted, his eyes bulging. Having put down his cup a few moments before, Brunul had raised his hands to his chest, which posture caused the archivist to smile.

"I won't hold you in suspense any longer. I shall read the rest without interruption. 'Domiciled in Jassy, No. 7 Strada Făinii, Jassy region . . .' I'm afraid you're out of luck here," said the archivist, breaking his promise not to make any further interruption. "At the request of comrade Bojin, I went to the address, but the building at No. 7 Strada Făinii has been demolished. There, you see? The city is a living creature; things change. A building is here today, gone tomorrow. Anyway, now do you understand why I began with a history of the city of Jassy? Because you are a citizen of Jassy. Not just now, but even before the . . ." He raised his hand to his head to suggest the accident. "But to continue," he said, seeing that Brunul made no reaction. "'Occupation at date of arrest: no occupation. In the past: no occupation. Property at date of arrest: no property. In the past: no property. Spouse's occupation: dash. Spouse's property: dash.' What else can I say if you never got married? 'Parents' present occupations: deceased. Parents' past occupations: industrialists.'" Here the archivist looked up from the form. "It says 'Italy' in brackets. There are other dashes, since your parents' property and suchlike are unknown. I'll skip marital status, since I've already mentioned that. 'Distinguishing features: height: 174 cm, forehead: broad, nose: medium, mouth: medium, chin: oval, skin: dark, eyes: blue, hair: brown, eyebrows: arched, beard: none, mustache: none, ears: medium, no distinguishing marks.' I'm telling you all this just so you can get an idea of what you looked like when you were arrested. But from what I can see, you haven't changed much," he said, looking Brunul up and down. "What else? Ah, yes, here comes a bit that will definitely interest you. 'Previous convictions: none.' But . . . But!" The archivist here smacked his lips and then heaved a sigh. Expecting a reaction from Brunul, he repeated the sigh. Not receiving any reaction, he went on, rather disappointed. "But! 'Registered on November 6, 1954 by—' the name of the legal organ isn't very legible, as you'll see for yourself '—arrest warrant issued for—' pay careful attention here '—for illegally crossing the border.'" The archivist put down the sheet of paper and gazed at Brunul fixedly. "That's what you did. Here, see for yourself." He proffered Brunul the sheet of paper. "It was hard for me to find it. But who else but I could have found it?" There was a hint of pride in what he said.

Brunul didn't take the piece of paper. He was trying to swallow the lump in his throat. He took a deep breath and, turning his head to comrade Bojin, looked him in the eye. Comrade Bojin immediately lowered his head and flexed the fingers of his right hand, as if their numbness were the most important thing to be dealt with right then; he sat there studying his fingers closely as he bent and unbent them. Only when this flexing of the fingers lost its justification, since no numbness of the hand could possibly last so long, did comrade Bojin raise his head to look at Brunul, and with his left hand he gave him a light, friendly pat on the back. But having done so he compressed his lips in scorn. It would have been hard for him to say whence arose the feelings that caused his lips to contract like that. Perhaps one thing alone could explain his reaction: the merry face of the archivist, beneath whose mustache could be seen a satisfied grin. But when the archivist gave him a wink, comrade Bojin mustered all the powers he had honed while practicing his balancing act between the two truths in which he still believed and, forcing his lips to contract into an answering smile, he closed and opened his right eye, aware for the first time in his life that such a gesture, one ultimately so common and simple, could become extremely difficult when your eyelids were clamped in the vice of obdurate thoughts.

The archivist had told him the building had been demolished, and so there was no point in his going there. No. 7 Strada Făinii. It was not far from the building where Eliza lived. They climbed the Gully, passed the Mihail Sadoveanu Lyceum, heading for Union Square. It was August 23: "Rumania's liberation from beneath the fascist yoke, the Rumanian people's most important national celebration," as numerous red placards, large and small, proclaimed. Since they had gone out for a walk anyway, they were curious to see how the square had been bedizened for the parades to be held later that day.

The stands were festooned with garlands of flowers, countless red flags, countless Romanian tricolors. The air of festivity excited Brunul, almost making him forget why he had left the house that Sunday. A number of huge portraits dominated the main viewing stand: the faces of the great teachers of the world proletariat, Marx, Engels, and Lenin. Above them towered the emblem of the People's Republic, with the prominent caption:

"1944–1959." Complementing the faces of the great teachers, but smaller in size, the portraits of comrades Gheorghe Gheorghiu-Dej and Nikita Sergeyevich Khrushchev were displayed above the other viewing stands. Between them was a sign, more beautiful than any that Brunul had painted for the Bahlui embankment building site, inscribed simply: "Long live Rumanian-Soviet friendship!" And lest there be the slightest shadow of a doubt as to that beautiful friendship, the slogan was repeated in Russian underneath: "Да здравствует румыно-советская дружба!" The broader history, in portraits, images, and placards, had made overwhelming preparations to receive the hundreds and thousands of narrower histories that were to fill the square throughout that day. So impressive were the square's decorations that Brunul would probably have lingered there longer, until it filled with people, until the speeches began, until the slogans were chanted, had not Eliza tugged him by the sleeve, interrupting his reverie, dissipating it, reminding him of the real reason for their walk.

Finally, they left the festive square and entered the boulevard. From there they had less than a hundred meters to walk, uphill. Finally, they came to Strada Făinii. It was more a narrow lane than a street, with tall-roofed houses huddled together on both sides. Nothing. Brunul felt absolutely nothing as he walked down that street. Nothing to suggest that he had ever been there before. He felt a vague excitement, vaguer than what he had felt in the square below. But even that vague excitement came from what the archivist had told him, rather than from inside him or from the buildings around him.

He was disappointed. He told Eliza so. No, it was worse than disappointment: in that moment, he hated his mind, his illness. He must have walked down that street thousands of times; the document he was holding could not lie. It was there in black and white: No. 7 Strada Făinii. But the illness caused by his accident blotted out all memory. Nothing.

There was almost nothing at number seven. An empty space. The archivist had been right. The building had been demolished. But nothing else had been built in its place. They came to a stop, gazing wordlessly at the heap of rubble at the back of the lot. Weeds had overrun the rubble, enhancing the feeling of dereliction, of nothingness, of time that erodes all memory. Brunul looked up in the air, as if tracing the roof beneath which he had lived as a lodger up until 1954, as comrade Bojin had told him after they left the archivist's office. He must have been a lodger, because if he had been the owner of the house, the Party would have returned it to him; they wouldn't have moved him into a one-room apartment in a different part of the city. Nevertheless, there were questions that remained unanswered. Why had he come to Jassy from Italy, if he had no memory of the city up until 1937? When had he come? How had he paid the rent on that house, or a room in that house, which had stood on that now vacant lot? And then there was the national subscription ticket, of which the archivist had also made a big thing. Comrade Bojin had told him that he must have been working to be able to pay the twenty-lei subscription. How then had he paid it if the registration form said he had no occupation? What was more, according to the document, he hadn't had any occupation even in the more distant past . . . And then there was his passion for puppets, which he was absolutely convinced must have come from the mists of his missing two decades. And then there was Vasilache. And then the fragment of text written in his own hand, in which could be found his thoughts about marionettes. And then, above all else, there was that flash of memory that had come to him at comrade Bojin's birthday party, only to sink back into the mist a moment later. In Italy he had probably learned about marionettes; the faces that had risen in his mind could not have been accidental; the words about the movement of puppets, uttered in Italian by that voice so profound, must have been important, otherwise they would not have come back to his mind. Was he to believe that he traveled from Italy to Jassy to live there without an occupation?

Comrade Bojin had tried to explain it to him: he had probably earned money in a less than honorable fashion, giving performances with Vasilache at country fairs and markets, where folk would have tossed coppers in his hat. His friend told him that he had read in the papers about beggars in the capitalist countries; people sang, danced, pulled faces, anything for a few coins. It had been the same in Romania in the old days. After the coming of the people's regime, beggary had gradually been eradicated; there was a job for everybody who wanted to work, but the old habits could not be changed in the blink of an eye. That is probably what Brunul had done: he had given street performances with his puppet and that was how he made his living. As for the subscription, Bojin supposed that Brunul must have had a job, since public subscriptions were usually collected in the workplace, although not necessarily, since the newspapers also wrote about them and anybody could contribute. Maybe Brunul had felt guilty about the money he had been making in a less than honest way and that was what impelled him to make a contribution. Who could now know? It was best not to think about it, said comrade Bojin, it was best that he did not remember that period, which as was now apparent had been less than savory. What good did it do to remember anyway? There was nothing he could change now. All he could do now would be to whine like Dona Siminică in one of his dirges . . .

Brunul had accepted comrade Bojin's explanations for want of any others. But his questions gave him no rest and continued to demand completely different answers, all the more so given that for the first time since he left prison that terrible guilt of his no longer overwhelmed him to the point of tears. Yes, he had done wrong; he had deserved to go to prison. But his wrongdoing had been understandable; he had not sinned with all his soul against the Party, which now showed itself to be so benevolent to him; he had not sinned against the people. After his meeting with the archivist, he was sure that the reason he had tried to cross the border illegally in that period lost in the mist had been ultimately decent: he had wished to visit his parents' grave. That must have been the reason. They had died in the war, of that there could be no doubt, especially since an official document claimed as much. That must have been his intention in 1954: to cross the border and return to Italy, only for as long as it took to lay some flowers on a grave. Why had he not tried to obtain a permit to cross the border? Perhaps he had indeed tried, according to comrade Bojin. Perhaps he had tried, but had not received permission. Why should he go back, if his parents were dead anyway? Why should he risk indoctrination at the hands of the capitalist elements who hated the fact that Romania had set out on a new road? Why should he risk not being allowed to return to Romania? No, the State provided people with everything they desired, everything they had ever dreamed of, but in return it asked just one thing: loyalty. The State could not risk people going to one of the countries that didn't share its values and which in fact hated those values. His action had been understandable, ultimately; such was Brunul's opinion too. Obviously, he felt sorry that he had not understood things in the same way when, in 1954, he had tried to cross the frontier near Timișoara, as was stated on the back of the document the archivist had given him, without further details. He was sorry that he had not thought in the same way back then, but all in all he was satisfied that his indubitable guilt had not gone further than that. Not one word or letter of the registration form said that he was ungrateful to the Party or his country. Quite simply it had been a mistake. For which he had paid the price. And now he could begin a new life, a life without further mistakes.

"Maybe we should ask the neighbors," said Eliza, who had not let go of his arm since they began their walk. "It's only been five years since then. There must be somebody who remembers you."

Brunul's face lit up. He was amazed that he had not thought of it himself. They went to the house next door. The old woman in a headscarf could make nothing of their questions. Finally a younger man came downstairs. On hearing what it was all about, he frowned. Without a word, he took the old woman, who was probably his mother, by the shoulders and moved her inside. He then shut the door, visibly put out.

Brunul nodded, already discouraged. But Eliza wouldn't give up. They crossed to the other side of the vacant lot where number seven had once stood. At the house on the other side, which had clearly been built or renovated quite recently, nobody came to the door. Eliza led Brunul to the next house, where a man in his fifties answered the door. After hearing their questions he shrugged and, without so much as a smile of apology, told them that he had moved there four years ago and so he had nothing to say to them. The same as the first man, he closed the door coldly, emphatically.

They went back to the other side, passed the old woman's house, and knocked at the next door. Eliza promised Brunul that this would be their last attempt. They knocked for a long while and finally a child of about ten came to the door. Smiling at him, they asked him how long he had lived there. Since before he was born, said the child, and then ran inside to call somebody else, leaving the door half open. Finally, an old woman appeared. Unlike the first old woman, she was elegantly dressed, in a hat and a black two-piece with a buttonhole; she looked as if she were just about to go out. She didn't have time to talk, she was in a hurry, she had to get her grandson dressed. She asked them to excuse her and to ask some other neighbor for the information they wanted. Eliza persevered, begging her to answer a single question. Brunul was then amazed when she asked the elegant old lady the same question as she had put to the child.

"Can you tell me how long you've lived here?"

"Three years."

The woman then closed the front door, making a final apology as she did so.

He washed Vasilache's clothes, cleaned his face, slowly, with care. The old clothes became white once more, even if some traces of dirt could not be completely removed, even if the shirt and trousers were fraying in places. He wiped him with a towel, rubbing his face, the rather faded black mask, the ringlets that poked from beneath the long, pointy hat. Returning to his room, for half an hour he darned all the holes in Vasilache's costume. Satisfied at last, he placed him on his knees and caressed the still damp clothes, as if he were trying to dry them with the warmth of his hands. He was indebted to the marionette. He was fully aware of how abnormal it was to feel indebted to a lifeless puppet, to a few carved bits of wood tacked together to look like a human. But he felt gratitude for everything that Vasilache had done for him in prison and after his release. He now knew very well that he had created for himself that friendship with a puppet: he had given it life because something within him impelled him to do so, even if back then, before he put Vasilache away in a cupboard, his mind sometimes refused to play along, the same as it did now that he had taken him out to restore him to his former animation. He was ill, but he was not mad; he had never been mad. But even so, he had talked to the marionette so many times, he had gone for walks with him so many times, and now he wished to resume their former relationship, which had been cast aside for a time, dumped among the clothes in the darkness of a cupboard.

Now what he wanted to do most of all was to cry. In the past he had cried with Vasilache in moments of deep sadness, in moments when it was as if the winds of the gloomy days filled a balloon within him to the point of bursting, creating an unbearable pressure that burst the dams of his eyelids and sent tears streaming down his face. He wept, and that lump of wood was there for him, understood him, accepted the tears and the heartrending sobs that were hardly acceptable in a man of almost forty.

And that was why he took him out of the cupboard. He needed a witness to his suffering. Eliza . . . It had been unexpected. Their quarrel had been final. It had come at the end of the day when they had walked to No. 7 Strada Făinii, a day that had given no sign of what was to come.

"No, it wasn't final. It was just a quarrel. But it was one that . . . I mean . . ."

Something had snapped. Vasilache no longer listened to him. Or else he no longer knew how to tell him what he had to say. Brunul laid Vasilache on the bed. He buried his face in his hands, trying to erase all the things that now came rushing into his mind, into his eyes, and above all Eliza's angry face, her yelling. The words she had shouted at him now filled his ears, more than an hour after they parted: "All this time I thought you were normal. Do you really not get it? All right, you've lost your damned memory; it's gone. But what about your mind? Where is your mind? It's not even madness; it's stupidity. I just don't get it: can't you see that nothing adds up? Can you really not think for yourself?"

He had tried. That old woman, dressed up like a lady, might have made a mistake. Or, more likely, the child had made a mistake. Three years, rather than ten . . . And even if the child hadn't made a mistake, wasn't it possible that both of them were telling the truth? The child had lived there with his parents ever since he was born. The lady must be his grandmother. What if she had moved in with them three years ago? Such a supposition was more than satisfactory. Not even now could he understand why Eliza had lost her temper when he tried to explain it to her. Not even now could he understand why she was so stubbornly silent on their way back, during which she had no longer held him by the arm. And above all he could not understand how she could have said all those things as they approached the building where she lived.

Somebody was lying to him, as Eliza had prefaced her remarks. Somebody wanted to hide the truth from him at all costs. Somebody had invented a past for him in Jassy. Somebody had filled his mind with nonsense. Somebody wanted him to believe that his parents were dead and that he was completely alone in the world (this statement had upset Brunul more than anything else). But what if it were not like that at all? What if, and here Eliza had stopped walking and looked at him fixedly, what if she told him that his mother was alive in Italy, that she continued to look after the family business, that she would help him if he fled there, that she would help him find a job, even help him to recover his memory? What if she told him that and it were true?

He did not think of Dr. Ustinenko and Varvara at the time. Eliza's words had rained down on him like a hail of stones. He had trembled, flinched in pain. Why all those insinuations aimed at comrade Bojin, the man who had helped him more than he could ever have imagined was possible? Why that insane fantasy about his mother being alive and in Italy? How could Eliza know that? And above all, after everything he had told her about his past, as much as he had been able to learn from the archivist, why that indifference, that downright malice on her part when it came to using the verb "to flee"? The very thought of it seemed to him a betrayal. To flee? Him? Why? What for? For the sake of Eliza's crackpot notions? For the sake of suppositions that could be easily explained? Perhaps not easily, but ultimately they could be explained. Certainly, they could be explained . . .

He didn't think of Dr. Ustinenko or of Varvara. He merely froze, staring wide-eyed at the woman he had loved for so long, unable to believe what he was hearing. He couldn't understand it. And because he could not understand, he was lost for words.

He could only watch as she walked away, having hurled all those insults at him and, having gotten no reaction from him, concluding: "Can you really not think for yourself?" He had gone after her too late, far too late to catch up with her. He had seen her enter her building without looking back at him. It was only when he came to a stop in front of the entrance to the building, hesitating as to whether he should follow her upstairs or not, it was only then that he had had time to realize that it all ended there, that their quarrel had been final, otherwise Eliza would not have left him in the middle of the road, she would not have entered without even looking back at him. That thought put an oppressive end to his hesitation. He continued on his way, not really knowing what to think about what had happened, not knowing exactly what he felt about Eliza.

He didn't think of Dr. Ustinenko and Varvara until he got back home. But now, with his head buried in his hands, he sensed that not even Vasilache accepted his tears and his sobs. His thoughts collected themselves and the face of the woman he loved was superimposed upon that of the woman Dr. Ustinenko loved. The mystery of his past had been unraveled to some extent. He had not been a doctor, he had not even had an occupation, and so he did not dare liken himself to the hero of the film that had made such an impression on him. However, Eliza did resemble Varvara all too much. Albeit not as clearly as the woman in the film, she demanded that he feel what he had felt once before, in the years now enveloped in mist, and thereby she wronged those who were now so good to him. The same as Varvara had demanded of Dr. Ustinenko, she demanded that he be himself, or rather that he be the same man as he had been in the past, the man she had despised for so long on account of all he had done. He could not. There was no possible way he could.

Just as he began to accept the idea of self-sacrifice, he was interrupted by a knock on the door. No, he would not go to Eliza, he told himself. Maybe they would meet again, the same as the characters in the film had met again, and then she would realize what a mistake she had made. But he would not go to her. Never. He kept repeating that "never" to himself and in the end it would have burst that balloon in his chest in which had collected the winds of gloomy days, it would have rid him of his tears and sobs, had there not been another, more urgent knock on the door.

Barely able to drag his feet, he went to the door. When he opened it, Eliza rushed inside, leaving him no time even to display surprise. She cupped his cheeks in her hands and gazed at him with wide, frightened eyes.

"Have you told anybody anything?"

He shook his head mechanically. Her sigh of relief was audible.

"Let's talk," she said, dragging him down the hall into his room, without taking her shoes or her flimsy summer jacket off.

They both sat down on the bed. Brunul picked up Vasilache and put him on the table, leaning him against the large red vase that had never held a single flower, the vase that had been there when he moved. Only now did Eliza take her jacket off, laying it on the bed beside her. She took a deep breath and looked down at her shoes, somehow bitterly. She shook her head.

Then she looked up at Brunul and began to talk.

# Chapter 14

OCTOBER. NOVEMBER. DECEMBER. January. February. The rush-matting months. They passed more torturously but also more senselessly than ever. And after the stupefying heat of summer, with the coming of the cold season, they brought Bruno into far too close contact with Captain Maromet and his smug jokes that gave both himself and the other guards no end of amusement, but at which the prisoners sometimes refrained from laughing, lest they get a beating (who gave them the right to laugh?), or at which they sometimes laughed, lest they get a beating (what, didn't they like the captain's sense of humor?). Then there was Brunul's quota, which the "technical bureau" had tripled since the captain became prison commandant. The reason for this tripling was simple: there were twenty-four hours in a day, not eight, as Maromet's predecessors seemed to have believed, completely erroneously. Twenty-four divided by eight equaled three, and therefore the quantity of rush mats had to be tripled. Sleep? What would all those dogs do after they croaked if not sleep? What did they need to sleep now for? There was a simple solution: let them croak sooner rather than later, since eternal slumber was the most restful sleep of all, as the captain quipped. He would then chortle, the guards would chortle, and the prisoners would chortle and get a beating for it, or else they would not chortle and get a beating for it.

But commandant Maromet could also be reasonable. Sometimes, he recognized that sleep was a nuisance that got in the way of the prisoners' eagerness to work longer than twelve or even fifteen hours on that frosty cement. At such moments he would feel a wave of goodness washing over his soul as powerfully as the blizzard that swept the yard set aside for the weaving of rush mats, and then he would send the prisoners to their cells to sleep. Obviously, he could not allow himself to show any weakness toward the class enemies, and so if the quota was not achieved, then punishment was a matter of course. In order to conceal his goodness and emphasize his authority, he would reduce the sleepy prisoners' rations the next day, and their food was given to the pigs on the prison farm, which were more deserving, since once slaughtered they would be of use to society. And whenever the prisoners' rations were thrown to the pigs, Nicolae Maromet never omitted to give his favorite educational speech, comparing what he saw as the two types of death: the altruistic death of the pigs, which was for the good of the people, and the selfish death of those dogs the prisoners, which was for the sake of their own eternal slumber.

Numerous selfish prisoners died for the sake of their own eternal slumber in the year after Captain Maromet took over the running of Galaţi Prison. Many of them died weaving rush mats in the "technical bureau," to which Bruno Matei had been assigned in the spring of fifty-four. What made Bruno curse the hours, days, and months he spent there was not the hunger, which, on the days when the pigs ate their fill, made the dry, whitish skin beneath his ribs tremble in time with his stomach; it was not the night frost roughened by driving snow, which sometimes numbed his hands so badly that he could no longer tell his fingers apart from the rushes; it was not the beatings. Uranus and the Peninsula had shattered his naivety, they had hardened him, they had created for him a system whereby to relate to the conditions and the people in prison, thanks to which he was able, even in the most terrible moments, to raise a shield behind which he could hide himself and his private thoughts. He beguiled his hunger by chewing slivers of reed for hours on end, which his mind imbued with different tastes; more often than not he shut off the cold by means of the thoughts that burrowed into his memories of the stupefying heat of summer, whereby he managed to content himself with the present winter conditions; for the most part he avoided the beatings, thanks to experience, which enabled him to react neither too much nor too little, but rather just enough so as not to be singled out. Of course, there were also collective punishment beatings. Apart from that, on occasion none other than Nicolae Maromet himself had kicked him in the teeth once, when he deemed Bruno to have been working too slowly; on occasion he had been punched in the back of the neck, slapped in the face. But no matter how painful all these might have seemed when considered from the outside, they were bearable once they became part of the daily routine.

What really tortured Bruno was old man Zacornea's marionette. The thought of it. The lack of it. After that night in the bathroom, when they had been secretly transported outside the prison walls, Bruno had not managed to preserve the reflexes he had rediscovered during that irrepeatable event. Rather, his reflexes, joined with those of the marionette, had instantly been transformed into desires, into yearnings, as he was to discover, firstly with a kind of joy, but then with increasing resentment as time wore on. He had sworn to himself so many times that he would reject any illusion, but again he had fallen prey to one: the illusion that the nocturnal performances might continue, even if for an audience whose only member was old man Zacornea.

Old man Zacornea was spared the rush mats, however. The conditions were too harsh for an elderly warden, and so over winter the prison management had assigned him to housekeeping, where he guarded the luckier prisoners, who, taking advantage of his preoccupation with other things, must have benefited from bigger rations, including the food diverted from the "technical bureau" to the piggeries; from greater warmth, albeit provided by the fresh garbage that warmed the air; and from fewer beatings. During all those months, Bruno merely glimpsed the old guard in passing a few times. With one exception, on the first day of 1954, their encounters were marked by exchanged glances only, from which Bruno was able to draw very little meaning. It was not until New Year's Day that they were able to steal a few moments in which to speak, since the commandant was absent, along with a number of the more assiduous guards, who had been allowed to spend the holidays with their families. From the brief conversation that took place between them, Bruno understood that the illusion was worth maintaining, since the doll had not yet left the prison. Old man Zacornea had hidden it in the hope that favorable moments would return and that their "project" might even reach the stage at which the old maker of figurines would learn to pull the strings in his own right and awaken the marionette to life. But for that, whispered the old man before walking away, spring was needed.

For old man Zacornea, the need for spring did not conceal any deeper meaning, it did not hint at some code, it did not hold forth any promise. In his need for spring, the old guard saw only the end of the rush-matting months, in which there were no fixed hours of day or night; in it he saw Bruno's return to the predictable labors of garden and field, where plans could be remade, where "projects" such as theirs could be woven, outside the completely unpredictable projects that arose from the prison commandant's whims.

But for Bruno the need for spring coiled around his heart like tangled strings around the wooden body of a marionette, hampering his movements and augmenting his agony. There ensued the hardest months of all the years he had spent as a prisoner. And when labor on the rush mats finally came to an end, when Captain Nicolae Maromet gave the order to disband the "technical bureau" team, every muscle of Bruno's body felt that spring had arrived, although the icicles had yet to melt;

although not one speck of green relieved the general grayness; and although his warm breath still created an icy tracery on the wall of his cell.

Some pulled weeds, while others, behind them, dug. The heaped, loosened earth exhaled, before being hoed by the third line of prisoners to form a seedbed that was like a long, squashed snake. The hoes carefully tamped the edges of the seedbed so that nothing would spoil the clean parallel lines. Such spring-time work was light, particularly for those who had survived a winter's labor in the "technical bureau." On their faces, even if they were frowning in concentration, you would, on closer in-spection, nonetheless have discovered the same expression, as if the rays of the sun lit each face at exactly the same angle and in exactly the same place: a reaction of happy amazement, mingled with the fear that the gift they had received might be taken back at any time. That amazement mingled with fear increased productivity far more than all the commandant's yells, beatings, and coarse jokes had ever been able to.

Not even Captain Nicolae Maromet had any reason to be dissatisfied that day in the vegetable garden. After an incident the same morning, when a luckless wretch had been sent off to solitary confinement, Maromet had strolled among the workers with his hands behind his back for about half an hour, taking a close interest at first, then feigning interest, and finally stifling his yawns and returning to his office, leaving it up to the guards to make sure that work continued at the same brisk pace.

The incident of that morning had not been unusual, but even now it still oppressed the other prisoners. One of them, a recent arrival, had not only responded to one of the captain's wonted jokes by joining in the general laughter to which the more experienced prisoners had given voice, sensing the prison commandant was in a good mood, but also he had reckoned that such a good joke was worthy of comment: "Very good gag, comrade director!"

For three seconds time stood still for the other prisoners, frozen in attitudes of labor, but not for Nicolae Maromet. In that interval of three seconds, Maromet strode over to the new arrival, who after uttering his words of congratulation had stooped back down to work. Within another fraction of a second Maromet's booted foot had bloodied the wretch's mouth.

"What did you say, dog? Do I look like I'm your comrade, you fucker?"

The following seconds were punctuated by the croaks of the man writhing on the ground. Each kick of the captain's boot in his head, ribs, stomach boomed like a gong, but it didn't occur to anybody to count them or even to look in that direction. The others simply got on with their work, as if nothing were happening. After the prison commandant had cooled down, he curtly ordered the guards to drag the new arrival away to serve three days in solitary confinement.

Nothing unusual had happened, indeed. It was merely the first day of work in the vegetable garden, following a wait that had extended long after the advent of spring, which Bruno had sensed after the disbanding of the rush-mat teams. The first day of work in the garden was without any unusual incident. But even if the first half of the day was utterly routine, before nightfall, the broader history was to transform it into one of the few days of his time in prison that Bruno would remember for the rest of his life, which was so much a part of the narrower, personal history. However, Bruno no longer bothered to differentiate between the two; the relationship of his own narrower history to the broader history had begun to weary him, to engender confusion and bewilderment, and so he had given up trying to understand it.

After the noon meals, taking advantage of the absence of the captain, who was resting rather than endure the boredom of such a day, Bruno, clutching his belly in pain, asked old man Zacornea, with whom he had been exchanging meaningful glances since that morning, to give him permission to go aside. For all his joy at finding himself once again in this situation, Bruno would still not have been able to hug the old guard, who, so it seemed to him, was more stooped than ever. He squatted with his trousers around his ankles, as he had done so many other times, assailing the guard with questions. Yes, the marionette was still in a safe place, no worry on that score. No, old man Zacornea had been unable to get himself assigned to another night shift, although not for want of trying. But he had talked to his old woman and he was thinking about applying to work normal shifts again, at least during the good weather, when his bones didn't ache the way they did in winter; this was what he would tell the management when he requested to be returned to regular duties. To Bruno's feeling of guilt and unease at the old guard's having to make such a sacrifice, old man Zacornea gave a nonchalant wave of the hand; he grinned and explained: "Do you think the night shift wears me out more than my old woman does?"

Then, immediately after Bruno pulled up his trousers, getting ready to go back to work, the old man stopped him, as if abruptly having remembered something.

"Listen, didn't you say that in the beginning they'd interrogated you because you had connections with that former minister?"

Bruno nodded, but nonetheless reminded him in a few brief words that he had never met Lucrețiu Pătrăşcanu personally, and so in the end they had convicted him of something else.

"In that case, you ought to be grateful that they convicted you of something else," murmured the old man, and then grabbed him by the arm, shoving him in front of him and yelling loudly enough to be heard from the vegetable patch: "Get a move on, you idler! I'm going to puke if I have to stand next to you much longer!" After which he lowered his voice and said, "If you never met him, then I can tell you without any worry."

As he walked, Bruno turned to glance at old man Zacornea.

"I read it in the newspaper and remembered that you'd said something about him. There was a trial, with a lot of people, but I can't remember all the names. Maybe you know them, but I'm just telling you what happened in general. They all got heavy prison sentences. But him they sentenced to death, and they shot him."

The others were already back at work after the meal. Bruno picked up his hoe, silently re-joined the line of prisoners, and set about molding from the crumbly soil a long, squashed snake with perfectly parallel edges to add to the rows of other identical snakes in the vegetable garden of Galați Prison.

Very old times, from a different world. He had almost forgotten them. He even had ceased trying to remember them. But now he was forced to do so. Elena and Lucrețiu Pătrășcanu. His father assuring him that in Romania he would enjoy the protection of the minister and his wife. But now the former minister was dead, and his wife languished in some prison like Bruno's, where she was terrorized by some other Maromet and dreamed of times past. The minister's wife. Back then she had had an elegant *coque de cheveux*. She had smoked long cigarettes, holding them with an aristocratic tilt of the hand. She had worn an expensive leather coat and light-colored two-piece suits. Now she was languishing in prison.

That night he would have fallen asleep thinking such thoughts. But in a place where news of such events was so hard to come by, where only the captain's whim changed the timetable and the type of work, the day decided differently. And it brought Bruno more than the news of his former benefactor's death. Since it had begun by bringing him sad news, the day did not prove to be clement; it didn't bring the necessary counterbalance. On the contrary, it drowned the sad tidings in a second piece of news even greater and perhaps even more unexpected than the first.

Returning to his cell before the sun had fully sunk behind the prison walls, Bruno was able to lie on his bed, crammed alongside a cellmate, for no more than an hour. The iron door suddenly opened; the prisoners got up and stood in line. They had not been brought food; they were not about to be taken to the latrine. The guard yelling at them was trembling. He had brought that trembling with him from somewhere on the outside, and it had nothing to do with the four men who had instantly stood to attention in front of him.

Within a few minutes, they were taken out into the yard. Not only them. All the prisoners in the cell block were lined up: almost a hundred men, murmuring at first, but then falling silent when Captain Maromet appeared in front of them, next to the guards. Captain Maromet first cast them a scornful look and then spat in disgust. He did not commence his monologue with a joke, as was otherwise his habit. He didn't even begin his monologue by yelling at them, as was also otherwise his habit. Rather, he ran up to the first row of prisoners and started kicking and punching them, cursing incoherently. When he finally calmed down, he walked away from the perturbed ranks of prisoners, straightened his uniform, and signaled to the guards.

A croak immediately rose from Bruno's throat, but his jaws checked it at the last moment, before it could leave his lips. His eardrums began to throb, the blood rushed to his cheeks, his eyes widened as they fastened helplessly on old man Zacornea, whom two guards dragged over to the captain. Two of his fellow guards. Bruno's thoughts deafened him, his terror drained down into his legs, and his muscles were barely able to sustain his weight. Their wooden marionette began to dance in front of his eyes, clouding the sight before him; it began to move as it had never done in real life, during that night in the washroom; it moved as if writhing, terrified, trying thereby to drive away the nightmare now unfolding, although night had not yet swallowed that day so different from the others, and although sleep, so often responsible for such nightmares, had not pulled Bruno down into its depths.

No traces of violence could be seen on old man Zacornea's face, only an overwhelming desperation, which had multiplied his wrinkles, shrunk his eyes, turned his hair even whiter. When he heard the captain's voice, the old man's head instantly bowed in a kind of supplication that cried out for forgiveness.

Amid enraged yells, Maromet demanded that the prisoners look at his eyes and his ears. Did they think that his eyes and ears were there on his head? Then they were mistaken. They had no idea how mistaken they were. The prisoners were fast asleep, they were living in clover, the dogs, roared the captain, if they didn't know where his eyes and ears really were. It meant they didn't know to look right, left, in front, behind. Sometimes, if they knew where to look, they would have been able to find Nicolae Maromet's eyes and ears right there inside them. As he yelled he gestured at the prisoners, pointing left and right at each of the dogs in front of him.

But Bruno's eyes sought old man Zacornea. Above the yells his ears strained to hear the slightest croak, sigh, or whisper that might have come from the old guard. But Maromet's roars and gesticulations now directed themselves at the old man, before any croak, sigh, or whisper could reach Bruno. The captain grabbed the old guard by the hair and dragged him to the front. The yelling erupted once more, informing all those present that the eyes and ears of the prison commandant never slept, and that was why treason would always come to light. Treason and stupidity, since only an idiot like the old guard would have helped the prisoners by bringing them news from the outside;

only an idiot would have slipped food parcels to lice like them, who were anyway glutted on the blood they had sucked from the people. What would become of the stupid, traitorous old codger now? He would spend the final years of his life in prison, the same as the other dogs . . .

Bruno held his breath throughout the yelling. Behind his pity, a terrified thought implored the old guard not to mention him to the prison commandant, not to say anything about the wooden doll. And that thought was immediately followed by another, even more dreadful, which whispered to Bruno, and to Bruno alone, that it was too late, that the marionette had been discovered, that old man Zacornea now found himself in this situation because of their "project," and that Bruno himself would soon have to endure the worst suffering of all his years in prison.

Something then happened that he could not have suspected. Old man Zacornea's eyes, which were now turned toward the prisoners after the captain had yanked his head up by the hair, met Bruno's terrified gaze. And after a few moments, the old man's eyelids spoke to Bruno, closing and opening, reassuring him. When Bruno understood what was being said to him, he was overwhelmed by a feeling not of liberation but of dreadful shame, a crushing guilt before that old man, who, in such a moment, had found in himself the strength to banish the prisoner's fear.

During the half an hour that Captain Maromet kept the hundred prisoners there, he learned no more than he knew already, and this despite the commandant's threats and promises that any additional incriminating information would be rewarded with a shorter punishment than would be meted out to those who had collaborated with the old guard once their names came to light during the investigation. The captain's ears had that very day provided him with the information that old man Zacornea had been doing favors for certain prisoners. His ears had informed him that old man Zacornea had secreted a food parcel from the relatives of one of the prisoners. But the same as always, the host of prisoners endured his curses, his threats, his outbursts of rage, his kicks, and his punches in silence. Finally, they were marched back to their cells, just as silent.

Only when he was back in his cell, where he would no longer have to wait for his portion of food, which that evening would be going to the pigs, only then was Bruno able to detach himself, to a certain extent, from the feelings that had overwhelmed him during the scene in the prison yard. Only then was he able to narrate the event to himself, having placed it in an order that helped him the better to understand its meanings. First of all he understood that old man Zacornea would never again appear in the prison yard. He then understood that since they had discovered his hiding place and found there only a food parcel for one of the prisoners, then the marionette must be elsewhere, within the prison, but in a place where it would probably lie concealed for all eternity, as a guarantee that those walls would never crumble, housing generation after generation of wretches branded enemies of the people. Finally, he understood that ultimately nobody could genuinely provide him with any hope, but only with snatches of hope, which would inevitably be annihilated, since no power in the world, no matter what it might be founded on, could endure before that gigantic juggernaut that had borne down on him over the last few years.

After he understood all these things, transforming them into liberation or into final submission, Bruno had still not been able to sleep, even if he forced his thoughts to avoid old man Zacornea. Even if he tore his thoughts away from the faceless name of his former benefactor, Lucrețiu Pătrășcanu. Even if he strove not to think about all the things that told him that in the more distant or more recent past there were times when he had been able to imagine that he didn't live completely alone, that he had reasons to trust in somebody else almost palpably close.

He was unable to sleep because his thoughts, submissive at first when it came to accepting the helplessness in which they were crammed together, finally rebelled, taking refuge in the few free spaces within the cell: between the cracks in the walls that had remained from the earthquake of 1940; in the distance between the lower bunk, on which he lay next to another prisoner, and the bunk above, likewise occupied by two prisoners; and even in the suffocating space between him and his bunkmate. They rebelled and had their revenge, conveying new fears to Bruno's mind. For, once banished from the only place in which they could create rational connections, his thoughts mustered their forces and conveyed insane, fantastical images of the captain's eyes and ears, which took on a life of their own and like spiders wove webs in the cracks in the walls and the distance between the bunks and the so-narrow space between him and his bunkmate.

That night, after tortured hours of sleeplessness, Bruno found the only solution, which was to gather his thoughts one by one, luring them into an idyllic space that could do him no harm, since it was from a completely different life, and providing them with a language that was not foreign to them, but which had nothing to do with the language of the judges who had sentenced him, or that of the prison guards, or that of the prisoners, or that of old man Zacornea and Lucrețiu Pătrășcanu. That space and that language belonged to the old puppeteers of Sicily.

It was almost morning when Bruno managed to fall asleep, by which time his thoughts had become accustomed to that space and that language, keeping for themselves the words of teaching once uttered by the head of the family of puppeteers: "*In uno spettacolo di marionette, bisogna tener presenti due condizioni essenziali. La prima: il pubblico non deve vedere altri movimenti all'infuori di quelli imposti dal gioco, provati e riprovati dall'artista che maneggia il pupazzo. La seconda: il pubblico non deve sentire altre voci all'infuori di quelle imposte dal gioco, provate e riprovate dall'artista che dà voce al pupazzo."*[3]

---

3    In a marionette show two essential conditions must be borne in mind. First: the public must not see any movements other than those imposed by the game, tried and retried by the artist managing the puppet. Second: the public must not hear any voices other than those imposed by the game, tried and retried by the artist who gives voice to the puppet.

# Chapter 15

A YEAR HAD passed since Brunul had, to a certain degree, been freed from the immediate and most agonizing effects of his illness. And he had imagined that he was rid of them for good. But things had lately gone awry.

In the final months of prison and then in the first months following his release, life did not much look like how comrade Bojin had striven to describe it to him. He had found it difficult to adapt to being alone in his cell, although gradually things had acquired greater meaning, and comrade Bojin had spent much time with him, sitting on the other iron bed, smiling at him more often than not and encouraging him. In a way, it was better even than in the hospital, where the tests and the bitter-tasting medicines he was forced to take sometimes drove him to the brink of despair, and where he was able to understand absolutely nothing of what was happening to him.

On the other hand, during the long hours when he remained alone in his cell, and even after he met Bojin, he had had to fight against a gigantic fear, which sometimes turned into desperation, so much so that he would press himself up against the walls, try to tunnel into them with his hands, not to get to the other side, but to make them tell him something about his past, to make them tell him anything at all. And the lack of the communication he so desperately desired tore repeated howls from the depths of his chest, howls he could not control and from which the warder would sometimes rescue him, entering, picking him up, hurling him on the bed, covering him with the blanket, until the darkness soothed his starting eyes, allowing them to retract back into their sockets so that his eyelids could cover them, and the warmth would gradually quell his trembling. Sometimes his howls would die down by themselves, and he would crawl into bed by himself, covering himself with the blanket without the warder's help.

Such episodes grew more seldom only after he learned to communicate with the marionette. After he realized that that wooden creature was more than just an object from his unknown past. After he understood that, unlike the walls, even if it was unable to answer him, the doll looked at him, and that even if it was unable to say so, it could understand him. Gradually, in the moments of terror, laughter had replaced the howls, and he quelled his body's trembling by clutching the marionette tightly to his chest. Later, after comrade Bojin gave it the name Vasilache, Brunul's closeness to that wooden figurine, which looked at him from behind its black mask and understood him, helped him to control his states of exhaustion, helped him to return to normality, more or less.

But immediately after his release from prison, his "seizures" began. Maybe the "seizures" had existed in his cell too, but there had been nobody there to notice them. And if Vasilache had noticed them, he was unable to tell him about them. It was only on the outside, after he had met a number of people, that Brunul found out about his seizures. Firstly in a food shop. He had been handing over the money for a loaf of bread to the woman behind the counter, and in the next instant another woman, who had appeared as if from nowhere, was shaking him, shouting at him, her eyes boggling, as if trying to make him wake up. Brunul had pushed her away, he had been as frightened as she was, he had almost broken into a run, but before he could do so he realized that the woman had been addressing him gently in fact, and that far from threatening him, she had wanted to help him. "You just froze," she explained. "You stood there like a rock with your eyes fixed on the wall. And then you started banging your hand on the counter, frightening everybody. Bang, bang, bang, again and again." And here the woman showed him how, banging on the counter. "The lady—" she pointed at the woman behind the counter "—kept talking to you, but nothing. She kept talking, but you didn't reply . . . Are you ill?"

It was comrade Bojin who had called them that. "You suddenly turn numb, like you're having a seizure," he had said. The second such event occurred a few weeks later, in front of his friend, during one of their evenings together. It had lasted maybe a minute at the most, Bojin told him. "I think it's something to do with your head," he opined, passing over the episode quite lightly. Another two such episodes followed in quick succession at work. A complaint was made to comrade Bojin; he was informed that Brunul had frightened his new colleagues. Comrade Bojin took his friend to hospital to see Dr. Petrovici. Nor did the doctor know what to make of it; he didn't have enough information, so he said, to be able to explain those moments of horror, which Brunul had, with shame, described to the man in the white coat, fearful that he would tell him, the same as comrade Bojin had, that he was insane. All the more so given that Brunul had agreed with comrade Bojin that it was paradise on the outside, just as he had been promised it would be, and that life was good: he had a job, a place to live; the Party had taken care of everything. But he repaid that care with those inexplicable moments when he suddenly became afraid, and fear and howls would well up in him out of nowhere. And as if that wasn't enough, now his "seizures" had appeared.

"Yours is a strange illness," the doctor had said, trying to reassure him. "But it's not insanity; it's something else. Don't listen to what other people tell you. All these things are symptoms of an illness. Be patient. You'll recover gradually." And so that he would recover, he prescribed him some medicines.

After the first months of freedom, particularly after he met

Eliza, things had settled down. The "seizures" had vanished. The medicines must have helped. The harrowing sadness still appeared from time to time, but he had learned to control it. He had learned not to plunge into it except when he was alone; he had given it a name, as the doctor had advised, and he had chided it whenever it arrived at an unsuitable moment, striving with all his might to drive it away. Most of the time he succeeded.

He had every right to believe that he had rid himself of all of this for good. He no longer took the medicine. He had embarked upon wonderful normality, as he often thought to himself. He had embarked upon a wonderful life, especially now that Eliza had responded to his silent waiting, to the signals he wished so much to give her, but had never dared to. For a time, the paradise comrade Bojin had promised him as he sat on the iron bed in his cell seemed to include him and to accept him.

But then, it was as if someone, or something, an invisible force, angry at the life he had made for himself, had swooped down on him and things had gone awry. Thinking about it now, thinking about recent events, Brunul could no longer tell when it had all begun. Had it been the subscription ticket? If he had left it there, buried in the snow in the yard of the Catholic church, would anything have changed? Would he have preserved the normality in which he had rejoiced so greatly? Perhaps not. Was it the building site? The building site . . . It would have been better if the building site had not existed. It would have been better if he had still been working at the State Puppet Theater. Perhaps none of it would have happened if he had not been moved. He had tried to be happy with his new job; he had even managed to take a certain satisfaction in it. But what if . . . Even so, it wasn't the building site. It wasn't because of his change of workplace that he was now suffering once again. Was it the television set? What if he hadn't seen those images of violins on television? What if he hadn't heard that voice from his past, which had spoken to him in Italian. Who knows . . . It was true that he wouldn't have found out what he had from the archivist. On the other hand, Eliza would have been the same, Eliza would have had the same thoughts, even if she had not told him them that evening. She would have postponed them; she wouldn't have told him them now, but what would have been the use? Normality would still have lasted only a few more days, maybe a few more weeks.

Clutching Vasilache tightly, sitting huddled up, rocking his whole body, Brunul thought that it would still have been good to obtain even a few more weeks. He would even have been content to forget everything he had discovered from his talk with Eliza, he would have been content if a new accident had shattered his brain, his mind, and blotted out the memories of the last few weeks. That was all he asked, to forget the last few weeks. But in the end, what would have been the use? Other people would have remained the same . . .

He would have liked to go outside with Vasilache and make a path through the snow. He went to the window and stood motionless, cradling the doll, gazing outside. In the distance the light of a streetlamp made the asphalt look white. But it wasn't snow; it couldn't be snow now, in late August.

He sat back down on the bed. He lowered his head to Vasilache, slowly, moving his lips to the coarse hair, then to the long, soft, white hat. He opened his mouth with the same slowness, as if calculating the distance between his lips; he opened his mouth and then gripped the marionette's hat between his teeth, clenching it more and more tightly. His body began to shake, from his depths sounds that were like squeaks rose to his throat, they became louder, turned into screams, into protracted howls.

The old cloth slowly came loose, and in place of the hat there remained the blank space of Vasilache's wooden pate, fringed with a few tufts.

Comrade Bojin had no way of remembering the last time he had
been inside a church. It must have been when he was a child.
At Easter and Christmas his mother used to drag him with her
when she felt the need to go to confession. But so long a time
had passed since then that it was impossible for him to remember anything about it. Later, his wife Toriţa had tried to persuade
him to go to church with her. That had been during the war,
immediately after he had managed to obtain an honorable discharge, thanks to the connections he had fortunately been able
to develop. Not only had he refused to go to church with her,
but he had been enraged at the very suggestion: the few months
he had spent in the trenches until his connections were able to
sort out his discharge had set him against the priesthood. As he
had observed at the time, the only rôle the priests played was
to pop up out of the holes in which they had been hiding, once
the battle was over, and to make the sign of the cross over the
corpses, all the while whispering words of no use to anybody.
They turned up like jackals, in their cassocks, bowing rhythmically, as if performing some insipid chore above the bullet-rid-
dled bodies of men who, a few hours before, had joked, eaten,
drunk, and harbored the illusion that they would survive. In
the few months he had spent in the war, he had learned that
priests played no other rôle than to consecrate death through
their stupid rituals.

   After the war, not only had he refused to go to church with
his wife, but he had forbidden her any display of unpleasant
piety in front of the priest, he had forbidden her to leave the
house on Sundays or feast days for any other reason than to
do the shopping. The world had changed, and he had changed
his job along with it. In the new times, not only did his own
antipathy make him have nothing to do with the Church, but
also his new status precluded anything of the sort. Without
relinquishing God, his wife Toriţa nonetheless accepted that

ultimately, if she wanted white bread to put on the table, as her husband often put it, she would have to forget about going to church.

But now, hidden in the darkness of the State Puppet Theater auditorium, comrade Bojin somehow felt as if he were in a kind of church. What was more, he felt a need for that church; from the outset, he had been driven there by a mad, inexplicable desire to confess. A desire he had never before felt, given that his childhood confessions had been obligations imposed on him by his mother. The evening before, he had had to meet with Brunul, however, and for the first time since being assigned to him, he woke up in the morning with a heavy, unbearable burden weighing on his soul, which had caused him to stop shaving, to grow rigid in front of the mirror, holding the razor close to his cheek in one hand and the soapy brush in the other, and to wonder what the hell was happening to him and where that damned feeling of guilt came from. Ultimately, why should it be his problem? He had always received orders and he had always obeyed them. And that was all.

That was all. Except that when it came to this particular intelligence objective, the orders bewildered even him. In the beginning, he had left him that doll in his cell on the doctor's recommendation. Later, after he was released, well, they'd ordered him to get him a job at the puppet theater. After that, consequent to the accurate reports he himself had submitted to them, their orders began to change. First of all, the puppet had to disappear. They had sent some policemen to confiscate it. Brunul's desperation, which likewise he had signaled in his report, had made them relent somewhat, and so Bojin himself had been obliged to go to the police station to recover the puppet and then give him it back. But he still wasn't done with it all: after a while, the orders said that it was no longer appropriate that Brunul be employed at the puppet theater. What if he regained his memory? But hang on, wasn't that what they had wanted from the very start? Yes, but . . . He himself wasn't supposed to know too much. He merely had to carry out orders. But even so, he had pressed them. He couldn't do his work unless he knew what his superiors were aiming at. Finally, he had been given an audience with somebody higher up. Not very high up, but high enough for him to find out a few things.

In the beginning they hadn't believed that the illness was genuine. There wasn't even a diagnosis for it. Who'd ever heard of anything so stupid: losing your memory of a period of exactly twenty years? Was he insane or wasn't he? That's why they had assigned Bojin to him from the very start, so that he could observe his behavior and convince himself that Brunul really couldn't remember anything. And in the end Bojin's reports persuaded them that no matter how strange it all was, they really were dealing with a genuine illness. That's why they had released him. Why the puppet theater? Because at first they had gone by what the doctor had said. He had to be provided with a familiar setting, that's what the doctor had told them, otherwise he would genuinely lose his mind. The doctor had vouched for it. And their man had recovered, little by little; this was demonstrated by no less than Bojin's reports. He had recovered, but without regaining his memory. And that was precisely what had to be exploited. Therein lay their opportunity. Had comrade Bojin heard of the Makarenko method for creating the new man? Of course he had heard of it, said Bojin, rather alarmed at the turn the discussion was taking, since he now vaguely remembered the method, from the time of the tedious lectures he had once sat through, although he would not have been able to go into any detail on the subject. Of course he had heard of it. Well then, if he had heard of it, what better material could there be for an experiment of that kind than a man who had completely lost the negative, counterrevolutionary part of his memory? Obviously, the high-ups themselves had played no part in erasing the man's negative memory, but nonetheless it had happened, and so why not try to take advantage of the situation? If that was the aim, then naturally he would be of no use to them if he did regain his real memories. What if his counterrevolutionary memories came back to him? No, the man had to be educated in the socialist spirit, and later, when his memories did come back—the doctor had assured them that this would happen sooner or later—it would be all the more interesting to observe how the subject would cope with them. Yes, it wasn't quite the pure Makarenko method, but wasn't it a situation worth following? Wasn't it worth studying in detail? Didn't comrade Bojin feel that he was participating in a genuinely special, challenging assignment, which many others would have been only too eager to take? Yes, certainly he did. And so wasn't it better that he carry out the assignment, rather than asking questions that wouldn't do any good? Yes, certainly it was.

After that audience, he repressed any further questions. "Makarenko it is then, if that's the way it has to be," he said to himself over and over again, particularly when some feeling of compassion popped up out of the blue, forcing him to waver between the two types of truth in which he believed.

That Sunday, however, Makarenko was of not much help to him. The meeting he was due to have with Brunul, his first since the visit to the Archives, made him feel a greater discomfort than any he had experienced thitherto. He needed to confess. After he came out of the bathroom, his first impulse had been to take his wife by the hand, sit her down, pull up a chair in front of her, and talk. Ultimately, he had told her lots of other things about Brunul, about the nature of their relationship, albeit without going into all the details, naturally. But now he would have liked to go into those details with her. However, the impulse persisted only until the moment in which he came face to face with her. No, she wouldn't be able to understand. What could she have told him? That he should go to church and confess? And anyway, why should he reveal himself to be weak in front of her? And how could she have understood, when not even he very well understood the reluctance, the thoughts, the feelings with which he had awoken that morning? Or did he understand them all too well? No, in fact he had no idea where they had come from.

He had no idea why his need for the confessional had prompted him to go to the puppet theater. What answers could he have found there? In the darkness of the auditorium, looking at the stage on which *Aladdin and the Magic Lamp* was being performed, he could find no justification even for his second reason for being there. Because, hiding the fact even from himself, comrade Bojin had for a long time wanted to return and watch rehearsals or a performance for the sake of those voices which had so strangely aroused him that time, pushing him to the verge of moral transgression in relation to his marriage. The women's voices, giving life to the animals, the childishly distorted, altered voices, had even for a time made him dream of all kinds of almost lascivious creatures preening in front of him, putting his feelings in a whirl, dredging up from his depths sensations made flaccid by the passage of time, sensations from his rather tumultuous youth. He had reined in his desires, which were not at all appropriate to a middle-aged married man such as himself. He had reined in his desires, which were not at all appropriate to a man in his line of work. But that Sunday, everything had come to a head, as if to drive him in the direction of the State Puppet Theater. The need to confess had made him think of church, whether he liked it or not, and the association he had then made with the hush of the theater auditorium had provided a substitute. Moreover, for him the theater was enveloped in a kind of respect associated with a period in which he had not felt so guilty, since it was there that he had seen Brunul happy on so many occasions. Even if Brunul had lost his memory, Bojin had known he somehow felt at home there. And in comrade Bojin's mind, the orders to find another job for Brunul had turned him into the instrument of the amnesiac's unhappiness. Finally, even if his reason rejected the idea, he had been driven there by the feeling that, allowing himself to be enchanted by those voices once more, he would escape from the oppression of another voice, that of his own awkward conscience, which refused to be pent up, at the command of the second type of truth in which he believed, within the boundaries of the first type of truth, the one that must never be spoken and above all never analyzed.

But even the voices were absent now. In *Aladdin and the Magic Lamp* not a single animal voiced by a female actress appeared onstage; there were only puppets with human faces, in a story that comrade Bojin was unable to follow, with the result that nothing could disburden him of the thoughts engendered by the prospect of his meeting with Brunul that evening. Perhaps he ought to have gone to see a film instead, he told himself, but not even the memories of the few films he had seen over the years could divert him for very long, memories with which, making an effort, he tried to blot out his guilty thoughts. At least if he had known where his guilt lay, if he had been able to clarify it to himself, he would have been able to find an explanation, a justification. But it was merely a feeling, which, in a flash, had first come to him in the office of the archivist, who had been spinning Brunul a tale completely divorced from reality, a feeling that he had ignored on the days that followed, but which had come back that morning, refusing to be explained away, erased, banished.

He tried yet again to follow the story being performed onstage. A boy and his so-called magic lamp, an embarrassing attempt on the part of the people behind the screen to bring to life lumps of wood using their hands. Some of the audience believed in it; the children around him could be fooled. But not him. He knew what the puppet storeroom looked like. Brunul had once shown it to him. He knew that those clothed bits of wood were nothing but lifeless dummies; they only appeared to acquire life when they were onstage, to eyes that did not want to see what was really to be seen. And this was the case even if each of them had a name, the way only humans have names: Brunul had shown him a ledger with the puppets' names: Hansel, Gretel, Păcală, Sînziana, Pepelea, Nikita, the Tsarevich Vazul, the Tsarina Nastasia. Beneath all the names to be found in that ledger was a detailed description of the movements, voices, songs, and clothes each puppet had to present to the audience. It was a kind of archive, thought comrade Bojin, his memory returning to his last meeting with Brunul. An archive of puppets, in which were recorded all the moments that genuinely mattered in their so-called lives. They existed only insofar as their puppeteers stuck to the instructions contained in that archive. And not even then did they really exist, and people with good eyesight, like him, knew it.

He didn't stay until the end of the performance. It was afternoon already and in any event he had lost the thread of the story. In fact, not for one moment had he been able to concentrate on the story. He left the State Puppet Theater, just as dissatisfied as he had been when he arrived, just as puzzled at all the feelings that assailed him. After wandering around at random for half an hour, not finding anything better to do, he entered a tavern and asked for two bottles of wine. He didn't even think to ask for a receipt so that he could claim them on expenses, as he usually did when he bought wine from a state food shop. He paid with his own money, put one of the bottles in a bag for later that evening, and asked the tavern keeper to uncork the other. He then asked for a glass.

Waiting for Bojin to arrive at eight o'clock that evening, as he had been instructed in the note the engineer had passed on to him the day before, Brunul thought of rebellion for the first time. But the thought was also accompanied by fear. Rebellion against and fear toward the man he had always regarded as his friend. But now this whole deluge of lies had come. His friend, who had stuck by him for so long . . . He didn't even want to ask him any questions. He would have liked merely to slam him up against the wall, kick him, yell at him, wring from him, from the last speck of soul that comrade Bojin must surely possess, a few words whereby he would acknowledge his guilt; yes, he would have dearly wished to do that.

But Eliza had asked that he make no reaction; she had even implored him. She had asked that he swear to keep their discussion just between themselves; it was the only way in which the plan would work, if Brunul ultimately agreed to it. But his rebellion, which the pressures of the last few days had prevented from erupting, now made Brunul wonder whether he would be able to keep his promise, his oath to Eliza; it made him fearful as to how he would react. Even before seven o'clock came around, he started pacing up and down his narrow room, looking more and more frequently at his watch, trying to calm himself by pressing his forehead against the window, entering the kitchen to find something to keep himself busy, peeling an onion for something he knew very well he would not cook that evening, leaving the kitchen, going into the bathroom, returning to the bed sitting room . . .

That hour had elapsed agonizingly, and now, at eight o'clock, he planted himself in front of the door, pressing his ear to it to listen for footsteps. Whenever somebody climbed the stairs, his heart started to pound. With difficulty he calmed himself as he heard the sound of footsteps recede, climbing the stairs to the other floors.

It was not until after half past nine that he abandoned his post by the front door. Comrade Bojin must have forgotten their meeting. He was somehow relieved, but also disappointed to a certain extent. It was not the first time that comrade Bojin had forgotten or had had other business, but this time it was to have been a special meeting, in a way, and so his disappointment was understandable. Maybe he would not have said anything to him; he would certainly not have said anything. But he would have studied the other man's face closely. He would have looked at his face differently, the way he ought to have looked at it long ago. And he would have seen something in that face; he would have read something there.

At around midnight, after he had fallen asleep, thinking bitterly about the meeting that hadn't taken place, he found himself obliged to jump out of bed and rush to the front door, on which somebody was pounding loudly enough to wake all the neighbors. In a fright, he opened the door, not yet having properly woken up, with his pajama top still unbuttoned. In the doorway stood comrade Bojin, his head bowed, tottering, steadying himself against the doorframe with one hand and holding a bag in the other. It was only after a few seconds, just as he was about to kick the door once more, that he realized it was now open. He raised his arms and flung them toward Brunul as if to embrace him, hitting him with the bag he was holding as he did so. Brunul was unable to avoid the bag, from inside which came the clatter of bottles, but at least it prevented comrade Bojin from falling headfirst into the small hallway of the one-room apartment.

"It's past midnight," muttered Brunul, trying to recover at least a part of the mood he had felt before going to bed.

He conducted comrade Bojin inside, propping him up. After managing to sit down on a chair, comrade Bojin thrust his hand inside the bag and pulled out empty bottle after empty bottle, placing them on the table. Four bottles in total. As he was trying to pull out the fifth bottle, comrade Bojin cut his fingertip and began to laugh. He put his finger in his mouth to stop the bleeding. A few moments later, he managed to slur, merrily, "There was another, but it broke."

And then, as if having completed his business, he got up and walked to the door, managing to keep his balance. Steadying himself with one hand on the door handle, he turned to Brunul and said: "Look, man, I don't know how to tell you so that you'll understand. But I've been thinking. And here's what I think. Why do you need somebody from Archives to tell you about your life? What do you get out of it? What do you gain? You understand what I think?"

Brunul shrugged and then, because comrade Bojin had looked away in the meantime, he said, "No."

Comrade Bojin waved his hand in annoyance. Then he shook his head, muttering something, and opened the door. From the other side of the threshold he muttered something else, which sounded like a swearword, and emphasized his annoyance with another wave of the hand.

He lifted his head, trying to look Brunul in the eye, and said, "What do you want from me, man? Want to hear me beg your forgiveness? Is that what you want? I'm not going to do it. Not a chance in hell of that. But here's what's what, just so you'll know: life is what you live today, not what's in the archives . . . That's what I thought I ought to tell you, understand? Because one person will tell you one thing, and another will tell you something different. But what's in there—" here he pointed a finger at Brunul's chest "—you alone know. Understand?"

He didn't wait for an answer. His feet started shuffling in front of him, as if dragging the rest of his body behind them. He descended the stairs with difficulty, hanging onto the bannister. Finally, Brunul heard the front door of the building close behind him.

# Chapter 16

ON THE THIRD day, after lights out, Bruno was unable to fall asleep straightaway because somebody was talking in a low voice about a certain Tcaciuc. It was late in the evening and the voice to which Bruno was listening with his eyes closed pointed out first of all that Tcaciuc was nicknamed "the butcher." He quickly realized, however, that in this particular case the word didn't have the meaning so familiar to him from his previous life in Italy. Vasile Tcaciuc "the butcher" had lived in Romania and had died in 1937, before Bruno and his family left the country.

Twenty years previously, whispered Bruno's cellmate, his sister-in-law had come to his house with a dog. After a very short while, the dog had grown agitated, scratching the floor, whining, barking. Finally, thinking that there was something wrong, he pulled up the floorboards in the spot that caused the dog so much agitation. He had not been able to believe his eyes: a man's arm, still clothed, although the material was tattered. He hadn't called the police straightaway, but fetched a spade and started digging, driven by unhealthy curiosity. He still didn't know how he had had the strength to unearth no less than six corpses. If he thought about it, he wouldn't have done the same thing now; he would have called the police from the very start, even if he had known what he would subsequently go through: investigation, treatment as a suspect, the terror of going to prison. Of course, there was no way he could have been guilty: he had only recently bought the house from Vasile Tcaciuc "the butcher," and the corpses were much older. In the end, he had been released without charge, but only because

Tcaciuc was already under arrest, for theft or burglary, he couldn't remember what. And who the hell knows why, but while the police were busy interrogating him, an innocent man, in one cell, Tcaciuc was confessing in another that he was the one who murdered the people whose bodies had been discovered by the dog. Twenty bodies. Twenty-six, counting the ones under the floorboards inside the house. Later, he found out that the butcher had managed to escape and was shot by the police.

Bruno's cellmate then gave a bitter snort and went on: "At the time I was terrified of going to prison. I thought: I'm an innocent man, I wouldn't even hurt a fly. And there I was, with six bodies under the floorboards in my house, I go to the police to report it, and they arrest me. It's all a question of fate. You can find yourself locked up and not have anything on your conscience. I had a terror of going to prison. But I was released, like I said. And it was as if I was born again. After I was released, I told myself: that was my big ordeal, I got through it, and that means I'll never again end up in the slammer. But here I am. I didn't go to prison for six people buried under my floorboards, but I'm here now because I had to go and get drunk with a neighbor who was a secret police informer. And I talked and . . . you know the rest. I let my mouth run away with me. How was I supposed to know he was with the secret police? If I'd known, I wouldn't be here talking to you now."

With that, the others left him to his bitterness. Later, just when Bruno thought he would be able to go to sleep, another whisper broke the silence.

"And you say all that happened here in Jassy?"

"Yes, here," confirmed the first voice. "All the newspapers in the country nicknamed him 'the Butcher of Jassy.' I've never lived anywhere else. I was born in Jassy, I've lived my whole life in Jassy, I found those corpses in my house in Jassy. I was arrested in Jassy and I ended up here in Jassy Penitentiary."

On the third night after his transfer to Jassy Penitentiary, in September 1955, Bruno Matei would have had the opportunity to join in the conversation between his cellmates. He would have had the opportunity to tell them about himself, to find out more about them, to ask them questions, rather than just listening to their stories. But for the last year and a half, since the time when he was in Galați Prison, since the day when he had seen old man Zacornea for the last time, the guard whom he had begun to hold dearer than he would have liked, he had avoided falling into such a trap.

Fortifying himself with the words of the head of the family of puppeteers, which in his cell in Galați had come to him from another life, from a completely different place, Bruno had for almost a year and a half been on strike. It was not a strike that might bother the prison guards or the soldiers, since he obeyed their orders, limiting himself to the words and movements strictly required. Rather, his strike distanced him from the other prisoners, who would have thought him deaf and dumb had it not been for the brief, sparse replies he gave the guards; they would have thought he suffered from a mental illness, which would in the end have resulted in his transfer from prison to an asylum. But this is not what Bruno sought. He sought merely to shun illusions.

He shunned illusions even after inspectors from Bucharest arrived at Galați Prison and Nicolae Maromet was sacked, shortly after the incident with old man Zacornea. And when he left, the captain took his jokes with him, his obscenities, his beatings, his triple quotas. He took away his brutal whims. But Bruno had no reason to believe that the former head of the prison had taken his eyes and ears with him, since the captain himself had said all too clearly that the organs in question only appeared to be attached to his head, when in fact they had long since burrowed into the prisoners without their knowing it. Although not directly motivated by the fact that the captain's eyes and ears might still be lurking among the prisoners around him, Bruno's attitude at least liberated him from any fear on that account. For, Bruno's strike, his refusal to communicate either by word or gesture, not only released him from the slavery of any illusion, but also lent him the status of model prisoner, from whom nobody could expect any trouble.

It was probably as a reward for this behavior that after a year and a half he was placed on the list of those to be transferred to a prison with a reputation less dire than Galați. At least that was what he instinctively thought when he found himself on that list. But he immediately repudiated the thought, since it concealed a new speck of hope. In the end, the reason for such a transfer might be anything at all; the prisoner himself didn't have to be informed. After driving out his instinctive thought, Bruno accepted that vague, meaningless "anything at all." He found it more satisfying, since he could treat it with a complete lack of interest.

Before the transfer to Jassy, after taking a long look at the yard as he was being taken to the prison gates, Bruno nonetheless allowed a little joy to infect his steps, which caused him to straighten his back and shoulders and adopt a posture that differed a little, but only a very little, from the one he usually presented to others; it even caused the corners of his lips to spread into a smile that nobody in the world apart from him could have noticed. That joy came from the final disburdening he needed. For, in the year and a half since the arrest of old man Zacornea and since he relinquished all communication, Bruno had nonetheless been eaten away by the trace of an illusion, which probably lay hidden somewhere in the walls of the cellblock, in some chink in the brickwork: the trace of the final passion of a guard who had molded clay figurines for a lifetime and who in his dotage had tried to turn his talent to woodcarving.

He had no need of that trace. He felt no need to look at the walls and wonder behind which brick the marionette was secreted. And the walls of Jassy Penitentiary, no matter how harsh, would at least spare him that final question.

On his third night in Jassy Penitentiary, the first in the large room that was to be his "abode" for a long time to come, as the guard who brought him there assured him, after two nights alone in a cell, Bruno Matei was unable to fall asleep until after the echoes of the tale of "the Butcher of Jassy" had died away. In the two years he had spent in a narrow cell in Galați, he had forgotten the thrum of a large room, where nearby whispers can be heard clearly, before fading into an indecipherable amalgam of sound, a rustling that to other ears, including the guards', was distinguishable only as a very low, almost inaudible background noise, but which to Bruno after years of silence was an almost deafening racket. In any event, it was a sound that prevented him from sleeping.

The fifty prisoners who were to be his dormitory mates, until the next transfer, thought Bruno, differed from both the prisoners on the Peninsula and those at Galați. He was able to determine this in the long hour he spent listening to them. Whereas on the Canal the men returned to the huts exhausted, seeking to gain as much time as possible for sleep, and whereas at Galați his three cellmates, who, after the sacking of Maromet, were reduced to one, so that they no longer had to sleep two to a bunk, had been grumpy and uncommunicative, keeping their silence, there in Jassy the draught that blew from the wooden door to the barred window, above which hung blinds, brought with it an air of freedom. The freedom of words, albeit spoken in low voices. This freedom, as Bruno was to observe in the days to come, could even be found in the faces of his fellow prisoners, which were less burdened by thoughts and fears; it could be found in their movements and gestures, which were less hurried when reacting to the orders and curses of the guards, and above all in the joking banter at the expense of those guards, as if there, behind the walls of that prison in the Copou district, from where the luxurious crowns of the trees were visible, Baba Samca and her ghosts had never set foot, as if no Iosif Lazăr or Nicolae Maromet had ever held sway.

Such observations gave Bruno joy at first, but as had been his habit in the last few years, he did not allow the joy any opportunity to take root. He quickly drove it away, giving it no opportunity to bring with it any glimmer of hope to the space of self-imposed silence and control over his own movements that he had created as his area of safety. He therefore did not allow himself the slightest change. The basic premises of the performance, in which he was the actor and the others, be they guards or fellow prisoners, were the audience, remained just as strict. Bruno provided his audience with no movements other than those he had imposed on himself and no words other than those that could not be avoided.

The first six months spent in Jassy Penitentiary brought constant reasons for amazement. This was mainly because of the work, which was so different from that in Galaţi, where the prisoners had made rush mats. In Jassy, they worked in the prison workshops, and Bruno, thanks to his experience of carving wooden puppets, was assigned to the carpentry shop. The workshop was makeshift and the work followed no fixed pattern. Most of the time, they made rolling pins, sometimes wooden spoons, which the management then sent to a state crafts enterprise. The same as the other prisoners who worked in the shop, Bruno sensed that the work was random, without any long-term organization. In a vague way, it justified the sentence of hard labor, but otherwise there were days when there was no wood to work, the quotas changed from one week to the next, more often than not being decreased rather than increased, to Bruno's amazement, and allowed an idleness to which he was unaccustomed. The fact that he was unaccustomed to idleness, combined with his custom of controlling his movements so that they would not place him in any danger from the guards, soon made Bruno the only worker to surpass his quota, without him necessarily wanting to do so. This brought him no praise on the part of the guards, however, and gave rise to sidelong glances from the other prisoners. Finally, one evening, it even brought him a nickname.

It was the first nickname that had ever been applied to Bruno. He had not had one in childhood. His friends mostly called him Matei, his surname, which therefore provided them with a suitable alternative, in their eyes, when they wanted to insult him or make fun of him: Bruno. His unusual first name, which sounded strange not only in his grandparents' village but also in Bucharest, served as the perfect nickname, sometimes provoking laughter that was inexplicable to him, but which also gave him an aversion to the name for many years; for a long time, he had even refused to answer when his parents called him by that name. He had blamed his mother for the name, and he was right: it had been the single concession that the Romanian George Matei had made to his wife, after adamantly refusing even to think about leaving Romania and going to Italy, where Mrs. Matei had, for the sake of love, left behind her wealthy family. And so George had agreed that their son be named Bruno, even if he dismissed out of hand a Catholic baptism, favoring an Orthodox ceremony, out of pride rather than religious belief. Bruno: even if it had been employed as an insult throughout his childhood, it could not be regarded as a nickname, since it was the name by which he was officially known.

Bruno's first nickname came into being one winter night early in 1956, in the large dormitory for fifty prisoners, in one corner of which he had his bed. It began with the scornful words whispered by the very same prisoner whom Bruno had heard telling the story of Vasile Tcaciuc on his third night in Jassy. This time, his whispers didn't tell of any butcher, but made obvious reference to the recent story of a man who had refused to be a butcher, in order to dedicate himself to a passion about which the others could not even speak without bursting into laughter. The whispers arose because of a certain Alexei Stakhanov, a Soviet miner, whose story the press had widely reported after 1945 and who had become a hero of the Soviet Union when, some ten years before he made the front pages in Romania, he had surpassed his quota sevenfold in a single night. None of those who listened to the story that night admired the Soviet worker's achievement. Quite the contrary. Not even Bruno admired it, after listening to the story with his eyes closed, but at first he did not realize how it related to him. But he was saddened after the others started calling him Alexei in the workshop, mockingly palatalizing the "I" to make it sound more Slavic, and afterward he overheard various jokes about that same Alexei, who, according to the prisoners, had infiltrated their ranks there in Jassy. He said nothing, since the plan he had followed for so long did not allow it. Having been overly attentive to his performance in front of the harshest audience, that made up of the guards, he now realized that he had come to ignore the other part of the audience, that made up of his fellow prisoners.

Once you have treated an audience offhandedly, it is hard to win it back. Bruno knew this, and so in the beginning he inured himself to his bitterness, without changing his behavior, allowing things to take their own course. In Jassy Penitentiary, he had noticed another aspect by which it differed greatly from the others: the weltering pace at which prisoners arrived and, even more so, left. At first he thought that he too would be caught up in the welter. The dormitory into which he had been thrust in the beginning was only his "abode" for around six months, as the guard had promised. By spring more than half the prisoners in the dormitory had been transferred to other prisons. Bruno could not help but notice that the penitentiary was mainly reserved for non-political prisoners. In the first part of 1956, of the almost one hundred "counterrevolutionaries" he had found there on his arrival, most of them in his dormitory, only seventeen remained. And now there were only eight in his dormitory. In spring, he was moved to a smaller cell with around half of them. The prison seemed to be dissolving around him. Day after day, he wondered what he was still doing there. Without joining in their conversations, he found out from his fellow prisoners that even among the seventeen remaining counterrevolutionaries not many expected to remain there long; each of them was somehow on the point of leaving, and each was already thinking about the next prison to which he would be taken.

Throughout 1956, taking note of the departures with a certain amount of joy and nurturing the hope that he himself would leave that prison, along with the nickname that had stuck to him there and the jibes to which he was subjected, Bruno could not help but feel a growing amazement: he had passed the half-way point of his sentence, unlike others there, who were still under investigation or at the beginning of their sentences, and so Jassy Penitentiary did not seem a suitable place for a prisoner in his situation, particularly given that the specification "hard labor," part of his punishment from the outset, had lost all meaning now that the workshop had been closed down and they spent most of the time in their cell. Waiting in vain for his transfer, Bruno was forced to concede a theory that had gradually found its way into his mind: through some bureaucratic mix-up, he had been forgotten, and if that were really the case, then it was possible that the day of his release had also been forgotten. In the years before his own imprisonment, he had heard of such things, of prisoners who had been sent to the wrong prison or had been released weeks or months or years late. But he did not allow himself to be overcome by this fear; the day of his release was still years away, and so, accepting his situation and abandoning himself to the care of time and the authorities, he focused his attention on counting the new arrivals and, even more so, the departures, in the hope that the welter would erase his nickname and the highly unpleasant status his fellow "counterrevolutionaries" had established for him.

But an idea, a name, earns the right to its own existence, seemingly independent of the people who come up with it, clinging to walls, to barred windows, to whatever can shelter it for a time, before returning in force to influence the minds and behavior of other men, who know nothing of how it first arose. Bruno was forced to come to this conclusion at the beginning of the following year, after yet another winter in Jassy Penitentiary, by which time the last of his original cellmates had been replaced. A number of "counterrevolutionaries" had accumulated in the prison once more, approaching a hundred, as they had when Bruno first arrived. Among them he recognized no more than three faces, and even them quite vaguely. He had never had any contact with those prisoners, he could not remember them ever having spoken to him. Nevertheless, none of the newcomers called him by his name, but rather by his nickname, as if it were branded on his face, and after they had had time to settle in and quell their initial fears, almost all of them adopted, as if out of nowhere, the same mocking attitude toward Bruno.

Subjected to such unpleasantness, which he had never seen coming, since all his senses had been focused on not creating enmity among the guards, Bruno gave ground a little, he withdrew from his performance somewhat, trying at least to exchange smiles with the audience, even a few brief words. In addition, because winter work had begun in the workshops again, now that there were sufficient counterrevolutionaries to man them, Bruno began to adapt his movements not only to the demands of the guards, but also to the demands of his fellow prisoners. While meeting his quota, he learned to mete out his time in such a way that he would not exceed it. But none of this was enough.

The eyes and ears of Nicolae Maromet had been left behind in a forsaken place near the Danube that Bruno had all but forgotten by 1957. In Jassy, there was no Iosif Lazăr to brandish his fists and threaten Bruno with a beating. The violent interrogations he had undergone in Uranus now seemed to Bruno a story he had learned, but which he no longer felt in any fiber of his being. As for Baba Samca and her ghosts, it was obvious they had gotten lost somewhere on the way, they had gone in the wrong direction, or perhaps they were too busy elsewhere to find that out-of-the-way corner of the country. But while he did not suffer pain in his flesh and bones here, while the cold of winter and the heat of summer were more bearable, while hunger gnawed his stomach more seldom, while the guards' curses and fists were milder, in keeping with the mildness that enveloped the prison, the humiliation he felt swelling in him after a year and a half in Jassy Penitentiary throttled Bruno to the point of tears.

# Chapter 17

IN THE LAST few days he had felt the need to cling to anything but his own thoughts. One afternoon, on his way back from the building site, he had gone into the Cartea Rusă bookshop, where, because the woman behind the counter had allowed him to look through the books before choosing one, he bought a volume which, as he had leafed through it, he was convinced he would read from cover to cover, no matter how hard it might be. It was a book about puppets, about the life of a creator of puppets, Sergey Vladimirovich Obraztsov, entitled *My Profession*. And even if now he knew he could not believe the things written in the registration form he had been shown in the Archives, even if he had begun to imagine that he had probably had some occupation other than the "dishonorable" trade of giving puppet performances on the street, even if now, questioning everything anew, he had returned to the unbearable mist that blotted out his past, something deep inside him told him that his profession, no matter what it may have been, clearly had some kind of connection with that described in the book he had purchased.

Despite all this, the book didn't snatch him from the path of the juggernaut that was questions and anxieties of late. He skimmed whole chapters, but what captured his attention, without him knowing why, were the passages in which the author narrated the performances he had given in Bucharest in 1945 with Mussolini as a character. When he read how Obraztsov had made the puppet that portrayed Il Duce sing an *arioso* that went something like this: "Am I to sing? When

I am in a delirium? I understand neither my words nor my gestures . . . But still I must act! What? Are you a man? No, you are a harlequin! Dress yourself and smear your face with flour!" when he read those words, Bruno was overwhelmed by powerful feelings, which came from within him, but from a place that he could neither point to nor explain, a place that seemingly occupied his entire body, his entire mind, and yet which was nowhere to be found in either his body or mind. Those words spoke to him, the harlequin in the image conjured up by the book spoke to him, but he did not understand those words and he did not know whence they came. "I understand neither my words nor my gestures," said the Mussolini on the page, and Bruno felt exactly the same thing. In the end, exhausted by his own impotence, he decided the feelings must come from the Soviet puppeteer's juxtaposition of two places familiar to him in the past: Bucharest and Italy.

Also to save himself from his questions and anxieties, he bought the newspaper for a few mornings in a row. He had never done so before then, although comrade Bojin had often urged him to. But he read only the headlines; seldom did any article capture his attention. One day, however, a short text about the "magnetogrill" made him think of his erstwhile friend, who, with his strange passion for gadgets, would have been thrilled at such an invention. The apparatus, built in Czechoslovakia, was based on the "principles of radar and diathermy," terms that were a mystery to Brunul. The "magnetogrill" was able to heat foodstuffs rapidly thanks to the absorption of radioactive waves by the vegetables or meat placed on its porcelain tray. It was an oven, in other words, but one which, if you believed the newspaper, acted only on the food, since the tray and the oven itself remained cold. The Czechoslovaks had called it the "magnetogrill." Perhaps at one time Brunul would have been overjoyed to remember such a news item and to demonstrate to comrade Bojin that he too was up to date on the great inventions

of the socialist world. But that "at one time" was firmly in the
past. Comrade Bojin himself was no longer the same, he could
no longer be his friend.

He had bought the newspaper that Sunday too, before
meeting Eliza. He had arrived in the park half an hour early,
and so he had read the headlines as he sat on an out-of-the-
way bench, quite far from the children who broke free of their
parents' hands to chase the pigeons. He had waited for her
outside the hotel one evening a few days ago and had walked
her home from work, but they hadn't talked. They had both felt
somehow helpless, neither of them had wanted to continue the
discussion which, on the evening of August 23, had changed
everything between them. Almost everything. On the way from
the Victoria Hotel to Eliza's apartment, apart from exchanging
a few flat pleasantries, all they had managed was to arrange a
meeting in the park that Sunday. And he had arrived half an
hour early and chosen an out-of-the-way bench, so that they
could talk undisturbed. He then attempted to calm his nerves
by reading the headlines in the newspaper and the weather
report.

The newspaper forecast rain for that Sunday. But the
weather itself stubbornly contradicted the forecast. The early
September sunshine turned the air to a shimmering haze
in front of him, a haze that was then in front of the two of
them, once Eliza arrived and, silent, awkward, sat down beside
him.

"Didn't we meet here so that we can talk?" asked Brunul
after a while, seeing that she was still reluctant to start the
conversation.

"Do you know what Yellow Gulley was called originally?"
she asked, attempting a smile.

He shrugged, rather annoyed. Did she intend to continue
with the pointless pleasantries today too? Was she still of a mind
to avoid the discussion?

"The Elisabeta Esplanade," she said, emphasizing the name of Romania's first queen.

Maybe he would have reacted differently not long ago. He would certainly have reacted differently. He would even have quipped: "They named it after you, in fact." She would perhaps have laughed; she would have pressed up against his arm. That was before so many other things came between them. And so little time had elapsed since then, but enough to change everything, enough to make Brunul now reply in a surly mutter: "At least they didn't name it the Elena Esplanade."

Eliza gave a short laugh and then shook her head for a few long seconds.

"You're not going to let it go, are you? If I hadn't had good intentions, I wouldn't have told you . . . I don't know what goes on in there, in your mind: you were like a child; I liked that. It's as if all of a sudden all those years you can't remember have come toppling down on you and you've jumped from sixteen to thirty-eight in a single day. It's my fault too, but . . . Can't you understand that I had to do it? Can't you see that I did it for your own good?"

"Are we in Yellow Gulley here?" said Brunul, raising his voice slightly. He looked at her fixedly and went on only after she shook her head, bewildered. "Then why do you bring it up? We're in the park. You told me it was important that we talk. I'm here; I want us to talk. What do I care that it was once named the Elisabeta Esplanade?"

"I have the same name, I merely thought . . . You're right. You're perfectly right. Let's talk. We'll talk. What do you want me to tell you?"

"In that file of mine it said that I wanted to flee the country via Timişoara. I've no idea whether it's true or not. But I've been thinking about it for the last few days: it seems strange to me that you want to take me there."

"That's where people leave the country," said Eliza, lowering her voice and gesturing for him to do the same. "Not from

Timișoara directly . . . But we need to reach Yugoslavia. That's the only route out."

"And what will we do there, in Yugoslavia?"

"There . . ."

Eliza sighed, took a deep breath, paused, searched for a handkerchief in her handbag with which to mop her brow. It was hot, far too hot for early September. Not even in July had it been so hot. With languid, drawn out movements she folded the handkerchief, to Brunul's irritation. Finally she put it back in her handbag, laying it there the way you would lay an ironed shirt in a drawer lest it crease.

"I don't have a very clear plan," she finally said, without looking at Brunul. "I don't know anybody over there," she added in an insinuating tone that did not escape Brunul.

"In Italy, you mean. Where, if I'm to believe you, I know people . . ."

"From Yugoslavia you can travel on straight to Italy. You know that, don't you? From Serbia we have to go west, to Zagreb or Rijeka . . . There, we could go to the police and report that our papers have been stolen. You have an Italian name. You can tell them that. I speak French . . ."

Brunul cast her a sharp look of reproach, whose meaning Eliza immediately understood.

"I speak French, but I didn't hide it from you," she said with an apologetic shrug. "The subject simply never came up."

"It never came up for more than a year?"

"Why would I have hidden it from you? Ever since I confessed all those things to you, you view everything I say with suspicion."

Her brow wrinkled, her eyebrows arched, tears welled up in her eyes. Never had she appeared to him like this and Brunul could not help but feel slightly guilty. But he didn't show it in any gesture of tenderness. He merely turned his head, looking at the children in the park, who were running up and down near their parents. Only now did he see that one of the children had come up to him and Eliza, making a buzzing sound with his lips and using a piece of wire with a hooked end to roll a small wheel along the concrete path. Brunul smiled at the child mechanically, as he had learned to do during his first days at the State Puppet Theater. The child came to a stop, frowned, brandished like a sword the rigid piece of wire with the wheel on the end, and then silently ran back to his mother a few dozen meters away. When he reached his mother, the child turned around and pointed at Brunul, who wondered how a mere smile could have so frightened him. But he was familiar by now with children and their odd reactions. But as he was thinking this, he failed to catch what Eliza had been saying and heard her words merely as a continuation of the boy with the wheel's buzzing lips. He turned to her and said, "Pardon?"

"You know very well I work at a hotel. You have to be able to speak at least one foreign language if you work there. You could have thought of that by yourself."

"I didn't think of it," said Brunul, more kindly. "All right, you speak French. How would that help us in Yugoslavia?"

"Ah, yes," said Eliza, as if suddenly remembering what it was they were discussing. "I would be French." She lowered her voice. "I would be your French wife. You would be Italian, I would be French. We could declare our papers stolen. They would check. That's what they would do, but they wouldn't find any evidence of us anywhere. But we could give them your mother's name. They would have to check. I know she's in Rome. She is . . ." She paused, carefully choosing her words, but then shook her head. "She's there. I can tell you that for sure."

"Do you know her address?"

"No."

"Why don't you know it, if we're tourists?"

"We lived at my house in France. In Paris. You quarreled with your mother a few years ago, because she didn't want to accept our marriage. You don't know where she is living now, only that it's in Rome. You wouldn't have wanted to contact her now, but we don't have anybody else to turn to, we're in a desperate situation, we've lost our papers. It's their job to check. And in the end, somebody would contact your mother. They would tell her: two people say they know you, one is your son, the other his wife. They would give her the names. And she would understand what it was about. After so many years . . . She must have tried to find you. It's only normal. All these years, she couldn't have just sat there in Italy doing nothing. She would understand as soon as she heard. And she must have connections. After all, she's an industrialist. She would intervene, get us out of Yugoslavia somehow. In any case, nobody would know that we're Romanian. We have a big opportunity, that's what I think. Otherwise, it's pointless. Somebody has to get us out of Yugoslavia . . ."

"Didn't you say your plan wasn't very clear?" said Brunul, smiling at her for the first time since they had sat down on the park bench.

"Well, it's not all that clear," said Eliza, looking at the ground. "Lots of things could crop up. We have to think about it. The Serbs will check to see where we entered the country, for example. We'll have to tell them how we entered the country. We'll say we're there on holiday. But then why isn't there a record of us at the Italian border? Did we enter the country illegally? No. Complications, you see? There'll be a lot of questions, but we'll have to stick to our story. In the end, there'll be nothing they can do. Even if they suspect us of all kinds of things, they'll not make the connection with Romania. And they'll still reach your mother. And once they reach her . . . You understand? But look, first we have to come up with a story. We still don't know the story, you see? That's why I said I didn't have a very clear plan. If you agree, we'll make one together. We'll prepare everything, the story, the journey . . . I've got money. I work at a hotel, I can even get hold of Yugoslav money, dinars. I

promise. It's important for you to want to do it, to agree to it.
You understand how much of a risk it is, don't you? I'm telling
you all this only because . . . You should know I care about
you. I care about you a lot. I trust you. And I'd like more than
anything for you to trust me."

She said these last words in a hurry, in an even lower voice,
nudging Brunul as soon as she finished speaking to signal
that somebody was approaching. Brunul turned his head and
saw the child with the wheel attached to a piece of wire, who
was with his mother. Or perhaps it wasn't his mother, Brunul
thought; she was too old to have such a small child.

"Excuse me, but I have a question," said the woman in a
trembling voice. She was frowning and Brunul felt slightly
afraid, thinking that the child must have told her about that
smile of his, which, in all likelihood, had frightened the boy
more than he imagined.

"I know you," Brunul heard Eliza say in a surprised voice.

"Of course you know me. Don't try to pretend," said the old
woman in the same trembling voice. "I don't understand what
it is you want from me. Why did you follow me here?"

Only now did Brunul realize why the woman's face had
seemed so familiar. Strada Făinii. The woman in the hat and
black two-piece suit. Her hair was now tied up in a bun. Brunul
looked at the child, but did not recognize him. Children all
looked alike. But it must be the woman's grandson, who had
opened the door to them and told them that they had lived
there since before he was born.

"At first, I really did think that it was you they were
following," said the woman, pointing at Brunul. "But now I
realize that you've got a problem with me, or with my family.
What have I done wrong? My son's an engineer, you know. And
he's a Party member. His wife's got an honest job too. She's
going to become a Party member. Neither they nor I have ever
caused any trouble. My husband was a kulak, it's true, but he

gave his land to the collective farm of his own free will. And besides, he's been dead for eight years. He can't do anything there in the other world."

Brunul wanted to answer her, to explain, but Eliza spoke up first, taking his arm and holding it tightly. She stood up and Brunul was obliged to do likewise.

"All we wanted was some information," Brunul heard Eliza say in a rather official-sounding voice; her tone was completely different than the one she had used when speaking to him up to then. "Don't be afraid. It's nothing to do with you. I expect that one of our colleagues visited you beforehand . . ."

"Yes. He told me that a man might come looking for me and ask me various questions about the street where we live, and not to tell him anything, to tell him only that we moved there three years ago. I've lived there for eight years, since my husband died. I came there from the country to help raise the little one." The old woman stroked the boy's head and pulled him toward her. "I thought," she said, looking at Brunul, "that they must have been talking about you. And I did what I was told, like you heard. I'm upstanding. But I see it can't be you, if you followed me here and . . . We're upstanding," she repeated, and the tremor in her voice turned her words into something approaching an imploration. "I've never done anything wrong. Think about the little one," she whispered imploringly.

"Madam, it's a coincidence," Brunul was unable to restrain himself from saying. "Nobody is following you. Everything will be fine. There's no reason for you to be afraid. We were here just by coincidence. We came out for a walk. I give you my word."

"You mean you're not from the—"

"Yes, we are," interrupted Eliza. "But you're not being followed; nobody is being followed. When we came to your house, we wanted to see whether . . . to make sure that there weren't any problems, that the citizens were following our instructions. The state's instructions, that is. Don't worry, everything is fine."

She smiled at the young boy and ruffled his hair. With her other hand, she almost yanked Brunul after her. Brunul followed her, barely having time to utter a kindly "goodbye" to the old woman and her grandson. Only after they had moved far enough away to talk undisturbed did Brunul voice his amazement.

"Why did you tell her we were from State Security?"

"How else could I have calmed her down? She'd just confessed that she believed we were with the authorities. Didn't you hear what she said? She's lived on that street for eight years . . . Think about it: what would have happened if we'd told her that we were the ones she'd been warned about and she'd put her foot in it by telling us the truth? Can't you see how scared she was?"

Only after they reached the straight road that led downhill to the Foundation did they slow their steps. Eliza remarked that they had no reason to rush like that. When they reached the University, Brunul snorted and said, "Comrade Bojin again! He was the 'colleague' you were thinking of, wasn't he? He made sure he went there before us, so that my so-called former neighbors wouldn't give me any ideas . . ."

Eliza came to a stop and for the first time that day, she showed tenderness toward him, clasping his hand between hers and looking him in the eyes.

"Who else? It's exactly like I've told you already. Do you still have doubts?"

That evening, which was impossible to forget not only because it had been the evening of the great August 23 holiday, after their walk to Strada Făinii and back, which had raised more questions for Brunul than it had provided answers, and after their terrible argument, when Eliza had insulted him for the first time, she had come to his one-room apartment and begun to talk to him: a long monologue, punctuated only seldom by Brunul's questions, and which had lasted until after midnight. She had made no attempt to sweeten it. Throughout her monologue, which was accompanied by detailed explanations, Brunul had scarcely dared to look at her. To save himself from the reality coalescing around him, he had fixed his clouded gaze on the large red vase on the table, in which he had never placed flowers, but which he had kept as an ornament, since he had found it there on the day when he moved.

First of all she asked him to remember the day when he himself had confessed to her. The day when he made use of Manolis Glezos to be able to tell her he had been a political prisoner. Did he remember? That was exactly how she too felt right then. She would have liked to have a Manolis Glezos with whom to make the connection, so that her confession would come more easily. Did he understand what she was trying to say? If so, then that was precisely where she should begin her explanation. From Manolis Glezos. Because to tell the truth, she had never really cared about the Greek revolutionary. Yes, she had read the newspaper articles to him, but . . . The same as with that film, what was it called? *My Dear Man*. Oh, and the visit to the building site at Ciric too, when she hadn't been able to stomach it any longer. None of it had come from conviction. She had lost her convictions long ago, if she had ever had any. It had come from . . . Brunul had not tried to help her as she confessed, he had not even looked her in the eyes to see her bitterness and the tears caused by her shame. It had come from the fact that she had been obliged to act out all those things in front of him. And this was the first difficult thing she had to confess to him: she too knew comrade Bojin. She had known him for a year, perhaps even longer. Shortly after they had become friends and Brunul had started waiting for her outside the Victoria Hotel, she had met comrade Bojin too. He had come to the hotel one day. Her manager had summoned her and, somehow humbled and frightened by Bojin, he had introduced him to her. Bojin had intimidated her even more than he had her manager when he showed her his identification.

She had then spent hours in an office in the State Security building. Nightmarish hours, although Bojin had spoken nicely to her throughout. But behind his nice words, she could sense the threats. In those few hours, he had given her special instructions regarding Brunul. First of all, she had to confess that when she discovered what it was all about, she had intended to break off her relationship with him; she did not yet feel anything toward him. But the secret police had not allowed it: she had entered the game of her own free will and now she had to go through with it to the very end, whatever the end might be. She had had to sign a piece of paper, an agreement, and only after that did the training begin. They had given her a different name: Elena. From then on Elena would have to provide as much information about the "target" as possible. And the "target" was he: Brunul.

Other meetings had followed, usually in a student residence hall, in the doorman's hut, or rather a separate cubicle of the hut, which contained a bed, something that she, as a woman, had found it even more difficult to accept: she and Bojin in that narrow room that contained only a bed. During those meetings, she had made statements and then received instructions. One of her first tasks had been to read him newspaper articles about Glezos and to express her enthusiasm for the Greek hero, which Bruno also had to embrace. At a subsequent meeting she was instructed to take him to see revolutionary films, as many as possible. On this point she could be proud, since she had taken him to just one film; after seeing his reaction, she had avoided taking him to see any more, she had sensed that it was too much, that it wasn't appropriate. What about the visit to the Ciric building site? How could he not have wondered why the man in charge of the building site had been so obliging? What engineer breaks off what he is doing to give casual visitors an exhaustive tour? It had been Bojin who had sent her there; she merely had to show the engineer her identity card. And many other things . . . She had expected him to realize what was going on. She had expected him to regain his memory. But he had preferred to bury, immediately to forget that brief flash of memory he had told her about: the voice talking in Italian. When a man loses his memory, so she had imagined, he would be desperate to get it back. But Brunul seemed to be afraid of it. It was as if he refused to regain his memory.

It was only at this point that Eliza paused, only at this point that Brunul looked her in the eyes. He did not realize he was trembling. He realized only when she laid her hand on his arm, not daring to caress him, not daring to make any other gesture, but merely holding her hand there, in a gesture that perhaps begged forgiveness. But he had pulled his arm away. In that instant he had not been capable of thinking about forgiveness.

She had another confession to make, she told him, looking away, and Brunul felt his spine turn to jelly. Did he remember that she had sometimes tried to make him think about his parents? It had not only been from a feeling of pity, not only because she felt suspicions. In her first meeting with Bojin, in the State Security headquarters in the Copou district, after she had signed the agreement, she had discovered something that probably she ought not to have known. When Bojin had given her her training, he had made use of a dossier which, so far as she could tell, contained everything about Brunul. Everything. Everything that he had done before he went abroad, his years in prison, everything. But the information provided to her had been vague. Bojin passed over many items of information in the file; it was obvious he was reading to her only the things she needed to know. And so she had not managed to find out anything about the real reason for his arrest, but she was convinced that Bojin knew. She had not found out very much about Brunul. But at one point, probably without him realizing it, Bojin had read out a sentence from which it was apparent that Brunul's mother was still alive and lived in Italy, in Rome to be precise. Later, she thought about it many times; she wondered whether it had been a slip on Bojin's part or whether the secret police had decided she needed to know. She inclined to believe that it had been a slip, because immediately after he read the sentence, Bojin had, rather threateningly, insisted that Brunul never find out. He insisted on the story that both Brunul's parents had died in the war. On the other hand, she had in her mind also accepted that it might not have been a slip: it was possible that the secret police, via Bojin, had told her this truth so that she wouldn't accidentally lead the conversation on to the subject of his parents. In other words, so that she wouldn't give Brunul occasion to ask any question. Anyway, Bojin had ended the discussion on that menacing note: she mustn't let the conversation get on to the subject of his parents. Eliza had to nip in the bud any attempt on Brunul's part to talk about his parents, to ask questions about where they were buried or whatever. They had died in the war and that was that.

At that point in the confession, Brunul had not reacted in the way that Eliza had expected. As if washing his hands of the whole story, he had stood up and gone to the window, trying to peer beyond the darkness outside. He had stood at the window for a minute, maybe two. He then sat down in front of her, rested his hands on his knees, and finally opened his mouth to speak, asking merely, "What will we do now?"

# Chapter 18

FOR DAYS IT had been the only thing they had talked about. The discussions around him, in which he did not take part, but which he could not help but hear, made even Bruno forget his misfortunes, which there in Jassy Penitentiary were caused by the other prisoners more than the guards or prison management. Two years had been long enough to convince him that even there, beatings and humiliation on the part of those with the power were still a matter of course, and so too was the contempt he encountered everywhere, particularly aimed at "counterrevolutionaries" like him. The essential difference was that Jassy Penitentiary held mainly non-political prisoners; the "counterrevolutionaries" were a minority, treated rather as transients unworthy of special attention. Although he was now the oldest "counterrevolutionary," Bruno was treated no differently than the others, since the guards seemed unable to remember individual faces, viewing them as a mass. This suited Bruno. What did not suit him, causing him a constant feeling of not fitting in with the others, a feeling he had never experienced elsewhere, was the fact that not even the political prisoners formed any kind of complicity between themselves, perhaps because of the atmosphere of precariousness created by their transitory status there. True, he didn't seek them out; he wanted isolation for himself, albeit of an amicable kind, the same as at Galați, where the others had understood his silences, his deliberate muteness, and where he had not for one moment felt alienated from others in the same situation as he was. At Galați, his withdrawal into himself had not banished him from the group, and his feeling of being part of a collective somehow protected him against the threats that arose day after day, at any moment and from nowhere at all. But in Jassy, this was something he never felt. He often found himself forced to endure the mockery of his fellow prisoners, which in many respects was more painful than that of the guards.

But in the last few days he had come to share in the others' hopes, imagining that he might be one of the few picked for the work gangs. The news had been passed down from the management at the beginning of the month, couched in the usual lofty, bombastic terms: the people required assistance. More and more new housing blocks were being built. Jassy was springing up as if from the soil, and the labor force outside the prison walls was too highly qualified to stoop to tasks such as shoveling rubble into trucks on the sites being cleared for the new blocks. Gangs of ordinary prisoners had already been recruited, eighty men in all, but the prison management was also preparing to reward twenty "counterrevolutionaries": those who proved themselves to be responsible and diligent over the next few days would be assigned to a week's labor on one of the building sites.

Excited by this prospect, more and more of Bruno's fellow prisoners became "Alexeis," "Stakhanovs." Watching as they worked industriously in order to get into the supervisors' good book, Bruno felt vindicated to an extent. All the men who had made fun of him for so long, some of them without even understanding the meaning of his nickname, now proved to be more zealous than he had ever been. Their zeal was repulsive in a way, manifesting a competitiveness that was almost vile: in their rancor toward the next man, if he managed to achieve a larger quota than they, their eyes would narrow, they would mutter under their breath, all but coming to blows. Even among the "counterrevolutionaries," although they saw themselves as so different from the horde of common criminals, fights would have broken out, if those seething with envy had not known that thereby they would have lost any chance of being among the lucky few.

Reconciled with himself, satisfied and disgusted at the same time by the behavior of those who for the last two years had not let up with their stupid jokes at his expense and had made him endure a lack of camaraderie such as he had not experienced in any other prison, Bruno decided not to alter his own behavior one whit. He met his quotas the same as he had always done, although the temptation to exceed them was great. As was his wont, he left the decision in the hands of fate, making no attempt to influence it. And when he was summoned to join the new brigade of twenty "counterrevolutionaries," who were to labor on the building site for a week, he made no outward reaction, although joy filled him for the first time since his arrival in Jassy, the least harsh, but also, in its own petty way, the most terrible of the prisons through which he had passed.

It was no longer so hard for him to endure the new avalanche of mockery to which he was subjected on the night before his first day on the building site. He even smiled when one of his fellow prisoners, whose zeal had failed to win him a place in the work gang, ripped a button off his shirt and then pressed it against his ribs, like a medal, whispering loud enough for the others in the dormitory to hear: "Let us salute the decoration of our new hero of socialist labor."

The others grinned and raised their hands to their foreheads in a salute, but for the last few days Bruno had no longer been affected by such insults. He was now immune to their contempt, and to him the grinning faces were nothing more than rigid, wooden masks unworthy of attention; they were the props and stage scenery in a story rather than the main characters.

He felt himself avenged the next morning, when his work gang was loaded into a truck with a brown tarpaulin and they drove through the prison gates, with an escort of not only prison

guards, but also a few soldiers from State Security. Behind him
he left numerous envious "counterrevolutionaries," who had
been denied even this small portion of liberty.

That portion of liberty was to take on a different meaning
at the end of the journey, however. A four-story block, white
on the upper floors and with a band of redbrick on the ground
floor, surrounded by huge heaps of rubble, chunks of concrete,
tree trunks split and rotted by the rain, piles of branches: this
was the image that confronted Bruno and the other prisoners
when the tarpaulin of the truck was lifted, abruptly quenching
their enthusiasm. Work in the shops and garden over the last
two years had not prepared Bruno for this. A week? The word
that had held such promise now sounded differently.

He looked hopefully at the far more numerous gangs of
common criminals. Under the watchful eyes of the guards, they
were moving away toward other, similar housing blocks. They
were hardier, more apt for such labor. But it was obvious that
they would not be working in the same place; it was obvious
that only the "counterrevolutionaries" would be responsible for
clearing the space that had so daunted them as they climbed
out of the truck. Bruno looked at his arms, as if seeing them for
the first time; they were only slightly thicker and less dry than
twigs. He looked around him once more. A week? Not even
Alexei Stakhanov himself, not even twenty Alexei Stakhanovs,
could have finished the job in a week, thought Bruno. And what
about liberty? The city? Nothing but other housing blocks all
around, some completed, others still clad in scaffolding, and yet
others only half built. Even the penitentiary vegetable patch was
a more pleasant sight. Here, the few patches of grass were gray,
withered, scorched in places, and the few trees that remained
standing seemed crippled, as if after a bombardment. A deserted,
apocalyptic cityscape where, apart from the prisoners, not a soul
was to be seen. But the prisoners were not people. They all knew
that. It had been bawled in their ears so many times that it

had sunk deep into their brains, and now not even they would have wished to encounter people from the outside. But having created that apocalyptic zone, the people from the outside had abandoned it. Only on the following days did Bruno discover, overhearing the resentful whispers of the prisoners who had fought to be brought there to that "liberty," that the people had all been sent away on holiday, for exactly a week, as long as it would take to clear the site, so that they could then return to work in a whole new set of conditions. So much for the portion of liberty. Grayness, surrounded by massive verticals of rectangular cement, higher than the three-meter prison walls, full of rubble, rubbish, dead vegetation, withered trees.

The guards didn't give them any time to feel sorry for themselves, however. Deaf to Bruno's thoughts as to how it would have taken twenty Alexei Stakhanovs more than a week, the guards informed the "counterrevolutionaries" that they had two days to clear the ground around each of the blocks and that they had to leave everything as spotless as in a hospital, as one of them underlined. Spotless meant making a single, large heap of rubble before loading it all into trucks at the end of the day. Bruno's team had been allocated three housing blocks. The plan was perfect and left no possibility of circumventing it.

That evening, after returning to the dormitory, no matter how hard he tried, Bruno was no longer able to turn the others' faces into masks that served as mere stage props. Some of those who had returned from the building site, utterly exhausted, had not been able to refrain from telling the others what it had been like. The envy-contorted masks of that morning were now transformed as if by miracle into faces of merriment, adorned with scornful grins, and from whose lips poured words of mockery. Yet again, for Bruno the voices created a background noise just as annoying as in the past.

The following evenings unfolded in more or less the same way. They returned exhausted, covered in dust, which, during the torrid nights, ate away at their skin, turning into a filthy, sticky film that wracked their sleep. The next evening it would be the same. The sarcastic remarks of the others. Bruno's self-isolation. His bitterness that although he had tried so many ways of surviving undisturbed in prison, nothing worked out the way he had imagined, and his attempts invariably ended in depressing, annoying failure, which, at least for a time, left him no other solution as to what different attitude he should take.

But he did not want to think about any end to this truth. He stubbornly refused to allow his hopes to cling to the day of his release. While all his other attempts to fool the prison walls, not to become embroiled in any conflict with those who held power in the prisons, to avoid even the problems that might arise with other prisoners, had come to naught, his principle of refusing to imagine the day of his release was the only thing from which he was never to deviate.

At least that was what Bruno promised himself on the fourth evening when he returned exhausted from the building site. After cursing the unrelenting background noise of the others' sarcastic remarks, he then allowed himself to think for a few seconds of the time remaining until his release, the two years that still separated him from completion of his sentence. But he then held his eyes tightly closed, clenched his teeth, and in that way refused to allow his hopes to travel farther than that June evening of 1957.

The fifth day on the building site brought a change. It had rained overnight, dissolving the dust that had cracked the prisoners' lips and leaving a cool, fresh taste in the air, which was enough to bring about a change in the laborers' mood, no matter how slight. The morning sun softened the drab prospect of the concrete housing blocks, even invigorating the few tufts of grass that still remained.

Moreover, on the fifth day at the vast building site, Bruno saw the results of organization more efficient than he had encountered thitherto in his two years at Jassy Penitentiary: the areas around the first two housing blocks had been cleared and were now spotless, as had been demanded of them. The last of the mangled, dusty trees had been uprooted and the holes filled in. The chunks of concrete had been broken up with pickaxes. And at the end of the gravel access roads for the heavy trucks there stood mounds of trash and rubble, no taller than a man, but extending for ten to fifteen meters. The area around the final housing block still remained to be cleared, but the experience the prisoners had gained on the previous days and also the air freshened by the overnight rain somehow dispeled the oppressive sense that they would not be able to complete the work on time, which, as the guards had warned them from the outset, would result in punishments. Either that or they would be made to continue working through the night, which in itself was sufficient punishment.

Like the others, Bruno began the day in a completely different mood than heretofore. Everything around him, the atmosphere, the evidently more relaxed faces, created for him a kind of comfort which, had it not been for the guards and the soldiers, might even have caused him to whistle to himself in a carefree way. After climbing out of the truck with the tarpaulin, walking to the third housing block, he himself was amazed at his mood, which was such as he could not remember feeling in all the preceding years. It was as if that soft, refreshing air instilled in him an indefinable expectancy of something pleasant or the fulfillment of a promise. He did not succumb to that expectancy, it would have been a stupid mistake, but nor did he make any effort to dispel the good mood he felt, which was so rare and ultimately so beneficial.

Unlike the other two blocks, which were almost ready, the third had been built but the interior had not been fitted out. The team of "counterrevolutionaries" therefore had to clear not only the area around the block but also the interior. On discovering this, a sense of oppression returned to some of their faces; the work seemed harsher and more time-consuming. But Bruno swiftly transformed his vague unease into a joy that was in keeping with his mood up to then. Along with four other prisoners, he had been assigned to the upper two stories of the four-story block. They were to throw down to the ground chunks of cement and other rubble, which the others would then clear away, piling up mounds ready for loading into the trucks.

From the third floor, where they began their work, there was a broad view over the city. Whenever he went up to a window or out onto a balcony, Bruno lingered for two or three seconds, briefly enough not to incur the wrath of any guard, and, taking deep breaths, he would steal a glance at the view. It was almost as if he had never beheld such a prospect before, because the years he had spent in prison had consigned any similar view to an inaccessible zone of nebulous memories.

He had never been to Jassy before. Not even in childhood, as far as he could remember, had he visited any large city outside Bucharest. But looking at the city from above, in two- or three-second snatches, it seemed to him the most beautiful place he had ever seen. The expectancy he had sensed since that morning, to which he could lend no meaning and which he had been unable to develop, now took on a solidity that he could not have foreseen. The city, at last. Numerous church steeples, countless trees among the buildings, swallowing them up, allowing only their red-tiled or silvery sheet-metal roofs to poke through the verdure. Chimneys. Small redbrick apartment blocks, very different from the ones around which Bruno had been working for the last few days. From time to time a motorcar lazily drove along the main road that vanished between other trees up the hill. And people. Walking down the street, carefree, absorbed in their own affairs. It never crossed their minds to look up in the direction of the building site. They had no idea that nearby there were other people, albeit prisoners, for whom the city viewed from the third or fourth floor of a gray, drab housing block was more important, more beautiful than it was for its rightful citizens, those who walked its streets day after day, without seeing the chimneys and the trees and the hills and the red or silvery roofs.

Gradually, as the sun climbed the firmament, casting varicolored rays of light over different corners of the town, Bruno prolonged his stolen seconds, taking advantage of every egress onto a balcony. He even began to drawl his warning shouts before throwing down the rubble, so that those below would be forced to ask him to repeat himself, thus allowing him to prolong his moment on the balcony. When he climbed to the fourth floor, which provided him with an even wider panorama, Bruno made the most of his weariness, leaning on the balustrades of the balcony for a good few seconds to catch his breath, despite the angry shouts and threats of the guards; it was worth overdoing his exhaustion in order to allow his memory to store as much of the view as it could.

When the sun sank behind the other blocks and the guards decided that work on the inside of the building was over for the day, Bruno grew alarmed at the thought that the third block had almost been cleared, and that the final two days of his so-called freedom would not allow him the view from the third and fourth floors, they would not allow him to breathe in the city from above, filling the depth of his lungs. He began to descend the bare concrete stairs, which had not yet been fitted with a bannister. He was trembling worse than he had on any previous day, not because of his exhaustion, to which he had become inured, but because of the view he was now forced to leave behind. And with each step he took, Bruno sensed how his long unshakeable determination not to form any image of the future, not to allow the thought of his release to burgeon in his mind, diminished with a rapidity far greater than his descent down the stairs. The thought no longer gnawed away at him somewhere at the back of his other thoughts, like a mouse behind the woodwork whose presence is betrayed only by a rhythmic scraping. Not even on the Peninsula, before he rejected any future hope, when he occupied his mind with counting down the days until his release, not even then had the thought taken on such solidity as it did now. Back then, he would not have known what to do at the end of the countdown; he had never considered it. He merely counted down the days, without ever thinking of the end point as a new beginning. But now, under the weight of that view across the city, as he descended the stairs from the fourth to the third floor of the counterrevolutionaries' final block, the thought of the days that would follow that end point swelled, filling his mind, creating images of him strolling carefree and fearless along the city streets, like the passersby who never even looked up at the building site as they strolled through the green parks and over the surrounding hills. The thought then descended to his chest, still swelling; it filled his body, his arms, his legs, causing them to tremble so that only with difficulty was he able to carry on down the stairs.

Descending the final stairs to the third floor, Bruno no longer felt in control of his movements; his bones and his muscles were wholly under the sway of that thought that had invaded and conquered him. Because his mind had been the first to capitulate, he made no reaction to the commotion that had sprung up around him, to the cries of the guards, which all but he could hear. Only when the thought was forced slowly to retreat, unable to hold out against the blows raining down on all the nooks of the body it had conquered, only then did Bruno feel that not only his mind was howling in pain, but also his muscles and bones; his mouth was howling too; even his eyes were howling, as they clung to the last sight of the city from above, to the view from the balcony onto which that thought had driven his body, oblivious to the guards' orders.

His hands clung to the concrete balustrade; he howled, struggled. The guards who had rushed after him finally managed to break his grip, dragging him back to the stairs, hitting him with their rifle butts, kicking him. His mind now freed of the thought that had driven him to that act, Bruno felt the blows, heard the curses, even if they were jumbled together, with each voice saying something different, although each was equal in its fury.

"You fucking moron!"

"Get us into trouble, would you, you fucker!"

"What the fuck, trying to escape over the balcony, were you!"

"Just you wait, you fucking dog!"

He put up no resistance. He went limp. They dragged him by the legs over to the other prisoners. He glimpsed them jostling to get down the stairs, terrified, flinching from the guards, who cursed him and rhythmically beat him as they dragged him. In the commotion, it was as if time stood still; he remembered his mood that morning, which had promised a day better than any he had experienced in a long time, and then he remembered the previous evening, when he had promised himself for the umpteenth time that he would not let himself be guided by hope. And in that strange dilation of time he also felt bitterness that, the same as all his other attempts to oppose the broader history in which he had been held in thrall for eight years, this attempt had ended in failure too.

Only when time began to flow once more did he realize that he was being dragged down the stairs by the guards and that he would not be released to make his own way down alongside the other prisoners. The back of his neck was striking each concrete step, dazing him, sending arrows of pain shooting into his eyes. He gathered his strength and tried to lift himself up, to fend off the blows raining down on him.

And then a cry bursting from many throats, perhaps the guards' and the prisoners' all at once. A knot of cries, a many-voiced moan, accompanied his fall down the stairwell from the third floor. He floated, the same as in the nightmares of childhood, when he would awake in bewilderment, his fingers gripping the arm of his grandfather, who alone was able to save him from his dream fall from the attic of the house. But now it lasted no more than a second. A dull thud. Thousands of sensations swarming into his head, into his eyes, but no pain. And a different thought, the last. He felt it slowly fade from his mind, grow flimsier and flimsier, sinking into the mist that enveloped him without any hope of his resisting it. The thought that here everything came to an end.

# Chapter 19

COMRADE BOJIN WOKE up with the same headache that he had had for almost a week. Torița had been sure it was a cold. She had treated him with sulphamide and cups of hot tea. She had dissolved a handful of rough salt in a basin of hot water, in which her husband then placed his feet. It was a remedy she had employed, most of the time successfully, since childhood, but which this time had no effect. Her husband submitted to it all not because he believed he had a cold, but because he had no mind to confess to his wife, knowing how superstitious and religious she had always been. What could he have told her? That the headache was not due to any illness but self-inflicted, the result of the stupid weakness to which he had succumbed these last few weeks? Deep inside, comrade Bojin was convinced that this was what lay behind his headache. And it annoyed him just thinking about it. His wife on the other hand would have said it was the curse and vengeance of the Lord Above, given all the things her husband had done. Women are weak, thought Bojin that morning, weak and stupid: they're happy to have all the good food their hearts desire, they're happy to live in a big house in the Copou district, they're happy to watch a Record television, but when the time comes to think about how such prosperity is obtained, they start going on about the Lord Above, as if the sky had fallen down on them, they avoid any mention of it, they even make the sign of the cross on the sly.

The unfortunate thing was that lately something had begun to change in him too. He wouldn't go so far as to make the sign of the cross, to visit priests or to whine like Dona Siminică, but for the last month he had started asking himself all kinds of questions, which he had never been prone to do before, he had wracked his brain with all kinds of slippages between the two types of truths in which he believed, in which he had believed his entire life. And comrade Bojin was convinced that this madness in his mind was at the root of his headache.

For a month, ever since the evening when his drunkenness led him to say things he shouldn't have said, he hadn't visited Brunul at home. He had visited Brunul's building site twice. By then Brunul was working with a pickaxe, as he had wished. He had moved on from the stage when they only let him be a kind of general drudge. Bojin had had some merit in that: he had asked the engineer to stop making a mockery of the guy, who was thirty-eight years old and didn't deserve to be a general drudge all his life, and the engineer had paid heed. How could he not have paid heed? He had also paid heed when he had asked him not to say anything about his visits; Bojin had been content to hide behind the engineer's hut, musing as he watched Brunul wield his pickaxe for a few minutes. It was his thoughts that annoyed him more than anything else, and this was why he didn't leave Brunul a note stating the time of their next meeting, although in a way he was even required to do so. During the course of the month, however, he did file two false reports about meetings that had not taken place, in which he declared that the target was developing in the spirit of labor and communist ideas. It was no big deal; he had filed fictitious reports two or three times before, albeit out of convenience, since he had had better things to do and knew that nobody would check on him anyway. But now it was down to the weakness in himself, the weakness that he had been cursing lately; he was quite simply afraid to face Brunul.

He was somehow ashamed. He had been assigned to people so many times before. Oho, so many times! In the beginning, he had worked directly with his targets. Later, as his superiors gained confidence in him, he had created his own network of informers. In the last few years, it was true, he had even given up direct contacts with his informers; he worked only with residents, the higher category of civilian collaborators, who in turn had their own unqualified collaborators who assiduously gathered information. Could this be the reason for his present weakness? The fact that he had been working only with residents for a good few years? Obviously, the residents didn't cause him any problems; they conscientiously submitted their reports, they saluted him nicely, and to them his word was law. When he met a resident, a smile spread across his face when he saw him clutching his hat in his hands and bowing his head; he felt reassured, perfectly safe. Over the years, the residents, all of whom were the same, all of them subservient, had made him forget the meaning of work in the field, of direct contact with a target.

This was why his assignment to Brunul had so amazed him at first. He was afraid that a demotion was in the works. But he quickly realized that on the contrary, the mission proved that his superiors' confidence in him had reached the highest level, since the prisoner who had just been discharged from hospital was a wholly special case, given his strange amnesia, which not even the doctors had been able to fathom. At first, Bojin thought he had been putting it on, all the more so given that the target had been an actor before his arrest, albeit at a puppet theater. Nobody had heard of such an illness—the loss of all memory of the last twenty years. They had all thought that there was a good chance that he was pretending in order to get released from prison. Nevertheless, they had still taken into account that the affliction might be real, especially since that was what the doctors claimed, and so they had assigned Bojin to untangle the threads. And that was what he had done: their man really did seem to have lost his mind. All right, he hadn't lost it completely; he just had no memory of that long period, as Bojin realized even as early as his discussions with him in his cell. Thence their amazement: apart from the two decades erased from his memory, he was more or less normal. Granted, he had difficulty speaking at first, difficulty talking, but that was only to be expected, so the doctors had said. But he wasn't insane.

Bojin had remained saddled with him after his release. He had become an important case. After Bojin's reports reached high-up offices where he himself had never set foot, they had decided to make something of the man. Some bigwig somewhere had cited Makarenko and his method. And whom had they appointed to become a Makarenko in Jassy? Bojin! As if that was what his career lacked. He began to read all kinds of books and typewritten dossiers, all of them deadly boring. Comrade Makarenko may have been Soviet, but when it came to reading, Bojin preferred the newspapers any day of the week, where his eyes were immediately drawn to the latest technical achievements of the Soviet comrades, which both amazed him and filled him with nostalgia: he was forty-six, but had he been younger, he would have liked to be an inventor. But here he was, having spent almost two years coming up with new methods of fooling Brunul, of inserting a history other than the real one into the twenty-year void in Brunul's mind, of transforming him into a "new man."

In the first phase he had somehow enjoyed it. Ultimately, it was a bit like inventing something technical: you take a man who is broken in places, you repair him, not with original parts, but with new ones, better ones, more appropriate to the present context of society, more advanced. The thought amused him. But after almost two years, that initial enjoyment had gone to hell. Maybe because he had been dealing with residents for too long, losing direct contact with the targets, he allowed himself progressively to go soft as a result of Brunul's behavior. Perhaps there was another reason. Who knows? What was for sure was that for a long time he hadn't felt an inventor's enthusiasm.

Ever since he realized that he was dealing with a man, not a mechanism.

For the last month, looking around him, at his large, nicely furnished house in the Copou district, at his Record television, his Strassfurt, Daugava, and Romanța radio sets, at his Pobeda, Iskra, Sportivnye, Kama, Molnia, and U.M.F. Ruhla watches, at his Lyubitel and Zorki cameras, at all the things that comprised his prosperity, of which others could only dream; and not even clinging to all those things, which he could never have possessed if he had chosen a different kind of life; for the last month, he had not been able to find any reason to meet with Brunul. And so, even if his wife Torița stuffed him with tea and sulphamide, even if she put his feet in basins of almost-boiling, salted water, he knew that his headache had a completely different explanation. And he hated that explanation.

That morning, however, after a restless night, he got out of bed in a determined mood: he would repair what he himself had broken due to the weakness that had gradually taken hold of him over the last month and reduced him to that pitiful state. There was no reason why he should put up with headaches and all kinds of stupid pangs of conscience. Ultimately, he was no Makarenko. If it had been up to him, he would have left Brunul in peace long ago. It had been the bigwigs that had come up with the whole charade, and he had been too insignificant a player to make any decisions. He had to do what he had been learning to do an entire lifetime; he had to obey. And in order to do that, he would have to pay Brunul a visit. An unannounced visit. But it was Sunday, and so he would probably find him at home. It would be a visit without any bottle of wine, but there was no need of one this time. This time he would need a clear head, he would have to be convincing enough to bring things back to normal, the way they always ought to have been.

He curtly summoned Torița, who was already busy in the kitchen.

"Listen," he said suddenly, after his wife entered the bedroom, wiping her hands on her apron. "You're always going on about God. Then tell me why the hell this God of yours, if He's so big and powerful, lets children die before their first birthday. Are they sinners or what?"

His wife looked at him in amazement. He had never asked her a question like that before. In fact, he had never asked a question about God before. Whenever she mentioned Him, he had always just told her to shut up. She was afraid to answer her husband now. He was looking at her, frowning, as if he were itching for an argument. And so she mumbled something unintelligible.

"Speak up, woman, I'm not going to hit you."

Bojin was making an effort to keep his voice calm, and so Torița finally found the tongue in her head.

"Who am I to judge the Lord Above? He does what He sees fit."

"Yes, right," said Bojin, nodding his head repeatedly, as if he had been expecting such an answer. "But what about wars? Why does He allow them? And don't you tell me that it's only the sinners get killed!"

"I don't know," answered Torița, sitting down limply on the edge of the bed. "He judges and does as He likes."

Such questions, popping up again in comrade Bojin's mind after the compulsory atheism classes that had bored him so greatly in his first years on the job, would not have taxed even a first-year theology student, but for poor Mrs. Torița they were far too profound, they demanded answers far too difficult, and so she was satisfied at least to have overcome her initial mumbling and to have uttered a few words, even if they left any explanation shrouded in divine mystery.

Her husband too was satisfied with her answers; he had not even been expecting anything more. He gave a mocking smile and then headed to the bathroom, without so much as glancing at Torița. He had not needed his wife to reconfirm his thoughts; he had not needed to include her in the decision he had taken. But it did him good to know that all people, be they employed or unemployed, be they churchgoers or unbelievers, be they women or men, be it he or Torița, were, whether or not they allowed themselves to be riven by uncertainties, subject to a plan from above. Or from on high.

He wetted the soap, rubbed his shaving brush with it, and lathered his face.

The whole of the recent period had altered Brunul's habits, his plans, his sleep. For two, even three weeks, he struggled to hold out against not only the illusions that Eliza constantly fostered in him, but also against the voice that had begun to gnaw away at him inside, a voice that spoke pedantically in Italian, and the memory of which, even if now he no longer heard it, he could not drive from his mind. The words in themselves didn't pertain to him in any way; their meaning was distant. He could not explain in what way "*il marionettista è una sorta di musicista*," but it was not the statement itself that tormented him. What disturbed his sleep and caused him moments of fear and sometime stark terror was the memory of the voice, arising in his mind out of nowhere, superimposed upon the new promise, made by Eliza, who was to take him to Italy, where he was sure he would discover that voice, the same as he was sure that he would discover the whole of the past now obnubilated in his mind. And when Eliza's words had coalesced into a plan, he had no longer been able to control that desire, a desire at times heartrending, to discover his past; he had no longer been able to balance it with the gratitude he had for so long felt toward the Party and comrade Bojin. Despite all the truths that had been revealed to him lately, that gratitude still struggled within him to regain its former place, and as a result of that struggle between gratitude and desire, Brunul no longer had any peace.

One day, he would allow himself to be inflamed by Eliza's plans, he would direct all his hatred toward the lies that had enveloped him for the last two years, he would lay the blame on comrade Bojin, on the Party, on the country to which, at such times, he no longer felt any debt whatsoever. The next day, sometimes even the same day, but a few hours later, he would no longer love Eliza in the slightest, his hatred would turn from Bojin and the Party toward her, who had tempted him with her reckless, stupid plans, thereby giving the Italian voice from his past the opportunity to torture him with questions, to subject him to the almost unbearable effort of creating a setting and a face for it, of trying to remember some other detail, no matter how small, anything.

Comrade Bojin had not paid him any visits lately, however. After the night when he had come to his door drunk, speaking words without meaning, but seeming to lend them some extraordinary meaning, his erstwhile friend had completely avoided him. And after two or three weeks, this had made Brunul feel less and less indebted to him; it had made him seek out Eliza almost every evening after work, it had made him think more and more about her plan, less and less about a future in that city that had not even allowed him to remain with his puppets, in his storeroom, but forced him to work on a building site, doing a job which, even if it was no longer that of sign painter or newspaper-cart attendant, still failed to appeal to him in any way.

He woke up late that morning, having only managed to fall asleep as dawn was breaking. Looking at the clock and seeing that there were still another two hours until Eliza was due to visit him at his apartment, he found no reason to change out of his pajamas. Sometimes he spent the whole Sunday without changing out of his pajamas into his day clothes, and lay in bed forcing himself to think of the times he could no longer remember, trying to picture them in various ways. It was not the case now, however; there was still enough time to change before Eliza arrived.

He made himself a cup of tea; he fried himself two eggs. He looked inside the bag that hung on the back of the chair, the only item of furniture that fit inside his narrow kitchen, and found only a stale crust from the loaf he had bought three days previously. It was enough, however. He needed only a taste of bread. Returning to his bedsitting room, he put his plate and mug on the table next to the red vase. He sat down and sipped his tea. Only now did he realize he was not hungry. He had fried the two eggs without thinking, because that was what he did almost every Sunday; during the week he skipped breakfast, he seldom ate lunch, and his evening meal was the only consistent one of the day. Looking past the vase, he espied Vasilache, who was lying sprawled, with one leg under the cupboard, his bald patch glinting in the spot where his large hat had once been attached. Brunul could not even remember when he had tossed him there. He snorted, thinking of his stupid relationship with that wooden puppet, which had gone on for so long. For a year and a half, almost two years, if he counted the time he had spent in his cell after leaving hospital, in that creature he had found a kind of friend; he had tried to believe in it as a friend. But after he had left the State Puppet Theater, the relationship had been broken. If he thought about it now, it was ultimately a sign of his recovery. As comrade Bojin once said, "Wood is still wood, man; no matter how much you talk to it, it still won't answer you." He hadn't had any "conversations" with the marionette in a long time; his last attempt had been on the evening when he had his first major argument with Eliza. But not even then had he felt close to Vasilache; he had no longer felt Vasilache was capable of answering him. Which is to say, he no longer saw in Vasilache a person worthy of a proper name, but rather he had begun to view him as a lifeless creature.

He stood up and went over to the marionette with a smile

on his face, laughing to himself. He picked Vasilache up, shook him lightly, and said, "Do you feel like talking?"

Obviously, this time he was aware that it was stupid, but it didn't stop him placing the marionette on the table next to the vase, propping the wooden head against the red glass.

"Let's talk, the four of us," Brunul continued, finding the game amusing, "me, you, the vase, and the plate."

He shook his head, smiling. He then raised his hand to his forehead and held it there for a few seconds. He looked up at the clock: there was still time before Eliza arrived. He looked at Vasilache again and suddenly felt guilty toward him. Yes, he was as lifeless as the vase, as lifeless as the plate with the two eggs, which were by now probably cold. But who was to blame? He was, he and his blasted memory. He stood up, annoyed at himself. He let Vasilache hang from his strings to touch the floor and holding the paddle with his left hand tried to make him walk.

"Come on. One step. Two. Three."

Vasilache took three steps, but he shuffled and jerked, and in no way resembled the hand puppets that were so full of life onstage, even if they lacked legs. Increasingly annoyed, Brunul started tugging on all the strings. "The marionettist is a kind of musician: he controls the strings of the puppet the same as the musician, by means of his bow, controls the strings of the violin." But in vain. Vasilache clattered chaotically, moving his hands and legs, but also waving his head in every direction, refusing to resemble a human being, refusing to convey a symphony, refusing to transcend his soulless, characterless clown suit.

"You're pathetic," said Brunul calmly, putting him back on the table and leaning him with his back against the vase.

He bent down and pulled a piece of paper from under the bed. He unfolded it on the table, pushing to one side the untouched plate of eggs and the mug of tea.

"Look," he said to the marionette, "I'm showing this only

to you. I'm not talking to the vase or the plate, but only to you. And I promise you that I'm not going to take them on the journey we'll be making, but I can't leave you behind, helpless as you are, I can't leave you here."

He ran his hand over the piece of paper in front of him, traversing the country from a dot in the east, marked "Jassy" in bold print, to a dot in the west, marked "Timișoara" in letters of equal weight. His index finger then descended to a smaller dot inscribed "Reșița" in slenderer script. The area was circled in pencil and within the circle, beneath a barely visible point, could be descried the name "Naidăș," not in printed letters, but in Eliza's handwriting. At Brunul's request, she had added the place-name in fountain pen when she had given him the map. It wasn't much use to him, but since Eliza had involved him in the whole story with such finality, he had felt somehow awed when she showed him the map for the first time, in her apartment, before carefully folding it up and putting it in a drawer. And so he had asked her for his own map. He had been so insistent that in the end Eliza had bought him one. On Eliza's advice, Brunul kept the map under his bed, lest some other person discover it. The other person to whom she referred was obviously comrade Bojin.

Naidăș, on the River Nera, upstream from Yugoslavia, was the village through which Eliza was planning that they flee the country. In the last few weeks she had assured Brunul countless times that it was the best place for their escape. There was also the possibility of swimming across the Danube, but she didn't know how to swim and since the city lido had closed after the end of the season, there was not enough time for her to learn. And so, according to Eliza, Naidăș on the Nera was the best option for the most important part of the plan: leaving Romania.

"This is the place we have to reach," Brunul said to Vasilache. "What do you think? Do you want to?"

With his right hand he made the marionette nod its head. He smiled.

"That's good. You're more determined than I am. But what do you care? If they catch us, I . . . You'll end up with somebody else, maybe somebody who'll know how to pull your strings. No matter what, you can't lose, can you?"

He placed his finger on the map, tracing a slender, convoluted blue line, like a vein on the foot: the Nera. But his finger turned back from the border with Yugoslavia, moving upstream to Semenic, near the river's source. He held his fingertip pressed against the brown area where he imagined the river began its journey and then moved it downstream once more, passing over the name inscribed in fountain pen. His finger paused at the border, lingering for a few millimeters, and then crossed it, with a kind of excitement, as if having overcome an obstacle, before rushing down to the Danube, where it was unable to continue its journey since upstream the course of the great river lay off the map.

He heard the knocking on the front door only when it grew louder. Without looking at the clock, shaking himself out of his reverie, he rushed to the door to greet Eliza; he did not realize he was still in his pajamas. Only when he saw comrade Bojin in the doorway rather than Eliza did he feel embarrassed; he quickly buttoned up his pajama top, apologized, and invited him inside. After his friend, his former friend, entered the room and pulled out a chair to sit down, Brunul felt the blood rise from his cheeks to the top of his head, where it froze and held him in a vice-like grip. He was unable to rush to the table, grab the map, and toss it somewhere out of sight, not because he didn't have time to do so, but because his legs felt as wooden as Vasilache's, unable to take a single step. It was as if his legs were attached to strings and his marionettist were as incapable of making him walk as he himself had been with Vasilache just minutes before.

Brunul sat on the bed, comrade Bojin at the table. Between them sat Vasilache, still leaning against the red vase. On the plate, the two eggs had congealed next to the stale crust of bread; the mug of tea was only half drunk. The map was not on the table. Nor did comrade Bojin hold it in his hands. After looking at it in deafening silence, as if tracing the same course as Brunul's finger just moments ago, comrade Bojin had slowly, carefully folded the map. He ran his fingers over the folds to flatten them and then handed the map to his host. Comrade Bojin said not a word as Brunul awkwardly thrust the folded map under the bed, where it should have remained hidden in the first place. On his third attempt, Brunul managed to push the map out of sight, in the almost mystical hope that a miracle would occur and it would not be mentioned during the conversation between them. Only now did his former friend speak.

"You wanted to see where you tried to cross the border before your arrest, did you?"

Brunul looked at him: comrade Bojin's narrowed eyes and the beads of sweat on his brow did not make his words seem sincere. Nor did comrade Bojin's forced, crooked smile reassure Brunul. But even so, Brunul clung to those words, seeking a reply among the welter of memories from the day he spent in the Archives.

"Yes," he said. "I didn't mean to . . . I bought the map thinking of what it said in the registration form. I mean . . . It's a question of my past, as you know. I wanted to see Timișoara . . . I can't remember anything. I thought the map might help."

"Via Naidăș? Have your memories come back?"

Brunul shook his head.

"What then? Did somebody tell you you'd fled via Naidăș? It's not even your writing."

"Yes it is. That's what I imagined. I . . . There's a river there, on the map. And it's on the border with Yugoslavia. That's why I wrote it."

"Show me the fountain pen you used to write it."

Comrade Bojin folded his arms across his chest. His eyes were still narrowed. His eyebrows somehow fell over his upper eyelids, pressing down on them, but apart from that he was making an effort to look calm.

"I don't have it anymore . . ."

"You mean you lost it," said comrade Bojin with a forced laugh.

"No, no. I wrote it in the bookshop. I asked for a fountain pen."

It seemed to him a terrible explanation. Maybe it would have worked, if everything had been limited to words only, but the expression on the face of his former friend annihilated it, made it seem like a shameful confession. It was hard to believe that he would be able to hold out under such questions; his temples were twitching and tears were welling up in his eyes.

"You thought of it in the bookshop," said comrade Bojin, shaking his head. "Did the name of that village come to you out of nowhere or what?"

Brunul made no reply.

"Did you ask the woman in the bookshop the names of the local villages? I say woman because it looks like a woman's handwriting. The women who work in bookshops nowadays are highly educated. It's not just anybody who gets to sell books. Or maps. You can't just take a woman who sells eggs, let's say, and give her a job in a bookshop. You need education," said comrade Bojin, raising his hand to his head, "you need a lot of knowledge to sell books nowadays. If somebody asks you a question, you need to know the answer, don't you?"

"Yes."

The "yes" was audible mostly in Brunul's mind; from his throat came only a vaguely affirmative noise, almost a groan.

"That would be one explanation," said comrade Bojin, chewing his lower lip. He then took a deep breath. "What does it matter whether you wrote it or whether it was the woman from the bookshop? Let's cut a long story short, shall we? It's all to do with your past. You did what you did and that's that. Why should we care about Timişoara? Now is now and we're in Jassy. If we keep dwelling on the past, what about the future?"

He had finally managed to regain the tone of voice he had prepared even before entering Brunul's apartment. His eyebrows seemed to release some of the pressure on his eyelids and on his face appeared a few benevolent wrinkles.

"Let me tell you why I'm here," said Bojin, after taking a deep breath. "I want to explain. Lately, I've been having some problems at home. And I must have seemed different to you. Not the same as before, in any case. It was nothing to do with you. They were personal problems."

Brunul's eyes grew wider and wider as he began to realize that Bojin was moving away from the subject that had suffocated him, choking off his words. Could he have gotten away with it? Could he have so easily fooled the man whom for a time he had regarded as his friend, believing him to be merely a comrade from the Party? It was hard to believe; his explanations would not have fooled even himself, but even so, comrade Bojin was now talking about something else entirely, as if the whole business with the map had been erased from his mind.

"That night, when I behaved—" here comrade Bojin groped for the right words, he made a studied gesture of regret, raising his hand to his brow, "—that night when I behaved inappropriately, it was all because of the drink, you understand? It was the same as my birthday, all over again. But in the end, everything I told you I tell you again: you don't need to pay attention to what it says on some registration form. That was in the past, but now you've become a man . . . a comrade in the full sense of the word, let's not beat about the bush. But I think that maybe you misunderstood, because I was . . . You saw yourself what drink does to me. That's what I wanted to tell you. Obviously, what's in the archives matters, but only inasmuch as it lets you know what you were in the past, so that you won't make the same mistakes. You understand? That's all. If you make a mistake once, it can be forgiven, and yours has been forgiven, erased. You've paid for it, and now you have a future; you don't have to pay anymore. But nobody will forgive you a second time. If you make the same mistake, it means you didn't learn anything the first time."

Brunul once more felt a cold shiver, but comrade Bojin, as if wishing to reassure him, fluttered his hand and smiled.

"That's all I'm going to say, so that you'll understand you're all right, that you won't make the same mistake a second time. And that's what I was trying to tell you then and what I'll tell you again now: don't cling to the past, because it doesn't matter. Think of the future. You've got a good job now, on the building site. You're part of things again; you're doing something useful for society. Stop asking questions. Forget about the past. Look to the future."

"Does that mean everything in the registration form is true?" asked Brunul, finally finding the courage to speak.

"The truth and nothing but the truth!" said Bojin, slapping the table top. "I knew that you were thinking of something else that evening. But this is the truth. You saw it with your own eyes in the registration form. Why would anybody lie to you? Who would lie to you? Me? Look at me! We've known each other for a long time: I don't lie to you. And I'm just as sure that you don't lie to me, isn't that right?"

Brunul nodded in answer to this question, which struck him like a blow. He nodded and then looked at the floor, avoiding comrade Bojin's eyes. Somehow, although it was clear to him that his former friend was feeding him lies even now, even now as he tried to prove to him that he was not lying, the contempt he had sensed in him during the last few weeks could still be felt in his words. As he listened to those words, a feeling of guilt made him lower his eyes. Ultimately, even if Bojin had lied to

him over the course of time, he had done him no wrong; quite
the contrary. It was to Bojin that he owed his apartment, to
Bojin his long period at the State Puppet Theater, to Bojin so
many wonderful evenings. He had lied to him, but maybe he
had had to because his job required it. Certainly, his job required
it. Bojin had provided Brunul with a host of good things. But
Brunul had repaid those good things with lies that arose from . . .
From what? Did he really want to leave? His mother might be
alive in Italy; he himself had begun to believe this was the truth.
But did he really want to see her again? Perhaps only in order to
find out things from his past that he no longer remembered. He
couldn't remember whether he had ever really cared about his
mother, even in childhood. She had been cold and uninterested
in her own child. Why then should he flee to Italy, showing
his ingratitude to those who had helped him, even if they had
lied to him? It wasn't at all for a better life: even if he didn't
like working on the building site, he had started to make a life
for himself and whichever way he looked at it, he had no great
reason to complain. It now became clear to him that he wanted
to flee only because Eliza demanded it of him. He had agreed
to it, betraying everybody, including comrade Bojin, because
although Eliza was Varvara to a certain extent, he himself was
in no way Vladimir Ustinenko.

He would probably have continued to think along those
lines, while comrade Bojin drummed his fingers in the silence
that had descended between them, had a knocking on the door
not begun to accompany the tapping on the table top. Brunul
got up, knowing that this time it was Eliza at the door. She
smiled at him when he opened the door, to which he shook
his head, despondently or perhaps pensively. Eliza stood with
her mouth half-open, gazing over Brunul's shoulder at comrade
Bojin, who had stepped into the small hall of the apartment.
She mumbled a greeting, and comrade Bojin went up to her,
ceremoniously extending his hand. Shaking her hand, he

introduced himself, to which Eliza made no reaction.

"I think it's time I left," said Bojin, turning to Brunul with a smile and concluding his playacting with a knowing wink. "When a man and a woman want to be alone, one can't play gooseberry," he added, with a friendly chuckle.

Taking his coat from the peg, he then said to Eliza, "Please, do go inside, I won't disturb you any longer."

# Chapter 20

FIRST THERE WERE sounds. They came from the dense, milky fog that enveloped him. He opened his eyes: still unrelieved whiteness, not a single image. Or perhaps he had not yet opened his eyes. Slowly, after seconds he was unable to count, he began to see. Fields flowing past him, hills, a river, briars, trees, mountains all of a sudden looming and coming toward him, passing him. And a choking bitterness: Italy. He didn't want to go to Italy, they had taken him by force, he hated them. He hated the man and the woman sitting next to him. Who and what was Italy? What was Italy? Why do we have to go to Italy? He didn't want to go to Italy. If he at least knew what Italy was . . . And then suddenly the dense fog once more.

"He's coming around!" said a woman's voice.

"Why is he struggling?" said a man's voice.

"I don't know. Step aside please," said another man's voice.

Hands grasping him as if in a vice.

"It's my job. We're here to guard him. After all, he's a prisoner—"

"You really think he'd be able to escape in this state?"

"I have my orders, comrade doctor."

"Yes, yes. Now step aside."

The words came from the milky fog that prevented him from seeing. He began to understand them once they accumulated in sufficient number to form a meaning. But even so, the meaning was nonsensical; they weren't talking about him. He was sleepy, terribly sleepy. That's why he couldn't see anything, why he kept his eyes closed. He opened his eyes. His mother sitting on a bench seat. Next to her his father. George. George. George and Clara. She was to blame; she was the one who wanted to go to Italy. Italy. A country. A different country. They were in Romania; she wanted to be in Italy. They were in the train. And he too was to blame. His father. He was even more to blame! His father. He hated him most of all. The hatred made his hands tremble, tensing his every muscle. "I've never dared to talk back to you, but it makes no difference anymore. What could you do to me that's worse than this." His father frowned, unable to believe it. "Found your tongue, have you?" "You don't care about me one little bit. You make decisions for everybody else, but have you ever asked yourself whether I care about being a stupid lawyer? I don't want to study law. I'm sick of you deciding my future for me!" "Mind your tongue! There are other people here!" He looked around him, looking to see where his father was pointing. Were there other people? Maybe. He couldn't see them. He didn't care. "I don't want to go to Italy. I don't want to hear about Italy." "What's gotten into you all of a sudden? Have you gone crazy?" "No, it's not me who has." "What did you say!" "It's you who's gone crazy!" A heavy slap from his father, fury overwhelming him there, in the train, and then despair. And then sleep. He was dreadfully sleepy. He closed his eyes again. White. Somebody was holding down his arms, his legs. He struggled to see once more. Through his eyelashes. The large window of the train. Mountains. A bend. The train entering a tunnel. That was all. And then black. Black. White. And then nothing, as if submerged.

Other words pulled him from the abyss, later, much later. He sensed it was much later. He opened his eyes with difficulty. The milky white abruptly changed to a sharp, painful white, which pierced his brain, forcing him to clench his eyelids shut, to shield himself from the so-strong light.

"Keep calm," he heard, "don't try to move."

The words made him try to do just that. But he immediately

felt helpless, it was as if he were moving without moving, as if his hand rose to float in the air, weightless, attached by strings to the hand of flesh and blood that remained below on the bed. He tried to speak, to ask a question, but the words could not find their way to his lips. He knew he had to ask a question, but he did not know what it was, as if the question in itself existed inside him, but not the words to express it. Where was he? Those were the words. He finally found them, they coalesced, they demanded to be spoken. Nothing more: Where was he? But the words went astray on their way from his mind to his lips, they no longer made any sense, he was unable to speak them. A vague answer: in the train on the way to Italy. Where . . . where . . . An argument. A tunnel. Nothing. But no, not there.

"You're in hospital," the voice said. "You've had a serious accident."

An accident. Where? In the train? His eyelids refused to open, terrified of the sharp white light, which might otherwise be able to pierce his brain. Finally, he persuaded them, he persuaded his eyelids, he dared to confront the light. Through the pain that overwhelmed him, he saw a warm shadow, which fought against the sharp whiteness, fending it off to an extent, a shadow which moments later acquired a face. A beard. But then his eyes were no longer able to resist. They closed once more. This was enough for sleep to return. The abyss. This time seemingly deeper.

When he awoke, his eyes opened before he gave them the command to do so. They opened. Darkness. Nobody there. A flickering light whose source he was unable to see. With difficulty he lifted his head from the pillow. He trembled in pain. For long moments he forced his hand to lift itself up; he forced himself not to be fooled by the other, floating hand. Finally he succeeded. He lifted his hand to his head, touched the bandage. He was in hospital, he remembered the voice having said. In hospital? An accident. Where? When? He forced himself to remember. In the train, came the answer, in the train on the way to Italy. But no, it could not be. The train to Italy had been long ago. Not his mind, but his whole body told him so. Long ago, in distant youth. The memories of the journey came as if it were yesterday, yes, it was as if it were yesterday, but a yesterday across which a long, long night had fallen. Something like that was impossible. Something like that made no sense, it was as senseless, he said to himself, as lying in hospital with a bandaged head, finding it difficult to make the smallest movement, wearing yourself out when you thought the slightest thought, struggling against a stubborn sleep that did not weaken for an instant, a sleep that could not be denied.

Bruno Matei. Nothing made any sense. Not even his name. Bruno. Bruno. Bruno. Bruno Matei. His name. He remembered it only when his hand and his head sank back down onto the bed, exhausted. It was as if they had traveled long kilometers in order to return, as if they had run headlong in order to traverse the small scrap of space that separated them from the sheets.

He was ashamed in front of the women. Only the appearances of the doctor with the beard, who had formed the first image he glimpsed in hospital, reassured him. The nurses, each time a different one during the first three days, helped him relieve himself, lifting him out of bed and seating him on a cold, silver-colored bucket that was rusted in places. He didn't want to do what they demanded of him, but he was unable to hold it in, no matter how hard he tried. The day after he woke up, the first of the days when he was unable to hold it in, shame made him beg the woman to leave him by himself. They were the first words he had spoken since he fully woke up, since he first managed to remain conscious for a number of consecutive minutes, perhaps even for an hour; they were the first connected words he had spoken other than "yes" and "no" on the first day. He himself was amazed at how hard it was to connect his words. It was as if, in order to connect them, he needed to make an effort far more painful than the one he had made on the first day, when, under the doctor's supervision, he had slowly moved his eyes, his hands, his feet.

The woman understood his plea only after asking him to repeat it a number of times. She spoke to him, saying words that made sense, but in a strange fashion, as if they kept clashing up against each other, caught up in a battle in which, although it was waged solely in his mind, he was nothing but a spectator.

"It's not possible yet. In the afternoon you'll talk to Dr. Petrovici. He'll tell you what you can and can't do."

Then the soldiers. In fact, two soldiers. One during the day. The second he discovered when he woke up during the night. They entered seldom, merely to cast a look, but it was enough to terrify him. He was not ashamed in front of them. He felt only a fear that probably came from his childhood. He could not remember clearly where the fear came from; he saw only an image of his grandfather pointing at the soldiers from the garrison near their village. But perhaps that wasn't where the fear came from. Perhaps it came from the thought they were there because of him. This thought took clearer and clearer shape and was all the more frightening for being inexplicable.

On the afternoon of his second day of consciousness, although this state was frequently interrupted by sleep, Bruno Matei made efforts to collect his thoughts when the doctor sat down next to his bed. With long pauses between them, he managed to utter another three words.

"Where am I?"

"In Socola Mental Hospital. But not in the . . ." The doctor smiled, raising his hand to his right temple and swiveling his splayed fingers. "You're in the Neurosurgery Section."

He couldn't understand what the doctor was saying, but he did not have the strength to construct a further question that might supply a satisfactory answer. Instead, he uttered another two words, heaving a sigh.

"But why?"

"You fell," said the bearded man in the white coat. Dr. Petrovici the nurse had called him. "Can't you remember? You fell from the third floor of a housing block. You were there with the other prisoners. They had taken you there to work on the building site. Can you remember that?"

Bruno would have answered the question, he would have said no, a single, short word, which required less effort, even a shake of the head would have been sufficient, but the doctor's other words had distracted him from the final question, bewildering him, frightening him more than if the soldier, or both soldiers at once, had burst into the room. But the doctor did not notice and, not receiving an answer, he carried on talking.

"It's normal for you not to remember everything at once. You were in a coma for eight days." Here the man lowered his voice and glanced at the door. "But they didn't bring you until three days before you came out of the coma. If they had brought you in time, we would have gotten you out of the coma more quickly. We're specialists in that area. But they kept you for five days in the prison infirmary, as if they could've done anything for you there . . . But anyway," he said with a smile, "a good thing you came here in the end, isn't it?"

"Prison?" stammered Bruno after a few moments.

He understood the word very well.

"What? You ought to remember that at least," said the doctor, narrowing his eyes. "From what I gather, you were in prison for a good few years. You can't not know . . ."

He looked at his patient for a few moments, as if seeing him for the first time. He got up from the chair and without taking his eyes off him placed his hand on Bruno's forehead, rubbing it gently, and then sat back down.

"What do you remember? Tell me the last thing you remember when you think about the past."

Bruno tried to please Dr. Petrovici, who seemed so friendly

and at the same time so concerned about his condition. He tried to sit up and no matter how hard it was, he tried to tell him about that day at the cemetery, at his grandmother's grave. Or rather, about leaving his grandmother's grave, when, in a different language, his father had spoken to his mother, telling her the following words that he understood very well even now: "*Le cose hanno preso la piega che volevi. Adesso ce ne possiamo andare. Non c'è più niente che mi trattenga qui.*" That seemed to be his final memory, words he understood very well, but which he knew even before he opened his mouth that it would be impossible for him to repeat to the doctor.

"Not yet," said the doctor, stopping him from making the attempt to sit up. "There's time for that yet. Tell me what you remember. Anything, even if it's just a snatch of an image. But the last thing you can remember."

The last? Even a snatch of an image?

"In the train. Talia . . ."

"Talia?"

"Italia," he said. "Italia."

On leaving his mouth for the first time, the word somehow amused him.

"What about the year? Can you remember the year?"

It didn't take him long to think of the answer. He shook his head.

"Can you at least tell me if it was before or after the war?"

"I hadn't been born when the war happened," said Bruno in a jerky whisper.

Or at least that was what he meant to say, but the doctor looked at him in astonishment, asking him to repeat himself. The words collected in his mind, they coalesced and set off toward his lips, but they must have sounded different, so different that the doctor said in amazement, "I asked you whether it was before or after the war. I can't understand your answer."

He was convinced that he had given the right answer, he

had heard his own words, and so he couldn't understand the
doctor's amazement, he searched for the words again, in order
to join them together and utter them once more. The war. To
his mind came images of the garrison at one end of the village
and his grandfather telling him about the Great War, which he
had avoided because he was too old to be called up. "If there's
another one," said his grandfather, ten years after the war, "it
will be a disaster. Look at that lot, look at them: you'd think
they were just playing at being soldiers. But if there's another
war, no matter how mild they may look now, they'll spit people
like pigs with their bayonets. There's nothing worse than war."
That was why he was afraid of soldiers. Even more so now that
he was being guarded by soldiers. They were guarding him in
a hospital. Because he had been a prisoner, so he understood
from the doctor, he had been in prison . . . He still didn't know
what it meant. But no. War was the word he was looking for.
He had to answer the doctor; he couldn't let himself get lost
among his memories.

"I hadn't been born when the war happened," repeated
Bruno.

The doctor made him repeat it twice more. Weren't they
speaking the same language? Bruno said it clearly; he said what
had to be said.

"Impossible," said the doctor finally, shaking his head.

After a few long moments, he asked another question, which
anybody other than Bruno would have found easy to answer.
The Second World War, the last one? Could he remember the
Second World War?

The discussion went on for another few minutes, with Bruno
having to give an answer once, twice, three times in order to
make himself understood. And then, even taking himself by
surprise, he told the doctor he felt sleepy. He didn't want to go
to sleep right then, when not only the doctor's questions but
also his own mind had begun to wrack him. But the exhaustion

he suddenly felt obliged him to say those words, fearful lest sleep force him to withdraw from the discussion against his will.

On the third day he was able to sit up unaided. The hospital room became smaller, so it seemed to him, when he viewed it sitting up. On the fifth day, he was freed of his shame at relieving himself in the bucket, when he was allowed to go to the bathroom by himself. But having been released from one shame, another took its place: on the fifth day, after he came back from the toilet, one of the soldiers guarding him came into the room and handcuffed him to the edge of the bed.

After the first difficult talk with Dr. Petrovici, the conversations became clearer, and Bruno was able better to understand what was said to him and to convey what he was thinking. But even so, he often used different words than he meant to say, and the doctor tried to correct him, providing him with the correct words when he understood the meaning of the whole sentence. Despite these difficulties of communication, however, Bruno discovered that he was a prisoner, that there in the hospital he was serving a sentence he genuinely didn't understand, but which, as the man in the white coat explained to him very clearly, he should on no account oppose. For his own good. For the good of both of them, doctor and patient: he wanted Bruno to remain there for as long as possible, since his condition was almost unprecedented, so he said. The doctor told him he had only ever read about it, in a medical review. He was certain he could treat it, but for that he needed Bruno to place his trust in him and above all not to provoke the guards in any way.

For Bruno, on the other hand, the situation was far more bewildering than it was for the doctor. They had calculated it together: he remembered nothing of the last twenty years, the period that had elapsed since he went to Italy by train. A whole war, more bitter even than the Great War? Prison, years in prison, of which he remembered absolutely nothing? It all seemed like a practical joke, played by people without any pity—this is what he had actually believed for a few seconds, that it might all be a nasty joke played on him by somebody. But his memories, even the most recent ones, were old, he sensed it, and they could not be part of some joke in bad taste. After he realized this, he thought he must be insane; there could be no other explanation. Socola. The Socola Hospital. He remembered from childhood, or maybe from his youth, without being able to pinpoint the memory, that the name was associated with madness. It was a hospital for the insane, this he knew, without being able to say how he knew. He must have gone mad. That's why he couldn't force his mind to remember anything, and after taking account of this possibility, he was afraid to continue taking his medicine. He told himself that it was probably because of the medicine that he couldn't concentrate on remembering anything beyond his childhood and early youth. In the end he had taken his medicine. When he had refused to take it, the nurse had called the doctor. The doctor's face did not lie, what he said must be true: he was in Socola Hospital, in Jassy, which everybody knew was a hospital for the insane, but no, he wasn't in one of those wards, but in the neurosurgery section, as the doctor had explained from the very beginning, it was perfectly normal for him to be there, since he had undergone a brain operation after his fall, otherwise he would have died.

In the first week he hid his fear and desperation from everybody except Dr. Petrovici. He hid it from the soldiers in particular. Or rather from the guards. He had learned to accept that they were guards rather than soldiers. When he remained alone with the doctor, at whose request the guards took off his handcuffs, Bruno did not hold back his feelings. He had even learned to weep in the presence of the man in the white coat, who did not stop him, but withdrew into a seemingly respectful silence, allowing him to exhaust the suffering caused him by his lost twenty years.

Every day, the doctor asked him whether he had divined anything about his past, whether he had gone beyond the train journey. Every day, Bruno discovered a fresh memory, but from childhood and early youth, never later than the train journey to Italy. Every day, the doctor grew more and more puzzled, more and more curious, and the patient became more and more oppressed by his own helplessness.

During the third week, the wound in his head finally healed, but the inner wound gaped ever wider, swallowing the hopes of both the doctor and the patient he was treating. Swallowing an entire war. Swallowing years of his life spent in other places, since the train leaving Romania must have stopped somewhere, and other trains had probably taken him to that destination he had feared so much. Swallowing what had become of his parents. Swallowing his return to Romania . . .

But he was content with the doctor's soothing presence. As time passed, the doctor tried to spend as much time as possible with him, asking him hundreds of questions, but also coming up with hundreds of solutions to deal with his patient's despair. The doctor became dear to him, and every time he entered the room it brought him salvation. It brought him the relief that only his friend, the doctor, could provide.

But toward the end of the third week after Bruno came out of his coma, Dr. Petrovici entered the room downcast, bringing news which, he said, he had been keeping to himself, but which he could no longer avoid telling him. Now that Bruno was physically well, he would have to go back to prison. The doctor confessed that he had made efforts to have him kept there. He had explained all the details of his illness to the authorities. But they had asked him whether he had encountered such an illness before and he had had to tell them the truth. He had never treated such a condition. He had come across something similar only in that medical review he had read, probably as a student, and this was sufficient for him to believe Bruno, particularly given that he had been studying him all this time. But this argument had not been enough for the authorities, who wanted him back in prison. They said they had consulted another doctor, and that in his opinion the patient was feigning his illness so as not to serve out the rest of his sentence. The doctor knew it was not the case, but his hands were tied.

"I persuaded them to keep you separate from the other prisoners, at least for a time. And to let me visit you in your cell from time to time . . . They have no way of knowing. What the hell, not even I would have believed it if you hadn't been here under my very eyes for the last three weeks."

"How long before I have to go back?" asked Bruno.

The news hadn't taken him completely by surprise. In the very first week, his daytime guard had warned him that as soon as he was back on his feet he could expect to re-join his "colleagues," as he had put it, in a rather menacing tone. The guard wanted to re-join his own colleagues, albeit in a different sense of the word. Bruno would have understood the guard's impatience, if he had had time to think about the two different meanings. But he registered only the menacing tone of voice and was gripped by a new fear at the thought of resuming a life that he had in fact never experienced. He had no memory of experiencing it. But in any event he had known that the moment would come. He had hoped that it would be long in coming, but he had known that it would come.

Dr. Petrovici shrugged, downcast.

"In a few days, that's what they told me. They've seen that you're able to walk around and so . . . If only you'd broken some other bone when you fell," sighed the doctor, pointing at his patient's legs.

And even if that sigh did not sound wholly appropriate, not only the man in the white coat, to whom Bruno had grown so close, but also Bruno himself regretted that the other bones of his body had proven tougher than his skull, that his fall from the third floor of a housing block had crippled only his mind and his memories, and not some limb, which would, at least for a time, have enabled him to avoid being sent back to prison, a place so alien to him.

They waited for him the whole afternoon. But Dr. Petrovici was late and the guards had been obliged to phone from the hospital to explain why the transfer of the prisoner was delayed.

It wasn't until evening that Bruno, already wearing prison fatigues, with a hospital gown on top, jumped out of bed and rushed to greet the doctor.

"I almost missed it," said the doctor who had treated him for almost four weeks.

"They've been about to leave twice."

"I almost missed giving you this, not your departure," said the doctor, holding up a bag for Bruno to see. "I knew they wouldn't leave; I had a word with the right person. I had to be able to give it to you myself . . . you'll see what it is."

He thrust his hand in the bag and with a broad smile pulled out a wooden puppet.

"How about that?" he said, shaking the doll by the head, from which dangled some strings to whose ends was attached a cross-shaped wooden paddle. "What do you have to say about this?"

Bruno looked at it carefully. The head looked too big for the body and was half-covered with a black mask. Black tufts of hair poked from beneath a long pointed hat. It was wearing a strange costume: baggy white trousers bunched at the knees, and a white shirt with a brown girdle. Should it mean something to him? After his initial smile, the disappointment on the doctor's face confirmed that his expectations had been different.

"It's yours. It was among your personal effects, which they kept for you after you went to prison. I had a hell of a time obtaining them. I don't know where they're from or what you did with them in the past. I don't have access to such information. And even if I did, I wouldn't be able to tell you anything about it. Every prisoner has personal effects, prior to going to prison. When I saw how your condition affects you, I asked for your personal effects. I'd hoped to be able to give you them sooner; maybe they would've helped you. But it took a long time, I don't know why. It was only yesterday that I received confirmation. And today I had to haggle for them; they'd changed their minds, said they wanted to give them to you. In the end I obtained permission. I hoped they would be useful to you in some way."

"They?" asked Bruno, pointing at the doll.

"Ah, yes, there's something else. I almost forgot."

From his breast pocket he took a piece of paper and handed it to Bruno, but without the same smile as when he had taken the doll out of the bag.

"I expect it won't mean anything to you. Nonetheless, it's your handwriting. That's what they told me . . . I think I'm allowed to tell you. It's a page from a manuscript that was confiscated from you when you were arrested. That's all I was able to obtain, just one page. But maybe it will help you. I've read it and it's . . . I know it's hard for you to read now, but in time you'll be able to again. Read this. What you wrote is wonderful. You'll see: it's to do with this marionette."

Bruno took the piece of paper. There was a rubber stamp in one corner. The page was filled with handwriting. Crowded letters. They said nothing to him. But unlike when he received the doll, now he was filled with a certain amount of excitement. He couldn't read what he had written, but the thought that he had written it, during his past life, which was now enveloped in the mist, was enough to make his hand tremble as he held the page.

"Does it say anything to you?" he heard Dr. Petrovici say in an impatient voice.

"No. But if it's my writing . . . Can I keep it?"

"Of course you can. The marionette too."

The doctor then struggled to put the marionette back in the bag and handed it to Bruno.

"They promised me you could keep it with you in your cell. I don't know how I managed to persuade them, but in the end I did. Maybe in time you'll remember. Try to read the page. They're your words, your thoughts. They'll have to say something to you eventually."

When the guards came in, Bruno was forced to give them the puppet and the piece of paper. They unshackled him from the bedstead, took off his hospital gown, and then cuffed his hands behind his back. Without giving him very much time to say goodbye to Dr. Petrovici, they took him down to the hospital yard and put him in the back of the van that had been waiting there for him half a day.

At the end of a not very long journey, during which he tried to allay his fears by listening to the rumble of the engine, the voices of the people outside, the motorcar horns, and the croaking of the crows, one of the two guards informed Bruno with a mocking smile that he had arrived home at last. Without making any reply, Bruno climbed out of the van and found himself in a narrow courtyard surrounded by high concrete walls topped with barbed wire, which he had never before seen in his life.

# Chapter 21

THERE WERE MOMENTS when he felt the urge to see comrade Bojin, even to go to his house and confess everything to him. One night, after hours of sleeplessness and cold sweats, he got out of bed, despairing, sick of all the anxiety, and ripping off his pajamas he got dressed. But he only got as far as the door, standing for long, exhausting moments with his hand on the door handle, trembling. He couldn't do it; he couldn't do that to Eliza.

There were other moments when he catalogued in his mind all the lies that his former friend had fed him, forcing himself to hate him, even to despise him deeply for it. One afternoon he even sat down at the table and began to list them on a piece of paper. Number one: the national subscription ticket. Number two: the death of his parents in a bombing raid. Number three: the house on Strada Făinii. Number four: the job he supposedly had had in Jassy. Number five . . . He stopped at this point. There were too many lies, they were too entangled with one another, he was unable to list them in order, and indeed he no longer even knew which were the lies and which were not. In the end, everything, absolutely everything was a lie, not only the things he had written down or wanted to write down on that piece of paper that now lay crumpled in the bin. But even so, precisely because they were too many, precisely because they were so tangled up with one another, precisely because together they made up a kind of truth or at least sounded like the truth when they had been served up as explanations by comrade Bojin, he was no longer capable of being outraged by them.

Eliza? Comrade Bojin? He felt, and this was the final argument, which he put to himself whenever his thoughts and his loneliness overwhelmed him, he felt closer to Eliza. True, he was no longer consumed with the longing he had felt at first, when he would fall asleep thinking of the moments he had spent with Eliza. Those beautiful thoughts had contracted into a not-very-distant memory, which now bothered him. Ultimately, she had lied to him too. Ultimately, this was the source of his depression: How could he know beyond all else that she had told him the whole truth? Ultimately, and here his depression became thornier, what if Eliza had never loved him, but was now merely using him, the same as comrade Bojin had used him, albeit for a different purpose? But even so he felt closer to Eliza. At least because with her it was the questions that caused depression, whereas with Bojin it was the answers that hurt.

Eliza. In the days that followed, he did not confess to her that comrade Bojin had seen the map on which she had written Naidăş in fountain pen. Nor did she bring up the unfortunate encounter with comrade Bojin in Brunul's apartment. It was a subject that needed to be set aside. Perhaps they would discuss it later, once Naidăş had become nothing but a memory.

More than a week after that Sunday, at the end of his day's work on the building site, Brunul had been informed that somebody was waiting for him at the engineer's hut. Eliza embraced him. To the morose engineer her broad smile must have suggested nothing more than that she was happy to see Brunul. But Brunul himself could not help but notice the worry in her eyes. A few minutes later, after Brunul had handed in his overalls, once they were out of earshot, holding Brunul tightly by the arm, Eliza almost groaned the words she had been bursting to say to him.

"Why didn't you tell me that Bojin had seen the map?"

Brunul stopped walking for a moment, but then let Eliza

drag him onward, continuing what had to appear to be nothing but a lovers' stroll.

"Nothing happened," he said, but it was clear that Eliza was not to be reassured by such an explanation.

"Nothing? I had a two-hour talk with Bojin in a hotel room today, during my working hours. You can imagine what my colleagues must have thought, what with me and a strange man in a room together for two hours. Nothing, you say. For two hours he asked me a thousand questions about you. At first I thought he knew about everything we've planned. He told me he recognized my writing . . ."

"I told him at first that it was mine, then that it was the woman from the bookshop's. In fact he was the one who suggested it and I agreed."

It was a gloomy afternoon. Crows croaked as they flew overhead, and heavy clouds were gathering, making the warm air of that early October suffocating. Beads of sweat trickled down Eliza's brow, perhaps because of the stifling air, perhaps because of the tension that had been building up in her throughout the day and which she was now releasing. She stopped, took a handkerchief out of her handbag, dabbed her forehead for a long moment, and then fluttered her other hand in front of her mouth. Having caught her breath, she continued speaking.

"I told him it was my writing."

"What!"

"I didn't have any choice," she said, casting Brunul a reproachful look. "You didn't tell me anything. I didn't know what you had said to each other. But it's better this way, I now think . . . It's better I told him. Things add up this way."

"How do they add up?"

"I told him you came to me with the map and that you wanted to find out where you'd tried to cross the border the first time. Not the first time, obviously, but where they'd told you you'd tried to escape. And then I told him that I'd drawn that place on the map because I knew about it from a cousin of mine. Which is in fact the truth," she said. "I then had to tell him all about my cousin . . . In the end, I convinced him. But I told him so as not to create bigger problems. Much bigger ones."

The confusion on Brunul's face made her shake her head bitterly.

"In a way, I revealed to him or . . . or at least I suggested to him a few things about our plan."

Their plan. Her plan. All the way to Red Bridge, and then along the narrow streets flanked by small cottages with gardens full of poultry and dogs that groggily poked their heads through the gaps in the fence pales before withdrawing so that they could bark freely at the passing strangers, cottages that didn't seem to belong to the city Jassy, Eliza told him her plan in detail for the first time. Their plan.

First of all, her story took him to a village in Bukovina. The village where she had been born. For an instant Brunul stopped walking; he realized that they had never before spoken about Eliza's past. It was as if his own past were so tangled, so shrouded in mist, that he would have felt guilty if he had questioned her about her past. Since they met, Eliza had told him two or three times that she was going "to the country, to her parents,'" and he had been satisfied with that explanation, without feeling the need to know any further details. They went on their way, amid the clucking of the poultry and the barking of the dogs, and she told him about a cousin of hers, with whom she had grown up and who was very close to her. Things had changed, the times had changed. She had come to Jassy and he had gone all the way to Timişoara, where he had found a job at the Banat sugar factory. They met once or twice a year in their native village, when they went back to visit their parents, at Christmas, at Easter, when the families gathered to celebrate together. Not long ago, back in the village her cousin had made a confession to her, after having too much to drink. That confession had remained seared into her memory: he had tried to flee the country with two friends. Via Naidăş, where they too planned to cross the border. Her cousin and his friends had planned their escape thoroughly; he even dreamed about the exact route at night. But in the end his heart had not let him. That was what he had told her, on the day before the planned escape, his heart had not let him. He would never have seen his family again; he would have had to forget about Easter and Christmas in his native village. He couldn't do it. They had prepared everything, but on the day of his escape, he had told his friends he was staying behind. The other two had managed to cross the border, however. Naidăş was a good place for it. They had crossed without problems. Her cousin later found out they had succeeded, after the secret police started investigating his two friends' relatives. But the two hadn't escaped in the end. They had ended up in prison, because the Serbs had caught them and sent them back over the border. They hadn't concealed the fact that they were Romanian; that had been the problem with their plan. They hadn't had anybody to help them get out of Yugoslavia. That had been their second major mistake. One that Eliza and Brunul would not make. Because Brunul had somebody in Italy. And not just anybody; his mother was there, she must be an influential person, if she ran a business, she would get them out of Yugoslavia, solve all their problems. The main thing was getting out of the country, and Naidăş was the best place for that. In the first phase, Eliza's cousin, whom she'd last met just a few months ago, back in their native village, would help them get out of the country. He'd promised. The plan was therefore simple: as soon as they were able to travel to Timişoara, she would telephone her cousin, but without giving any details; they had settled on this the last time they met. She would merely telephone to say she was coming to Timişoara. After that everything would go smoothly. She hadn't told

Brunul all these details before now in order not to burden him and cause him additional worry. He didn't have anything to worry about. She would deal with everything. Hadn't she asked him to leave everything up to her?

By now they had passed the Palace of Culture. So caught up were they in Eliza's story that they did not notice when the clucking and the barking gave way to the din of the city.

"And you told Bojin all this? Why?" asked Brunul at last.

"Obviously I didn't tell him all this. But I had to tell him that I'd found out about Naidăş from my cousin. I had to allay his suspicions, didn't I? I didn't tell him my cousin had wanted to escape, but just that he knew about that place, that in Timişoara he'd heard about people who'd crossed the border at Naidăş. I didn't tell him the story that I've just told you. A lie isn't any good unless it's based on at least half a truth . . . But even so, the problem is that I've drawn his attention to it. In fact, if I think about it, it wasn't me, but you, when you let him see the map."

Brunul shrugged, half apologetically, half annoyed at being blamed. But he didn't say anything, since her eyes were not accusing; it even seemed to him for a moment that he recognized in her gaze the feelings that she had confessed to him recently.

"We have to hurry," Eliza said.

Brunul looked up at the sky. The clouds were now lower, darker, and beyond the housing blocks distant flashes of lightning, as yet unaccompanied by thunderclaps, heralded a downpour. He lengthened his stride.

"I don't mean now," said Eliza with a smile, but then looked up at the sky and added, "Now too, of course, otherwise we'll get soaked. I don't have an umbrella. When I said we have to hurry, I meant something else . . ."

Brunul looked at her, not understanding what she meant.

"I meant our departure," she explained. "We have to hurry. It's October already. We can't cross the border in the snow. They'll see our footprints and we'll get caught straightaway. Also,

I don't want to give Bojin too much time to think. I've already drawn his attention to it. If we delay much longer, things could get very complicated. Two weeks, three at the most. Although I'd prefer even sooner. But whatever happens, we can't let October pass."

Brunul continued to hurry in silence. He even quickened his steps, dragging her behind him so that she was almost forced to run. A long silence. Hurried footsteps. Deeper and deeper breaths, quicker and quicker breaths. Near a tram stop, he let go of her arm and broke into a run, all but throwing himself at the tram that had just stopped and holding the doors open until Eliza caught up with him. The tram had started moving when Eliza climbed aboard, clinging to Brunul's outstretched arm. They then both found a seat. Brunul had somehow stupidly hoped that Eliza's words would be left outside, that they would be washed away by the rain, through the cracks in the asphalt, down the drain, but as the tram doors closed, he realized that despite his running, the words had followed him and now rang in his ears like a gong.

Two weeks. Three at the most.

Very few Yugoslav dinars. Two hundred German marks. A hundred dollars. Eliza had obtained the money from the hotel. Foreign tourists had occasionally stayed at the hotel, and when it was possible, when the guest didn't appear to be a danger, money could be changed on the sly. Unfortunately, although there had been a few Yugoslav guests in recent months, most of them had been officials; it was impossible to change money with them. She had received the small change in dinars from a German journalist, who had also given her the deutschmarks. He had traveled through Yugoslavia and gave her the small change without asking for anything in return, just because he liked her and the subject had come up. She had asked him what money he had apart from deutschmarks and he had taken a handful of coins out of his bag, a mixture of Czechoslovak korunas and even Russian kopecks, and he had let Eliza choose whichever she liked.

Then a kilogram of pepper. It wasn't sold by the kilo, but in small bags of a hundred and fifty grams. She had bought seven hundred-gram bags and six fifty-gram bags and then emptied them all into a bigger bag. Brunul was surprised at the pepper, but Eliza explained that it was for the dogs. It had been part of her cousin's preparations. A kilo of pepper throws the border guards' dogs off the scent. The opposite of Hansel and Gretel: a trail of pepper that nobody can follow.

A thick black coat for Brunul to replace his beige raincoat. As black as night. They had scoured the shops for three days in search of it. Eliza had become exasperated and at one point come up with the idea of dyeing a blue coat, but finally, in a small local shop in an outlying district, they had found that long black coat. Eliza promised to shorten it to ten centimeters above the knee, sewing a new hem, so that if they had to run Brunul wouldn't trip over it. And it was a foregone conclusion that they would have to run.

Every afternoon after he finished work and when Eliza was not on duty at the hotel, Brunul silently, docilely accompanied her on her almost maniacal expeditions to gather all the things they needed for their departure. He followed her and in his mind he cursed his inability to tell her what he really thought. And what he really thought was that things had gotten out of control; that their fleeing would come to no good; that the world on the other side could not be nicer than the one here; that comrade Bojin, for all his lies, had helped him more than his own mother ever had, his mother, whom Eliza now viewed as their salvation and whom in her mind and often in her words she portrayed as a kind of Saint Sunday from the children's fairy tale. A gentle, warm, loving Saint Sunday, driven by desperate love for her son, who, living on the other side of the River Saturday that was as wide as Yugoslavia, would send her dog Swift-as-the-Wind-Heavy-as-Stone to rescue him from his misfortune. A Saint Sunday in whom Brunul did not believe any more than he believed in other fairy-tale godmothers, since she did not convey to him any feeling of real hope or faith across the mist that lay between him and his distant childhood. She did not convey to him any face, but only an outline behind his father, which only seldom spoke, uttering a word or two in Italian, refusing to learn Romanian even to talk to her own son.

This is what Brunul believed as he followed Eliza, silently, lacking the courage to give voice to such thoughts or deeming it pointless. And when she informed him, without asking his opinion, that the date of their departure from Jassy would be Friday, October 23, that they would spend the Saturday night in Timişoara and cross the frontier the next day, since these were the only two consecutive days off that Eliza had been able to obtain at work, it had become clear to Brunul that his life was going to change completely. It became clear to him that there was nothing he could do, that things had already been decided: they would soon board a train, leaving behind forever the only city he had known in his adult life, the only place that he had been accustomed to regard as home.

He met comrade Bojin in the week before their departure. It was a Tuesday. Bojin was waiting for Brunul when he left the building site. His manner was friendly, as if everything between them had been resolved since the Sunday visit he had paid him. Brunul would have liked either to have met him earlier or not to have met him at all before the departure. But it was not until now that he realized there had always been a problem to their relationship, one he had never been aware of, or which at least he had never viewed as a genuine problem: namely, their meetings had always been arranged by comrade Bojin. Even if Brunul had perhaps sometimes felt the need to see comrade Bojin, especially in the period when he regarded him as a real friend, he had viewed the manner of his meetings with Bojin as a given; he had never thought that he might get in touch with his friend, or rather his former friend. However, now that the preparations for departure had advanced so far, on a number of occasions he greatly desired to see Bojin. But all he knew was where Bojin lived, and to visit him at home seemed inappropriate. Moreover, he realized that such a visit would have raised a number of questions. Even so, he would have liked to see him, to see his face, to try to discover whether all the illusions he had nurtured regarding Bojin might be salvaged in some way, by some friendly expression on Bojin's face, for example; to try to discover whether all the fears he had harbored about him might not somehow be dispelled by a smile on the part of the man on whom his life since the accident had depended so much. But in the final week before the departure, when it had become more than clear to Brunul that there was nothing more to be done, it was precisely a potential friendly smile on Bojin's part that made Brunul not wish to see him. Not because it would have made him change his mind, since it was too late for that, and in any event, even if he had changed his mind, it was not up to him, but rather because it would have made him regret his departure even more, it would have made him hate himself even more for not finding within himself the strength of a Dr. Ustinenko or a Manolis Glezos, characters who, even if they had enabled others to manipulate him, still remained inside him, sometimes stirring up his feelings and making him feel small before their greatness, small and power-less, cowardly even.

A warm, friendly smile. And an embrace from comrade Bojin, immediately after they met that Tuesday afternoon. Then, a surprise: his former friend led him to an elegant black chauffeur-driven car.

"I have a short trip to make, and so I decided to take you for a ride in this beauty," said Bojin, spreading his arms wide to indicate the black motorcar. "Coming?"

He knew that Brunul would come. The question was merely a polite touch aimed at easing the strain that had affected their friendship of late. Even if he had been due to meet Eliza, Brunul would not have declined, especially now, when he had to be more careful than ever when it came to comrade Bojin. But Eliza would be working late, into the night, since on November 1 a new hotel was going to open in Jassy: the Continental. Frightened at the prospect that their plans might be affected or even that her two days off might be canceled, Eliza told him that her managers had decreed overtime for all the workers at the Victoria, since they would be in socialist competition with the new hotel when it opened and they couldn't afford to be outdone.

Brunul climbed into the back of the motorcar. Comrade Bojin sat down beside him, having climbed in by the door on the other side. Before driving away, the chauffeur respectfully but mechanically saluted Brunul, proof that he had no idea who he was; it would seem that comrade Bojin had not told the chauffeur anything.

"What do you think of her?" Bojin asked Brunul and then bumped up and down on the soft seat a few times. "Comfy, eh? It's not mine, but if I could afford a car, this is the one I'd get: a Pobeda M20. There's nothing can beat it. I don't mean overall, because overall it's nothing special, but as far as the suspension goes. You can't even feel the road. Three gears, plus reverse. Four cylinders. Two liters. It'll do eighty, won't it?"

Brunul was taken aback by this question, but immediately saw that it was in fact addressed to the chauffeur.

"About eighty. The clock goes up to eighty kilometers an hour, but I've never done more than seventy, comrade. Best not to strain the engine."

"You don't need to do more than that. Does it consume more than twelve liters?"

"Never. Twelve liters per hundred kilometers, comrade. That's what it says in the manual."

Brunul sensed that the conversation was for his benefit; he

also sensed that he ought to make some appreciative exclamation or at least nod his head, but it all sounded so foreign to him, and the words, particularly Bojin's, conveyed an enthusiasm that meant nothing to him. And so Brunul smiled at his former friend, and Bojin smacked his lips, satisfied at the reaction.

"You see? I'm casting pearls before swine."

Bojin then nudged him and winked, to show he was joking.

Before they reached the road through the Păcurari district that led to Lețcani, comrade Bojin cast another few pearls before swine, telling Brunul about the rocket the Soviets had sent to the Moon, a truly epochal event, since it had touched down on the surface of the heavenly body in mid-September. He would have told him about it before now, but they had only met once since then, and even that meeting had been interrupted by "the lady comrade," and here he winked once more. Coming back to the rocket, he told Brunul about how for all eternity there would be flags on the surface of the Moon, with the symbol of the Soviet Union and the words "Union of Soviet Socialist Republics. September 1959." Only now did Brunul look at him closely, troubled by a question.

"Was it a rocket without people in it?"

"That's a good one," said comrade Bojin with a shrug. "Now you want people in it."

"Then how did they leave those flags on the Moon?"

Comrade Bojin looked at him steadily for a few moments and raised his hand to his cheek.

"In the newspaper it didn't say. But they must have robots or something. They left them there somehow. They're clever, after all."

By now they had left the Păcurari district. There was nothing but fields around them. A long period of silence. It was not at all usual that the garrulous comrade Bojin, who normally lost no opportunity to tell Brunul about what he had read in the newspaper, making his head spin with all kinds of uninteresting technical details and asking him question after question, now found nothing to say to interrupt the unpleasant rumbling of the car engine. Only when the motorcar finally came to a stop in Lețcani did comrade Bojin break his silence, pulling a file from his bag and saying, "I'll be back in five minutes," and adding with another wink, "You'll wait, won't you?"

Although the playful question had been addressed to Brunul, it was the chauffeur who answered: "But of course, comrade. Aren't I driving you?"

Bojin climbed out of the car, without bothering to explain to the chauffeur that he was joking. Brunul spent the next half an hour in the car, which was parked next to a sidewalk. He peered along the side street down which comrade Bojin had vanished, from time to time looking at his watch, a Pobeda make, the same as the car, the watch that his former friend had given him a long time ago. All the while he tried not to think of anything; he tried not to think of either Eliza or the departure, which, if her job didn't get in the way, would occur four days thence; he tried not to think of why comrade Bojin had brought him on that trip out of town, although from the very beginning this question had taken precedence over all his other thoughts. He tried to count the number of houses on the side street. He then turned his attention to the tiles on a roof, constantly losing count and starting all over again. When at last comrade Bojin appeared in the distance, he started counting the number of steps he took on his way to the car, looking only at his feet. But he had gotten no further than ten when another thought interrupted him: after he left the country, this was the only memory he wished to preserve of his former friend, a memory of approaching feet without a face, without lying smiles, without words that concealed different meanings. Nothing but feet that trod the ground the same as his or anybody else's.

"Sorry it took so long," he apologized as he climbed back in the car.

"Never mind, comrade, I'm used to waiting, it's part of my job," said the chauffeur, although Bojin had not been addressing him this time either.

The journey back was shorter, since they didn't have to cross the city from one end to the other to reach Brunul's building site this time. Not even now did comrade Bojin see fit to ask Brunul about the banal details of his life, in which he had always been so interested before. Nor did he mention their last meeting. Without much enthusiasm he tried to break the silence with a few jokes, illustrating them with gestures. Giving a forced laugh, and as if talking to himself, he spoke of an American rocket, which, unlike the Soviet Moon rocket, had been a failure. The Americans were a joke: their Polaris rocket, which wasn't even interplanetary, but just a submarine-launched missile, had broken up after jettisoning its second stage and fallen into the ocean near Cape Canaveral. But Brunul didn't join in the laughter, since comrade Bojin declined to develop the subject further, but merely grinned scornfully for a long part of the way, which said a lot about his opinion of the Americans.

The car finally came to a halt in front of Brunul's building, somewhat to his surprise, since, although he had seen the direction in which it was heading, he had not been expecting the meeting to be purposeless and without any concrete discussion. Not even when he heard Bojin give the chauffeur directions to his building had he thought the car would stop there. Nonetheless, he climbed out of the car, concealing his amazement. When he saw his former friend climb out of the car too, for a moment he thought of an explanation, in alarm: Bojin would come up with him to his apartment and the real discussion would take place there. Even if he didn't know what the content of the discussion would be, he knew it would be unpleasant, because otherwise Bojin would not have taken the trouble to drive him to Lețcani and back, somehow holding him prisoner in the car, to make sure he wouldn't escape it.

But comrade Bojin came up to him with a broad smile on his face, he embraced him, for the second time that day, although Brunul could not recall him ever having done so before. He then stepped back and placed his palms on Brunul's shoulders, gazing at him for a few moments, without altering the benevolent expression on his face.

"This is it," he said. "Did you enjoy the trip?"

"Yes," murmured Brunul, no longer able to conceal his amazement.

"What's up?" asked his former friend, fastening him with his gaze. "Is there something you want to tell me?"

"No," said Brunul, shaking his head, moving away slightly, thereby obliging Bojin to lower his hands.

"Well then . . ."

Bojin waved goodbye and climbed back inside the car. It was only then that Brunul suddenly remembered what he and Eliza had agreed he should say to his former friend in the event of a meeting.

"Actually, there is something," he said, bending toward the car.

Bojin poked his head out of the window and Brunul straightened up.

"This Saturday I'd like to go to Eliza's parents' village in Bukovina. She's invited me to meet her parents. You know, our relationship is . . . I mean . . . I'd like to go there on Saturday. She has two days off."

He spoke the final words in a rush, annoyed at his own stammering.

"I understand," said Bojin, nodding, this time without a smile. "You can ask for a day off at the building site. I'm sure they'll understand."

He withdrew his head back inside the car and the chauffeur started the engine. Brunul took two steps back, toward the entrance of his building. He had already asked for a day off and the engineer had granted it to him; he hadn't been asking for Bojin's permission. What had he been asking, in fact? What had he expected? The truth was that he didn't understand anything of that meeting, that parting. He didn't understand why Bojin hadn't asked him a single question, not even now, at the end. He hadn't even told him the name of the village in Bukovina, even though with Eliza he had prepared all the answers to every potential question. In the past, his former friend had been interested even when Brunul had taken an outing to the area surrounding the city. Once, in the months after his release, Bojin had even berated him when he had gone for a walk on his own to the Cetăţuia Monastery just outside Jassy, curious as to the view from up on the hill. Bojin had been furious and made it clear that as Brunul's protector he had to be the first to know if his ward took any such further initiatives. After that, Brunul had taken care not to err again. He had refused even to set a date for the picnic in Ciric, where he had had his first argument with Eliza, until Bojin had given him his permission to go. But now it didn't matter that he would be away for two whole days? Bojin had not even asked the name of the village, although Brunul had clearly told him it was in Bukovina, which was two hundred kilometers away.

The chauffeur turned the car around so that he could drive back the way he had come. The car slowed down as it approached the entrance to Brunul's building and comrade Bojin wound down the window.

"Bon voyage," he said to Brunul, winking at him for the umpteenth time that day.

Brunul did not have time to reply. He merely raised his hand to chest level, waving timidly, as if all the questions that assailed him weighed down on his hand, preventing him from raising it any higher. He then watched as the Pobeda M20, the only car comrade Bojin would have bought, had he been able to afford one, turned onto the main road, some fifty meters from the entrance to the building, and vanished behind other concrete buildings, leaving in its wake a faint, not entirely unpleasant, whiff of petrol.

# Chapter 22

"You must have done something. You're guilty of something. Don't whine like Dona Siminică. Nobody would have put you in prison if you weren't guilty. The important thing is for you to think about what you're going to do when you get out. To see what your perspectives are, that's what I'm trying to say."

His perspectives. A space of a few square meters, cold, dark walls, two beds, one of which he lay on, the other vacant. The same perspectives for a good few months already. Nobody to talk to. Dr. Petrovici had visited him three times since he left the hospital. In despair, he had asked him why he didn't come more often. He would have liked to, but it wasn't up to him, came the reply. And he had no reason not to believe him. Ever since he had become a prisoner, or rather gone back to being a prisoner, everything had been secret. And more importantly, everything was forbidden. If he himself came up against so many obstacles, why should he not believe the doctor when he said it was forbidden to visit him more often? He was physically healthy, as Dr. Petrovici had complained at each of their three meetings in the first few months. Things would have gone differently if he had been able to declare him unfit. Ill. But physically, he was sound. As for his memory . . . Here, even he, the doctor, had been treated with skepticism. Nobody completely believed him. He had told him this in a whisper, on the third visit. The last. Everybody thought he was pretending. In order not to serve the rest of his sentence.

And now here was this plump man older than he, sitting in front of him. "I'm forty-four," he had told him from the very first, "and in all my life I've never heard of anybody not having any memories whatsoever. All right, if you were an old crock, I'm not saying it couldn't happen. Old crocks lose their memory. It's old age. But not to remember anything, absolutely anything about the last twenty years. I've never heard the like, really I haven't."

He was from the party. That was how he had introduced himself, without specifying which party. Without explaining what business any party might have with him, a prisoner, who didn't even know why he was in prison. He didn't look like a party man. A memory from childhood: his village, a visit by a member of the Liberal Party, or maybe the Peasants Party, it no longer mattered which. He was wearing a hat and a pin-striped suit. He entered their yard, talked cloyingly to his grandparents. Finally, one of his men had left a sack on their veranda: pork sausages, red apples, cheese, eggs, other things too, but these he couldn't remember. They had deposited the sack and then quite simply left. Only he, the child, had noticed the sack. His grandfather saw it only after they left. He had been angry, kicked the sack, scattering its contents all over the yard. That was how he found out what was in the sack. His grandfather had shouted at his grandmother: Did they think he was a beggar or what? He was the village headman! What did he need their hand-outs for? Such was his memory of a politician: a man who talked cloyingly and wore a hat and pin-striped suit.

But the man who had entered his cell was wearing ordinary clothes and didn't have a hat. Ordinary trousers, without a pinstripe. A jumper whose color wasn't apparent in the faint light. A round, friendly face. Ruddy, freshly shaven cheeks. Small eyes beneath bushy, untidy eyebrows. A bald patch that made his short hair look like a tongue wrapped around his head. "Bojin Dumitru," he said his name was. "You can call me comrade Bojin." He then gave him a friendly wink. "Matei Bruno," he said, as his father had taught him as a child, giving first the surname and then the first name. "Yes, I know," said Bojin Dumitru. "I even thought about it on my way here: Bruno is a funny name. I take it it's Italian. I look at you and I see that you really are brown. *Brun.* And if you're brown, that's what I'll call you: the Brown. *Brunul.* We're in Romania after all."

For the last two hours since he met him they had been talking, chatting, but not so much about what Bruno would have liked to talk about: How much longer would he be kept there? He was losing his mind between those four walls without anybody to talk to. More than anything else he was losing his mind because he couldn't remember anything; months had passed and he could still remember absolutely nothing. Why was he in prison? This was the question that tortured him the most, a question that the guards refused to answer. All of them refused to tell him. He was sure that Dr. Petrovici would have told him, but he too was forbidden to do so. He was allowed only to talk about Bruno's medical condition. But why was he in prison?

"You must have done something. You're guilty of something. Don't whine like Dona Siminică. Nobody would have put you in prison if you weren't guilty. The important thing is for you to think about what you're going to do when you get out. To see what your perspectives are, that's what I'm trying to say. And anyway, it's not all that bad: I see they've given you that doll of yours, so you're not all alone, are you? If you only knew what it was like for other people in prison . . . You've got it easy: nobody makes you work, nobody bothers you. You sit by yourself in your cell, you've got a bed to sleep on, food to eat. All you have to do is think, make an effort to think about those twenty years you claim not to remember."

Bojin Dumitru paused after saying all this, picking up the wooden doll and rattling it gently.

"Oho, Brunul, there are people who'd do anything to swap

places with you. All right, not people on the outside, because we're living in different times now, completely different to the ones you say you remember. People are starting to have a good life on the outside. But here, inside . . . How many people would swap places with you, oho!"

After more than two hours, comrade Bojin left, leaving nothing but questions behind him. Many questions. Questions that in different circumstances would perhaps have been far more torturous. But the man promised that they would meet again very soon, that they would meet quite often in the period to come. And Bruno felt well that day. He didn't weep, clutching his doll to his chest. He didn't recite obsessively the words he had learned by heart from the piece of paper Dr. Petrovici had given him on his release from hospital. During the first days in his cell he had struggled to read it, letter by letter, word by word, sentence by sentence. "Every marionette has a soul. You need only know how to reveal it. Perhaps the same as in humans, it resides within. But of course some people would give it a different name, and so we shall call it the center of gravity. A marionette's every movement is based on . . ." He had recited it during the first days in his cell, without understanding its meanings, striving to the point of desperation to explain to himself how such a text, which he himself had written, so he had been told, could no longer say anything to him. His thoughts were set down there, thoughts that now refused to yield their meaning to him. After a few days, or perhaps weeks, he had learned it by heart. And he had recited it thousands of times; he even recited it during his nights of insomnia. But now, after the first visit from the man "from the party," he no longer felt the need to mask his solitude with those empty words, reciting them to himself or to the doll beside him. He no longer felt the need to subject himself to questions, to the new questions left behind by his visitor. He liked him, since besides the questions, which perhaps at any other time would have been torturous, he also left behind a friendly face, smiles, and above all hope. The hope of further meetings that would alleviate his loneliness. Even the hope of answers.

Matei Bruno, Brunul, slept well after that first meeting with Bojin Dumitru. And before falling asleep, he thought for a good few minutes, perhaps for a whole hour, about perspectives.

His perspectives constantly widened in the following weeks and months. Not his perspective on the past, although in the case of Bruno Matei this would have been a necessary perspective, which held more hidden dangers than the future, but also, who knows, its own beauty. Nevertheless, it was not about the past that he spoke with comrade Bojin, who kept his word, visiting him often, sometimes even three times in the same week. Rather it was about the present and the perspective from outside his prison cell. And from time to time it was even about the future.

The present, as Bruno Matei, Brunul, discovered little by little, no longer had any connection with that stretch of past he could remember, his life up to the age of sixteen. After a second world war, a war crueler even than the first, in which the Romanians had fought heroically against the Germans, albeit not from the very first, things had changed dramatically. The people had made a revolution, they had overthrown the exploiters headed by King Michael, and defeated once and for all the bloodsucking bourgeoisie. All enemy elements had been eliminated, rooted out like weeds from a cornfield, when the corn has not yet grown tall and is not strong enough to triumph on its own. And now, thanks to the people's revolution, the corn had grown tall and shone in the sunshine, and the corn had produced large, nourishing cobs such as the country deserved. Everything had changed. Everything. The peasants no longer depended on the boyars and the kulaks. They had their own land, which the majority of them had decided to share or donate to the collectives. Collectivization meant that the land belonged to

the state, but the state was theirs, the peasants' and the workers',
and so state land was also their land. For the state, and this was
the most important thing, the state itself had changed. There
were no longer different parties to quarrel among themselves,
each trying to steal as much as it could. There was no longer a
king to do whatever he liked whenever he liked, living off the
backs of the poor. There was a single party, the workers' party,
led by the workers. On the outside, so comrade Bojin said, the
heaven that the charlatan priests had talked about in the past
was being built right here on earth. Rather than a heaven after
death, fashioned from lying fantasies, better a paradise on earth,
during this life, one you work for and which grows around you
as fast as the eye can see.

Although he couldn't fully understand what he heard, and
although many of the words were alien to him, Bruno Matei
created in his mind luminous, even astonishing scenes, full of
joy and sunlight, full of a lust for life, which so overwhelmed
him that many nights he was unable to fall asleep for thinking
about them; he was gripped by a new and thrilling sense of
what life would be like after his release. For yes, he could think
about such a thing, and comrade Bojin had even encouraged
him to do so. Without giving him a definite date, comrade
Bojin had told him that if things went well, he would soon be
released and would be able to experience to the full the paradise
on the outside, to live there with all the others. If things went
well—this was the only problem, since comrade Bojin didn't
elaborate on it; he didn't tell him how exactly things should
go in order that they go well. Even so, Bruno sensed that the
plump, friendly, rosy-cheeked man with the bushy eyebrows
would decide whether things were going well. He sensed that it
depended on comrade Bojin, and within a few weeks he came
to live for his meetings with him, he came to dream of them,
and he began to have feelings toward his visitor that were hard
to define, all the more so given that he had never experienced

such feelings before, but it was as if they resembled what he had felt toward his grandfather when he was a child. Comrade Bojin gave him the feeling that the whole world was moving within the same moment as he was, that the air took on a fresher scent when he entered the cell, that a single word from him was sufficient to lend life to the dark walls and fill that cell with bright colors. Comrade Bojin gave him a feeling of safety and great, great hope.

The moments of despair dwindled. True, they still occurred, particularly when the visits were late in coming, when days on end elapsed during which Bruno had to re-accustom himself to the curt, surly words of the guards, who still forbade him to leave his cell, requiring him to eat there and relieve himself there, in the wooden bucket that stank even after it had been emptied and rinsed. But even the moments of despair found alleviation thanks to comrade Bojin. For during one of their meetings another perspective had changed for Bruno: his perspective on that doll from his past, given to him by Dr. Petrovici. In just a few words, his friend—he regarded him as a true friend—had given life to the doll. Even if you clutch it to your breast when you weep, even if it be the mute witness to a speech you have learned by heart from a piece of paper, a thing remains inanimate so long as it has no name. But comrade Bojin had given it a name. He had picked up the puppet, studied it for a while, and then told Bruno, "Once when I was younger, maybe even a child, I can't remember when exactly, I went to a fair. And I saw a puppet show there with one of these. It was a long time ago, but I remember the puppets' names. There was one who was called Mărioara, and another, a man, who was like yours, and his name was Vasilache. I wouldn't have remembered, but I heard the same names again after that, at puppet theaters. It's not like in the old days now; puppets don't perform at fairs in the mud anymore. There are puppet theaters now. Did you know that? Anyway, it's a good name for a wooden puppet. Vasilache." Vasilache. And when he said its name, the puppet began to listen to Bruno. It still couldn't speak; the wooden mouth still couldn't open. But it was enough for him to say his name for Vasilache to listen. It was enough for him to ask Vasilache a question. For Vasilache had answers, even if he expressed them by nodding his head or moving his hands. It was enough for him to say Vasilache's name for the puppet to share in his moments of despair, to help him, to understand him. Vasilache seemed to help him understand better the speech he had learned from the sheet of paper. Vasilache stood in for comrade Bojin during his long periods of absence, and for many days the guards heard coming from the dark cell not only sobs, not only mechanical whispers, but also the most natural conversations, lively conversations and even stories, which Bruno now salvaged from his memories prior to the mist and recounted to Vasilache, who listened attentively, conscientiously. He learned by listening.

Sometimes, comrade Bojin brought the newspapers. *The Spark. The Jassy Flame.* He read them to Bruno, thereby proving that the paradise on the outside was experienced not only by him, a representative of the Party, but by numerous other people, by everybody. He read letters from those people, published in the newspapers, letters in which they thanked the Party from the bottom of their hearts for the wonderful achievements of the last few years, for the so-radical change in their lives and working conditions. Sometimes, comrade Bojin read to him about the achievements themselves. New railway lines. Electrification. Production quotas enthusiastically surpassed in various factories. The construction of new housing blocks for the working class. The construction of culture clubs in the villages, to enlighten and edify the peasantry. Parks for recreation. Polyclinics, hospitals. Perspectives.

Most of all, however, comrade Bojin liked to read to Brunul, as he always called him, without ever mentioning his old name, about the technical achievements of the new world. Every article that described an invention, a success, particularly on the part of the U.S.S.R., since it was Romania's vast, friendly neighbor that blazed every trail to the future, Bojin read to him with great pleasure and satisfaction, making enthusiastic exclamations. This is how Bruno Matei found out about the motorcar of the year 2000, although he was unfamiliar even with the motorcar of the present, except the rare examples he remembered from his childhood. But he was filled with the same enthusiasm as his friend when he found out that by the year 2000 half of all motorcars would have atomic engines and the other half electric engines. He tried to show the same broad smile as his friend when Bojin reached the part of the article that talked about the high-voltage electric cables that would stretch under the vast motorways of the year 2000. He strove to picture the cars of that year, his imagination carried away by Bojin's excited voice: "A special antenna device beneath the motorcar will capture the electromagnetic energy field created around the cable. In fact the cable beneath the motorway is an emitter and the car engine is a receiver. The high-frequency energy field captured by the receiver is transformed into continuous currents that drive the motors located directly beneath the wheels. Journeys by such cars will be completely safe, the driving will be automated, and the car will not make any inappropriate maneuver: the passenger will reach his destination in the shortest time." The paradise of the year 2000 was to be much more spectacular than the paradise that already existed in 1958, although unlike comrade Bojin, Brunul could not perceive all the details of the present paradise. But even so, Brunul made the calculation in his mind, adding forty-two, the number of years that remained until the paradise of 2000, to his present age of thirty seven, and he rejoiced at the thought that, although the wait would be long, there was still a chance that he would live to see those times and in his old age he would forget the less happy times of the present.

But long before he arrived in that paradise, Brunul needed to know about the present paradise from which, for the last few months, comrade Bojin had arrived on his visits. And when, that spring, his friend entered his cell and, after giving him a broad smile, which lingered long on his face, he at last gave him the long-awaited news, Brunul suddenly grew dizzy, he was unable to breathe for a few seconds, his knees turned weak, and only the fact that Bojin had grasped him by the shoulders, supporting him, prevented him from falling.

Formalities. Signatures. With comrade Bojin always at his side. A spring day. April the thirteenth. "April the thirteenth, nineteen fifty-eight," stated a man in uniform in an official tone, before signing one of the documents. The day when Bruno Matei, Brunul, was to step through the prison gates and enter a city with which he was unfamiliar, but of which he had high expectations.

At last, in the middle of the day, after shaving, after washing, after shedding his prison fatigues and dressing in different clothes, not necessarily new, but different, clothes supplied by his friend, at last came the walk to the prison gates. He remembered them. He had entered them last summer. The courtyard was unchanged. Narrow. Tall concrete walls. Barbed wire on top. But there was a big difference. Now he was about to go out of the prison gates. A guard opened the door reverently. He gave a respectful bow. Addressed to comrade Bojin, however, not to Brunul. Comrade Bojin was the first to step through. Brunul followed him. A short salute and the door closed. The outside.

They came to a stop. Brunul stopped, and comrade Bojin waited for him a little way ahead, next to a car with two open doors. Brunul stopped and turned around to face the closed gates. He took a few paces backward, the better to view them. Vasilache was indifferent, hanging inert from Brunul's right arm. What did Vasilache care? For him nothing much had changed. Vasilache needed only Brunul, nothing more. Vasilache was a listener. And he would have Brunul on the outside the same as he had had him in prison. For the former prisoner, however, the image of the tired, old gray building that now presented itself to him from the outside was important. It was an image that he had to imprint firmly on his memory. He could not allow himself the luxury of losing this memory along with the others. Even if it was not a good memory. But it was, it had to be, an important memory.

And then a hand on his shoulder.

"Come on, man. We've got a hard day ahead of us. Hard for me, that is, because it'll be nice for you. There'll be surprises, too. You'll see."

The whole journey was full of amazements for him. Jassy University, a vast edifice. The first in the country, as his friend proudly informed him. The Library. The statue of Mihai Eminescu. Yellow Gully, with its spectacular architecture. The train station, hurrying travelers laden with luggage. Housing blocks. Streets. Lanes. Housing blocks. It wasn't until they came to a stop in front of one such block that Brunul thought of asking, "But where are we going?"

It was a question that he should have asked much earlier, even before they left the prison walls. But it had not come to him. He had not thought of it even for an instant. He knew they were going to the outside, and that had been enough. He was to leave the dark, narrow cell. And he was to do so alongside comrade Bojin, who, of this he was sure, would solve everything, decide everything; comrade Bojin was a man in whom you could place your trust without asking yourself questions. And he hadn't asked himself any questions. But now he felt the need. In front of the old four-story apartment block. Next to which the car had come to a stop.

"You'll see," laughed his friend.

They climbed to the first story. Comrade Bojin came to a stop in front of a door, took out a key, opened the door. He entered. Brunul waited on the other side of the threshold.

"Don't be scared," said comrade Bojin from inside.

A hall. To the left, a door. Comrade Bojin opened it.

"This is the bathroom."

Then another door, also on the left. Comrade Bojin opened it.

"This is the kitchen."

At the end of the hall, a larger door. Comrade Bojin pressed the door handle and entered.

"Come on. This is the bed sitting room. There's just one room, but it's enough, isn't it?"

A bed. A cupboard. A large table in the middle. On the table, a red vase, with nothing in it. Two chairs on either side of the table.

"Well?"

"Nice."

"You still don't get it, do you? Come on, sit down on a chair. Let me help you understand, since I see you can't on your own."

Brunul sat down. His friend sat down on the other side of the table. From his bag he took a bottle. He looked around for something.

"They didn't think of that. Glasses. They didn't bring any glasses."

He got up and went into the hall. He went through one of the doors and quickly came back with two cups.

"These will do. Now let's celebrate. I've brought a special wine for the occasion. We have to celebrate."

He poured the wine. Brunul raised the cup to his mouth straightaway. A scent he didn't recognize. A sharp scent. But pleasant.

"Hold on, what are you in such a hurry for? I want to make a speech. Do you think that all this comes without a speech?" said comrade Bojin with a laugh. "What did I tell you in prison? Do you remember? What did I tell you? Didn't I promise you that if things went well, you too could experience all these, these . . .

what should I call them? All these joys that an ordinary person has in the present. I promised. And as you can see, I've kept my word. Not only me. Because I can't do everything by myself. We work for each other. All for one. And they've worked for you too. They've allocated you this apartment. It's yours. Make yourself at home. Now let's clink."

Brunul mechanically stretched out his cup and they clinked. He didn't taste it or smell it, he didn't even hear the merry words that comrade Bojin now spoke. His apartment? His home? He could not yet understand the words that were whirling in his mind; he would have liked to have caught them, extracted them from among all the other thoughts, separated them, rejoiced in them. But he couldn't. Not for a good few minutes. He was able to only after comrade Bojin filled the cups for the second time. Only on his second cup did he taste and smell the wine. Only then did he begin to hear.

". . . for everybody who isn't an idler, for everybody who does an honest day's work. We're going to find you a job. You have to earn a living, reintegrate. But what's important is that the Party won't leave you homeless in the meantime. We'll help you when you're in need. You've paid your debt to society. Now you're clean. And so now we're doing our duty to you."

"Is this my home?" stammered Brunul.

"It's yours. Can't you believe it? It's yours. Which is to say, you'll live in it. And after we find you a job, you'll pay rent, because that's only right and proper, isn't it? We give and you pay us back. What's important . . . What's important is that you've convinced me you're innocent. Your illness, I mean. Let me put it to you straight: I didn't believe you at first. Nobody believed you. Not even the doctor who treated you was able to convince us. He kept saying: comrades, I've never seen the like. To lose all memory of twenty years of your life. Comrades, I've never seen the like. That's why we talked all those times. Because we had to know. We had to make sure you were being honest with us. And if you're honest with us, then we're honest too. That's what life is like."

Over the next two hours they emptied the bottle. In the meantime, comrade Bojin provided answers, many of which Brunul had been seeking for the last few months. Cup after cup, answer after answer. Not about the past. When the past isn't good, it's not worth talking about; it's better forgotten. An illness like Brunul's was even a blessing, that's what Bojin told him, it was a blessing if you thought about it. Why have memories of things that landed you in prison? The past no longer matters. The answers were to do with the future alone. To do with perspectives. And from the answers Brunul understood that he was to be helped. He understood that in a society such as the new one, a man was never alone. A man couldn't be alone, because he was part of a whole that always thought and acted as a whole. The construction of paradise on earth could be achieved only when men were united. It could be constructed when a people united and shared a common goal: development, success, communism.

Brunul understood that he was no longer alone. And he didn't even feel alone when comrade Bojin, the wine and the speeches having finished, got up and, promising to return the next day, left. He didn't even feel alone when, still quite a few hours till evening, he got into bed. He placed Vasilache beside him and began to gather his thoughts. One by one. He placed them in order. And he joined them all, he connected them to a single meaning. He connected them to his perspectives of which his friend comrade Bojin had spoken so many times that day, the same as he had spoken of them so many times before.

# Chapter 23

HE DIDN'T WAIT for them at the station. She had his address written on a piece of paper. Ticu. Eliza's cousin. He didn't want to take the risk, Eliza explained to Brunul. He wasn't the one who was leaving the country. Why risk coming to the station? Why risk being seen with them? He was exposing himself to danger even as it was by letting them stay at his house overnight.

Saturday evening, October 24. Timișoara station. They had set out from Jassy almost twenty-four hours before. A long journey, abominably long, so it seemed to Brunul. He had not slept for a minute, although Eliza had insisted he try. Fast train no. 604, departing at 22:45 hours from Jassy, stopping at Tecuci, Buzău, Ploiești South, Bucharest North. Arriving in Bucharest at 06:30 hours. Their tickets were to Bucharest. Almost every other word Eliza spoke was "risk." Why should they risk it? If somebody in Jassy caught on, he would think they had gone to Bucharest. No farther than Bucharest. It would be a problem, because Bucharest is not in Bukovina. But it would be a lesser problem than if that somebody found out they had gone to Timișoara.

They had had an hour in which to buy new tickets. Another route. Another fast train. Bucharest–Timișoara. Brunul didn't catch the number of the train this time. It would be traveling via Pitești, Piatra Olt, Craiova, Turnu Severin, Orșova, Caransebeș. Departure at 07:30 hours. Arrival at 19:35 hours. Numbers. Times. The names of towns he could not remember ever having heard. And a long journey, this time even more uncomfortable. The tiredness accumulated over a sleepless night combined with the sun, with the bright daylight, to torture him. He would have liked to sleep. Other people were asleep on the bench seats. He would have liked to catch up on the night's sleep he had lost because of anxiety. But a new anxiety arose. Sleep might have sent him into a tunnel. A new tunnel, a new mist. And so he forced his eyes to remain open, to store all the fields and valleys seen through the window, all the hills, all the mountains, all the forests, to store them inside himself, to keep them there, not to miss a single detail. He strove to keep awake, lest he be carried into a tunnel, lest he lose sight of his thoughts for an instant. As far as Timişoara. As far as Timişoara station, where an early, unexpected sleet was falling as they alighted from the train. In the middle of the night. The train had been delayed. For long hours.

Ticu. Eliza's cousin. Eliza told Brunul that it was a good omen, a piece of luck that Ticu lived near the station. Following the directions on Eliza's piece of paper, they arrived on foot in less than half an hour. The train had been late. How would they have gotten there if he had lived farther away? Time was not on their side. The next day they had to continue their journey. They had to cross the border as quickly as possible. It was vital that nobody in Jassy should ask any questions before they crossed the border. That was the plan. Eliza's plan. Which had to be followed to the last detail. Her plan. The only salvation.

Ticu. When he opened the door, his eyes were bulging in fright. He quickly ushered them inside the apartment. He had feared the worst. The delay had led him to imagine all kinds of things. He imagined that they had been caught in Jassy. Worse still, he imagined that his telephone conversations with Eliza at the post office had been monitored. And even if they had taken precautions, talking offhandedly and in code, without making any direct reference to what they were planning, he had still feared they had been discovered. In which case he would have been in trouble too. That was how he had spent the hours in which the train had been delayed: thinking about how he was now in trouble too. He hadn't known whom to expect when he heard knocking on his front door: them or State Security.

Mugs of tea. Drunk with the lights out. It was past midnight. There was no point attracting unwanted attention.

"There's no point in our taking a risk," Eliza told Brunul, apologetically.

"There's no point," reiterated Ticu.

Ticu. Eliza's cousin. A man of around forty, with thick, blond hair, large eyes, a broad forehead, trembling hands. He kept making abrupt movements. Maybe it was in his nature or maybe it was because of that night, during which he had stored up so many fears. A mild man, with a low voice that came in barely a whisper. He had a harelip, as Brunul had noticed straightaway. A hoarse voice. He smoked cigarette after cigarette, drinking three cups of tea to their one cup.

"You're really going to do it," he concluded, after too long a pause. "I didn't believe you," he added, looking at Eliza.

The only light, from a bulb on a telegraph pole outside, lent a faint glimmer to the outline of their faces and was enough to prevent them from speaking blindly into the dark.

"You've always wanted to do this, ever since you were a little girl," Ticu went on.

"Not quite since I was a little girl. I didn't know what a foreign country was when I was a little girl."

"All right, then ever since your youth," said Ticu, smiling. "You went on and on about it so much that in the end I wanted to do it too. You realize it was because of you that I thought of doing it?" He then turned to Brunul and said, "She's probably told you that I wanted to leave. But I couldn't go through with it . . ."

"She told me," said Brunul.

"Whenever we met back in the village, we'd end up talking about it," Ticu went on, addressing Brunul. "My mother, her aunt, tried to talk sense into her. 'You want them to kill you, girl? You want them to kill us?' The only one who encouraged her was my father, her uncle. Isn't that right that he encouraged you?"

"They're old," said Eliza, waving her hand, bothered by the turn the conversation had taken. "They'll not do anything to them. There'll be an investigation, and then they'll leave them alone. I didn't even tell them. After the last time I talked to you, I didn't tell them. They've got no idea that I'm here."

"Ever since I told her about that attempt of mine," Ticu went on, talking to Brunul in a hoarse whisper, "she's been obsessed. She had to know everything. I had to tell her everything. And then you turned up. The man with connections on the outside. If it hadn't been for you, I'm telling you, she wouldn't have left. Nor should she have even tried. Without somebody to get you out of Yugoslavia, it's as if you put the noose around your own neck."

"Do you really think we've got time to chatter?" said Eliza, raising her voice, trying to silence her cousin.

Brunul saw her eyes in the faint light. She was frowning, angry. She glared at Ticu for a second. Her lower lip was quivering, the way it always did when she was angry.

"I've brought everything. Even pepper for the dogs, like you told me."

"The pepper is essential."

"And a torch."

"Turn it on only if it's essential. Best not to turn it on at all. If the weather had been better, you wouldn't have needed it . . ."

"Damned sleet."

"Maybe it'll pass by tomorrow night."

"Maybe."

"What about food?"

"A few things. I didn't want to bring tins. Even if you peel off the labels, they'll recognize them as Romanian. Nothing from the shops. Just some smoked bacon, sausages."

"From the village?"

"Whatever I had left."

"Good. Speaking of food . . ."

He got up and went into the kitchen. While he was gone, the other two spoke not a word to each other. Brunul was bothered by something in the conversation he had just heard. He still did not know what exactly, but Eliza's annoyance and the instant in which she had glared at her cousin had conveyed something unpleasant, something he knew he ought to try to understand, but couldn't. It was these thoughts that prevented him from speaking.

They ate, still with the lights out. Bacon fat, cheese, bread. A few apples afterward. Talk of their plan continued as they ate. Without further reminiscences, without further complicities that excluded Brunul. Advice from Ticu. Lots of it. Some things they could count on. Other things were in the hands of fate. On the night when they crossed, for example, the wind would have to be blowing, neither too strongly nor too lightly, but just enough to cover any rustling sound they might make. It wasn't up to them, they couldn't control the wind, but Eliza's cousin liked to demonstrate to them that he knew everything, that only by following his advice would they succeed. Or maybe it merely gave him satisfaction to tell them. Maybe because he had not gone when he had the chance, he at least wanted to contribute to a successful escape. Maybe he was trying to create a reason for himself to take pride in later. A feeling. Maybe he could see himself still working at the Banat sugar factory in a year, in two years, three years, but knowing that on the other side, which for him had never taken shape, but which he knew without a doubt was better, two people would be living a completely different life thanks to him.

They did not go to bed until three in the morning, perhaps later. On waking, Brunul knew even before he opened his eyes that he was about to experience a day like no other. He knew that when he went to sleep again it would be somewhere else.

In another country. Maybe in a train. Maybe in a bus. Maybe even in a field. But in another country. The thrill caused by this thought as it budded did not have time to turn into a cold sweat, however. It did not overwhelm him. The exhaustion accumulated during so many hours without sleep proved more powerful than all the fears that crowded his mind.

Ticu had not noticed Vasilache the previous evening. Eliza and Brunul had left their two bags in the hall and the marionette had been invisible in the darkness between them. But in the morning Brunul awoke to the agitated whispers of the two cousins, on the verge of an argument.

"I can't ask him to do that. It's dear to him, I can't—"

"Is he mad or what? It's just a shitty doll. A bald one at that! What the hell! It'll draw attention. Everybody will be looking at you. And besides, at night . . . it's white."

Brunul got up from the bed, still exhausted. He took a step toward them.

"Vasilache," said Eliza.

"It's white!" said Ticu, looking at Brunul accusingly. "You can't take it with you. Especially at night. It would be as if you were carrying around a target for them to shoot."

"We could at least put it in another bag," said Eliza. "A black one."

Her cousin waved his hand in disgust and said, "Right, like you're going on holiday, with half a dozen bags . . ."

Brunul rubbed his eyes, trying to brush away the mist that obscured his vision like cobwebs. He then sat down on a chair, shaking his head. What they said made sense. Everything made sense. Except the fact that two people who now seemed alien to him, who went back a long way together and were part of the same family, were now shouting at him. Albeit shouting in a whisper. He had agreed to everything. For Eliza's sake, he had agreed to make a mockery of everything he had learned and experienced over the last two years. He had agreed to a torturous, far-too-long train journey. A journey during which she had already begun to seem like a stranger to him. He had agreed even to resist that feeling of his, to drive it out, thinking of the wonderful times they had spent together long before he found out that she wanted to flee and drag him into it. For the sake of those times, he had agreed to everything. But did he really have to agree to this? Vasilache had long ago ceased to be his friend, perhaps also because of Eliza. In the meantime, lately, Vasilache had become nothing but an inanimate marionette. But even if he knew this now, he still owed that marionette a great deal. For there had been a time when the marionette had meant much more to him than it meant now. And if he was going to leave, if he was going to cross the cursed border, he wasn't going to leave Vasilache behind. Nor would he stuff him in a bag. It was just a marionette, but it was one that had seen his struggles, his pain, his sobs, his despair; it was one that had listened to him. And now, on that day so different from any other in his whole life, he owed Vasilache at least that much. He owed it to him to be a witness to that day. No, he would not leave him behind, he would not stuff him in any bag.

"No," said Brunul.

"It's white," whispered Eliza imploringly, going over to the chair on which Brunul was sitting.

"I'm taking him with me no matter what. Otherwise I'll go back."

"You can't do that. They'll arrest you."

"Arrest me for what?"

"For helping me escape," she said, lowering her eyes. "You're here. It's done already. You're with me. You can't go back."

"No. Vasilache is coming with us. And I'm not stuffing him in a bag."

"It's stupid," interrupted Eliza's cousin. "I've never heard anything like it."

"I'm not going anywhere without him!" said Brunul, raising his voice, no longer abiding by the rule that they speak only in a whisper.

Ticu went to the table and sat down on a chair. Eliza did likewise. A few moments of silence. Eliza's cousin made a sweeping motion with his hand.

"Boot polish," he said. "We'll daub him with boot polish."

Brunul frowned.

"It'll wear off in the end. But at least it won't look so white. I'm also thinking we could dissolve some boot polish in a basin of water and dye its clothes."

Brunul said nothing. He looked at Vasilache's clothes. Old, shabby, and threadbare as they were, they were still white, far too white. Perhaps he shouldn't have washed them to prepare for the journey.

"The train leaves in two hours. You have to be on that train. Otherwise the next one isn't until evening. You'd arrive in Reşiţa late, and you wouldn't catch the bus to Naidăş. If we dye it now, we'll dry it in the oven."

"Come on," Eliza begged Brunul, more impatient now.

Brunul allowed a few moments to elapse before agreeing. In the end he had no objection. Vasilache in black clothes was still Vasilache, the same as he had still been Vasilache after he had torn his hat off with his teeth, leaving him bald. But nor did he want to give in so easily. He was sick of other people deciding for him, of hearing Eliza tell him what was best and what was not. But even so, he was too white.

"All right," he said finally. "We'll dye him."

A few minutes later, Vasilache looked dirty rather than dyed, horribly dirty. After Eliza's cousin wrung them out, the white clothes, which Brunul had washed so carefully, were stained black in places, gray in other places. Dirty rather than black. But at least they had allowed him to take Vasilache with him. As the marionette was drying in the oven, Brunul contented himself with the thought that they had let him have his way, that he hadn't given in this time. He wasn't interested in what they were talking about. They had sat down at the table. Ticu had given Eliza a map of the place where they were to cross the border, which he had drawn himself before they arrived. They pored over the map for a long time. Ticu explained to Eliza what they had to do, step by step, where they had to go once they reached Naidăş. But the discussion was between them, between two people who were more or less strangers to Brunul, on whom he now depended only because he had not had the courage to break away sooner. There was no turning back now. It was too late. But at least he had not given in when it came to Vasilache.

Ticu did not step outside the apartment when they left. They parted there, by the front door. There was no point in risking it. He gave them more pieces of advice, most of which he had already given them the previous evening. He shook Brunul's hand. Hereinafter the risk was theirs alone.

The rest of the day went largely according to plan. Reşiţa. An empty train station. After getting off the train they remained on the platform for a while because Brunul wanted to find a toilet. They then remained on the platform for a further while because they didn't know which way to go. Finally, Eliza got her bearings, and Brunul followed her in silence. They didn't have far to walk to the bus station, a tiny booth that sold tickets. Including to Naidăş.

Nonetheless, there was one deviation from the plan. Vasilache. For whose sake Brunul had opposed Eliza and her cousin. Now, as they waited for the bus that would take them to Naidăş that Sunday afternoon, Vasilache was in a bag. A brown cloth bag, purchased from a state food shop, in which not Eliza but Brunul had stuffed him. But this was because he himself had decided to do so, not because she had demanded it of him.

He had decided to do so after they got off the train and they had had to look for a bathroom, where Brunul had spent long minutes scrubbing the black dye off his face and hands. It was Vasilache's revenge for the way his clothes had been treated. And Brunul had taken his revenge on Vasilache by stuffing him in a brown bag bought from a state food shop. In the end, it had been one of the pleasanter episodes of the day. For a short while, Brunul's stubbornness when it came to the doll had relieved the tension, it had made them laugh together, as they had in past times, times for whose sake Brunul now found himself waiting for the bus to Naidăş.

A small, rattling bus, which belched black smoke as it came to a stop and more black smoke as it set off again. A crowd of passengers, mostly old, men and women returning home from town with empty bags, having taken food from the village to their children or perhaps grandchildren. Tired, silent faces. Nor did Brunul feel any need to break the silence between himself and Eliza during the journey.

The sleet was still falling. A pane was missing from one of the bus's upper windows and cold, wintry air blew inside, although they were in the southwest of the country and it ought still to have been warm there in late October. Maybe not warm, but in any event not wintry. The draught at times whistled through the missing windowpane, a sound that created an oppressive atmosphere, all the more unbearable when dusk began to fall, reducing visibility, which was already poor because of the sleet. An increasingly oppressive feeling caused Brunul to breathe heavily. His fear returned and, rising almost to terror as the bus jolted along, it now mingled with the cold, whistling air, with the shadows of evening, with the encouragement whispered by Eliza, who from time to time leaned her face toward him reassuringly, forcing a smile.

At one point the bus stopped amid some hills or mountains, Brunul was unable to tell which, because of the darkness.

The driver opened the door and got out. He then erupted into a torrent of curses—what a shitty fucking life for this to happen here of all fucking places. A puncture, the passengers soon discovered. The driver told everybody to get off the bus. They had been forced to deviate from their plan, from Eliza's plan, thought Brunul. Eliza's face revealed the same frightened thoughts as his as she stood next to him.

The driver, a fat, swarthy man, trembling with irritation, asked for the passengers' assistance. He divided them into two teams, a men's team and a women's team. The men all had to come to the right side of the bus and lift it on his command. Neither too much nor too little. Enough for a boulder to be rolled under the bus. The boulder was the responsibility of the women's team. With his hands, the driver showed them how big it should be. He sent them off in search of such a boulder, which they would then roll back to the bus. Then it would be the men's turn. They would lift the bus so that it would rest on the boulder. One of the men complained. Why should the women do all that work while the men only had to lift the bus when they got back? The driver explained to the comrades that first of all he was in charge, and secondly the labor had to be divided. Some had to lift the bus, others to bring the rock. In the end, in an equal society, labor had to be divided equally. And besides, concluded the driver in his speech to the comrades, anybody could see that rolling a rock was easier work than lifting a bus.

Within a few minutes, the women had completed their task. From a distance, Brunul saw Eliza pushing the boulder more desperately than the other lady comrades. She was obviously frightened, time was slipping away, and they still had a long way to the border. The driver encouraged them, waving his arms, shouting, pointing to where the rock should be dragged. Once the rock was positioned next to the bus, the driver turned his attention to the men's team. Further curses, further instructions.

The passengers, including Brunul, groaned in unison, lifting the bus, or rather pushing its side. The entire operation unfolded to the sound of the driver's copious swearing and took almost half an hour. Despite the combined strength of all the men's arms, the weight was too great and so the women were forced to bring other, smaller rocks to support the bus centimeter by centimeter, high enough for the wheel to be removed. Finally. An hour or more after the driver first detected the puncture, he gazed in satisfaction at the new wheel and demanded a final effort from the men and women: the former had to raise the vehicle a little so that the latter could remove the boulder from under it.

Once they re-boarded the bus, the atmosphere changed. The passengers were now smiling, satisfied at the bus being able to continue their journey as a result of their labor. Eliza too was satisfied, noticed Brunul. They had not been delayed very long: an extra hour wouldn't ruin their plan.

"You made a big effort and no joke," an elderly woman sitting on the seat opposite told Eliza once the bus was in motion again. "I was all out of breath, but you were pushing that rock like you wanted to ride it back home."

She laughed, revealing a few gold teeth. She didn't say it unkindly, even though her words made her sound as if she were scolding. Eliza merely smiled in reply. But the old woman was obviously in the mood to talk.

"Where are you going?" she asked, pointing with her chin at Brunul to show that she included him in the question.

Eliza frowned. She hesitated. But she had to answer.

"Naidăș."

"Well I'll be!" she exclaimed happily. "Who are you visiting? My sister lives there. I'm going to visit her. I know most of the folk in the village. I've been going to Naidăș ever since I was young. I used to go to the church there. There was a good priest back in the day, but I don't know where he is now. Oh what a good mass he used to give. They'd come from all the villages around to listen to him say mass. Then he left. It wasn't up to him, though, if you get my meaning," said the woman and gave them a complicit smile. "He was a priest from the times before now. He had his faults, but he said a wonderful mass. Who did you say you were visiting? I'm sure you're not from around here . . ."

Brunul could see that Eliza's frown had turned into fear and annoyance both at once. But it was the fear that made her open her mouth to answer.

"I don't think you know him. I've got a cousin. He's only just moved there. That's why we're going—" here she pointed at Brunul "—to help him. We live in Timişoara. That's where my cousin moved from. We're going to whitewash the house, do the cleaning. He's not married and he needs somebody to do the woman's work. The roof has got a hole in it too. That's why I've brought my brother—" again pointing at Brunul, "—to help us."

"Phew!" exclaimed the woman, almost managing to whistle through her puckered lips. "How about that. Folk moving to Naidăş. What for?"

"To engage in agriculture," said Eliza quickly, without a moment's hesitation.

Brunul admired her sangfroid. For a few moments he rejoiced that she was so clever—he wouldn't for the life of him know how to extricate himself from such a situation, but she had immediately found a suitable explanation. And she had said it so confidently, without hesitation, that she would have convinced even him if he hadn't known how things really stood. She had set out from her real cousin, and then the story had come of itself, flowing smoothly, without impediment, as if she had had it ready in advance. He rejoiced for a few moments that he had her with him. On the other side, in Yugoslavia, things would come of themselves just as easily. More easily even, given that they had been working on their story for longer; they had often rehearsed it together. And if he let Eliza tell it, no matter to whom, then he had no cause to worry.

Then, as he listened to Eliza talk to the old woman who had a sister in Naidăş and admired her, Brunul found his thoughts, which had ranged as far as Yugoslavia, returning to the previous night and lingering on the exchange of glances between Eliza and her cousin. His thoughts lingered there, seeking something in the words that Ticu had said, but without him realizing even now what it was they sought. It was only after the bus stopped in a village, letting off the old woman and other passengers, and only after Eliza turned to Brunul and whispered that they only had a little way to go, perhaps only a few minutes, and that it was a relief to have gotten rid of the old lady, it was only then that his thoughts tore themselves away from the memory of the previous night and coalesced into a question, asked in a low voice: "When was the first time you told your cousin about fleeing the country?"

Eliza narrowed her eyes, thereby asking him not to talk about it even in a whisper, even on a bus that rattled so loudly it was impossible for the passengers to hear each other unless they raised their voices, as had been the case when she had talked to the old woman.

"Nobody can hear us," said Brunul. "When did you tell him?"

This time he raised his voice, not to make himself heard, but because those thoughts of his, springing from the previous night, were impatient for an answer.

"I don't know," said Eliza with a shrug.

"How can you not know? Don't you remember when he wanted to flee?"

His voice was too loud. Eliza made wide eyes and looked around her in alarm.

"Two years ago. What the hell is wrong with you? Do you want to ruin everything?"

"Two years ago. And when did you find out about my mother? How long have you known she's in Italy?"

"What's wrong with you?"

"Tell me!"

"I told you . . ."

She had told him. Eliza had found out during her first meeting with Bojin, who had let slip that Brunul's mother was alive and in Italy. Brunul had believed her when she told him that. Why would he not have believed her? It was on the evening of August 23, when Eliza had come clean, when sincerity had riven her soul, and her confession had come of itself, flawlessly. It had come of itself more smoothly and connectedly than even what she had said about her cousin who had moved into a new house in Naidăş.

Nonetheless, Brunul felt, he intuited, that some connection was missing, some connection that could not be found there on that rattling bus, during a night of sleet, and with the wind whistling through a missing windowpane, bringing wintry air at such an inopportune moment. Particularly there in southwestern Romania, a region which in late October ought to have been having milder weather.

# Chapter 24

ON THE MORNING of April 13, 1958, Dumitru Bojin woke far earlier than usual. He was not in any great hurry, although he had a hard day ahead of him. Fresh air streamed through the window that gave onto the park, which he had left wide open overnight. In the last few days the skeletal trees, made haggard by winter, had come back to life, and Copou Park wafted the aroma of lindens into the house along with the waves of fresh air. Or rather the illusion of that aroma, since the scent that enveloped the whole hill, the whole city even, had not yet come into its own. The lindens would not be at their best until June. But even the sight of the trees coming into leaf was encouraging enough for his nostrils to seek the aroma in the spring air and even to get the impression from time to time that they had discovered it, that they had managed to capture it and convey it with a slight tremor throughout his body.

A quarter past six. He looked at the hands of the clock. A quarter past six, which meant he would not arrive at the Penitentiary until eight o'clock. He hadn't woken Torița. He went to the kitchen and without haste made himself some tea. It was all he needed for breakfast. He had long since given up eating early in the morning. Lunch was his first meal of the day. He washed and dressed while the water boiled, and then went out onto the terrace with his tea, lit a cigarette, took a couple of puffs, threw it away. He wasn't a heavy smoker, but in certain situations, when drinking with friends for example, it was pleasant. Smoking a cigarette when irritated was less pleasant, although calming when the pressure of work became too great, when they demanded of him things that gave him no pleasure whatsoever, and such things happened, they did indeed happen. However, the two types of truth in which he believed helped him to maintain a benign face in front of his bosses, even when the task they assigned him was unpleasant. The two types of truth and a calming cigarette.

In the last few months, however, he had been doing his job with increasing pleasure. It wasn't at all what he had at first imagined it would be—he had been alarmed at first, he had viewed it as a demotion, since they were assigning him to work in the field, they were assigning him to just one man, which is the kind of work he had done years ago, before assembling a network of collaborators. But for a long while, whenever it had been a question of a particular target, his informants and residents had done their jobs well; overall, he had nothing to complain about with them. They had made his life easier, even if he sometimes missed work on the ground, and from that point of view he could say with a certain amount of bitterness that although his life had become easier, it was also a lot more boring. The excitement of working directly with people, the strategies he hatched in his mind for each individual target, the play of ideas, the ingenious tricks, all the things that ultimately made life worth living, since they nurtured his creative side, all these things had, in the majority of cases, become the responsibility of his informants and residents lately. Sometimes he envied them. On the other hand, sometimes he consoled himself with the thought that he wasn't a dull sort of man, unlike many others he knew, and he had other interests with which to fill his life. All the latest technical discoveries filled his days and alleviated his boredom. Ultimately, his collaborators' stories were also various and sometimes stimulating, and so not even at work could he say that his life was devoid of satisfaction. Obviously, his collaborators included all sorts of people. Some he held in contempt, but all of them he viewed as working tools. A carpenter lends shape to wood, a steelworker forges steel, but the raw material of Dumitru Bojin's work was people. The difference with his job, one that made it all the more special, was that whereas carpenters and steelworkers use various tools to shape wood or steel, Dumitru Bojin and his colleagues shaped people using other people. Dumitru Bojin sometimes found amusement in the thought that they had gone from an age in which man exploited his fellow man to an age in which, using modern means, the final goal was for man to shape his fellow man.

But after his initial fears, he soon realized that his present mission brought together all the things that had once given so much satisfaction. The first phase: knowledge, gathering information. Accomplished. More than accomplished, even. The second phase commenced today, which was a turning point: the man he had been in charge of for the last few months was going to be released from prison. Bruno Matei. He liked him. He had worked hard for him precisely because he liked him. At first he had treated the target with suspicion; the whole situation was fishy. How could he lose his memory? And what was more, his memory of exactly twenty years, as if somebody, the Lord Above or the Lord Below, to go by his wife Torița, had chopped his life into segments with a cleaver. And not just any way, but to the millimeter, like an expert butcher. Chop! Twenty years of your life, you can have the rest, but we'll be taking these, because we need them. Come off it! You can't expect me to believe that! This is what he had thought at first. But a few weeks had been sufficient for him to realize that the butcher, the Lord Above or the Lord Below, really had been at work with his chopper. Which is to say, the man in prison wasn't lying to him; he wasn't lying to anybody. He was in a desperate state. He was thirty-seven years old, but all he could remember was his life up to the age of sixteen. It's a highly intricate thing, the human mind, but that's what he liked about this assignment: getting to the bottom of something so intricate. It took another few weeks for him to convince his superiors, writing report after report. But in the end he had succeeded.

The next step came of itself: his reports had been sent higher up, higher and higher, perhaps all the way to the top, given that now Bruno Matei was being released early. And what was more, a plan for the future had been put together. Once their man was released, phase two would commence: the shaping of man by his fellow man. And who was responsible for implementing it? None other than Dumitru Bojin. The reports had to continue; observation of the target had to be kept up without interruption. He was a special case of reintegration into society. Obviously, lessons could be learned from this, given appropriate surveillance. He was to provide him with an apartment, which within a short time the target would pay for by himself, since as part of the second phase Dumitru Bojin was responsible for finding him a job so that his reintegration would be active and productive. On the advice of the psychiatrist who had looked after the man, Dumitru Bojin had found their man a job at the State Puppet Theater—the file had shown that he had had some kind of obsession with puppets, and so it would be better if during the period of reintegration and recuperation he could do a job to which he was physically accustomed, even if he had no memory of it. That's what the doctor had told them: their man shouldn't be placed in a completely alien environment, because it could aggravate his illness even to the point of complete insanity. In which case all their efforts would have been in vain and the whole idea of reintegration and studying the said integration would have gone down the drain.

He finished his tea. Five past seven. Still too early. But there was no point in his sitting there on the terrace, even if the morning air was very pleasant. It would be even more pleasant on the way to the penitentiary. It was a twenty-minute walk at most, at a comfortable pace. He left the house without waking Torița; there was no point in waking her.

During his extended walk, with pauses to sit on benches around Copou Park, he felt that everything in his life was as it should be. Perhaps it was spring that prompted such positive thoughts, perhaps the feeling that that very day and perhaps over the days, weeks, and months to come he was to play a decisive rôle in the life of a man who was in effect starting from scratch. He stopped two or three times, thinking about it: he had the opportunity to work on a man in a way that probably nobody ever had before. In the way that you would raise a child from an early age in the spirit of your ideas. Except that in the case of Bruno Matei, Brunul, things were far more spectacular: he wasn't a child, he was a grown man, approaching middle age. And nonetheless he was starting from scratch, as if he had not been born into that new world, but leaping into it directly from the old world, passing over all the throes of creation with his eyes closed, over the whole arduous process through which Bojin had had to pass. Ultimately he was a lucky man, that Brunul. There it was: amnesia could be a piece of good fortune. He would be spared the struggle, the fears, the labor everybody else had had to go through, and he would enjoy nothing but the benefits. And Bojin was the one who was to create the new Brunul, a Brunul wholly adapted to the new world; Bojin had created the expectations, and he was to be the creator of the fulfillment of those expectations.

Turning right onto the road to the Penitentiary, Bojin brushed away all these pleasant thoughts. They were intoxicating, like poetry or a song by a crooner on the record player. But now the day was taking tangible shape; there were still a few minutes until eight o'clock. He had business with Brunul and he had to finish before noon, which was when he had a second piece of business, connected in a way to the first, and to his personal contribution to the first, to be more precise. He had arranged to meet one of his residents at a rendezvous house. The script laid out by his superiors was interesting and he would follow it to the letter. But why not make his own contribution to the script? No matter how tasty the steak made for him by Torița, Bojin always added a little salt and pepper. And he would add a little salt and pepper here too. But before he did so he had to deal with all the formalities.

After they stepped outside together, having passed through the prison gates, Dumitru Bojin sensed that Brunul wanted to be left alone for a few moments. He stepped aside, waiting by the car that had arrived in the meantime to pick them up. He waited for a few minutes, watching with a kind of joy mingled with pity as the man with the puppet dangling from his arm looked back at the prison building as if he had left the whole of his life behind. In fact, absorbed in his contemplation of Brunul, Dumitru Bojin liked to imagine what he was thinking, and the part about Brunul leaving the whole of his life behind was a product of Dumitru Bojin's imagination. Ultimately, that was more or less the truth of it, even if Brunul still preserved memories of his childhood. But properly speaking, mused Dumitru Bojin, a man's life only really begins after his youth. It's all a game up until then. Up until then you don't have your own life, you're subject to other people's demands, on the one hand, and to instincts a young mind can't control, on the other. Dumitru Bojin sometimes liked to philosophize about life, as any man is bound to do every now and then. And so as he waited for the newly released prisoner to take his leave of the prison, he had nothing better to do than indulge in a little philosophizing. But in fact he had no way of knowing what Brunul was really thinking during those minutes. True, he ought to have been thinking along those lines: that he was leaving the whole of his life behind, everything in life that he had known up to then. But who could know what a man who lacked any memory of the last twenty years was really thinking?

He went up to him. He had other business and couldn't wait there forever. He placed his hand on his shoulder.

"Come on, man. We've got a hard day ahead of us. Hard for me, that is, because it'll be nice for you. There'll be surprises, too. You'll see."

The biggest surprise was the one-room apartment. But he didn't want to tell him anything about it yet. He wanted to enjoy seeing how Brunul would react when he saw what was replacing his wretched, narrow prison cell. The whole way there, Dumitru Bojin said nothing, thinking only about the moment of the big surprise. Another surprise was the wristwatch he had in his pocket. A Pobeda, from his own collection. Obviously it was a lesser surprise than the one-room apartment, but it was a present he would give with all his heart. And it was a personal contribution. He didn't have a receipt for the watch; he hadn't filed a report or sought authorization for the present. It was simply something he personally wished to do, and wasn't bothered by the thought of reducing his collection. True, he had other watches of the same make, but that one was special, if he thought about it, since it had been bought on his only trip to the Soviet Union, on a work exchange visit a few years ago. The present was therefore special. And it was for a special man, as he intended to say when he gave it to Brunul. And it was true: for many reasons, Brunul was special.

He enjoyed the former prisoner's joy in the moment when he told him that the one-room apartment was now his home. After placing a bottle of wine on the table, he showed him around: the bathroom, where there were a few towels, three bars of soap, a razor and shaving brush, and even a brand-new dressing gown; the kitchen, where there were plates, cups, a ladle, knives, forks, spoons, but no glasses—they had forgotten the glasses; the bed sitting room, with the cupboard in which Dumitru Bojin proudly showed Brunul the clothes provided by the Party: a pair of pajamas, two pairs of trousers, one thin, one thick, a jumper, two shirts, a jacket, which, although it did not match the trousers, would still come in useful, and a raincoat—

all these in addition to the clothes and the pair of shoes Brunul was wearing, which the driver had brought to the prison for his release; and the hall, where, explained Bojin, there was a pair of overshoes, for winter. The Party took care of him; this was something that needed to be emphasized. The Party took care of all those who were deserving.

And for the next two hours, until they finished the bottle of wine, Dumitru Bojin insisted on talking to Brunul from the bottom of his heart, on telling him everything that needed to be said and, of course, everything that he was allowed to tell him. He became impassioned during that talk, because he felt himself turning into a teacher. Having been a rather awkward tutor, sitting on an iron bedstead in a prison cell, he now became the teacher of a free man, who absorbed his teachings like a sponge as he prepared to embark upon a life created by those very teachings. Dumitru Bojin had become impassioned and felt powerful. Thitherto, in the harder or easier years since he started working for the Securitate, he had felt powerful, but he had never rejoiced in it. It was a power he had wielded over people, who in the majority of cases were guilty and frightened and toward whom he felt contempt. People who begged forgiveness. People who, although well aware of their guilt, cunningly tried to conceal it. But his power over such people was invested in him by the institution he represented. It brought no satisfaction. It was not his own mind and his own power that allowed him to dominate those people, but the power of the whole system behind him. Moreover, even the power he wielded was illusory, since his domination over such people, and over his informants and residents, was immediately counterbalanced by the domination of those higher in the hierarchy than he.

But with Brunul the power depended on him alone. Brunul didn't even know he was from the Securitate, and if he had known, he wouldn't have understood what it meant. And it was very well that he didn't know . . . All the perquisites of dominance were to be enjoyed by Dumitru Bojin alone. Teacher, guide, aid. Without his realizing it in the beginning, Dumitru Bojin had provided himself with a huge satisfaction such as his work had never offered him before: that of shaping a man with his words, words that came from deep within him, albeit along the channel of just one of the truths in which he believed. They came from deep within him, and not from the printed pamphlets his bosses shoved down his throat.

When he left Brunul, after spending two hours with him in the one-room apartment, Dumitru Bojin realized he was dizzy. Granted, it might have been because of the wine. But in large part, as he had to admit, that dizziness was caused by a kind of enthusiasm for which he had not yet found an explanation, but which he wanted to preserve within him for as long as possible.

The discussion at the rendezvous house did not go on any longer than Dumitru Bojin had intended. After briefing his resident, providing her with a series of facts from the dossier, no more than were required, he gave her an official handshake. The same as always, he was thrilled by the warmth of her hand, but concealed it by clearing his throat in an official sort of way. He then felt the need to add, although he had said the same thing at the beginning of the meeting: "Nothing special, I should emphasize. Just a friendship to make him feel less lonely. I'll be there for him as much as I can, but he needs more than that. And until such time as he makes new friends, who else can take care of him but us?"

A small grin accompanied these final words. He didn't feel it coming, but his face demanded it. It was more natural that it be there, and in relations with a resident it was never inappropriate.

"The main thing is that you never bring up the things he has forgotten but which we know. It would be unjust. Let him remember by himself. That was what the doctor recommended anyhow. If we told him things, we'd make his madness even worse. What would be the point? Our job is to help him rediscover the world and re-adapt to it. You'll have access to further information as and when I receive it. As for how you make contact with him, it's entirely up to you. There's no hurry. Two, three months, even. My priority is to get him a job. After that, you'll find a way. I've got no worries on that score. Just keep me up to date."

The woman had already risen to her feet, and so Dumitru Bojin showed her to the door. She was his contribution to the plan. If indeed there was a well-structured plan. She was a woman who had won his approval over the last few years, ever since he took charge of her as an informant. Back then, naturally, she was younger, and her beauty even aroused envy among his colleagues. She had chestnut hair and large, dark, sparkling eyes; above her mouth she had a mole, barely visible, but enough to lend an especial charm to her smile. If he were honest with himself, it wasn't the thought of Torița that had stopped him from trying anything, but rather the fact that he was a professional above all else. In any event, he couldn't get mixed up with an informant. And in no event could he get mixed up with a resident—a woman who had attained a higher status solely due to her professional qualities. Rarely had he come across an operative so devoted; rarely did the information supplied by his collaborators surpass the usefulness of that provided by Elisabeta Stancu. Not even now had she lost the brilliance of her early years. She was thirty-five now. A few faint wrinkles could be detected around the lips that gave her that special smile of hers, but she was still a beautiful woman.

At the door, he shook her hand once more. The same sensation; in all those years he had never been able to rid himself of it. A beautiful resident, with a warm hand. She smiled at him from the doorway, making him lower his eyes in embarrassment and say, as if he hadn't said it already, "You'll manage. You're clever."

He remained alone in the room, trying to gather his thoughts. He didn't get up until a few minutes later. He searched in his pocket for the keys. They weren't there. He saw them on the table. But while he was looking for the keys in his pocket, he found the Pobeda watch from his collection, which he had intended to give Brunul as a surprise. For a moment he looked at the watch in his palm, as if unable to understand what it was doing there. Then he slapped his forehead with his other hand. He had forgotten. Carried away by the enthusiasm of his own words, carried away by those two hours in which he had shown himself how wise he was and provided Brunul with so much advice and so many teachings, he had completely forgotten.

The watch showed half past seven. It wasn't late. He could go to the one-room apartment and give it to him. But he would have to take a long detour and he didn't have a car at his disposal. And besides, maybe Brunul was already asleep. It was still early, but a day like that, in which he suddenly found himself with a home and a whole new world, must have been overwhelming for Brunul.

As he was locking the door to the rendezvous house, Dumitru Bojin's mind wandered off to Brunul's one-room apartment, before he could decide whether he would go there or leave his personal present for the next day, when he had in any event promised to visit him. And he put himself in the place of the former prisoner, he sat down on that soft bed, so different and so pleasant smelling compared with prison beds. Descending to the street, still undecided, looking now at the watch, now at the evening sky between the housing blocks, he replaced his own feelings, heightened by the spring wind, with Brunul's feelings, or rather what he suspected Brunul must feel. And there, in that one-room apartment that lay halfway across the city from him, he felt happy first of all, the way the former prisoner also must have felt. He then felt overwhelmed by the view he discovered from the window. He felt drawn to that view, which his mind's eye now associated with the green freedom of the hills and with the sunset freedom of the evening sky that showed through the gaps between the buildings. He felt drawn to it so strongly that, adding up the months of non-freedom he had taken upon himself, he was suddenly overwhelmed by the need to set out toward that horizon, to free himself of the recent past. Brunul's past. The past of the man into whose mind Dumitru Bojin had penetrated too deeply, without wishing to. The past of the man in whose mind Dumitru Bojin now discovered what he had not foreseen a moment ago. He discovered the acute need for freedom and to touch that freedom. The need to flee.

The need to flee. The words almost brutally summoned his imagination back. There on the street in front of the rendezvous house, there was no longer any place for the imagination, but only a fear springing from a reality too dangerous to be allowed. The need to flee suddenly took on a different meaning for Dumitru Bojin. He rushed to catch a tram and fretted as he rode for a number of stops, trying in his mind to make it travel faster along the rails. Then he ran to Brunul's one-room apartment, from time to time wiping the sweat from his brow.

He hammered on the door with his fist, clenching in his other hand the Pobeda watch from his own collection and hoping there would still be somebody to give it to. No reply. In the dark, he feverishly searched for his own key to the apartment. He opened the door and burst inside. Only after he saw the frightened face of the man in the bed, who had only just woken up and was holding in front of him the marionette as if it could protect him, only then did Bojin manage to hold his hand over his heart, trying to stop it thumping.

"You're here," he said, breathing heavily.

"Where else could I be?" said the man in bed, astonished, only now laying aside the doll and with his other hand trying to cover his chest with his pajama top. Calming down, he then said, "You said you would come tomorrow. I went to bed . . ."

Bojin sat down on a chair, nodding. He sat for a few moments and then unclenched the fist in which he was holding the present. He got up and went over to Brunul.

"I forgot to give you this," he said. "I came because I ought to have given you this watch. And I forgot. You'll need it. From now on, other people won't be keeping time for you. You won't be reckoning the passage of time by when you get your meals or when the guards are changed. You'll need a watch from now on."

He didn't tell him that it was a special present for a special man, as he had intended to in the speech he had composed in his mind the evening before. Although he certainly was dealing with a special man. A man whose mind, as he now realized, it was impossible to enter. Even if his imagination had striven to do so, it had remained nothing but his own imagination. But Brunul wasn't going to flee. He had no reason to. He had nowhere to go. Between him and flight stood not only too long a time, but also too wide a space. Twenty years contain space and time that you can't grope your way across.

But for Dumitru Bojin, Brunul's twenty lost years were contained in a file. For him, the information created a map, albeit a very schematic one, which his mind, transferred for a short time into that of the former prisoner, knew how to use. And so, at the end of that day of so many feelings hard to define, a new and oppressive feeling insinuated itself. For in Dumitru Bojin's life was beginning a period that was different, not only a period of satisfactions, as he had viewed it up to now, but a very difficult period.

The map hidden in the pages of the file had to be kept far away from Brunul.

# Chapter 25

BEFORE IT SNOWS. These were the words that Eliza had been repeating for the last few weeks. It was an essential condition of their attempt to leave the country. They had to leave Jassy before it snowed. But now, as they groped through the darkness, large snowflakes were falling thickly. Eliza's fear was blunted only slightly when the snowflakes seemed to melt as soon as they touched the ground. They had been trying to follow the directions Eliza's cousin Ticu had written on a piece of paper. But the sleet that had followed them from Timişoara and which they had cursed aloud now took its revenge, becoming a snowfall that heralded the onset of winter. Far too soon. Here of all places. Now of all nights.

The River Nera had been their guide at first. On leaving the village, they had crossed a bridge over the river and then followed its course, with its purling always on their right. This was the easy, clear part of the way. As far as the first large bend in the river. It was there that they buried their identity papers. Eliza placed them in a bag to keep them dry. They would no longer need them. And even if they did, even if something happened and they were unable to cross, it was hard to believe that they would be able to return to the river bend and recover them. But even so, Eliza placed them in a bag, uprooted a small shrub, and placed the documents in the hole. She poked the shrub back in the hole and made a pile of wet earth around it.

Ticu had told them that this was where they had to part with the Nera, carrying on in a straight line. When you have to confront darkness and snow, a straight line, so easy to keep to

when landmarks are visible, will start to bend and contort, and
you will end up moving like a pendulum, in a desperate attempt
to get back on track, to realign yourself with the only course
available to you.

They were lost. They spent hours searching for the frontier.
There was no sign of dawn, but they both knew it was long
past midnight. They knew it even before they passed the bend
in the Nera, even before the river flowed left in search of its
own ingress to Yugoslavia, at a distance far away, in a spot
where, according to Ticu, it was even harder to cross the border
because of the numerous guards. They were lost. Whenever they
heard a sound, they flung themselves to the ground. Sometimes
one of them would even fall to the ground because of some
sound the other had made. They had gone so far astray that
even Eliza, usually so calm and self-assured, was now trembling
with nerves, and her gestures betrayed that her exasperation was
now giving way to despair. But Brunul, as if devoid of thoughts
and objections, remained silent and let himself be led. As they
wandered lost he gave up all thought of any landmark other
than Eliza. He didn't even answer the whispered questions she
asked at rare intervals. He merely shrugged, perhaps waved his
hand, pursed his lips; but Eliza could not see these gestures in
the darkness, and Brunul's muteness augmented her slide into
despair and exasperation.

After a time much longer than the journey they had made
so far, Eliza placed her hand on Brunul's chest and he froze. She
had done this a few times before, but now she was not mistaken;
it was not another false alarm. In that wilderness barely outlined
by the faint shadows of night, men's voices could be heard, as
yet far off. For a moment they huddled behind some damp
branches, the remnants of a tree recently cut down or felled
by a storm, and waited as the voices came nearer. Just as it was
becoming painful for them to crouch stock-still, the darkness
acquired form. Two shapes. Two men. Border guards. They

were talking about food, but their lilting, strange Banat accent made it hard for Eliza and Brunul to catch all the meanings of the conversation. Kneeling with their elbows and hands resting in the freezing mud, Brunul and Eliza strove to breathe in time with the guards' voices. But in the too-long pauses between the guards' words, Brunul had no other sound behind which to hide the beating of his heart, which was now thudding furiously for the first time since he set out from Jassy on that journey which he had to make, although not even he knew why he had to make it.

The border guards didn't have dogs. They seemed unconcerned, not paying any attention to what was going on around them. Their conversation was friendly, almost cheerful. For them that pitch-black snowy night was just one of many that would fade from their memories because of the absence of any dramatic event, or rather any event whatsoever. Nor could the fugitives hiding behind the branches of a felled tree wish for anything more than that the night be ordinary and devoid of incident for the two border guards.

Not even after the voices faded away, moving in the direction opposite, did Eliza and Brunul dare to move. After a few minutes during which no sound of a voice could be heard, Eliza finally whispered that the border must be in front of them, since the guards would be patrolling parallel to it. They had to move forward as quickly as possible before the patrol came back.

The sucking sound made by their shoes in the mud now sounded deafening to them. Eliza came to a stop; she stopped Brunul. She knelt down and asked him to do the same. She began to crawl, followed by Brunul. Ten, twenty, thirty meters. Perhaps fifty. The sound of dogs in the distance, in the darkness to the right. They threw themselves flat in the mud, first Eliza, then Brunul. They would have to continue on their bellies, with the cold mud seeping through their clothes, entering through their collars and their waistbands. They had to go on, because somewhere ahead, at a distance still hard to gauge, but now close, rose the fence: you just had to lift your head from the mud a little way in order to see it. Perhaps also because the snow had eased off—the flakes were now mere specks—perhaps because the clouds had been depleted and now allowed faint traces of moonlight to shine through on the horizon, unless it was the light of a premature dawn.

The barking of the dogs was now closer. Perhaps the dogs were with the two guards they had seen. Perhaps the guards had been on their way to fetch the dogs and only now were they beginning their patrol. Only now were they coming directly toward them. Eliza strained to crawl to the fence more quickly. The darkness still protected them, but the way did not seem to grow shorter. Eliza stopped, looked at Brunul, and then stood up, stretching out her hand to him.

Brunul stood up, grasping Eliza's warm hand. He looked around, gaining a whole new perspective on his surroundings. In places the snow had laid thin white patches on the mud. A few patches lay between them and the fence.

They began to run toward the fence. The squelching sound no longer mattered; nothing mattered any longer. Nothing mattered but running in a zigzag to avoid leaving footprints on the white patches; nothing mattered but running to the fence, which loomed higher and higher, overwhelmingly high once they reached its base.

Eliza did not hesitate. Time was not on their side. It opposed them with a force far greater than the weave of barbed wire in front of them. She took the two bags they had lugged with them, which were sodden with mud and far heavier than they had been on their departure from Jassy, and she threw them over the fence. She then took the bag from Brunul's hands, took out Vasilache and tossed him over the fence. The wooden doll rolled into the ditch that was the final obstacle to leaving Romania.

Seeing Vasilache sprawled on the ground with his arms splayed on either side, Brunul suddenly felt like laughing. And his stifled laugh, prompted by the sight of the marionette lying in the ditch, released him from all the fears he had accumulated up till then. A ditch on the other side of a fence. As if those who had dug it wished to convey a message: that's what awaits you if you want to leave the country, a ditch, nothing more, a deep ditch, in which you will break your legs, your arms, your neck. But rather than sending a chill down Brunul's spine, that final message seemed to him rather ironic; it made him smile.

But Eliza didn't have time for such thoughts. She told him to follow her, to do exactly what she did. Covering the barbed wire with the bag that a moment before had contained Vasilache, she began to climb. As she climbed, it seemed to Brunul that the fence leaned first toward him and then toward the ditch on the other side. As Eliza straddled the fence, it stopped swaying and remained still for a few seconds. And then Eliza jumped. Unlike Vasilache she did not roll, she did not sprawl on the ground. She straightaway picked herself up and went back to the fence. She passed the bag to Brunul through the barbed wire. Her head barely came up to Brunul's knees. Her lips uttered something comical. Or perhaps the words themselves were not comical, and anyway he couldn't even understand what she was saying; perhaps it was only the laugh he had stifled shortly before that made them seem comical.

"What are you waiting for? We haven't got time."

The dogs once more. The barking was now distinct. It came from two hundred, a hundred meters away. But it was far enough away to allow Brunul the time to kneel down and move his face close to Eliza's frightened face on the other side of the fence.

Dawn was breaking; a mist was rising.

"What are you doing?"

She could barely control her voice. She felt like shouting at him to jump. The dogs fell silent, as if on command. The only sound now was Eliza's frantic breathing.

"What's gotten into you? We haven't got time . . ."

He had never asked himself how a single woman, a childless woman of thirty-five, as she had been at the time, never missed a puppet show. He had had no reason to ask himself. Not even after the theater director had brought her backstage and to his storeroom to see the puppets; not even then had he had any reason for astonishment. Not even after she invited him to a café and showed herself to be fascinated by his work. Not even after they had befriended each other during the summer of the previous year and her questions about his work had dwindled away to nothing, not even after she stopped wanting to go to the puppet shows in the autumn of the same year, claiming to be too tired, although she had been so interested at first. He had had no reasons to ask himself such questions at the time. Eliza was Eliza, the woman whom he barely dared to look at, the woman whose words made his cheeks burn, whether they were outside on a chilly evening or inside in the warmth of her apartment, the woman in whose company he could barely speak, his words lodging in his throat or barely escaping his lips in a whisper. He had had no reason to ask such questions. Their time had not yet come. But now, in that instant when his fears melted away, thanks to a stifled laugh, now their time had come, although nobody but he could have understood why. Or at least the time had come for one question, which his mind had not been able to rid itself of even under the pressure of the fears he had experienced before reaching that fence.

"How long have you known my mother lives in Italy?"

She gave no answer but looked at him, with an expression in which reproach seemed to give way to resignation.

He got up from his knees, rising above the faint mist that seeped from the ground. After the sleet, after the snow, the morning air, which ought to have been colder than that of the night before, now warmed him. He took a step back, which brought a glimmer of hope to Eliza's face.

"Are you coming?"

A firm shake of his head forestalled any further plea.

Eliza looked up at him for a few seconds. She then turned and picked up the two large bags. She noticed Vasilache and hesitated for an instant. She bent down, wrapped the strings around the puppet's body, and tucked it under her arm. She came to a stop before the other slope of the ditch, as if seeing it for the first time. She put the bags down and threw just the marionette up onto the other side of the ditch. She began to clamber up the side of the ditch. She slipped a few times but finally gained the top. Not even at the top, standing at the same level as Brunul, did she turn around to look at him. She picked up the marionette, smeared with boot polish and mud, and began to run. Brunul remained motionless on the other side of the barbed-wire fence, watching as she receded into the distance. He turned his back to the fence only when he was no longer able to see her, even in the dawn light.

The barking of the dogs was no longer to be heard. But in any event he no longer had any reason to fear. He was on this side, not the other side. True, he didn't have any identification, but even if he had known where to find his papers, he wouldn't have wanted to. Eliza's papers were there too; he didn't need additional anxieties. Supposing he recognized the shrub by the bend in the Nera, what if somebody caught him while he was digging them up? Border guards. Soldiers. They would have found out about her. He didn't want that. In no event did he want that. Eliza had always wanted to leave. Now she was far away. She deserved to be there. She deserved the opportunity to get as far away as she could, without anybody knowing. She no longer existed as Eliza. Her documents were hidden under the roots of a shrub. Now she was just some other woman, maybe a

Frenchwoman, that had been the plan: a Frenchwoman covered in mud, running through a remote corner of Yugoslavia. At the thought of it he felt like laughing again. That was what she would have to remain, a Frenchwoman running through remote corners of Yugoslavia, until she reached the other side, even farther away. Italy perhaps. Anywhere. She was clever. She could manage. And he had no need of documents. He would tell them who he was. His papers? He had lost them during the journey. He was careless, yes, but not guilty. He would tell them everything, how he had taken the train from Jassy to Bucharest. On his own. How he had gone on to Timişoara. On his own. Reşiţa, by another train. Naidăş, by bus. On his own. He had gone there to see the places where, according to his file, he had tried to leave Romania, in the past, when he was much younger and still had no idea about life. He didn't want to leave now. He had come just as a visitor. As a tourist. Would it be incomprehensible? Comrade Bojin would understand. In any event, comrade Bojin did understand. That was for sure.

He looked around him. The horizon was turning bluish-white, yellowish in the east. He had no idea which way to go. How much time had elapsed since the patrol terrified them? Maybe twenty minutes, maybe half an hour, but no more than that. He could no longer tell in which direction the guards had vanished. He walked away from the fence. It was now no longer behind him but to his left. To find the patrol he probably ought to have walked to the right, which was the direction in which they had been heading. But instinctively he went in the direction from which he had heard the dogs while he was beside the fence. But now he realized that he had heard them on the other side. It meant there was more than one patrol. One of them would find him. Why run? Why hide? Why expend further emotion? He could wait right there. With his back to the fence, at a distance from it. So that it would be clear to them he wasn't trying to escape.

He espied a large patch of snow in front of him. He smiled once more. He would wait there for them. He started treading over the thin snow, which immediately turned soggy underfoot. How many times would he need to cross in order to make a path of mud through the soft late-autumn snow, which was nothing like the stiff, resilient snow of winter. A single crossing, if he dragged his feet. He looked behind him and in dissatisfaction saw the clear, all-too-clear path. He would have to lift his feet, to lend outline to his footprints. He began to walk with longer strides, perhaps too long; it was not an ordinary gait. But it was better that way; he did not know how long he would have to wait. One, two, three. Ten. Twelve. Sixteen paces. Seventeen. The patch of snow came to an end, dissolved into the mud. He turned around. Further long strides, between the footprints he had already left. Taking care. One, two, three . . . This time not to the end of the patch, there would be no point, but to the place where the separate footprints became the continuous path he had made by dragging his feet on the first crossing. There were sixteen steps to that point. He had made a mistake. Could he really make a mistake on such a narrow strip? One step too few.

He waved his hand in dissatisfaction. Then he shook his head. Ultimately it's not important, he said to himself. It's not the number of steps that counts. He turned around, for a third crossing. It was not until the third step that he heard the dogs. And when he did hear them, all too suddenly, barking deafeningly, it was enough for him to turn his head slightly in order to see them. They were both rushing at him, making a kind of drawn-out whine, which was framed, this he knew, although he could see nothing except the approaching jaws, framed by the shouts of the dogs' handlers. He put his hands up, crossed them above his head, a reflex gesture, although in the not-so-distant past, when they were preparing their escape, Eliza had told him again and again to do just this if he was

caught. It would save him, Eliza had assured him. But it didn't
work. Not now. The dogs toppled him in the muddy snow, right
there on his path. He began to implore the dogs, since the men
were still too far away. He felt no pain, but it horrified him that
the dogs were biting him, they must be biting him, they didn't
have muzzles, he had seen their fangs when they rushed at him.
The fangs had blotted out every other image a few moments
before and they must now be sinking into his flesh, although
he was screaming at the top of his voice that he was innocent,
that he didn't want to flee, that he was just a tourist, nothing
more. When at last he could no longer feel the dogs on top of
him, when he felt a few kicks in his belly, when he saw the two
rifles pointing at him, at his head, he struggled to take a deep
breath, only now realizing that during the dogs' attack he had
forgotten to breathe—he had screamed and screamed without
taking breath. Only now, having caught his breath, did he hear
the men's voices.

"You're lost, my friend," said one of them, poking him in the
forehead with the barrel of his rifle.

"Lucky it was us who found you," added the other, poking
him in the cheek with the barrel of his rifle.

"Don't move!" both voices said together when Brunul tried
to turn his head toward them and get a better look.

"Not one word!" the two voices said in unison, when Brunul
tried, without moving, to explain why he was there.

They forced him to get up, yanking him by the arms. One of
the guards planted himself in front of him, with his rifle raised.
The other tied Brunul's hands behind his back with some string.
Not handcuffs, but string. This helped Brunul imagine that he
wasn't under arrest; they couldn't arrest him like that, without
handcuffs. Especially since he hadn't done anything wrong. He
was not guilty of anything. He tried to explain the situation to
the guards once more. But he had barely managed to speak two
words when the guard behind him hit him in the back with the
butt of his rifle, making him fall to his knees.

He remained kneeling. The guard who had tied his hands behind his back went over to the dogs and calmed them with a few friendly words, after which he fitted their muzzles. He then returned and with the help of the other guard he lifted Brunul to his feet. They began to drag him through the soggy snow, following the trail he had made before the dogs attacked. He tried to move his legs and it was only now that he felt the bites. Everywhere: on his hips, his ankles, on his arms, which the two guards were pressing painfully as they dragged him. He wasn't afraid, however. Not even now was he afraid. All the more so since the dogs were now walking alongside them, as if nothing had happened a few minutes before, as if it had all been in Brunul's mind. He wasn't afraid; he was, in a way, merely ashamed. He would have liked to walk on his own two legs and not to hang limply in the two guards' grasp. He tried to walk, but his ankles were somehow numb and painful at the same time. He gritted his teeth. He managed to take a few steps, but then, exhausted, he let himself be dragged once more. From time to time he felt the need to plant his feet on the ground, from time to time he gritted his teeth, and then gave up once more.

He had no way of knowing how long a distance they had covered or how much time had passed, when, on top of a low hill, a guard tower appeared before his eyes. They were dragging him there, making quite an effort; they too had tired by now. The two guards saluted the soldier at the top of the hill, who gave no sign of puzzlement, no sign of amazement. For all three it was a morning whose ordinariness Brunul in no way altered. The two guards propped him up against the base of the guard tower.

"He can't move," said the one who had tied him up. "You'll just need to keep an eye on him. We'll send a car when we finish our patrol. We can't carry him. He doesn't look heavy, but over a long distance . . ."

Brunul now heard the voice of the man up in the watchtower.

"I don't feel like shooting anybody today. It's such a beautiful day, after all that sleet and snow. It feels warmer, too, doesn't it?"

"It does feel warmer," said the guard who had hit Brunul in the back with the butt of his rifle. "Don't worry. You won't have to shoot him. His legs are in ribbons. He can't run."

"My dogs did their duty," said the third guard, with a kind of pride in his voice. "Come on," he told his comrade. "Another half an hour." He looked up at the soldier in the watchtower. "A car will come. There's no point in our carrying him."

The two guards walked away. Brunul watched them until he could no longer crane his neck to see.

"I'll shoot you if I have to, you know," said the soldier from up in the watchtower. "It's going to be a beautiful day. You don't want to die; I don't want to kill you. But I'll shoot you if I have to."

"I can't move," said Brunul, but then took fright, waited a few moments and then added in a low voice: "Am I allowed to talk?"

"You can talk. Just don't try to run."

"I can't run," repeated Brunul, "not even if I wanted to. But I don't want to. I'm innocent. I wasn't trying to cross the border."

"It's pointless your trying to convince me. My job is to stand up here with this rifle. You don't need to convince me of anything. But they caught you at the border, didn't they? I don't know what more needs to be said."

"I only came to—"

"Don't give me any explanations, just don't try to escape, that's all, because you'll force me to do something I don't want to do. I'm just telling you, so that you'll know. Never mind the explanations. Save them for the others. Not that explanations will do you any good. I've never heard of anybody getting caught and then being let off."

"I didn't want to flee," said Brunul.

"Then what were you doing here? Do you live around here?"

"No. In Jassy," he said, almost in a whisper.

"Where?"

"In Jassy . . ."

He heard a kind of chuckle from up in the watchtower. Or maybe it only seemed to be a chuckle; maybe the guard was merely exhaling deeply. Maybe he had snorted. In any event, Brunul waited for the soldier to continue the conversation, but no further sound came from above. Brunul still felt the need to speak. He decided to narrate to the soldier, whose voice seemed friendly, his whole story, or what he remembered of it. But without mentioning Eliza. Or Vasilache, since he too had left, along with his erstwhile girlfriend. He would tell him the story as if neither Vasilache nor Eliza had ever existed. He would tell him about comrade Bojin, about how he had looked after him for so long. He would then tell him that he hadn't known how to appreciate comrade Bojin and now he regretted it. He would tell him that he had been carried away by all kinds of thoughts, but when he had reached the fence, the final obstacle, he had abandoned those thoughts. In front of the fence, he had felt that he had nowhere to go, that in the end there was no other home than the one you know. But he had no way of knowing any other home, Brunul's thoughts urged him to tell the soldier. His home was the only place in the world where he would have liked to be right then. Sitting opposite comrade Bojin at the table with a bottle of wine. He wanted to tell the soldier, but then he realized that in addition to these thoughts, which were so clear, there was a host of other thoughts, which were less clear, but just as important. A host of thoughts that would have impeded his words and caused him to say extremely little, and extremely unconvincingly. Thoughts which if told over the course of half an hour would have meant absolutely nothing. Thoughts that he would have been able to tell only over the course of days, months, years.

"I've lost my memory," said Brunul, even though he had just decided to say nothing, to leave his explanations for later, as the soldier himself had warned him shortly before, to leave them for the years to come.

For a moment he thought that something had happened to the soldier, since he made no reply. He tried to get up, but his ankles and leg muscles were useless and sent pain coursing throughout his body, making him groan, making him tremble, no longer able to hold back his tears.

"Sit down," said the soldier finally. "I don't want to shoot you."

"There's no reason for you to shoot me," said Brunul sinking back down.

He gazed at his trembling legs, forcing his muscles to relax. He then raised his head, craning his neck to look up at the watchtower against which his back was leaning. He could not see the soldier. He opened his mouth to say something, held it open for a few moments, but then closed his dry lips and lowered his eyes. Better that he say nothing, no matter how kind that soldier might seem, whose face Brunul had not managed to glimpse when he was being dragged to the watchtower. Nor would he ever see it. And so he abandoned any thought of saying anything to him.

Dawn now lit up the sky. It did indeed look like it was going to be a warm day.

# Author's Note

It is appropriate from the outset that I should express my gratitude to a number of people who were kind enough to provide me with various pieces of information highly useful in the writing of this novel. I thank them for the patience with which they consented to my pestering them with all kinds of questions, some of which must have seemed odd to say the least, and I remain in their debt, convinced that a string of phrases in which I express my thanks is by no means sufficient, although it is certainly necessary.

Let me begin by thanking excellent translator Ileana M. Pop, who helped me to sketch out the protagonist's time in Italy. I am equally grateful to Professor Anca Ciobotaru of the Georges Enesco University of the Arts in Jassy, whose passion for puppet theatre has been found its way into the pages of the novel. Historians Andrei Muraru and Dumitru Lăcătuşu, researchers at the Institute for Investigation of the Crimes of Communism and at Memoria Exilului Românesc, helped me to overcome difficulties that I had been unable to solve by recourse to various bibliographical sources: I remain in their debt for their efforts and the promptness with which they provided me the necessary information. Dr. Bogdan O. Popescu, one of Romania's leading neurologists, Secretary General of the Romanian Neurology Society and member of the European Federation of Neurology Societies Scientific Board for Demetia, provided me with vital assistance in developing the protagonist from the medical standpoint. It was my good fortune that Bogdan is also a well-known and highly talented writer, and so he understood very well the requirements of my novel.

Without listing all their names, it is nevertheless necessary that I express my special thanks to those friends who read my manuscript and gave me useful comments. Also for her comments, I thank my wife, Adela. I am additionally grateful to her for bearing with me throughout the phases of the writing of this book and, I must admit, throughout my not at all likable changes of mood that came about, depending on the development of my characters.

I cannot conclude without making the following remark: the requirements of the narrative sometimes forced me to abandon documentary accuracy, and in places I stretched the historical framework, fictionalizing it where necessary. In all such instances, the responsibility falls solely on me, rather than on those who gave the book their support, whether directly or by providing bibliographical material. In other words, the scholarly expertise was excellent, and the decision to deviate from it in places was mine alone.

Lucian Dan Teodorovici (b. 1975) is a novelist, author of short fiction, and screenwriter. His novel *Our Circus Presents* was published in English translation by Dalkey Archive Press in 2009. *Matei Brunul* (2011) has earned widespread critical acclaim in Romania and won a number of major national awards.

A native of Sunderland, England, Alistair Ian Blyth (b. 1970) has resided for many years in Bucharest. His many translations include: *Little Fingers* by Filip Florian; *Our Circus Presents* by Lucian Dan Teodorovici; and *The Bulgarian Truck* by Dumitru Tsepeneag.

MICHAL AJVAZ, *The Golden Age.*
*The Other City.*
PIERRE ALBERT-BIROT, *Grabinoulor.*
YUZ ALESHKOVSKY, *Kangaroo.*
SVETLANA ALEXIEVICH, *Voices from Chernobyl.*
FELIPE ALFAU, *Chromos.*
*Locos.*
JOAO ALMINO, *Enigmas of Spring.*
IVAN ÂNGELO, *The Celebration.*
*The Tower of Glass.*
ANTÓNIO LOBO ANTUNES, *Knowledge of Hell.*
*The Splendor of Portugal.*
ALAIN ARIAS-MISSON, *Theatre of Incest.*
JOHN ASHBERY & JAMES SCHUYLER, *A Nest of Ninnies.*
GABRIELA AVIGUR-ROTEM, *Heatwave and Crazy Birds.*
DJUNA BARNES, *Ladies Almanack.*
*Ryder.*
JOHN BARTH, *Letters.*
*Sabbatical.*
*Collected Stories.*
DONALD BARTHELME, *The King.*
*Paradise.*
SVETISLAV BASARA, *Chinese Letter.*
*Fata Morgana.*
*In Search of the Grail.*
MIQUEL BAUÇÀ, *The Siege in the Room.*
RENÉ BELLETTO, *Dying.*
MAREK BIENCZYK, *Transparency.*
ANDREI BITOV, *Pushkin House.*
ANDREJ BLATNIK, *You Do Understand.*
*Law of Desire.*
LOUIS PAUL BOON, *Chapel Road.*
*My Little War.*
*Summer in Termuren.*
ROGER BOYLAN, *Killoyle.*
IGNÁCIO DE LOYOLA BRANDÃO, *Anonymous Celebrity.*
*Zero.*
BRIGID BROPHY, *In Transit.*
*The Prancing Novelist.*

GABRIELLE BURTON, *Heartbreak Hotel.*
MICHEL BUTOR, *Degrees.*
*Mobile.*
G. CABRERA INFANTE, *Infante's Inferno.*
*Three Trapped Tigers.*
JULIETA CAMPOS, *The Fear of Losing Eurydice.*
ANNE CARSON, *Eros the Bittersweet.*
ORLY CASTEL-BLOOM, *Dolly City.*
LOUIS-FERDINAND CÉLINE, *North.*
*Conversations with Professor Y.*
*London Bridge.*
HUGO CHARTERIS, *The Tide Is Right.*
ERIC CHEVILLARD, *Demolishing Nisard.*
*The Author and Me.*
MARC CHOLODENKO, *Mordechai Schamz.*
EMILY HOLMES COLEMAN, *The Shutter of Snow.*
ERIC CHEVILLARD, *The Author and Me.*
LUIS CHITARRONI, *The No Variations.*
CH'OE YUN, *Mannequin.*
ROBERT COOVER, *A Night at the Movies.*
STANLEY CRAWFORD, *Log of the S.S.*
*The Mrs Unguentine.*
*Some Instructions to My Wife.*
RALPH CUSACK, *Cadenza.*
NICHOLAS DELBANCO, *Sherbrookes.*
*The Count of Concord.*
NIGEL DENNIS, *Cards of Identity.*
PETER DIMOCK, *A Short Rhetoric for Leaving the Family.*
ARIEL DORFMAN, *Konfidenz.*
COLEMAN DOWELL, *Island People.*
*Too Much Flesh and Jabez.*
RIKKI DUCORNET, *Phosphor in Dreamland.*
*The Complete Butcher's Tales.*
RIKKI DUCORNET (cont.), *The Jade Cabinet.*
*The Fountains of Neptune.*
WILLIAM EASTLAKE, *Castle Keep.*
*Lyric of the Circle Heart.*
JEAN ECHENOZ, *Chopin's Move.*

STANLEY ELKIN, *A Bad Man.*
*The Dick Gibson Show.*
*The Franchiser.*

FRANÇOIS EMMANUEL, *Invitation to a Voyage.*

SALVADOR ESPRIU, *Ariadne in the Grotesque Labyrinth.*

LESLIE A. FIEDLER, *Love and Death in the American Novel.*

JUAN FILLOY, *Op Oloop.*

GUSTAVE FLAUBERT, *Bouvard and Pécuchet.*

JON FOSSE, *Aliss at the Fire.*
*Melancholy.*
*Trilogy.*

FORD MADOX FORD, *The March of Literature.*

MAX FRISCH, *I'm Not Stiller.*
*Man in the Holocene.*

CARLOS FUENTES, *Christopher Unborn.*
*Distant Relations.*
*Terra Nostra.*
*Where the Air Is Clear.*
*Nietzsche on His Balcony.*

WILLIAM GADDIS, JR., *The Recognitions.*
*JR.*

JANICE GALLOWAY, *Foreign Parts.*
*The Trick Is to Keep Breathing.*

WILLIAM H. GASS, *Life Sentences.*
*The Tunnel.*
*The World Within the Word.*
*Willie Masters' Lonesome Wife.*

GÉRARD GAVARRY, *Hoppla! 1 2 3.*

ETIENNE GILSON, *The Arts of the Beautiful.*
*Forms and Substances in the Arts.*

C. S. GISCOMBE, *Giscome Road.*
*Here.*

DOUGLAS GLOVER, *Bad News of the Heart.*

WITOLD GOMBROWICZ, *A Kind of Testament.*

PAULO EMÍLIO SALES GOMES, *P's Three Women.*

GEORGI GOSPODINOV, *Natural Novel.*

JUAN GOYTISOLO, *Juan the Landless.*
*Makbara.*
*Marks of Identity.*

JACK GREEN, *Fire the Bastards!*

JIŘÍ GRUŠA, *The Questionnaire.*

MELA HARTWIG, *Am I a Redundant Human Being?*

JOHN HAWKES, *The Passion Artist.*
*Whistlejacket.*

ELIZABETH HEIGHWAY, ED., *Contemporary Georgian Fiction.*

AIDAN HIGGINS, *Balcony of Europe.*
*Blind Man's Bluff.*
*Bornholm Night-Ferry.*
*Langrishe, Go Down.*
*Scenes from a Receding Past.*

ALDOUS HUXLEY, *Antic Hay.*
*Point Counter Point.*
*Those Barren Leaves.*
*Time Must Have a Stop.*

JANG JUNG-IL, *When Adam Opens His Eyes*

DRAGO JANČAR, *The Tree with No Name.*
*I Saw Her That Night.*
*Galley Slave.*

MIKHEIL JAVAKHISHVILI, *Kvachi.*

GERT JONKE, *The Distant Sound.*
*Homage to Czerny.*
*The System of Vienna.*

JACQUES JOUET, *Mountain R.*
*Savage.*
*Upstaged.*

JUNG YOUNG-MOON, *A Contrived World.*

MIEKO KANAI, *The Word Book.*

YORAM KANIUK, *Life on Sandpaper.*

ZURAB KARUMIDZE, *Dagny.*

PABLO KATCHADJIAN, *What to Do.*

JOHN KELLY, *From Out of the City.*

HUGH KENNER, *Flaubert, Joyce and Beckett: The Stoic Comedians.*
*Joyce's Voices.*

DANILO KIŠ, *The Attic.*
*The Lute and the Scars.*
*Psalm 44.*
*A Tomb for Boris Davidovich.*

ANITA KONKKA, *A Fool's Paradise.*

GEORGE KONRÁD, *The City Builder.*
TADEUSZ KONWICKI, *A Minor Apocalypse.*
*The Polish Complex.*
ELAINE KRAF, *The Princess of 72nd Street.*
JIM KRUSOE, *Iceland.*
AYSE KULIN, *Farewell: A Mansion in Occupied Istanbul.*
EMILIO LASCANO TEGUI, *On Elegance While Sleeping.*
ERIC LAURRENT, *Do Not Touch.*
VIOLETTE LEDUC, *La Bâtarde.*
LEE KI-HO, *At Least We Can Apologize.*
EDOUARD LEVÉ, *Autoportrait.*
*Suicide.*
MARIO LEVI, *Istanbul Was a Fairy Tale.*
DEBORAH LEVY, *Billy and Girl.*
JOSÉ LEZAMA LIMA, *Paradiso.*
OSMAN LINS, *Avalovara.*
*The Queen of the Prisons of Greece.*
ALF MACLOCHLAINN, *Out of Focus.*
*Past Habitual.*
RON LOEWINSOHN, *Magnetic Field(s).*
YURI LOTMAN, *Non-Memoirs.*
D. KEITH MANO, *Take Five.*
MINA LOY, *Stories and Essays of Mina Loy.*
MICHELINE AHARONIAN MARCOM, *The Mirror in the Well.*
BEN MARCUS, *The Age of Wire and String.*
WALLACE MARKFIELD, *Teitlebaum's Window.*
*To an Early Grave.*
DAVID MARKSON, *Reader's Block.*
*Wittgenstein's Mistress.*
CAROLE MASO, *AVA.*
HISAKI MATSUURA, *Triangle.*
LADISLAV MATEJKA & KRYSTYNA POMORSKA, EDS., *Readings in Russian Poetics: Formalist & Structuralist Views.*
HARRY MATHEWS, *Cigarettes.*
*The Conversions.*
*The Human Country.*
*The Journalist.*
*My Life in CIA.*

*Singular Pleasures.*
*The Sinking of the Odradek. Stadium.*
*Tlooth.*
JOSEPH MCELROY, *Night Soul and Other Stories.*
ABDELWAHAB MEDDEB, *Talismano.*
GERHARD MEIER, *Isle of the Dead.*
HERMAN MELVILLE, *The Confidence-Man.*
AMANDA MICHALOPOULOU, *I'd Like.*
STEVEN MILLHAUSER, *The Barnum Museum.*
*In the Penny Arcade.*
RALPH J. MILLS, JR., *Essays on Poetry.*
CHRISTINE MONTALBETTI, *The Origin of Man.*
*Western.*
NICHOLAS MOSLEY, *Accident.*
*Assassins.*
*Catastrophe Practice.*
*Hopeful Monsters.*
*Imago Bird.*
*Natalie Natalia.*
*Serpent.*
WARREN MOTTE, *Fiction Now: The French Novel in the 21st Century.*
*Oulipo: A Primer of Potential Literature.*
GERALD MURNANE, *Barley Patch.*
*Inland.*
YVES NAVARRE, *Our Share of Time.*
*Sweet Tooth.*
DOROTHY NELSON, *In Night's City.*
*Tar and Feathers.*
WILFRIDO D. NOLLEDO, *But for the Lovers.*
BORIS A. NOVAK, *The Master of Insomnia.*
FLANN O'BRIEN, *At Swim-Two-Birds.*
*The Best of Myles.*
*The Dalkey Archive.*
*The Hard Life.*
*The Poor Mouth.*
*The Third Policeman.*
CLAUDE OLLIER, *The Mise-en-Scène.*
*Wert and the Life Without End.*

PATRIK OUŘEDNÍK, *Europeana.*
*The Opportune Moment, 1855.*

BORIS PAHOR, *Necropolis.*

FERNANDO DEL PASO, *News from
the Empire.*
*Palinuro of Mexico.*

ROBERT PINGET, *The Inquisitory.*
*Mahu or The Material.*
*Trio.*

MANUEL PUIG, *Betrayed by Rita Hayworth.*
*The Buenos Aires Affair.*
*Heartbreak Tango.*

RAYMOND QUENEAU, *The Last Days.*
*Odile.*
*Pierrot Mon Ami.*
*Saint Glinglin.*

ANN QUIN, *Berg.*
*Passages.*
*Three.*
*Tripticks.*

ISHMAEL REED, *The Free-Lance
Pallbearers.*
*The Last Days of Louisiana Red.*
*Ishmael Reed: The Plays.*
*Juice!*
*The Terrible Threes.*
*The Terrible Twos.*
*Yellow Back Radio Broke-Down.*

RAINER MARIA RILKE,
*The Notebooks of Malte Laurids Brigge.*

JULIÁN RÍOS, *The House of Ulysses.*
*Larva: A Midsummer Night's Babel.*
*Poundemonium.*

ALAIN ROBBE-GRILLET, *Project for a
Revolution in New York.*
*A Sentimental Novel.*

AUGUSTO ROA BASTOS, *I the Supreme.*

DANIËL ROBBERECHTS, *Arriving in
Avignon.*

JEAN ROLIN, *The Explosion of the
Radiator Hose.*

OLIVIER ROLIN, *Hotel Crystal.*

ALIX CLEO ROUBAUD, *Alix's Journal.*

JACQUES ROUBAUD, *The Form of
a City Changes Faster, Alas, Than the
Human Heart.*

*The Great Fire of London.*
*Hortense in Exile.*
*Hortense Is Abducted.*
*Mathematics: The Plurality of Worlds of
Lewis.*
*Some Thing Black.*

RAYMOND ROUSSEL, *Impressions of
Africa.*

VEDRANA RUDAN, *Night.*

GERMAN SADULAEV, *The Maya Pill.*

TOMAŽ ŠALAMUN, *Soy Realidad.*

LYDIE SALVAYRE, *The Company of Ghosts.*

LUIS RAFAEL SÁNCHEZ, *Macho
Camacho's Beat.*

SEVERO SARDUY, *Cobra & Maitreya.*

NATHALIE SARRAUTE, *Do You Hear
Them?*
*Martereau.*
*The Planetarium.*

STIG SÆTERBAKKEN, *Siamese.*
*Self-Control.*
*Through the Night.*

ARNO SCHMIDT, *Collected Novellas.*
*Collected Stories.*
*Nobodaddy's Children.*
*Two Novels.*

ASAF SCHURR, *Motti.*

GAIL SCOTT, *My Paris.*

JUNE AKERS SEESE,
*Is This What Other Women Feel Too?*

BERNARD SHARE, *Inish.*
*Transit.*

VIKTOR SHKLOVSKY, *Bowstring.*
*Literature and Cinematography.*
*Theory of Prose.*
*Third Factory.*
*Zoo, or Letters Not about Love.*

PIERRE SINIAC, *The Collaborators.*

KJERSTI A. SKOMSVOLD,
*The Faster I Walk, the Smaller I Am.*

JOSEF ŠKVORECKÝ, *The Engineer of
Human Souls.*

GILBERT SORRENTINO, *Aberration of
Starlight.*
*Blue Pastoral.*
*Crystal Vision.*

*Imaginative Qualities of Actual Things.*
*Mulligan Stew.*
*Red the Fiend.*
*Steelwork.*
*Under the Shadow.*
ANDRZEJ STASIUK, *Dukla.*
*Fado.*
GERTRUDE STEIN, *The Making of Americans.*
*A Novel of Thank You.*
PIOTR SZEWC, *Annihilation.*
GONÇALO M. TAVARES, *A Man: Klaus Klump.*
*Jerusalem.*
*Learning to Pray in the Age of Technique.*
LUCIAN DAN TEODOROVICI,
*Our Circus Presents . . .*
NIKANOR TERATOLOGEN, *Assisted Living.*
STEFAN THEMERSON, *Hobson's Island.*
*The Mystery of the Sardine.*
*Tom Harris.*
JOHN TOOMEY, *Sleepwalker.*
*Huddleston Road.*
*Slipping.*
DUMITRU TSEPENEAG, *Hotel Europa.*
*The Necessary Marriage.*
*Pigeon Post.*
*Vain Art of the Fugue.*
*La Belle Roumaine.*
*Waiting: Stories.*
ESTHER TUSQUETS, *Stranded.*
DUBRAVKA UGRESIC, *Lend Me Your Character.*
*Thank You for Not Reading.*
TOR ULVEN, *Replacement.*
MATI UNT, *Brecht at Night.*
*Diary of a Blood Donor.*
*Things in the Night.*
ÁLVARO URIBE & OLIVIA SEARS, EDS.,
*Best of Contemporary Mexican Fiction.*
ELOY URROZ, *Friction.*
*The Obstacles.*
LUISA VALENZUELA, *Dark Desires and the Others.*
*He Who Searches.*

PAUL VERHAEGHEN, *Omega Minor.*
BORIS VIAN, *Heartsnatcher.*
TOOMAS VINT, *An Unending Landscape.*
ORNELA VORPSI, *The Country Where No One Ever Dies.*
AUSTRYN WAINHOUSE, *Hedyphagetica.*
MARKUS WERNER, *Cold Shoulder.*
*Zundel's Exit.*
CURTIS WHITE, *The Idea of Home.*
*Memories of My Father Watching TV.*
*Requiem.*
DIANE WILLIAMS,
*Excitability: Selected Stories.*
DOUGLAS WOOLF, *Wall to Wall.*
*Ya! & John-Juan.*
JAY WRIGHT, *Polynomials and Pollen.*
*The Presentable Art of Reading Absence.*
PHILIP WYLIE, *Generation of Vipers.*
MARGUERITE YOUNG, *Angel in the Forest.*
*Miss MacIntosh, My Darling.*
REYOUNG, *Unbabbling.*
ZORAN ŽIVKOVIĆ , *Hidden Camera.*
LOUIS ZUKOFSKY, *Collected Fiction.*
VITOMIL ZUPAN, *Minuet for Guitar.*
SCOTT ZWIREN, *God Head.*

*AND MORE . . .*